Henry Barton Baker

Stories of the Streets of London

Henry Barton Baker

Stories of the Streets of London

ISBN/EAN: 9783744750660

Printed in Europe, USA, Canada, Australia, Japan

Cover: Foto ©Andreas Hilbeck / pixelio.de

More available books at **www.hansebooks.com**

Stories

of the

Streets of London

BY

H. BARTON BAKER

AUTHOR OF "OUR OLD ACTORS," "THE LONDON STAGE FROM 1576 TO 1888,"
"FRENCH SOCIETY FROM THE FRONDE TO THE GREAT REVOLUTION,"
ETC., ETC.

WITH PORTRAITS AND NUMEROUS ILLUSTRATIONS

BY

CHARLES G. HARPER

"Truly the universe is full of ghosts; not sheeted churchyard spectres, but the inextinguishable elements of individual life, which having once been, can never *die*, though they blend and change and change again for ever."—RIDER HAGGARD.

SECOND EDITION

LONDON

CHAPMAN AND HALL, LIMITED

11 HENRIETTA STREET, COVENT GARDEN, W.C.

1899

TO THE READER.

THE author's endeavour in the following pages will be to present a series of pictures of the many phases of London life, of the past as well as of the present, and of the people in their habits and homes, as they lived; to tell the stories of its historic and romantic events, of the celebrated personages who have walked its streets; and to render the volume equally amusing to the Londoner who knows his London by heart and to the stranger who is desirous of knowing it.

CONTENTS.

CHAPTER V.

CHAPTER VI.

CHAPTER VII.

CHAPTER VIII.

CHAPTER IX.

CHAPTER X.

CHAPTER XIV.

CHAPTER XV.

CHAPTER XVI.

CHAPTER XVII.

CHAPTER XVIII.

CHAPTER XIX.

CHAPTER XX.

CHAPTER XXI.

CHAPTER XXII.

CHAPTER XXIII.

!LLUSTRATIONS.

CHAPTER I.

THE STORY OF ST. PAUL'S.

HOW few among the millions that daily swarm in the streets of the great metropolis have any real knowledge of this wonderful city of ours! The crowds hurry on, bent on business or pleasure, in ignorance or obliviousness of the associations connected with those thoroughfares, among the ruins of which, if not Macaulay's New Zealander, some other race in the remote future will meditate in such awestruck wonder, as does the pilgrim of to-day over the fragments of the capital of the Cæsars, and endeavour to fix the sites of those world-famous events of which London[1] has been the scene.

[1] The first mention of London (Londinium) is to be found in Tacitus. Various antiquarians have given various definitions of the name: one derives it from two Celtic words—*Llyn-Din*, the Lake City (the Thames was much broader and more lake-like at this point than it is now); another derives the word from *Lun-Dun*, the Grove City (meaning a clearance in the forest); a third from *Llong-Dinas*, a City of Ships, for even when Cæsar landed London traded with the Continent; while another group are in favour of a Norse derivation. But all the probabilities are in favour of the Celtic origin.

I

And these very Englishmen, who are so contemptuously indifferent to our modern Babylon, will
take the deepest interest in the *rue* or *strasse* or
church of some petty continental town that can
boast one famous man and half a dozen remarkable
events.   Yet it is scarcely too much to say that every
stone of inner London has its story, its leaf of history,
its page of romance, its human document.   Think
how exhaustless must be the annals of a city which
for eight hundred years has been the heart of this
mighty empire of England !   And during that period
there has been scarcely an Englishman whose name
is graven upon the scrolls of fame, and few foreign
celebrities, who have not at some time endowed it
by their presence.   But the stories of its streets are
written in sympathetic ink, in characters invisible to
the unknowing eye, but pregnant with meaning to
those who have the secret of making them start to
light.

To elucidate this vast cryptogram within the limits
of a modest volume would be impossible, therefore I
must confine myself to the more ancient and historic
neighbourhoods.

As my object is to endeavour to present a living
picture of London and its people as it appeared to
contemporaries at different periods of the city's history,
I shall put aside all dry-as-dust disquisitions in favour
of the more romantic aspects, so that these stories
may be acceptable to all who are interested in our
grand metropolis.

HOUR BELL AT ST. PAUL'S.

What better spot could I start from than the summit of that hill upon which rises Sir Christopher Wren's stately edifice? Century after century the life-blood of England's mighty heart has flowed and reflowed through this central artery. The glories of war, the triumphs of peace, the pageants of death, the pomps of civic state have been celebrated here. It is identified with religion, state-craft, scholarship, with art and science and glorious deeds, and with the great dead who repose within its walls. St. Paul's dominates the metropolis. Approaching it from the heights of Hampstead or Highgate, looking down upon it from Kent or Surrey hills, entering it by the Thames, still through the murky atmosphere looms the dome of the great cathedral, glittering and sceptred. It is to London what the Acropolis was to Athens, the Capitol to Rome. St. Paul's is a ghostly place upon a dark winter's night, when the great human hive has swarmed away from shop and warehouse and the city is deserted. Wheels rattle along frequently enough, but there are few pedestrians ; the electric lamps cast a cold glare of light, but they are powerless to dispel the awful shadow of the great temple, black with centuries of London smoke, brooding in eternal silence over the past.

And what a past !

When Cæsar landed in Britain there was a town, probably no more than a collection of huts, on the north bank of the Thames, of which the spot now dedicated to St. Paul was the centre, all to the north

of it being a dense forest. Here, says tradition, the
Romans built a temple to Diana or to Jupiter ; scalps
of kine and oxen—which were sacrificed to the
Olympian godhead — dug up in the fourteenth
century, pointing rather to the latter deity.

Ethelbert, in 610, soon after his conversion,
erected upon this ground a wooden church, which
was burned down in 961 and rebuilt the same year.
In 1087 the second church was destroyed by fire.

"Maricius, the bishop," says Stow, " began therefore the foundation of a new church of St. Paul, a
work which men of that time judged would never be
finished, it was so wonderful to them for length and
breadth ; also the same was built upon arches or
vaults of stone, for defence of fire, which was a
manner of work before that time unknown to the
people of this nation, and the stone was fetched from
Caen in Normandy." So densely populated was this
part of London even then that Maricius' successor,
Richard Beamor, had to buy up large streets and
lanes of houses to make room for the great building
and the churchyard, which was surrounded by a wall.
And still Finsbury and Moorfields were desolate
swamps, and the wolves howled and attacked travellers on the slopes of Highgate. Not until the latter
part of the reign of Henry III. was the colossal edifice
completed. Its length was 596 feet, its breadth 130,
its height from the ground to the top of the spire 520.[1]

[1] The dimensions of the present cathedral are 630 feet in length,
440 in breadth, width of nave 220, height 437.

In the new cathedral, as yet unfinished, assembled the barons and prelates to discuss the stipulations of the great charter, afterwards signed by tyrant John at Runnymede. In the dark days of Edward II. a bloody and sacrilegious deed was enacted on the threshold of St. Paul's. The Bishop of Exeter and lord high treasurer of England held London for the king; but Queen Isabella's party was paramount in the city, and after sacking his palace they dragged the prelate from his horse at the north door of the cathedral, to which he had fled for sanctuary, and beheaded him close by. Hither was brought Wycliffe, the first of the Protestants, to answer for his heretical doctrines, but so strong were his supporters, numbering among them John of Gaunt, the king's son, that they threatened to drag proud Bishop Courtenay, who had cited him, out of the cathedral by the hair of his head. And here "time-honoured Lancaster" was laid in a splendid tomb.

In the nave of St. Paul's was exhibited for three days the shrunken, murdered body of Richard II. Many a turbulent scene was enacted within the walls of the sacred edifice during the Wars of the Roses; hither was brought the naked corpse of Warwick, the kingmaker, from the field of St. Albans, and exposed for days to strike terror to his adherents; and a month afterwards the remains of the unhappy Henry VI. to lie in state. Both Richard III. and his conqueror, Henry of Lancaster, gave thanks for their accession at the high altar, before which, thereafter, Prince Arthur was wedded to Catherine of Arragon. Here Henry VIII. celebrated the thanksgiving for the peace between England, France and Spain; the king habited in purple velvet, powdered, with pearls, rubies, sapphires and diamonds, and Wolsey wearing a collar studded with carbuncles as big as walnuts. Charles V. was proclaimed emperor in front of St. Paul's. The defeat of Francis I. at the battle of Pavia was celebrated by a bonfire before the western entrance and a *Te Deum* within. Confusion worse confounded reigned here during the early Reformation days : now crucifixes were pulled down, then Protestants were tried there before being sent to the stake at Smithfield. Hither at the reception of Cardinal Pole came Philip of Spain with his splendid retinue—English, German and Spanish—as his father, Charles V., had before him.

On St. Paul's day a fine buck was brought up the steps of the high altar; the dean and chapter, apparelled in copes and vestments embroidered with bucks and garlands of roses on their heads, then forming in procession, the head of the buck was borne upon a pole before the cross, and so marching to the west door where the keeper who brought it blowed the death of the buck, and the horners of the city answered him in like manner. So Stow sets forth, and further informs us that the presentation of a buck and doe to St. Paul's was the tenure by which a certain nobleman held certain lands.

But these are antique cameos, and it is not until we

arrive at the glorious reign of Elizabeth that the dramatists and pamphleteers give us the means of peopling
St. Paul's with men of flesh and blood.   Can we not
picture that truly regal sovereign seated in a coach,
the first ever seen in England, drawn by four white
horses, and attended by her gorgeous court, coming here
to celebrate the victory over the Spanish Armada, with
the tattered banners of Spain waving on the towers ?
Fine as was our recent pageant, it must pale before
that ; for how can we compare our hideous, gloomy,
modern dress with the splendour and artistic beauty
which marked the costumes of that period ?

St. Paul's, however, in the days of Elizabeth was no
edifying spectacle, and rather resembled that temple
from which the usurers were driven than a temple of
Christ.   The Reformation by abolishing forms and
ceremonies destroyed all reverence for sacred things,
for the pagan spirit of the Renaissance had taken the
place of the old religion.

In the reign of Edward VI. Protector Somerset had
ordered all images to be torn down, the walls white-
washed to obliterate the paintings, and the priceless
plate to be carried away for his personal enrichment.
And although Mary reinvested the cathedral with
something of its old beauty, under her sister it went
from bad to worse.   The chantry was converted into
a lumber room ; the chapels were used as a school, as
a glazier shop, and for other unworthy purposes ; while
a trunkmaker plied his craft in the cloisters ; a baker
set an oven in one of the buttresses ; and in the vaults

were a carpenter's shop and wine stores. Upon
Sundays and all festival days, as late as 1631, the
children of the two neighbouring parishes came into
the church after dinner and played and shouted and
screamed until dark, so that the voice of the preacher
could not be heard in the choir. Let me attempt to
picture the middle aisle of St. Paul's and its frequenters
as they appeared to the looker on in the reigns of
" Gloriana " and her successor.

It is a public thoroughfare : porters carrying their
burdens, women with baskets of fruit and fish poised
upon their heads, even mules and donkeys laden with
goods, pass through it from east to west and west to
east ; costers are crying their wares and selling them
to the loungers who chaffer and bargain as in a market-
place ; on the pillars of the aisles are stuck printed
bills, advertising for servants or puffing the goods of
some enterprising tradesman—there is nothing new
under the sun, not even puffing—or setting forth how
the professors of the new art of tobacco smoking will
instruct pupils in the most fashionable way of " drinking tobacco," as the phrase goes. Here struts the
young gallant, resplendent in velvet and gold, beside
the sober citizen in woollen stockings and shining
shoes ; the sour-faced Puritan, gloomy as his dress ; the
soldier fresh from the wars, scarred and travel-stained,
clanking his ponderous sword and garnishing his talk
with oaths in English, Italian and Spanish, ready to
be hired by any one who will pay for his blade—did
not Falstaff " buy " Bardolph " in Paul's "?—hungry

gamesters, who having lost their last coin have come
to dine with Duke Humphrey,[1] which is the proverb
for going dinnerless ; serving-men aping the airs and
insolence of their masters ; and pickpockets plying
their avocation—few people troubling even to doff
their hats.

That gaily-dressed, devil-may-care young gentleman, from whom Shakespeare might have drawn
Mercutio or Gratiano, is arranging with that cunning-
faced scrivener, who carries pen and inkhorn in his
belt, for a *post obit.* on his gouty father, who lives
penuriously down in the country; while a fiery Tybalt,
in deedy converse with that truculent-looking ruffian
from Alsatia, is plotting an attack upon a successful rival, who may be killed outright or only drubbed
within an inch of his life. Behind one of the pillars a
courtesan and her gallant are toying ; merchants are
discussing the price of goods and making bargains ;
through the babel of ribald and profane tongues breaks
at times the chant of the choir from one of the chapels.
Suddenly the clamour takes a fiercer tone : a Cassio
and a Montano, having partaken too freely of the wine
cup, have fallen into a quarrel. It is a word and a
blow: there is a clash of swords and the two are at cut

---

[1] This has always been the common phrase, but Stow tells us that
it is incorrect, that the tomb so called was that of John Beauchamp,
constable of the Tower, and a younger son of the Earl of Warwick,
who was buried in the body of the church on the south side, 1358,
" where a proper chapel and fair monument remaineth of him. He
is by ignorant people misnamed to be Humphrey, Duke of Gloucester,
who lieth honourably buried at St. Albans."

and thrust. Friends try to part them, but there is a
general stampede of the idlers, for the civic guard is
coming, and they fear to be implicated in a sacrilege
which is punished by exposure in the pillory and the
cropping of ears. Indeed all these things that I have
described are penalised by laws that are daily broken.[1]

May we not detect among the crowd the gentle face
of Shakespeare, rugged Ben Jonson, handsome Beaumont, and his *fidus Achates*, Fletcher ; or those swash-
bucklers of genius, Robert Greene, George Peele, Kit
Marlowe, Tom Nash, debauched, unprincipled, thrift-
less, poverty-stricken, but with the *divine afflatus*
burning beneath their threadbare and tarnished finery,
the most pregnant group of Lucianic wits that ever
flourished at one period ?

Soon after eleven o'clock the loungers in Paul's,
save those who "dine with Duke Humphrey," repair
to the ordinaries, of which there are several in the
vicinity to suit all pockets, ranging from three pence
to twelve pence ; all are humble in accommodation,
with rushes or sand upon the floors, the plainest of
substantial furniture, wooden benches and trenchers :
but then the fare is of the best—joints, poultry,

---

[1] Even in the last century the jingling of spurs in the cathedral
often drowned the voice of the preacher. As the disturbance could
not be put a stop to, the dean and chapter resolved to inflict fines
upon all who wore spurs within the precincts of the cathedral, and
the beadles and choristers were commissioned to collect them. So
the moment the sharp ring fell upon the ears of the boys they crowded
round the offender, who would throw some silver among them, for
which they would scramble even while the service was proceeding.
There was a similar custom in the Chapel Royal, St. James's.

game. All is animation, for the spirit of youth is over all, youth with its virtues and vices, all in excess; youth in its ebullience, its roseate visions of futurity; there is no cynicism, no pessimism, it knows not the eternal sneer; yet it values not life at a pin's fee; it will fight to the death for a straw. There is a Benvolio who has just given his cloak and sword to his page, but is quite ready to try the *passado* upon any man in the room who "hath a hair more or less in his beard" than he has; there is Osric, in his lace-like shirt, exquisitely wrought by the needle in patterns of fruits and flowers, and even historical scenes; his yellow satin doublet richly laced, and shoes with yellow roses on them;[1] or perhaps Spanish leather boots, ruffled with costly lace, and wrinkled low to show off his silk stockings; loose-plaited breeches of enormous size, over which the shirt is bulged, in panes or partitions of different colours, and fastened to the vest by tags and loops, and girdle embroidered with gold and pearl and precious stones; a gilt-edged ruff bristles round his neck; his French murrey or beaver hat, the brim plaited with gold twist and spangles, and encircled by a gold cable band, from beneath which hangs down upon his shoulder a long love-lock,

---

[1] "Garters and roses, four-score pounds a pair," says Satan in Jonson's *The Devil Is an Ass.* Yellow was the fashionable colour. On his bridal night it was customary for the bridegroom, instead of unfastening his costly togs, to tear them off and throw them on the floor, and his friends to scramble for them. For curiosities of costume and tobacco smoking, I refer the reader to the comedies of Jonson, Beaumont and Fletcher, Rowley, Marston, Dekker, Middleton, Chapman, etc.

either worn shaggy or wreathed with silken twist;
maybe his hair falls upon his forehead in spaniel-like
curls, or is thrust up to a *toupet*, and a knot or rose of
ribbons is set jauntily against his left ear; then his
beard may be fashioned like a spade or a bodkin, or
like an alley, or a quick set hedge, or the letter T.
Nor must we overlook the gorgeous cloak of plush
which has cost three pounds ten shillings the yard.
He is discussing the last new fashion. Fastidious
Brisk is discoursing pedantically upon "drinking,"
tobacco, the "whiffe, the ring, the euripus, the Cuban
ebolition," and such like jargon of the day. Here is
another with arms crossed, and posing in the melancholy attitude, much affected by young gentlemen, as
Shakespeare tells us, now and again complacently view-
ing his face in the small mirror he carries in his hat.
Near at hand is Bobadil in big boots of untanned
leather, scarlet doublet, much frayed and stained, buff
jerkin, Spanish beaver with ragged feather, a huge iron-
hilted sword clanking at his heels, fiercely twirling his
moustache as he brags of his deeds of "derring-do," and
looking out for a gull to pay for his repast. In the
background is a party intent upon Gleek or Primero,
two highly scientific games at cards, while another
group of gallants is eagerly discussing the last new
play at the Blackfriars or the Fortune, or the last new
poem or satire. After dinner most of the company
return to the cathedral, where they will lounge until
it is time for the theatres.

The ancient churchyard of St. Paul's was of much

greater circumference than the present. On the north side was the famous Cross, which was almost as important as the cathedral itself. There in mediæval days the citizens assembled to elect magistrates, to discuss public affairs, and sometimes to try criminals. When these functions ceased to be performed there the Cross was used for all royal and civic proclamations; a pulpit was erected, also covered galleries for the mayor and aldermen, used occasionally by the king and court, who came to hear the preachings delivered by some of the greatest divines of the age. Here penitents were exposed to the gaze of the mob. Hither, barefooted, wrapped in a white sheet, a taper in her hand, came Jane Shore, the unhappy favourite of Edward IV., whom Richard of Gloucester, as all readers of Shakespeare will remember, accused of plotting with Lord Hastings to destroy him by the powers of witchcraft. "In her penance," writes Holinshed, "she went in countenance so womanly, that albeit she were out of all array, save her kirtle only, yet she went so fair and lovely that . . . many folks that hated her living (and glad were to see sin corrected) yet pitied they more her penance than rejoiced therein, when they considered that the Protector procured it more of a corrupt intent than any virtuous affection." The story of Jane Shore perishing of starvation is apocryphal, as Sir Thomas More, in his *Life of Richard III.*, describes her in her old age, and they tell you at Eton that she died within the precincts of the college.

There were stormy doings at the Cross during the struggles of the Reformation, and preachers alternately denounced, upheld, and again denounced the Pope and the Romish Church, and burned each other's sermons and missals and images, and sometimes tried to assassinate one another. The Cross was finally demolished by the Puritans, and upon the ground on which were enacted centuries of English history only crowds of women now gaze in at shop windows upon mantles and bonnets!

London House Yard marks the site of the bishop's residence, where Edward III. and Philippa were lodged during a great tournament in Smithfield, and Edward V. remained previous to the mockery of his coronation. The Chapter House now occupies a portion of the site. On the north-east side of the churchyard stood a belfry, or campanile, which contained the great bell that summoned the citizens when their presence was required at the Cross. On the south-west of the thoroughfare was a parish church dedicated to St. Gregory, and above it a prison, in which heretics were confined up to the end of the sixteenth century.

Until the cathedral was enlarged, in the time of Henry III.—Edward I., the church of St. Faith was a distinct building, standing on the eastern side of the edifice; it was taken down between 1256 and 1312, after which a portion of the vaults was given up to the parishioners and called St. Faith in the Crypts. After the fire the parish was joined to that

of St. Augustine; but the parishioners of St. Faith
still hold certain privileges in the cathedral.

During the reign of the first Stuart the grand old
Gothic temple fell into sad decay. James made some
movement to obtain funds for its restoration, but it
came to nothing, until his son and successor and Archbishop Laud took up the matter in earnest, and that
great architect, Inigo Jones, was commissioned to
do the work; sheds and houses that obstructed the
western entrance were cleared away, and it was proposed that all the shops in Cheapside and Lombard
Street, except goldsmiths, should be done away with,
so that a grander approach might be formed from the
east. But the great Puritan rising swept away all
these plans, and the church was plundered of its plate
—the unco guid always look to the siller—the monuments were destroyed, the graves desecrated, the choir
was turned into a cavalry barracks, shops were put up
in the aisles, where the soldiers played at ninepins;
and a saw-pit was opened in the body of the building.
Melancholy indeed was the aspect of the venerable
pile when Sir Christopher Wren was commissioned
to undertake the work of restoration.

The scaffolding is erected, all is ready for a commencement. On the night of the 2nd of September,
1666, the watchman who is on guard, while dozing
away the dark hours, becomes conscious of a red glare
in the eastern sky, denoting a fire some little distance
off; but conflagrations are so common among the
wooden houses of old London that he thinks nothing

of it and falls asleep again. But by-and-by he is roused by a strange hurtling in the air, wailing voices and great clattering of feet, as though the stragglers of a routed army are sweeping by. Again he starts up and sees that citywards the sky is like molten brass, shot with tongues of flame and lurid spirals of smoke. He runs down and questions some of the sobbing, affrighted people hurrying past; but when he learns that the fire is away in Eastcheap he comforts himself with the reflection that it must certainly be stopped before it reaches Paul's, and goes to breakfast with the philosophical calm of selfishness. Each moment the fugitives increase and their cries grow more terrible: "Woe, woe to this wicked city, for the judgment-day has come!" is shrieked by a hundred voices. The air is hot and becoming almost unbreathable, it is so thick with the pungent odour of burning; and the roar and swirl of the flames, the thunderous fall of buildings can be heard coming nearer and nearer. Filled with horror he once more ascends the tower.

Perhaps not since Nero gazed upon burning Rome has such a sight met human eyes; the sun is shining, but the awful glow, the billowy clouds of smoke obscure the day; beneath this canopy, that might be the roof of hell, blazes the city; it is a second Gomorrah; fire rains down upon it, fire surges up from it; streets, churches, houses are a red-hot mass; London Bridge is a cascade of flame, the river beneath a burning lake. Dense showers of glittering spangles borne on the east wind come nearer and nearer until they burn

2

the watchman's clothes; people in the houses round
about are wildly dragging out their furniture; tremendous explosions—they are endeavouring to stop
the conflagration by blowing up houses—add a new
horror to the hurly-burly; but all in vain, walls of
flame, like the sand clouds of the desert, come whirling
onwards, driving shrieking wretches before them.
Almost paralysed by terror the watchman descends
and rushes into the stream of panic-stricken people
fleeing down Ludgate Hill. When he turns to look
he sees the flames like fiery pythons twisting round
the scaffolding, and soon the old cathedral is a moun-
tain of fire, while with redoubled vigour, like the blast
of a sirocco, the winged flames still speed onwards.

Had Sir Christopher Wren been allowed to have
his own way in the rebuilding of London by making
St. Paul's the centre, and running from it broad, noble
streets, east and west and north, what a grand city
it would be! But when did Englishmen show any
reverence for beauty of design if it were opposed to
utility? Even the cathedral itself suffered from our
insular crassness, and until within these few years,
and then only after much owlish opposition, remained
a mere husk, cold, lifeless, and unmeaning.

Commenced in the June of 1675, without any
ceremonial, new St. Paul's[1] was inaugurated on 2nd
December, 1697, to celebrate the Peace of Ryswick;
but the king, much against his will, was not present,

---

[1] The cost of the building was under £800,000. The carvings in the
choir were executed by Grinling Gibbons for the sum of £1337 7s. 5d.

as a Jacobite rising was feared.   During Anne's reign
there were no fewer than seven thanksgivings for victories, all of which were attended by the queen.   It
was in 1713, at the Peace of Utrecht celebration, that
the charity children first attended.   The great architect received the usual reward meted out to English
men of genius—that is to say, he was snubbed, harassed,
and treated with contumely, and at eighty-six years
of age, when the glorious House of Hanover came to
the throne, he was dismissed from his post of Sur-
veyor of Public Works simply because he had been a
servant of the Stuarts, and an imbecile, named Benson,
put in his place; and though Benson's conduct
of affairs was so infamous that he had to be dismissed,
the king consoled him with some profitable places.
When Sir Christopher became too feeble to walk the
grand old man was carried once every year into the
cathedral to gaze upon his glorious work ; and when
at last he passed away at the age of ninety-one, in
1733, he was the first to be laid to rest within its
walls.   Was not that some consolation for the petty
malice of an ignorant German boor, whose sceptred
hands were not worthy to tie his shoe strings ?   And
what an epitaph he has: "Si monumentum requiris, cir-
cumspice".   " Kings for such a one might wish to die."

  It is suggestive that from the day on which George
I. went to St. Paul's to celebrate his accession, 1715,
no king of the House of Hanover entered the national
cathedral until 1789, when George III. went to offer
up a thanksgiving for his recovery from dementia.

The four greatest events connected with St. Paul's during the present century have been the burials of Nelson and Wellington, the thanksgiving for the recovery of the Prince of Wales, and the diamond jubilee of Queen Victoria.

Thirteen hundred years of history had rolled over the hill, and five different races of men had been masters there when the great Gothic cathedral was completed — the woad-stained Celts, the splendid legionaries and togad patricians of the Cæsars, the savage Saxons, the fierce Vikings, and the mail-clad Normans. There the white-robed priestesses of Diana, or the gorgeously arrayed flamens of Jupiter had offered up sacrifices to the deities of Olympus ; there, perhaps, had been worshipped the bloody gods of Walhalla, and there St. Augustin raised the cross of Christ. All had played their parts in the inscrutable drama of life and made their exeunt into eternity.

Since that time another six centuries have passed away ; centuries of storm and stress that have carried with them the pomp of papal Rome, the mighty Plantagenets, the masterful Tudors, the doomed Stuarts, and alien governors and strange religions and a new order of things have taken their places ; yet still the glory of the historic hill is undimmed, still it is the centre of the greatest city of the modern world, the symbol of our splendid empire of eternal sunlight.

CHAPTER II.

AFTER the cathedral and its belongings, the great
school, dedicated to its patron saint, now removed
far away, claims first attention. Many of us can still
remember that dark - cloistered recreation ground,
enclosed above and on both sides and barred in from
the pavement, like a prison, on the eastern side of the
churchyard; the ground is now covered by huge
warehouses.

"Paul's School," says Stow, "in place of an old
ruined house" (seemingly a religious establishment)
" was built in a most handsome manner by John Colet,
Doctor of Divinity, Dean of St. Paul's, for one hundred
and fifty-three poor men's children." It has been the
nursery of many good and some illustrious citizens,
chief among them John Leland, one of the earliest of
our Greek scholars, John Churchill, the great Duke of
Marlborough, John Milton, Camden, Pepys, and Sir
Philip Francis. Education was free in those days : each
boy paid fourpence at admission, and found his own
candles—only wax were allowed—and that was all.[1]

---

[1] St. Paul's was very severe in its discipline, even well into the
present century. Serjeant Ballantyne, in his *Experiences*, gave a

(21)

The scholars pay enough now. Verily the Charity Commission is a thing to be thankful for (?). Dean Colet's house perished in the great fire and was rebuilt by the Mercers' Company in 1670.

In the old days taverns and coffee-houses were numerous in the churchyard. There was the Mitre— famous for its musical entertainments and museums of curiosities—thereafter the Goose and Gridiron,[1]

gruesome description of the tyranny practised there in his boyhood's days. The three instructors under the head master, Bean, Edwards, and Durham, he says, " were all tyrants—cruel, cold-blooded, un-sympathetic tyrants. Armed with a cane, and surrounded by a halo of terror, they sat at their respective desks. Under Durham the smaller boys trembled. Edwards took the next in age. Each flogged continuously. The former, a somewhat obese personage, with a face as if cut out of suet pudding, was solemn in the performance of this, his favourite occupation. The Rev. Mr. Edwards, on the contrary, though a cadaverous-looking object, was quite funny over the tortures he inflicted. . . . One of the favourite modes of inflict-ing pain adopted by these tyrants was, when the boys came in on winter mornings, shivering and gloveless, to strike them violently with the cane over the tips of the fingers. . . . Bean was a short, podgy, pompous man, with insignificant features. His mode of correction was different in form, and I can see him now, with flushed, angry face, lashing some little culprit over the back and shoulders until his own arm gave way under the exertion."

[1] Larwood, in his *History of Signboards*, tells us that the Swan and Harp was a common sign for the early music houses. A swan with his wings expanded, within a double tressure, counter, flory, argent, was the arms of the Company of Musicians; this double tressure might have suggested a gridiron to the unsophisticated, and when the traditions of the Mitre were forgotten the swan would easily be transformed into a goose.

Music was in great vogue at this time, and fiddlers, in threes, attended all taverns and ordinaries, many of which were called " Musick Houses ". In the old dramatists we continually come across the expression " a noise of fiddlers," not in a depreciatory

which disappeared only the other day. Sir Christopher
Wren, when the cathedral was building, opened a
Freemasons' Lodge there, of which he was Grand
Master, and Caius Cibber, the sculptor, Colley's father,
one of the Grand Wardens ; Paul's Coffee-house,
patronised by the clergy ; Child's, a resort of Addi-
son's ; the Queen's Arms, frequented by Garrick and
Johnson, where he started a city club ; and the Chapter
Coffee-house, patronised by publishers and authors.

THE GOOSE AND GRIDIRON.

Even in Shakespeare's days the churchyard was
noted for booksellers, and at the sign of the White
Greyhound the poet's *Venus and Adonis* and *Rape of*

sense, but as a common term ; each band was known by its leader's
name, so it was " Mr. Cartwright's noise," or " Mr. Creake's noise ",
Every barber kept a cittern or lute for his patrons to play upon while
they waited, as his successor keeps newspapers ; and a viol de
gamba, frequently played by ladies, held a conspicuous place in the
best room of every gentleman's house.

Lucrece were published; and in this same neighbourhood *The Merry Wives of Windsor, The Merchant of Venice, Richard II., Richard III., King Lear* and *Titus Andronicus* were first issued in book form.

At the north-west corner of the churchyard was the shop of John Newbery, so highly eulogised by Goldsmith in the *Vicar of Wakefield;* he was the publisher of *The Traveller,* and commissioned the poor poet to write *The Citizen of the World* for *The Public Ledger.* Cowper's *Task* was also issued from this house, and some of Wordsworth's and Coleridge's earlier works. But it was for children's books that Newbery's was chiefly noted: *Goody Two Shoes,* supposed to have been written by Goldsmith, *Valentine and Orson, The Seven Champions of Christendom,* and others of that ilk, dear to the childhood of our ancestors. Another famous old bookseller of the churchyard was Joseph Johnson, who published Cowper's first volume of poems, *Table Talk,* and *The Olney Hymns;* he was imprisoned in the King's Bench nine months for the publication of Gilbert Wakefield's political writings. His successor, William Hunter, was noted for his Friday literary dinners, at which Fuseli and Godwin were frequent guests.

A better known name is that of John Rivington & Sons, whose shop bore the sign of the Bible and Crown; they were the leading publishers for sermons, and to them the country clergy brought their bundles of soporiferous theology: they were the first publishers for the Society for Promoting Christian Knowledge.

Paternoster Row, Stow informs us, was built without the walls of the churchyard by Henry Walles, who was mayor in the year 1282. "The rents of those houses," says the chronicler, "go to the maintenance of London Bridge. This street is now called Paternoster Row, because of stationers or text writers that dwelt there who wrote and sold all sorts of books then in use, namely, A.B.C., with the Pater Noster, Ave, Creed, Graces, etc. There dwelt also turners of beads, and they were called paternoster makers, as I read in a record of one Robert Nikke, paternoster maker and citizen, in the reign of Henry IV., and so of other."

In the time of Queen Elizabeth this thoroughfare was also noted for its ordinaries, where the gay gallants who frequented the middle aisle of St. Paul's took their midday meal. The best patronised of these was the Castle, the great resort of the actors of the Blackfriars, who, at the beginning of the seventeenth century, were as much petted and as eagerly sought after by "the great folks" as they are to-day.[1]

---

[1] "He is not counted a gentleman that does not know Dick Burbage and Will Kemp. There's not a country wench that can dance Sellinger's Round but can talk of Dick Burbage and Will Kemp."

"England affords these glorious vagabonds,
That carried erst their fardels on their backs,
Coursers to ride on through the gazing streets,
Sweeping it in their glacing satin suits,
And pages to attend their masterships,
With mouthing words that better wits have framed,
They purchase lands, and now esquires are made."
          —*The Return from Parnassus.*

The Castle (afterwards Dolly's Chop-house) was kept by Dick Tarleton, that "fellow of infinite jest," whom Shakespeare is supposed to have described as Yorick. Dick, after being one of the twelve players that formed the queen's company, was appointed court jester. "He could make Elizabeth smile in her sourest mood, tell her more of her faults than her chaplain dared, and cure her of melancholy more effectually than all her physicians." At last, however, he fell into disgrace for speaking scurrilously of the favourites, Leicester and Raleigh, and so was sent packing. But he is now host of the Castle, and hither come all the wild young bloods of the time to listen to his quips and cranks, droll stories and merry sayings, which keep the table in a roar. There he sits at the head of the board, a broad-faced, broad-nosed, sturdy-looking fellow, telling a story he has told scores of times—but his infinite variety never stales, and everybody roars as though he had never heard it before. How, having made merry at an inn at Sandwich and run up, as Falstaff did at Dame Quickly's, a long bill for sack, he found himself without money to pay it, so he instructed his boy to accuse him of being a popish priest in disguise ; the alarm was given, and when the officers of the law arrived they found him upon his knees crossing himself and telling his beads. So paying his bill, they carried him off a prisoner to London and took him before Fleetwood, the Recorder, who at once recognised him, and so enjoyed the trick he had played that he took him home to dinner with him.   All this is told with appropriate mimicry, convulsing the hearers.   Who would think now that the day will come when merry Dick will grow sour and puritanical !   It will be the old story, " When the devil was sick," etc., but as Dick did not get well again the devil remained a saint to the end.

Paternoster Row is associated with one of the darkest secrets and mysteries of the reign of James I. Here lived the notorious Mrs. Anne Turner, the milliner, who first introduced the use of yellow starch, for getting up linen, into this country.   It was at the house of Mrs. Turner in Paternoster Row that Lord Rochester and that vile woman, the Countess of Essex, held their assignations.   How the countess obtained a divorce from her husband and was married to her paramour, then Earl of Somerset ; how Sir Thomas Overbury, the king's secretary, for opposing this marriage—and other things—was marked out for vengeance, thrown into the Tower and done to death by poison, are events known to every reader of history. It was the woman Turner, assisted by a fortune-teller and an apothecary, who prepared the poisons which were mixed with every article of food used by the doomed Overbury.   The tools were brought to justice and executed, the earl and countess, after five years' imprisonment, were pardoned, as was Sir Thomas Monson, the king's falconer, who was also involved in the accusations, because, it is said, the king *dared* not drive to extremities the people who knew so many guilty secrets of his life.

That terrible mania for secret poisoning which raged throughout the seventeenth century in France and Italy had just begun to spread in England. It has been asserted that Henry Prince of Wales was poisoned by Buckingham to make way for Charles, without the latter's knowledge, however; and that James himself shared the same fate at the hands of his unscrupulous favourite. These accusations, however, are only *on dits*. Sir Anthony Weldon, in his *Court and Character of James I.*, relates that when the king was first informed of the cruel fate of his secretary, he sent for the judges, and kneeling down in the midst of them invoked God's curse upon the heads, not only of them but of himself and his posterity for ever, if they or he spared the criminals. The criminals were spared, and the invocation was terribly answered in the fate of his successors.

Paternoster Row in the days of the Stuarts was chiefly occupied by mercers and lacemen, and was so crowded with carriages and footmen during the day-time as to be almost impassable to foot passengers. The great fire brought about another change in the character of the locality; the fashionable trades migrated westward to Covent Garden, though even as late as 1720 the Row was noted for milliners and tire-women's shops; but the booksellers and publishers were now rapidly elbowing out all rivals. The most ancient of these firms is Longman's, the founder of which purchased the business of a Mr. Taylor, the publisher of *Robinson Crusoe*, in 1724; and all other

dealers in books who have taken up their business
quarters there are the merest parvenus when compared with the venerable Longman.   In the first half
of the present century "the Row" had almost a
monopoly of the trade, the publishers living over
their shops.   Readers of Thackeray's *Pendennis* will
recall to mind Bungay and Bacon, their jealousies and
the little dinner in the Row, "to which Pen and
Warrington and Captain Shandon and the Honourable Percy Popjoy, to give it a flavour of aristocracy,
were invited".   Then publishers, as the mercers and
lace-sellers did before them, began to move westward,
and the glories of the Row at one time seemed to be
in danger of extinction ; but the neighbourhood has
of late once more become one of the chief emporia of
the trade.

"At the end of the Paternoster Row," to continue
the quotation from Stow, the supreme authority upon
London antiquities, "is Ave Maria Lane, so called
upon the like occasion of text writers and bead
makers then dwelling there; and at the end of that
lane is likewise Creed Lane, late so called, but some
time Spurrier Row, of Spurrier's dwelling there ; and
Amen Lane is added thereunto betwixt the south end
of Warwick Lane and the north end of Ave Maria.
At the north end of Ave Maria Lane is one great
house, built of stone and timber, of old time pertain-
ing to John, Duke of Britain, Earl of Richmond, as
appeareth by the records of Edward II., since that
it is called Pembroke's Inn, near unto Ludgate, as

belonging to the Earls of Pembroke in the times of
Richard II., the eighteenth year, and of Henry VI.,
the fourteenth year. It is now called Burgaveny
House, and belonged then to Henry, late lord of
Burgaveny." (Now the Abergavennys.)

For the continuation of this history we must turn
to another of London's chroniclers, Pennant. "Burgaveny House (some time after the reign of Elizabeth) was finally possessed by the Company of
Stationers, who rebuilt.it of wood, and made it their
hall. It was destroyed by the great fire, and was
succeeded by the present plain building."

This famous hall, that figures so conspicuously in
literary history, is hung round with portraits of celebrated literati—Steele, Prior, Richardson, Dr. Hoad-
ley—taken from life. Here, in 1680, was instituted
the St. Cecilia Society, to commemorate that patron
saint of music; for its initiation Dryden wrote his
fine ode, "A Song for St. Cecilia's Day," and two
years after the yet greater "Alexander's Feast,"
perhaps the two grandest odes written since the days
of Pindar. They were set to music by Jeremiah
Clarke, the organist of St. Paul's. "Alexander's
Feast" thereafter found a much greater interpreter in
glorious Handel. Formerly Stationers' Hall had the
sole monopoly of publishing almanacs; it was from
there the venerable "Moore" was first issued.

In Panyer's Alley, on the north side of the Row,
there is a curious stone, built into the wall of one of
the houses, on which is carved the figure of a boy

STATIONERS' HALL.

seated on a pannier or wicker basket, with the following inscription underneath :—

When you have sought the city round,
Yet still this is the highest ground.

According to Stow this was a sign, but apropos of what he does not explain ; the date upon the stone, however, 1688, is a century later than the time of the old chronicler. Panyer Alley originally led to the

THE BOY IN PANYER'S ALLEY.

Church of St. Michael and Bladudum. Parallel with the alley westward runs Ivy Lane, "so called," again to quote Stow, "on account of ivy growing on the walls of the prebends' houses, but now the lane is replenished on both sides with fair houses, and divers offices have been there kept, by registers, namely, for the prerogative court of the Archbishop of Canterbury,

IVY LANE.

3

the probate of wills, which is now removed into
Warwick Lane, and also for the lord treasurer's
remembrance of the exchequer, etc."

At the King's Head Beef-Steak House in Ivy Lane
Dr. Johnson in his earlier years started one of his
many clubs; the members were merchants, booksellers,
physicians and clergymen, over whom he dogmatised
in his usual Aristarchian fashion. After a time the

GUY, EARL OF WARWICK.

doctor ceased to attend the meetings, which soon
languished for want of his commanding presence.
One December day, when the great lexicographer
was nearing his end, a meeting of the surviving
members was held at the Queen's Arms, St. Paul's
Churchyard. "We had not met together for thirty
years," wrote the doctor to Mrs. Thrale, "and one of

us thought the others grown very old. Our meeting may be supposed to have been somewhat tender. We were as cheerful as ever, but could not make so much noise." His voice had been weakened by a slight attack of paralysis.

"This [Ivy] lane," writes Stow, "runneth north to the west end of St. Nicholas Shambles. Of old time was one great house sometime belonging to the Earls of Britain, since to the Lovels, and was called Lovel's Inn." Warwick Lane, originally Eldenese Lane, was so named from an ancient house there built by an Earl of Warwick, the memory of whom is preserved by a stone similar to that in Panyer Alley, bearing a figure of Guy, Earl of Warwick. Here again the date attached is much later than that to which the stone belongs.

Retracing our steps and crossing the churchyard to the south, we are confronted by reminiscences of another dead and gone institution—Doctors' Commons, which dated back to the reign of Elizabeth. To us of these later times, Doctors' Commons is chiefly associated with the white-aproned men who used to stand at the entrance and tout for marriage licences. "Licence, sir; licence," was the cry, with a touch of the hat, much as a Clare Market tradesman cried his wares on a Saturday night. The scene is comically described by Dickens in *Pickwick*, and touched upon with a soberer pen in *David Copperfield*: "Doctors' Commons was approached by a little low archway. Before we had taken many paces down the street beyond it, the noise of the city seemed to melt, as if by magic, into a softened distance. A few dull courts and narrow ways brought us to the skylighted offices of Spenlow and Jorkins "—to whom David was articled. Doctors' Commons disappeared in 1867.

That ancient narrow thoroughfare called Knight Riders Street is said to have been so named as being the usual route taken by knights on their way to and from the Tower. Close to St. Andrew's Church is a secluded court, approached by a covered opening, quite an old-world place, with trees and quiet, quaint houses, one of those forgotten spots which have escaped the flood of " improvement," and that are becoming fewer and fewer every year. This marks the site where, in the fourteenth century, and for some centuries afterwards, stood the Royal Wardrobe. Richard III. stayed there for a time. It is frequently referred to in Pepys' *Diary*.

A network of ancient streets and lanes and churches that occupied the ground between St. Paul's and the Thames was swept away to make Queen Victoria Street ; in the thick of these was hidden that fine old mansion, the Heralds' College, which is now one of the handsomest ornaments of the new thoroughfare. It need scarcely be said that the original building, formerly the house of the Earls of Derby, was destroyed by that universal exterminator, the great fire, and that the present belongs to the Stuart period

Not far beyond, at the western end of Thames Street, the name of one of the ancient London

fortresses still survives in Baynard's Castle. Baynard
was a follower of William of Normandy; and he
erected a feudal stronghold on the banks of the river.
In the reign of King Richard it had passed into the
possession of the great baron, Fitzwalter, about whom
and his daughter Matilda tradition has woven a
pathetic romance. At a great festival held in the
castle, Prince John conceived a passion for his host's
daughter; but his licentious suit was spurned with
indignation, both by Matilda and her father. In
revenge, the vile John, who soon afterwards became
king, laid the castle in ruins, banished the baron, and
pursuing the unfortunate lady, who had taken shelter
in a nunnery, had her despatched by poison. Three
of the Elizabethan dramatists availed themselves of
the theme : Robert Davenport in *King John and
Matilda*; Anthony Munday in *The Downfall of
Robert, Earl of Huntingdon*; and Munday and
Chettle in *The Death of Robert, Earl of Huntingdon.*
After being rebuilt, and burned down in 1428, the
castle was taken over by the Crown, and it was at a
great council held there that Edward IV. was first proclaimed king. The famous scene between Buckingham
and Gloucester, in *Richard III.*, takes place in the
court of Baynard's Castle ; and, according to Shakespeare and history, it was there the Lord Mayor
tendered Gloucester the crown. In 1553 the castle
was the scene of another momentous historical event.
Having been again rebuilt, by Henry VII., it had
passed into the hands of the great Earl of Pembroke,

who, Edward VI. having just died, convoked a council
of the nobles and clergy, which there decided to proclaim Mary queen in opposition to Lady Jane Grey.
The last of Baynard's Castle perished in the great fire.
That dreary-looking wharf, an epitome of the most
sordid side of commerce, in one of the dreariest and
most sordid of London's commercial localities, seems
to be a strange spot for such memories of romance,
of fierce passion, pomp, splendour, and intrigues that
have helped to fashion the destinies of England.
Who would think of looking for mediæval romance in
a Thames Street wharf!

CHAPTER III.

THE BLACKFRIARS THEATRE—LUDGATE—NEWGATE
—NEWGATE STREET; ITS GREAT SCHOOL, AND
REMINISCENCES OF ITS SCHOLARS.

IN the middle ages the great Dominican monastery,
which has given the name Blackfriars to the whole
locality, stretched from Ludgate almost to the Thames,
while on the opposite side of the Fleet, then a broad
river, stood the Palace of Bridewell, a residence of
Saxon, Norman and Plantagenet kings, rebuilt by
Henry VIII. for the reception of Charles V. It
was given by Edward VI. to the city for a hospital
and endowed with the revenues taken from the Savoy;
in Elizabeth's time it became a prison. All that
remained of the palace perished in the great fire,
and upon the site was erected the notorious gaol which
figures in one of the plates of Hogarth's *Harlot's
Progress.*

The monastery was destroyed by the Tudor tyrant,
and a church within its precincts, dedicated to St.
Anne, was converted into a storehouse for properties
used in court entertainments; and here "the Children
of Paul's," who had been actors since the days of the

(39)

Miracle Plays, rehearsed.[1]   In the next reign it became
a tennis-court, and in 1596 James Burbage converted
it into a theatre, the renowned Blackfriars, greatly
to the horror of the Puritans, who swarmed in this
neighbourhood, and who presented endless petitions
to both Elizabeth, James and Charles to suppress
this "sinful" place, as the crowds who flocked to it
so blocked the thoroughfares that people could not
get to their shops.   It is worth noting that these
snuffling hypocrites were dealers chiefly in feathers,
pins and looking-glasses, and such like vanities, and
that the players were amongst their best customers.

No picture of the theatre, in which many of Shakespeare's masterpieces were first produced, is known to
exist; but from contemporary plays, more especially
those of Ben Jonson, it is possible to give a vivid
presentment of the interior of the building during a
performance.   The Blackfriars was a private theatre—
that is to say, it was chiefly supported by noble patrons,
who subscribed for boxes, and consequently it was
conducted with greater decorum than was the Globe

[1] "The Children of Paul's," who figure so largely in the dramatic
history of Elizabeth's and James's reigns, were the choristers of the
cathedral. Plays were frequently represented by them, not only in
their schools and in the private theatres, but sometimes at court.
The Blackfriars, before it was taken over by Burbage and his partners,
seems to have been devoted entirely to their use. The players
were very jealous of their popularity, and it is to them that Hamlet
alludes in the lines: "There is, sir, an aery of children, little
eye-asses, that cry out on the top of the question, and are most
tyrannically clapped for't; these are now the fashion," etc., etc. *See*
Hamlet, iii. 2.

or the Fortune, or such like. Again, it was entirely
roofed in, while the public theatres were partly open
to the sky ; and there were seats in the pit, a luxury
not vouchsafed to "the groundlings" in the others.

To eyes accustomed to the glare of gas and electric
light, the interior, lit up simply by candles, will
appear plunged in semi-darkness. A silken curtain,
which runs upon an iron rod and opens in the middle,
at present conceals the stage. On three sides are
tiers of galleries, to which the prices of admission are
sixpence and a shilling, and to the small boxes or
rooms beneath, two shillings and two and sixpence ;
these latter are rented by the aristocracy. The pit,
in the public theatres, is filled with a noisy, nut-
cracking, apple-eating, ale-drinking, card-playing,
romping, flirting, riotous crowd, whose clamour frequently drowns the voices of the actors ; but no
such licence is permitted here, nor would those sober
citizens who sit attentive on their benches desire it.

In a balcony on one side of the stage are the musicians, who play before the play and between the
acts, like the orchestra of a modern theatre ; and
very excellent music it is, for the musicians pay for
the privilege of performing at the Blackfriars, as it
recommends them to the nobility.

Hark ! there is the triple flourish of trumpets, which
announces that the play will now begin, and the cur-
tains are drawn back on each side. As a tragedy
is to be represented the stage is hung with black,
and like the halls of the nobles, the boards are strewn

with rushes; there is another curtain at the back, which is still closed ; the walls at the sides are hung with arras.

Although the actors have not yet appeared, the stage is already half-filled with ladies and gallants, seated upon three-legged stools, some of the gentlemen lying upon the rushes at their ladies' feet and fanning themselves, *à la* Hamlet and Ophelia. Here we have the *jeunesse dorée* of the court, the Mercutios, the Tybalts, the Romeos, the Benedicks, who in the play will see themselves reflected as in a mirror, just as in the dramas of our day we attempt to show " the very age and body of the time, its form and pressure ". We have met the gallants strolling in the aisles of old St. Paul's, and dining at Dick Tarleton's Ordinary, noted their close-cropped hair, their huge ruffs, monstrous trunk-hose, their feet half-hidden by the splendid roses in their shoes. But here are the ladies in their pearled stomachers, their expansive farthingales, stiff with gold and silver embroidery, and their yellow-dyed hair and glittering winged ruffs. At the back of each gallant stands a page, a veritable Moth, whose duty it is to keep his master's pipe, moulded in silver or clay into many curious shapes, supplied with tobacco from " fine lily pots " that upon being opened smell like conserve of roses, while between a pair of silver tongs he holds a glowing coal of juniper wood to ignite the Virginian weed, so that the atmosphere resembles that of a modern music hall.

When the curtain at the back is undrawn it reveals

an upper and a lower platform; the former, raised upon pillars ten feet high, is used when the scene[1] requires a double action; it serves for Juliet's balcony and the ramparts from which Prince Arthur casts himself. The actors are richly dressed in the costumes of the day; many of the nobility send them their cast-off suits. But they were not dependent upon these, for Henslowe has entered in his *Diary* such items as the following: "£21 for two piled velvet cloaks at 20s. and 5d. a yard; £6 13s. for a lady's gown; £19 for one cloak". To appreciate the sumptuousness of this apparel we must bear in mind the relative value of money in that day and this.

And now the play begins, and proceeds amidst loud comments from the audience, complimentary and otherwise. If they do not like it, there are cries of "mew!" "blirt!" "ha, ha!" "light, chaffy stuff!" Would I could describe how Burbage and Will Kempe and Lowin and Shakespeare looked and acted, but of that we have no record; and here the wings of my Pegasus fail him and we drop down upon nineteenth-century ground again.

Whether the postern, from which looked down the

---

[1] Whether or not scenery was used in these *private* theatres is a point by no means certain. Considering the wonderful scenic effects which were common in the court "masques" (see Ben Jonson's *Masques*), I think it more than probable; how otherwise can we understand the stage directions in the plays of the period which indicate not only scenes but sets? This is no place to enter into such a discussion, but let the reader take up his Shakespeare, or Jonson, or indeed any Elizabethan dramatist, and consider the matter for himself.

images of King Lud and his two sons and gave its name to the hill, was originally called Ludgate, or Fludgate, as being the barrier against the inundations of the Fleet River, I leave to antiquaries to decide ; but it reminds us that it was here that the gallant warrior-poet, Sir Thomas Wyatt, made his last stand against the troops of Mary, just in front of the ancient inn, La Belle Sauvage, which was on the western side of the gate, and was driven back, with some thousands of rebel followers, to Temple Bar, where he surrendered himself to Sir Maurice Berkeley, and so sealed his own fate and that of poor Lady Jane Grey. From the time of Richard II. until 1794 Ludgate was a poor debtor's prison, and, as at the Fleet, the wretched captives solicited alms at barred windows from all who passed, this being their only means of obtaining sustenance.[1]

"There happened to be a prisoner there," writes Strype, "one Stephen Foster, who was a cryer at the grate. As he was doing his dolorous office, a rich widow of London hearing his complaint inquired of him what would release him. To which he answered Twenty pound ; which she in charity expended ; and clearing him out of prison entertained him in her service ; who afterwards falling into the way of merchandise, and increasing as well in wealth as courage, wooed his mistress, Dame Agnes, and married her." Then, in 1454, he became Sir Stephen

---

[1] Prisoners still begged at the grating of the Fleet in the early decades of the nineteenth century.

Foster, Lord Mayor of London ; but he forgot not
the poor prisoners of whom he had once been one,
and did much for their relief and comfort, rebuilding
a part of the prison and erecting a chapel therein.
Rowley's play, *A Woman Never Vexed*, is founded
upon the story.

A famous hostelry in Elizabeth's time, and long
before and long afterwards, was La Belle Sauvage ;

THE ELEPHANT AND CASTLE.

here Banks the showman exhibited his wonderful
performing horse, " Morocco," so frequently referred
to by Elizabethan writers (Shakespeare in *Love's
Labour's Lost*, Raleigh in the *History of the World*, and
others).   Morocco by his marvellous tricks with cards
and dice quite anticipated the trained animals of to-
day.   According to Jonson, both he and his master
were burned on the Continent as sorcerers.   In the

courtyard of the inn plays were acted on movable stages before any theatre was built in London ; and the galleries which surrounded these inn-yards, and from which the spectators witnessed the performances, served as a model for the playhouses.

There are several explanations of this curious sign. Stow tells us that one Isabella Savage gave it to the Cutlers' Company, whose coat of arms, the Elephant and Castle, is still to be seen upon a stone in the yard. " Mr. Spectator " says that in his time the sign was a savage standing beside a big bell. Or it might have been the union of two separate signs, apprentices, when setting up for themselves, often using their former masters' signs in combination with their own.

Passing into the Old Bailey—a name so ancient that even Stow had to confess his ignorance of its origin, though he supposes it to have been derived from some antique court that was held there—we come upon that great gloomy house of terror, the silent remembrancer of centuries of sin and suffering, and the vengeance of the law. Newgate, the old Elizabethan chronicler informs us, was erected in the reign of Henry I. or Stephen, and, like all the other city gateways, served as a gaol. The story of Newgate prison has filled good-sized volumes, and cannot even be glanced at here : it has been well told by Major Griffiths in his *Chronicles of Newgate*. Of the awful condition of the old gaol, even as late as 1750, he relates the following anecdote : " At the May Sessions of that year a hundred prisoners were arraigned, and the whole of these had been incarcerated for some time in two rooms, fourteen feet by seven, and only seven feet in height; when brought into a court, which was only thirty feet square, they spread a pestilence around: four of the judges died plague-stricken, forty others were seized with the distemper, and only two or three escaped with their lives". Major Griffiths confirms Harrison Ainsworth's wonderful stories of Jack Sheppard's escapes, and adds others, of which one Daniel Malden was the hero, in 1735-6, scarcely less wonderful.

The strangest feature, however, in the criminal history of the eighteenth century is that these atrocious miscreants, as soon as they were condemned to death, became heroes, and men and women of the first fashion rushed to visit them in the condemned cell. Walpole, in one of his letters to Horace Mann (18th October, 1750), writes: "Robbing is the only thing that goes on with any vivacity, though my friend M'Lean [a notorious highwayman] is hanged. The first Sunday after his condemnation three thousand people went to see him; he fainted away twice in the heat of his cell. You can't conceive the ridiculous rage there is of going to Newgate; and the prints that are published of the malefactors, and the memoirs of their lives and deaths." More than half a century previously Claude Duval had been equally honoured: when he was captured, dames of the highest rank visited him, and interceded for his pardon; after his execution the corpse lay in state with all the pomp of wax-lights and black

hangings, and was gazed upon by scores of disconso-
late and weeping fair ones. Writing to Mann, 23rd
March, 1752, Walpole says : "It is shocking to think
what a shambles this country is grown! Seventeen
were executed this morning, after having murdered a
turnkey on Friday night, and almost forced open
Newgate. One is forced to travel, even at noon, as
if one was going to battle." [1]

The old prison perished in that terrible conflagration
raised by the Gordon rioters in 1780, of which no finer
picture can be found than that given by Charles
Dickens in *Barnaby Rudge*. Something yet remains,
however, of ancient Newgate, in some heavy, low-
arched cellars, without any means of ventilation,
which might have been the veritable cells in which
the hundred prisoners were confined, or Jack Sheppard himself. And the condemned cell has more
than a hundred years of ghastly traditions. During
the first half of the nineteenth century the rage for
seeing criminals hanged was as great as that for visiting them in the eighteenth, and the owners of the
houses opposite the place of execution made fabulous
sums by letting their windows to sight-seers. *Vide* the
Ingoldsby ballad of *Lord Tom Noddy*.

[1] Newspapers, journals and gossip of this time are full of references
to the anarchical condition of the London streets and suburbs, and
the daring robberies and deeds of violence daily and nightly perpetrated in them. There is an advertisement in *The Public Ledger*, in
1744, stating that on certain nights a horse patrol would be stationed
on the new road between the Sadler's Wells and Grosvenor Square
for the protection of visitors to the Wells. I shall have more to say
upon this subject when I come to Bow Street.

Glancing up Newgate Street our eyes fall upon
another landmark of old London which has been
doomed by the iconoclast, Christ Hospital. It is
a pity to break up such a noble mass of traditions
as those associated with the old school.

What a host of memories has gathered about that
small spot of ground on which, in the early decades
of the thirteenth century, the Franciscans within a few
years after the order was first established (1208) built
a monastery! In 1327 the Greyfriars was one of the
most splendid churches in London. Stow gives an
enormous list of illustrious personages, including
queens and the daughters of kings and great nobles,
who were interred there, and of nine monuments of
marble and alabaster in the choir alone, and seven
score gravestones of marble, all of which were thereafter sold by a zealous reformer, one Alderman Sir
Martin Bowes, for £50! Among the notable dead
was Isabella, "the she-wolf of France," queen of
Edward II., and there was a tradition among the
bluecoat boys that her ghost walked the ancient
cloister that had once formed part of the church.

It is generally supposed that the school was founded
by Edward VI., whose apocryphal reputation for such
like acts of beneficence has been so ruthlessly dissipated
by recent historical investigations; but Christ Hospital was founded by Henry VIII. in the thirty-eighth
year of his reign—it is unjust to ignore one of the
very few good acts of the Tudor despot—and the
grant was only confirmed by his son.

The roll of scholars and great men who received their training at this fine old school is a noble one ; to mention but a few : Stillingfleet, Samuel Richardson,

CHRIST CHURCH PASSAGE.

Coleridge, Lamb, Leigh Hunt. And what charming reminiscences the two last have left us of the old house—the first in the *Essays of Elia*, the second in

his autobiography. Both write bitterly upon the hard
life of those school days; the breakfast of half a three
half-penny loaf "moistened with attenuated small
beer," that "tasted of the pitched leathern jack it was
poured from," says Elia ; "our Monday's milk porridge
blue and tasteless, and the pease soup of Saturday
coarse and choking. . . . The Wednesday's mess of
millet somewhat less repugnant (we had three banyan
to four meat days in the week). In lieu of our *half-
pickled* Sundays, or *quite fresh* boiled beef on Thurs-
days (strong as *caro equina*), with detestable marigolds
floating in the pail to poison the broth of our scanty
mutton scrags on Fridays, the rather more savoury,
but grudging portions of the same flesh, rotten roasted
or rare, on the Tuesdays." Yet it was an unwritten
law among these half-starved boys that the fat of
fresh boiled beef should never be eaten ; it went by
the name of gags, and a gag-eater was a creature held
in horror. He tells a pathetic story of a boy who had
been seen to gather up these forbidden things, and
was regarded as no better than a ghoul by his disgusted schoolfellows until it was discovered that he took
them to his parents who were in dire want. Sometimes the boys were given a day's leave and were
turned out from breakfast till night into the burning
streets of summer or the frost and snow of winter to
shift for themselves. One of the greatest sufferers by
these enforced holidays was Coleridge, who had no
friends in London ; in fine weather he swam in the
New River, or haunted old bookstalls, and in wet

days tramped round and round Newgate Market until the gates were opened again.

The discipline of the upper school under the Rev. James Boyer was Spartan. "He had two wigs. . . . The one serene, smiling, fresh powdered, betokening a mild day. The other, an old, discoloured, unkempt, angry caxton, denoting frequent and bloody execution. Woe to the school when he made his morning appearance in his *passy* or *passionate wig*. . . . Nothing was more common than to see him make a headlong entry into the schoolroom from his inner recess or library, and with turbulent eye singling out a lad, roar out, 'Ods my life, sirrah! I have a great mind to whip you!'—then, with a sudden and retracting impulse, fling back into his lair, and after a cooling lapse of some minutes drive headlong out again, piecing out his imperfect sense, as if it had been some devil's litany, with the expletory yell '*and I* WILL *too!*' In his gentler moods, when *rabidus furor* was assuaged, he had resort to an ingenious method, peculiar, from what I have heard, to himself, of whipping the boys and reading the debates in the newspaper at the same time; a paragraph and a lash between." [1]

Here is a picture, from the same charming pen, of an illustrious schoolmate: "Come back into my memory, like as thou wert in the dayspring of thy fancies, with hope like a fiery column before thee—the

---

[1] Coleridge, however, admitted that he owed great obligations to this Gamaliel, who flogged infidelity and false taste in poetry out of him.

dark pillar not yet turned—Samuel Taylor Coleridge,
Logician, Metaphysician, Bard! How have I seen
the casual passer through the cloisters stand still, en-
tranced with admiration (while he weighed the dis-
proportion between the *speech* and the garb of the
young Mirandula), to hear thee unfold, in thy deep
and sweet intonations the mysteries of Jamblichus
or Plotinus (for even in those years thou waxedest
not pale at such philosophic draughts), or reciting
Homer in his Greek, or Pindar—while the walls of
the old Grey Friars re-echoed to the accents of *the
inspired charity boy!*"

How remote those old bare-footed friars, those
royalties and great nobles appear to be from us of
to-day, and yet their ashes lie within a few feet of the
crowded pavement of Newgate Street, while the very
stones are still haunted for us by the spirits of men
who yet live and breathe in their immortal thoughts!

Christ Hospital is not the only place in Newgate
Street associated with memories of Lamb and Coleridge. On the south side, nearer to Cheapside, stood,
until burned down in 1883, a notable old tavern
called the Salutation and Cat.[1] It is now rebuilt as a
modern public house and restaurant. During the
eighteenth century it was a favourite rendezvous of
literary men, especially of Richardson the novelist,

---

[1] The Salutation means the Annunciation, and was figured by an
Angel appearing to the Virgin. The addition of the Cat can only
be explained by such a combination of signs as is explained in my
note upon La Belle Sauvage.

Cave of *The Gentleman's Magazine*, and William Bowyer the antiquary. Coleridge, in one of his morbid moods, took up his abode at the Salutation for a while. He and Lamb frequently met there to talk of poetry and fate and free will, and Samuel Taylor would recite his last poem. There is a pretty allusion to these evenings in one of Lamb's letters to Coleridge : "When I read in your little volume your nineteenth effusion, or what you call ' The Sigh,' I think I hear you again. I imagine to myself the little smoky room at the *Salutation and Cat*, where we have sat together through the winter's nights, beguiling the cares of life with poetry " (10th June, 1796). How deep was the impression left upon Lamb by those evenings is shown in the following passage from a dedication of his works to that same friend : " Some of the sonnets, which shall be carelessly turned over by the general reader, may happily awaken in you remembrances which I should be sorry should be ever totally extinct—the memory of ' summer days and delightful years,' even so far back as those old suppers at our old inn—when life was fresh and topics exhaustless — and you first kindled in me, if not the power, yet the love of poetry, and beauty, and kindliness ".

It is but a step down King Edward Street, formerly Butcherhall Lane, into that quaint corner of old London, to which the Earls of Brittany, who lodged there in ancient times, gave the name Little Britain. In days gone by it was a " Booksellers' Row " filled with old bookstalls, in which the hunter for rarities picked up for a mere song many a choice treasure that would now set the *cognoscenti* at Puttick & Simpson's bidding against each other by the hundred. Milton's *Paradise Lost* was published in Little Britain, and for some time the copies lay as so much waste paper on the bookseller's shelves.   But one day that Mæcenas of his time, the poetic Earl of Dorset, Dryden's great patron, came into the shop in search of some book. Taking up a copy of the epic by chance, he dipped into it here and there, and, being greatly struck by some passages, bought it. Then the bookseller begged him to speak of it to his friends. His lordship sent the poem to Dryden—and so it was launched upon the world. The first numbers of *The Spectator* were published here. One of the most charming papers in Washington Irving's *Sketch Book* is devoted to Little Britain and the jolly doings of " The Roaring Lads." who met at the Half Moon Tavern, and opened every club night by trolling forth the famous old drinking song from " Gammer Gurton's Needle " :—

> Back and side go bare, go bare,
>   Both foot and hand go cold ;
> But belly god send thee good ale enough,
>   Whether it be new or old.

CHAPTER IV.

AND now let us turn into Giltspur Street, along which pranced and spurred and clattered the knights of old on their way to the tournaments in Smithfield, past the noble hospital, founded by that king's pious jester, Rahere, which has been doing Samaritan work unceasingly for nearly eight hundred years, and let us pause at the ancient gateway leading to the glorious old Norman church of St. Bartholomew the Great, in which Rahere is entombed.

Had they the power of speech, what stories those black stones could tell of the long, long centuries that have passed since the hands of the mason set them ; of the splendid pageants, the misery, the human agony, the horrors, the comedies, the tragedies that have been enacted before them. Smithfield was the scene of most of the grand tournaments in the days of the Plantagenets. Here assembled the splendid court of Edward III. to witness that joust at which the kings of France and Scotland were present ; and that seven days' tournament, given in honour of

(56)

ST. BARTHOLOMEW.

Edward's beloved mistress, Alice Perrers, "the Lady of the Sun"; and here were celebrated those yet more gorgeous pageants of chivalry in the reign of Edward's grandson, Richard, to which journeyed knights and nobles from France and Flanders, and many other foreign countries.

I give a picture from old Stow, who copied it from Froissart : "When Sunday came—the Sunday after Michaelmas, 1379—about three o'clock, there paraded from the Tower of London sixty barbed coursers, ornamented for the tournament, and on each was mounted a squire of honour. Then came sixty ladies of rank mounted on palfreys, most elegantly and richly dressed, following each other, every one leading a knight with a silver chain, completely armed for tilting ; and in this procession they moved on through the streets of London, attended by numbers of minstrels and trumpets, to Smithfield. The knights, being in the king's party, had their harness and apparel garnished with white harts (the king's device) and crowns of gold about the harts' necks." Can we not imagine these *preux* chevaliers in their damascened armour and gorgeously emblazoned surcoats ; the ladies in their rich velvets stamped and embroidered with armorial bearings, mottoes and devices, their hair confined in nets of gold surmounted by jewelled coronets, or by golden horns from which hang veils of Spanish or Flanders lace ? Now the demoiselles are seated in the raised gallery, and the king, queen and attendants have taken their places in

a splendid pavilion : without the lists is a swaying
crowd that fills the whole great area of Smithfield ;
the champions, lances in rest, range themselves in two
serried lines.   " Largesse, largesse ! Glory to the
brave ! " shout the heralds ; the trumpets and clarions
send forth shrill blasts of defiance ; then there is a
thunderous tramp of hoofs, a glitter, a flash, and
an awful crash of arms—and horses and riders and
plumed casques are rolling in the dust, while the
victors, amidst the acclamations of the spectators and
the frantic waving of ladies' handkerchiefs, kneel
before the throne of " the Queen of Love and
Beauty" to receive the guerdon of their prowess.

Not long afterwards a sterner scene was enacted
here, when twenty thousand rebels, under Wat Tyler,
Jack Straw and John Ball, confronted the sybaritish
king and would have slain him but for the loyalty and
prompt valour of Mayor Walworth, who killed Wat
Tyler on the spot.

In front of the old gateway during the reigns of
Henry VIII., Mary and Elizabeth, Londoners were
almost as frequently treated to an *auto-da-fé* as were
the subjects of Philip of Spain.   Now it was some
Papist or Papists who were burned for refusing to
acknowledge the king's supremacy ; then a Reformer
for rejecting the doctrines of Rome ; anon a Protestant
who denied the real presence ; and by-and-by an Ana-
baptist for blaspheming against the accepted codes
of both Catholics and Protestants.   And the faggots,
smeared with pitch and oil, are piled up in the great

open space, and the mob, whose instincts are always
cruel, and who are equally eager for scenes of death,
whether they be of the guillotine, the block, the gallows
or the faggot, gather about the funeral pyre and wait
as impatiently for the gruesome show as did their fore-
fathers for the jousts and tournaments. And now is
heard the distant solemn chant of the *Miserere*, or the
swell of some Lutheran or Calvinistic hymn, and the
ghastly procession of victims and executioners is seen
slowly approaching.

Soon there is a glare, and billows of black blinding
smoke, borne on the wind, drive back the gaping
ghouls; and chants and prayers swell louder and
louder, until they are drowned in the awful swirl and
roar of the flames. The differences of faith seem to
make no difference in the heroic bearing of these
votive offerings to the demons of bigotry, and the
same unblenching courage distinguishes both Papist
and Protestant; a cry of pain is seldom wrung from
them in their terrible agony, or a sign of apostasy.
Why, the stones of the old gateway are blackened by
the smoke from the funeral pyres of the martyrs!

Not wholly splendid and tragic, however, are
the scenes which the old gateway has looked upon.
During seven hundred years it witnessed the great
London saturnalia, St. Bartholomew Fair. Stow tells
us that Henry II. granted the privilege of a yearly
fair to the priory, and that clothiers and drapers
came thither from all parts of England with their
goods. It was open during three days in the month

of September. It ceased to be a cloth fair in Elizabeth's reign, as it had long been given up chiefly to horses, cattle and sheep, and booths and shows. The three days were afterwards extended to fourteen.

Ben Jonson in his comedy, *Bartholomew Fair*, has unctuously pictured the humours of this Cockney carnival in the days of the first Stuart. Several references to the Fair occur in Pepys' *Diary*. Under date 30th August, 1667, he writes: " I to Bartholomew Fair, there to walk up and down ; and there among other things find my Lady Castlemaine at a puppet play ". Frederick, Prince of Wales, the father of George III., frequently honoured it by his presence. And some of the principal actors of the patent theatres, such as Dogget, of coat and badge memory, and Pinkethman, eulogised by Steele, found it profitable to forget that they were ". His Majesty's Servants " and open booths there. Most famous of all theatrical booths was that of Richardson, under whom Edmund Kean appeared. Here any of Shakespeare's tragedies could be played within half an hour ; and contended with fire-eaters, rope-dancers, wild beasts, mermaids, fat boys, girls with two heads, cows with five legs, bearded and pig-faced ladies, strong men and women, and every other species of monstrosity that may now be seen at Barnum & Bailey's show. Vice and ruffianism, however, at last disgusted a more decorous age, and when, in September, 1850, the Lord Mayor, as had been the custom with all his predecessors, proceeded to Smithfield to open the fair by proclamation, lo, with the exception of a few gingerbread stalls, the ground was deserted! Bartholomew Fair was not suppressed : it died of pure inanition.

Among other strange sights that the old gateway has gazed upon have been wife selling and wife burning. *The Times* of 30th March, 1796, tells us how one John Lees sold his wife for 6d. to Samuel Hall, and she was delivered up with a halter round her neck, and the clerk of the market received 4d. for toll. Two cases of this kind happened even in 1832. Evelyn records that in 1652 he saw a woman, who had murdered her husband, burning in Smithfield, that being the usual punishment—not hanging—for murderesses. Smithfield was also a chosen spot in the middle ages for single combats and ordeal by battle. In the seventeenth and eighteenth centuries it had become such a rendezvous for bullies and bravoes that it was known as " Ruffians'-hall ".

In the first half of the nineteenth century, Dickens, in *Oliver Twist*, grimly limned some of the sights the old gate frowned upon.

" It was market morning, the ground was covered nearly ankle-deep with filth and mire, and a thick steam perpetually rising from the reeking bodies of the cattle and mingling with the fog. . . . The whistling of drovers, the barking of dogs, the bellowing and plunging of beasts, . . . the roar of voices that issued from every public-house, the crowding, pushing, driving, bleating, whooping, hideous and

discordant yelling that came from every corner of
the market confused the senses."

And knights and ladies, Plantagenets and Tudors,
all the pomp of chivalry, martyrs and persecutors,
and—oh ! terrible descent into bathos—all the riots
and humours of seven hundred years of Bartholomew
Fairs have passed away like the baseless fabric of a
vision, and the old archway has survived them all !
Think of the tiny England of the Norman kings,
without nationality or even a language ; think of the
mighty England of to-day with its world-wide tongue,
no word of which was in existence when those stones
were fashioned ! And city vandals proposed to sweep
them away to make room for an ugly, modern
thoroughfare !

Let us pass through the gateway, down the neglected
churchyard, formerly the nave of the church, and take
one glance at all that remains of the grand priory of
St. Bartholomew—the choir, the most superb specimen
of Norman architecture in the metropolis. For once
restoration has not spelt destruction, and all the
solemn beauty of the old edifice has been preserved.
Beneath the dim religious light reposes the effigy of
King Henry's jester, who, repenting of the vanity of
his life, made a pilgrimage to Rome, and having been
favoured by a vision of St. Bartholomew, on his return
in 1123 founded the church and hospital.

The north door of the church opens into one of the
most curious relics of ancient London yet left, Cloth
Fair. High walls nod to each other, and roofs almost

Back Court,
Smithfield.

meet; tall, gaunt houses with their overhanging
storeys and gable-ended roofs leave but a streak of
day visible above our heads; the dust and dirt of
centuries lie upon everything, upon the dark, dingy
shops, upon the eaves and every projection.   Here are
gaps where buildings have been wholly or partially
pulled down, showing the walls and windows of the
church behind.   Here are ghostly-looking houses
with every window smashed in, waiting for the pick-
axe and the spade.   Here is a *cul-de-sac* so narrow
that from the windows of one side you might easily
press your hands upon the black wall opposite, and
so dark that, summer and winter, a perpetual twi-
light reigns there.   As you advance farther, narrow
thoroughfares of ruinous houses and blind courts
branch right and left.

At the corner of one of these, leading into Long
Lane, stands "Ye Dick Whittington," which claims
to be the oldest licensed tavern in London, and, after
looking at the picture of it we here present, the claim
may be allowed.   It is probably as old as the days
of the famous Sir Richard himself.

And now, O reader! can thy imagination again
transport thee so far as to obliterate from thy mind's
eye the dreary and soul-depressing gloom of the
Clerkenwell of to-day, and picture in place of it fair
gardens and terraced vineyards and a bright blue sky,
and, on the slope passing westwards from the Green
to Ray Street, a noble monastic pile from which the
chants of the monks mingle with the ecstatic song of

the lark ?   Just at the bottom of what will hereafter
be Ray Street is Skinner's Well, almost as famous

YE DICK WHITTINGTON.

for its healing powers as Lourdes or St. Winifred's
will be in time to come.   But a more enduring fame

will cling to it as the spot where the parish clerks of London, on a raised stage or pageant, for centuries performed the Miracle and Mystery plays. And so it came to be called Clerk's Well.

Except when presented in churches, as were frequently the case, these plays were performed in the open. The stage was made up of three platforms, one above the other. On the uppermost sat God the Father, surrounded by His angels ; on the second the saints ; the third was for the mortals. On one side of the lowest platform was a yawning gulf representing hell, from which fire and smoke issued, and the yells of demons who occasionally showed themselves to the spectators. Such were the arrangements of the earlier Miracle plays. Subsequently some attempt was made at a rude kind of scenery, even to the building of a castle and a ship. The subjects of the plays were always scriptural : " The Creation of the World," " Job's Sufferings," " Dives and Lazarus "—all acted in very realistic fashion, and with much admixture of gross indecency and buffoonery in the character of " The vice," or Devil, who was the comic personage, and the progenitor of the clowns of a later date. As the centuries went on, these performances fell into the hands of the laity, and became so abominable and blasphemous that, sometime before the Reformation, the clergy suppressed them. *The Miracles* and *Mysteries*, however, greatly influenced our earliest dramatists, as readers of Dodsley's *Old Plays* will discover.

Richard II. and his queen attended these performances, and in the reign of his successor, Stow tells
us, "a great play was played at Skinner's Well,
which lasted eight days, where there were to see the
same the most part of the nobles and gentles of
England. And forthwith began a royal jousting in
Smithfield between the Earl of Somerset and the
Seneschal of Hainault, Sir John Cornwall, Sir Richard
Arundell and the son of Sir John Chesny against
certain Frenchmen."

When the clerks deserted Skinner's Well, all kinds
of barbarous sports took the place of *The Miracles* and
Mysteries. A bear garden was formed, and the bulls
and bears, on some occasions covered with fireworks,
were baited by savage dogs ; there were wrestling
and cudgel and single-stick play, and "champions"
challenged one another to bouts with backswords,
sword and dagger, sword and buckler, and slashed one
another to the huge delight of the spectators, as you
will read in the *Spectator*, No. 436. The place was
known for many generations as Hockley in the Hole.
The site of this notorious resort was marked until
within the last year by a very old tavern, The Coach
and Horses, at the bottom of Ray Street, originally
Rag Street.

Yet notwithstanding the ruffianly character of the
neighbourhood, some of the highest nobility, the New-
castles, the Berkeleys, had their town residences in
Clerkenwell until the end of the seventeenth century,
and are still remembered in the names of streets.

And now as a contrast to this turmoil and pother
let us look in upon Thomas Britton, " the musical small-
coal man," who carried on his trade in Jerusalem Passage, Aylesbury Street, in the earlier decades of the
eighteenth century.   Here is his shed, which was a
stable the other day, and above it is what was then
the hay-loft, but it now forms the proprietor's entire
ménage—kitchen, parlour and bedroom combined.   It
can only be approached by these outside steps.
Don't shrink back ; the red-heeled shoes and silken
coats and brocaded sacques of noble lords and ladies,
who are members of the musical club held here every
Thursday night, mount them weekly.

Hark ! do you hear those strains of grand music ?
Some master hand is sweeping the keys of a harpsichord, and those long, deep, full rich notes of a viol
de gamba can only be drawn out by a fine bow.   Let
us ascend ; it is a poor place, but take off your hat
and bow reverently, for you are in the presence of
a mighty genius.   The big, heavy-looking man at the
harpsichord is no less a personage than George Frederick Handel, who frequently attends and plays at these
musical meetings ; and he with the viol de gamba
between his knees, in a blue smock frock, is Thomas
Britton himself, a musician of the highest class,
theoretical and practical.   There are other players,
noted executants of the day : Sir Roger L'Estrange,
Dr. Pepusch, Mr. Bannister, Mr. Charles Jennens,
Madame Cuzzoni, and the ladies and gentlemen who
crowd the mean room are distinguished personages,

I assure you — dukes and duchesses, wits and philosophers.[1]

Thomas Britton, notwithstanding his very humble occupation, is no common person. If you will look in at Mr. Bateman's, the bookseller of Paternoster Row, any Saturday afternoon, you will probably see our musical enthusiast drop down a sack of coals at the door, enter the shop, salute the beaux assembled there in their velvets and laces, and fall into their conversation, aye, and be listened to respectfully, though among them we may recognise supercilious Horace Walpole and pompous Dr. Burney; for Thomas Britton is a collector of rare books and MSS., and owns twenty-seven musical instruments. Yet he will never be anything more than a small-coal man. How different all this would be now! But would it be better? No. There was a noble simplicity about this man that would have been destroyed by the gush and snobbery of an age which, while pretending to be in love with the spirit of democracy, imitates the most contemptible side of aristocratic exclusiveness.

[1] Ward, the author of *The London Spy*, wrote:—

    " Upon Thursday repair
    To my palace, and there
    Hobble up stair by stair;
    But I pray ye take care
  That you break not your shins by a stumble;
    And without e'er a souse
    Paid to me or my spouse,
    Sit as still as a mouse
    At the top of the house,
  And there you shall hear how we fumble ".

To exhaust the memories of Clerkenwell and its surroundings would require a volume, and I must pass over many an old building, old street, old lane, old tavern that would furnish much pleasant gossip, and merely glance at two or three of the more remarkable places.

Of the great Priory of the Knights of St. John of Jerusalem, founded in 1100, only the crypt of the church and the well-known Gateway remain. The former, seven hundred years old, beneath the Church of St. John, is one of the most interesting antiquities of London. The priory went with the other monastic establishments in Henry Tudor's reign; and in that of his son Protector Somerset carried away the stones to help build his great house in the Strand.

In the room above the Gateway Garrick made his first appearance in London (1738) in an amateur performance of Fielding's *Mock Doctor*. And in that room the great actor, Johnson, Goldsmith and Cave afterwards formed a club. Until within these twenty years the room in furniture, fittings and appearance was much as it might have been when it was a rendezvous for those four *illustrissimi*, but the present possessors have swept and garnished it in the true spirit of vandalism, leaving only the walls. At the Gate was first issued *The Gentleman's Magazine*, and here young Samuel Johnson, hungry, shabby, and almost shoeless, toiled for a crust, translating from foreign languages, composing parliamentary debates and speeches; yet with all his industry was sometimes obliged to walk the streets all night for want of a lodging. The Gateway after " Sylvanus Urban's " time, and perhaps *in* it, was a tavern called " The Jerusalem," wherein all the antiquities were reverently preserved until the advent of the iconoclasts.

In the old Square, of which little remains, the Carlisles, the Essexes, the Norths had mansions in Charles II.'s time. Hick's Hall, from which all distances to and from London were formerly measured, stood just about the spot where the Sessions House was built. It may be worth noting that Wadebridge Street marks the site of the old Red Bull Theatre of Elizabeth's time, which, in the style of its performances, resembled the Surrey or " Vic." of forty years ago.

Close at hand is a famous monument of the olden time. The Carthusian Monastery, thereafter known as the Charterhouse, was founded by that brave knight, so familiar to all readers of Froissart, Sir Walter Manny, in 1371. Adjoining it was a burial-place called Pardon Churchyard, in which, when the Black Death raged, in 1348, fifty thousand corpses were buried. To this Golgotha Sir Walter added thirteen acres, and Stow calculates that up to his time a hundred thousand bodies had been interred within the area. The monastery was dissolved for refusing to acknowledge Henry VIII. as head of the Church : nine monks were starved to death in Newgate, and a fourth was executed; Prior Houghton having been

previously put to death, and his head, with those of
two others, and portions of his body, spiked over the
gates.   The house afterwards successively fell into
the possession of the Duke of Northumberland, Lord
North, and the Howards, and was finally purchased
by Thomas Sutton, who, after being Master General
of the Ordnance under Elizabeth, became a goldsmith or usurer, and a man of enormous wealth.   It
has been said that he was the original of Jonson's
Volpone in *The Fox.*   Be that as it may, he paid
£13,000 for the old hospital, and endowed it to be
a home for aged men and a school for poor children
(1611), and when he died his funeral procession,
which numbered six thousand people, was six hours
in passing from Paternoster Row to Christ Church
chapel.

The original gateway and some ancient buildings
just within it on the right, together with the chancel
and south wall of the Jacobean Chapel, are all that
remain of the old monastery of the Carthusians; but
the main building is a fine specimen of Jacobean
architecture.   It is a delightful old-world spot, and
was quiet and secluded before Wilderness Row
became a portion of Clerkenwell Road, and brought
a racket of traffic past the tall boundary wall; but
still much of that air of calm and leisure, so precious
from its scarceness in this age of restless hurry, reigns
over the place.   The master's house has noble apartments, adorned with some very fine historical portraits
and furniture and hangings, among which you live

back in the late Stuart days, and dream of velvet coats and flowing periwigs.

Thackeray has shed an immortal halo around the old "Greyfriars," and it is almost impossible to enter or even think of Charterhouse without the image of grand old Colonel Newcome rising before you. Of all the flesh-and-blood people associated with the place none are so real to us as that creation of the great novelist's brain. And yet these mortals are a goodly crew, including such notable persons as Crashaw and Lovelace, the cavalier poets; Dr. Isaac Barrow, Joseph Addison, Richard Steele, John Wesley, Sir William Blackstone, the Earl of Liverpool, Lord Ellenborough, Sir C. Eastlake, Thackeray, Leech. But what are these names to the smug, heavily mulcted, middle-class young gentlemen, the Carthusians of Godalming? You cannot transport that subtle influence called prestige that clings about the stones, the ground, the air of our famous buildings, and the Surrey "Charterhouse" is no more *the* Charterhouse than would be a spick and span new church, built on Salisbury Plain, Westminster Abbey, because the ecclesiastical establishment of the London minster had been translated thither. Charterhouse School has passed away, and a country academy been established on its endowments. The same will be the case with Christ School. The boys of Merchant Taylors' now occupy the Charterhouse.

CHAPTER V.

> Who that rugged street would traverse o'er
> That stretches, O Fleet-ditch! from thy black shore
> To the Tower's moated walls ?   Here streams ascend,
> That in mixed fumes, the wrinkled nose offends.
> Where chandlers' caldrons boil ; where fishy prey
> Hide the wet stall, long absent from the sea ;
> And where the cleaver chops the heifer's spoil,
> And where huge hogsheads sweat with trainy oil,
> Thy breathing nostrils hold !   But how shall I
> Pass where in piles Cornavian (Cheshire) cheeses lie '

SUCH is Gay's description in *Trivia* (1716) of the
thoroughfare we now know as Farringdon Road and
Farringdon Street, through which ran—and still runs
beneath it—the Fleet River, then little more than a
ditch of Stygian blackness, upon the slimy banks of
which, wherever the rows of pigsties that clustered on
the western side left openings, were thrown refuse
and offal of all kinds, and the grunters roamed about
and fattened on the putrid garbage.   The ditch was
spanned by three bridges, one at the foot of Holborn
Hill, another at the end of Fleet Street, and a third
opposite Bridewell.   Little more than 200 years ago
ships anchored at the bottom of Ludgate Hill, and

(75)

thence passed into the Thames, into which the Fleet flowed.

All about this foul stream during the eighteenth and first half of the nineteenth centuries gathered a maze of narrow streets, courts and alleys, in which lived some of the most desperate characters of the metropolis. The most notorious of these haunts was Chick Lane, better known as West Street, that ran near the end of Field Lane. The Red Lion Tavern, which stood there within the last fifty years, and was a very ancient house, was supposed to have been one of the abodes of the infamous thief-taker, Jonathan Wild. It had sliding panels, secret hiding-places and trap doors opening over the river, convenient for the disposal of murdered victims; many other of the houses had similar conveniences. Most of this foul neighbourhood was swept away by the Smithfield improvements, between forty and fifty years ago, and by the Metropolitan Railway.

On the eastern side of the ditch, just about the spot where the Memorial Hall now offends the eye, stood for seven centuries the notorious Fleet Prison. "Abandon hope, all ye who enter here" should have been carved over the portals of that iniquitous den, the horrors of which culminated under the rule of Bainbridge in the first half of the eighteenth century. The tortures of the Inquisition were inflicted upon poor debtors who resisted the infamous extortions of this wretch; they were shut up with lunatics, lodged with people sick of fevers and small-pox, chained to

the ground, burned with red-hot irons, and were battered to death with sticks. In the common yard might
have been met peers who had shone at St. James's ;
preachers who had stirred thousands of hearts by their
eloquence ; brave generals who had lost their limbs
in the service of their country ; authors whose works
have been a delight to posterity ; merchants great
upon 'Change ; murderers, pimps, cheats, gamblers,
highwaymen, prostitutes, fine ladies, pious wives and
mothers, pure young girls, all mingled together like
the refuse of things once beautiful and dainty and
good to look upon, which was swept down the Stygian
stream that ran beside this pandemonium. Wat
Tyler burned down the prison, so did the Gordon
rioters ; but it rose again to be depicted in its last
days by the pen of Dickens. The locomotive now
puffs over a portion of its site ; but little dreams the new
generation of the silent records of strange romances
and crimes, of love and devotion, of hideous vice and
awful human misery it is passing over. Wonderful
are the untold stories of the streets of London !

But there are other records of the prison—comical,
sentimental, tragical—those of the Fleet marriages.
A person who stationed himself opposite those black,
frowning walls any morning in the early decades
of the last century would have witnessed a sight
amusing enough on the surface, but sadly suggestive
upon reflection.

All sorts and conditions of men and women are
making for the prison, and every Jack has his Jill :

some come in hackney coaches, some in gay chariots, others are picking their way on foot among the garbage cast out from Fleet Market that stands in the middle of the roadway, all are hurrying to this gruesome Temple of Hymen. That old harridan, patched and painted and in white satin sacque, looks more fitted for the grave than the bridal chamber ; she shakes with palsy as she leans upon the arm of her young, handsome but threadbare cavalier, upon whom she hideously languishes ; that is my Lady Ogleby, who amorous at seventy has bestowed her parchment hand upon Jack Wannop, a ruined gamester, and fearing the interference of her children has consented to a clandestine marriage at the Fleet. Poor old woman! That fierce, military-looking man is a " Derby captain," one of Marlborough's officers, and the fat, buxom widow, who hangs upon his arm a little nervously, is the hostess of a tavern where the brave captain has been living at free quarters and of which he is now to become the master ; the fear of interfering relatives has driven her also to the Fleet. Well, they will jog on with not more than the usual allowance of matrimonial skirmishes and scratches, perhaps. I don't know what to say about the next pair ; that bumptious-looking young fellow and that yellow, snub-nosed girl ; Tom Idle has induced his master's daughter to jump out of her bedroom window to hang herself in the halter of Hymen ; the story of that handsomely attired, dissipated-looking young fellow with that very plain and frightened-looking girl clinging to his arm is some-

what similar—Miss Chrysos, the rich heiress, has eloped
from her boarding-school with Dick Hopeful. Poor
girl! There are a lad and a lass whose united ages
scarcely number thirty-four years; it is a terrible case
of calf love. But oh, when they are man and woman
how they will hate one another!

Outside the prison lounge some half-dozen tatterdemalions, with bristly chins, drink-bleared eyes, their
rags, which serve both for day and night, reeking of
the pot-house. They are on the watch for these
victims of Cupid and Mammon, and, hat in hand,
surround them. "D'ye want the parson, my noble
young gentleman?" "This way, beautiful lady!"—
this to my Lady Ogleby, who sniggers and simpers
and hides her raddled face with her fan. "The
doctor's at the Pen and Hand." "This way to the
true and ancient register." At the entrance to the
prison the candidates for matrimony are met by rival
parsons in cauliflower wigs, rusty and ragged cassocks,
who each obsequiously presses for the honour of performing the ceremony. But while the unfortunates
are in danger of being torn to pieces by contending
divines and drunken touts, a powerful, forbidding-
looking woman elbows her way through the throng,
and with an air of authority, that seems to overawe
the rivals, beckons the couples to follow her; Jack
Wannop and the Derby captain succeed in doing so,
but parsons and touts close round the rest, like hungry
dogs over a heap of bones.

The female guide conducts her captives to the

frowsy room of a public-house, within the precincts
of the prison, where a huge, fat man, attired in clerical
garb, with a pewter-pot before him, is awaiting votaries ;
when you look at his nose of Tyrian purple, his leering,
squinting, watery eyes, blotched cheeks and thick
lips, and hear of his blasphemy and debauchery, you
may not wonder that these distinctions have won for
him the nickname of the " Bishop of Hell ". For a fee,
ranging from five shillings to a guinea, according to
the quality of his patrons, this priest of Hymen will
in a few minutes make a couple miserable for life.
But even now the days of his vile calling are numbered ; an Act of Parliament will soon be passed,
rendering such performances of the marriage ceremony
criminal. It will only drive erratic lovers to Gretna
Green, however, where the blacksmith will tie the
fatal knot as readily as did the Bishop of—the Fleet.

When, in 1737, a great part of the Fleet ditch was
arched over, the Old Stocks Market, which had
occupied the site of the Mansion-house, was transferred to a spot nearly opposite the prison, and opened
for the sale of fish, meat and vegetables. But, in
1829, it was found to be such an obstruction to the
increasing traffic that it had to be demolished, and
Farringdon Market, which has now also disappeared,
was erected in its place. The site and building of the
latter cost a quarter of a million of money, and a
handsome affair it was considered to be, strange as
such a dictum may sound to those who remember it
only in its days of decay and desertion.

FARRINGDON MARKET.

Until the construction of the railway line which joins Ludgate to Holborn Station there was, behind and beside the Fleet Prison, another network of unsavoury courts and alleys, extending to the Old Bailey and Smithfield. Of these was Green-arbour Court, in which poor Oliver Goldsmith passed a year or two of his bitter struggle for bread and did some of his earlier work. Washington Irving, in *Tales of a Traveller*, 1829, describes how, through alleys, courts and blind passages, traversing Fleet Market and thence turning along a narrow street to the bottom of a long steep flight of stone steps (they were known as " Break-neck Steps "), he made his way up to Green-arbour Court. " Here were the tall, faded houses, with heads out of window at every storey ; the dirty, neglected children ; the bawling, slipshod women ; in one corner the clothes hanging to .dry. . . . Without question the same squalid, squalling colony, which it then was, it had been in Goldsmith's time. He would compromise with the children for occasional cessation of noise by frequent cakes or sweetmeats, or by a tune upon his flute, for which all the court assembled. . . . He would risk his neck nightly at those steep stone stairs ; every day, for his clothes had become too ragged to submit to day-light scrutiny, he would keep within his dirty, naked, unfurnished room, with its single wooden chair and window bench. Such was Goldsmith's home." Yet perhaps even this was better than Axe Lane, where he had to herd with the beggars.

But what a curious picture the anecdote conjures up : the lean, hungry, tattered poet, standing in the squalid court, the centre of a ring of frowsy women and open-mouthed children, unkempt heads thrust out of the broken windows, tootling upon his flute. Must it not have recalled that self-drawn picture of himself acting the same part, but in far different scenes, as given in *The Traveller* :—

> How often have I led thy sportive choir
> With tuneless pipe beside the murmuring Loire,
> Where shading elms along the margin grew,
> And, freshen'd from the wave, the zephyr flew !
> And haply, though my harsh touch, faltering still,
> But mock'd all time and marr'd the dancer's skill,
> Yet would the village praise my wondrous power,
> And dance forgetful of the noontide hour.

Under Queen Elizabeth the condition of authors was most lamentable : that exquisite lyrist, Robert Greene, dying in abject destitution ; that awful cry of bitter despair from Tom Nash in *Pierce Pennilesse ;* the revelations of Henslowe's *Diary;* Edmund Spenser expiring almost of want—are terrible tales. It is a curious fact that although, with the exception of Charles I., the Stuarts displayed no particular generosity towards literary men, from the accession of James the condition of the author rapidly improved. Contrast the circumstances of the later contemporaries of Shakespeare with those of the earlier : if the Heywoods and Massingers were needy they were not always flourishing ; we hear no more of such horrors as Greene's death and Nash's anathemas. James was certainly a better patron and a truer encourager of literature than his predecessor.

Up to the death of Queen Anne authors of ability, who were moderately prudent in their lives, did not starve ; but with the coming of the Hanoverians, literary men fell into a state of poverty and degradation such as had not been known for more than a hundred years. Yet what could be expected when the king raged like a mad bull at the sight of a book, and was as unlettered as one of his own German peasants. And his son was no better. When he went to see *Richard III.* he thought nothing of Garrick, all that struck him was the Lord Mayor ! Literature was out of fashion, noblemen no longer patronised authors, and there was no reading public. What a sordid record is the literary life of the eighteenth century ; you cannot take up a biography, a play, a novel of the period without coming upon some trait of it. Pope and Foote and Smollett and Fielding and Goldsmith satirised or grew cynical or pitiful over it. In " A Modern Glossary " (*Covent Garden Journal*) Fielding defines "AUTHOR—a laughing-stock. It means likewise a poor fellow, and, in general, an object of contempt."

" Where are the great protectors and patrons of the liberal arts ? " inquires Governor Cope in Foote's farce, *The Author.* " Patron !—the word has lost its use ; a guinea subscription at the request of a lady, whose chambermaid is acquainted with the author, may be now and then picked up. Protector ! Why, I dare believe there's more money laid out upon Islington

turnpike in a month than upon all the learned men in
Great Britain in seven years." In another scene the
Printer's Devil brings the author his weekly pay for
the newspaper, five and sixpence, and treats him with
contemptuous insolence. " Here's a man on the stairs
wants you," he says as he is going away; "by the
sheepishness of his looks, and the shabbiness of his
dress, he's either a pickpocket or an author."

There is little exaggeration in this satire. Chatterton was paid half a guinea for sixteen songs, the same
price for a poem of 270 lines, and two shillings for a
couple of contributions to a magazine; for four months'
hard work he received four pounds fifteen shillings
and ninepence. In grim earnestness what can surpass those lines of Goldsmith's—" The Description
of an Author's Bedchamber"—probably a self-drawn
picture?—

> In a lonely room from bailiffs snug
> The muse found Scroggins stretched beneath a rug ;
> A window patch'd with paper, but a ray
> That dimly show'd the state in which he lay ;
> The sanded floor that grits beneath the tread ;
> The humid wall with paltry pictures spread. . . .
> The morn was cold ; he views with keen desire
> The rusty grate, unconscious of a fire ;
> With beer and milk arrears the frieze was scored,
> And five crack'd tea-cups dress'd the culinary board ;
> A night-cap deck'd his brows instead of bay,
> A cap by night—a stocking all the day.

We have seen Johnson homeless and foodless, and
pages might be filled with similar stories. Truly
here were few Chattertons or Johnsons in Grub

Street ; there were more Eusdens, Elkanah Settles, Nahum Tates, Gildons, Flecknoes, the dunces of *The Dunciad*. Some of the unfortunates, like Savage, of whom I shall have more to say presently, owed much of their misery to dissipation. Yet how much of that might have been induced by the precariousness of their lives, by that reckless despair in which there is nothing between temporary oblivion and madness· Let us judge leniently their errors and their vices.

CHAPTER VI.

ELY PLACE — HATTON GARDEN—BROOKE STREET
—THE HOLBORN INNS OF COURT—SOUTHAMP-
TON HOUSE—HOLBORN—SHOE LANE—FETTER
LANE.

THERE had been a time when the foul Fleet of Pope,
Gay and Swift was a clear river, taking its rise in the
springs of Caen Wood, and flowing down through
Kentish Town ; always turbid on account of its *fleet*
current, and given to flooding its banks, for which
riotous conduct, however, much blame was attached
to the River of Wells, a branch of which rose at
Holborn Bars (to give its modern name) and rushed
with the force of a torrent down Oldbourne, or Hil·
bourne, and swelled the waters of the northern stream
at Oldbourne Bridge.   But even as early as 1307,
Lacey, Earl of Lincoln, complained that whereas
in times past the course of water running under Old-
bourne and Fleet Bridges into the Thames had been
of such breadth and depth that ten or twelve ships at
once were with merchandise once able to come up to
those bridges, the course was now so filled up with
the filth of tanners and such others and the raising of
wharves and the diversion of currents for mills that

this was no longer possible. In answer to this plaint the river was cleansed, though it could never again be brought to its former depth. It was cleansed again and again in the succeeding centuries, until the nuisances increasing beyond control it was left to its destiny.

As late as the reign of Elizabeth the slopes of Old-bourne on the north side were covered with fair gardens, the memories of which still linger in the names of Saffron Hill, Vine Street, Field Lane, names so strangely incongruous with such hideous rookeries. Further north the rural character of the banks of the Fleet survived to a much later date, for at Bagnigge Wells Nell Gwynne had a delightful country residence, lying in charming grounds which were afterwards converted into a spa and place of public resort, where fashionable London came to drink the waters of a chalybeate spring, as they did at Sadler's Wells.

The gardens in which the saffron and the vines and fruit trees flourished, and the strawberries were so excellent, belonged to Ely Place, founded by John de Kirkeby, Bishop of Ely, in the latter part of the thirteenth century. It was not exclusively inhabited by ecclesiastics, as John of Gaunt died within its walls.[1] And in after reigns the Earl of Sussex and the Earl of Warwick lived there. But its most celebrated inhabitant was that high favourite of

[1] *See* Shakespeare's *Richard II.*, Act ii., Scene 1, and *Richard III.*, Act iii., Scene 4.

Queen Elizabeth's, Sir Christopher Hatton. How curious it reads at the present day that one of the stipulations in the lease by which he held it was that the bishops should have the privilege of walking in the gardens and gathering twenty baskets of roses yearly !

Sir Christopher spent a large sum upon beautifying the house and grounds, and lived in high state and splendour. It is said that he won the queen's favour by his handsome person and graceful dancing, at all events she doted on him and raised him to the dignity of Lord Chancellor. Elizabeth's avarice, however, was even greater than her amourousness ; Sir Christopher was indebted to her £40,000, which he hoped she would forego, but Her Majesty pressed so hard for payment that it broke her lover's heart. In her remorse, it is said, she came herself to his sick bed ; yet not even the royal presence could heal the wound, and the good knight passed away in 1591.

All that remains of Ely Place and its magnificence is the beautiful old chapel of St. Etheldreda.[1] It was probably built at the close of the fourteenth or beginning of the fifteenth century. The destruction of the gardens is marked by an entry in Evelyn's *Diary*, 7th June, 1659 : " To London, to take leave of my brother, and see the foundations now laying for a long street and buildings in Hatton Garden, designed

---

[1] Etheldreda was the daughter of a king of the West Saxons who did much towards founding Ely Cathedral, of which she was elected patron saint.

for a little town, lately an ample garden.'   There
are pictures of Ely House, however, standing on a

ST. ETHELDREDA.

grassy lawn and shaded by trees, taken in the second
half of the eighteenth century.

The shade of Charles Dickens hovers over the

whole of this neighbourhood. The old Saracen's Head on Snow Hill, which has given place to a modern hotel, was the scene of Nicholas Nickleby's first meeting with Mr. Squeers, and was the house at which John Browdie and his wife put up on their honeymoon trip. Field Lane and Saffron Hill are reminiscent of Fagin and his pupils and of Oliver Twist. No. 54 Hatton Garden was the old police court presided over by Mr. Lang, the Fang of the novel, before whom the poor little parish boy was arraigned. Bleeding Heart Yard is an important background in some of the scenes of Little Dorrit.

Leather Lane (Stow writes it " Lither ") was the western boundary of Ely Place garden, and is very ancient. The clearance made for the new Assurance offices has swept away the Old Bell Tavern, with which a well-known legend of the Commonwealth was associated ; it was one of the last, if not the last, of the old galleried inns of London. And Furnival's Inn, founded in the reign of Henry IV., and associated with memories of Sir Thomas Moore and of Charles Dickens, who there wrote the first numbers of *Pickwick*, has gone with it.

That gloomy and depressing thoroughfare, Brooke Street, though it has been lately modernised, has a fund of interesting reminiscences. Upon the spot now covered by St. Alban's Church stood the mansion of Fulke Greville, Lord Brooke. Courtier, statesman, poet, the friend of Sidney, Shakespeare and Ben Jonson, who must often have visited him here, the author himself of two tragedies, *Alaham* and *Mustapha*, which, though ponderous, are not without merit, and of some pleasant poems. Lord Brooke was a man of great importance in the days of Queen Bess and her successor, and great was the consternation when (1628) the news went abroad that he had been murdered by one of his servitors for some imaginary grievance, and that having done the deed, the assassin fell upon his own sword. I cannot discover when the mansion ceased to exist, but in Charles II.'s reign its name was changed to Warwick House, Lord Brooke having been created Earl of Warwick, under which title it is referred to by Pepys (3rd March, 1660). Twenty-three years later it was inhabited by the Earl of Clare, who had then just quitted his mansion in Drury Lane.[1]

But the interest attached to Brooke Street is chiefly centred in two dark romances—one of the seventeenth, the other of the eighteenth century. In Fox Court, which, until Gray's Inn Lane was widened, was an ancient and gruesome spot, in the year 1696, a masked lady was brought thither to the house of a midwife and secretly delivered of a child. The mysterious female was the notorious Countess of Macclesfield, her lover was Lord Rivers. Until Mr. Moy Thomas thoroughly investigated the story it was universally believed that that miserable but clever scoundrel-poet, Richard Savage, was the offspring of the amour. He always persisted that his mother was the wicked

[1] *See* Clare Market.

countess, denounced her for her unnatural conduct in forsaking him, and, in fine, traded upon his alleged aristocratic bar sinister. Mr. Moy Thomas has indubitably proved that Savage was the son of a cobbler, and that the countess's child died soon after it was christened. Savage was an idle, drunken debauchee. He killed a gentleman at Charing Cross, but was saved from the gallows by Queen Caroline, upon whom he had succeeded in imposing his fabrication, and Her Majesty granted him a small pension, which ceased at her death. Johnson met him when he first came up from Lichfield, and for a while they were brothers in starvation. Savage died of fever in a Bristol gaol at the age of forty-six. Two of his poems, "The Bastard" and "The Wanderer," have much power.

Fielding, in *The Covent Garden Journal*, tells a good story of Savage, which might be applied to the present day. His poems had found no purchasers until the poet was thrown into Newgate. The next day the bookseller advertised the works of Mr. Savage, now under sentence of death for murder. The whole impression went off immediately. The cunning trader then offered him a good price for his dying speech and confession, which should be made at Tyburn. Savage was pardoned. But nevertheless the speech was written and published—and sold prodigiously.

Far more striking and pathetic is the episode which connects the name of Chatterton with Brooke Street. He had removed from Shoreditch to a house on the western side, which was standing not many years

ago.   How he worked and starved I have shown in
the previous chapter. And here came the end. Locked
in his garret, he had eaten nothing for two days. On
the third morning his landlady broke open the door,
found the floor strewn with torn papers, and the poor
youth lying dead upon his bed. He had poisoned
himself with arsenic or opium. Without prayer, or
knell, or kindly tear, he was interred in the burying-
ground of Shoe Lane Workhouse, upon which Farringdon Market was built. He was only eighteen.[1]

It was at the Hole-in-the-Wall Passage, Brooke
Street, that the Cato Street conspiracy (1820) was first
concocted to kill Wellington, Canning, Eldon and
other cabinet ministers. The arms and powder were
kept there.

"Port Pool, or Gray's Inn Lane," writes Stow,
"so called of the Inn of Court named Gray's Inn, a
goodly house there situate, by whom built or first
begun I have not yet learned, but seemeth to be
since Edward III.'s and time,   is a prebend to St.
Paul's Church in London. This lane is furnished
with fair buildings and many tenements on both
sides, leading to the fields towards Highgate and

---

[1] This is no place to enter into the question as to who was to blame
for the sad catastrophe.   Much odium was thrown upon Horace
Walpole ; but what man would have acted differently to what he
did when convinced that the Rowley poems were a forgery ?   Here
was the deceit by which Chatterton destroyed himself ; and it was
one of the most curious aberrations of intellect on record.   Had he
admitted himself to be the author of those wonderful poems, written
by a schoolboy, there is little doubt that, even in that Bœotian age,
he would have been taken by the hand and acclaimed a genius.

Hampstead." Some famous people had inhabited those old, overhanging, gabled-ended houses, which became so gruesome in their squalor and mouldering decay before they fell into the hands of the house-breaker. Here resided both Hampden and Pym, and previous to them James Shirley, the last of the mighty dramatists of the Shakespeare and Jonson age, and other persons notable in their day. Jacob Tonson, the noted bookseller, had a shop just inside Gray's Inn Gate.

This famous Inn of Court was originally the residence of the Lords Grey of Wilton ; the exact date of its foundation has never been discovered. Although Gray's Inn can show a most illustrious roll of great men, who have studied within its walls, including Gascoigne, the great chief-justice who committed Prince Hal to prison for contempt of the law ; Thomas Cromwell, Henry VIII.'s minister ; the great Burleigh, Sir Nicholas Bacon, Chief-Justice Holt, Sir Philip Sidney, Sir Samuel Romilly, and, greatest of all, Francis Bacon ; while it has numbered among its chaplains five famous archbishops of Canterbury, Whitgift, Bancroft, Laud, Juxon and Sheldon ; and amongst its residents George Chapman, one of "the Elizabethan" dramatists, and a translator of Homer ; *Hudibras* Butler, William Cobbett, and, for a very short time, Johnson and Goldsmith ; yet nothing like the romance, the interest, and charm of association which pervade the Temple attach to this Inn. The garden, with its noble trees, until very lately the home of a colony of rooks, and its bright, smooth greensward, bounded south and east by the tall, grey, venerable walls of the Inn, silent remembrancers of the generations and generations of eyes, extinguished in eternal night, that have gazed down upon it from those long narrow windows, is still a grateful and beautiful contrast to the weary desert of dingy brick by which it is encompassed. It was a favourite resort of the great author of the *Novum Organum*, the man who overthrew that Aristotelian philosophy that had prevailed for nearly two thousand years. Often did he walk and meditate over some of his great work upon that very ground, many of his essays being dated from Gray's Inn. The shade of Francis Bacon overshadows all other memories of the ancient house of " Pourtepole ".

In the seventeenth century the Garden was a fashionable promenade. Mr. Pepys frequently took his walks there. He also notes (1667) a curious incident—a rebellion of the students against the Benchers, who outlawed them, but adds : " now they are at peace again ". The Garden is also mentioned as a place of assignation between fine ladies and gentlemen by the dramatists of that period ; but at last the doings therein became so disreputable that it had to be put under regulation and closed at certain hours.

The hall, finished in 1560, is very handsome, with fine carvings and portraits and emblazoned windows. Queen Elizabeth held Gray's Inn in high favour, probably on account of Burleigh's connection with it, as well as for the splendid entertainments they provided for her delectation, not only here but at Whitehall. It is said that the bench tables, now used, were her gift, and on all great occasions her "glorious, pious and immortal memory" is still drunk with much formality, only three benchers rising at a time, and then passing it on to three more, and so finally to the students.

From the reign of Henry VIII. Gray's Inn was celebrated for its Christmas, Twelfth Night and Shrovetide revels, and masquings and mummeries; they were suppressed under the intolerant Puritan régime of his son, but revived with greater splendour in the reign of Elizabeth. The grandest and most costly of all these masques, however, was given in the reign of Charles I., an account of which I shall reserve for my chapter on Whitehall. Of late years the Benchers have on several occasions revived these ancient forms of amusement in "The Masque of Flowers".

Crossing Holborn we come upon the most unique piece of ancient domestic architecture left in London, Staple's Inn, with its oak-beamed frontage, overhanging storeys, latticed windows, pointed roofs and quaint chambers, which have housed centuries of students. The Inn is as old as the reign of the fifth Harry, and is said to have been originally an hostelry for the reception of the merchants of the wool staple. The hall, or portions of it, date back to 1500, but most of the quadrangle is not older than the last century. Here again we meet with the two ubiquitous names of London, Dickens and Johnson. Here were the chambers of Mr. Grewgious, of *Edwin Drood*—the entrance to which is marked on a stone above the doorway J.T.—and here the doctor wrote *Rasselas*.

Barnard's Inn is very old, and here again the irrepressible Boz confronts us in the persons of Pip and his friend Hubert (*Great Expectations*). Yet more ancient is little Thavie's Inn, for Mr. Thavie, its patron, founded it in 1348. The old place was burned down in a later decade of the eighteenth century, and houses were erected upon the site.

West of Staple's Inn and Holborn Bars, in the reign of Henry I., the Knights Templars, whose order was then just established, raised the first Temple, which, Stow tell us, was built of Caen stone, and round in form like the later one by Temple Bar. It seems to have been abandoned in 1184.

Great interest attaches to Southampton Buildings, which adjoin Staple's Inn, as having been the site of the magnificent mansion of Henry Wriothesley, Earl of Southampton, Shakespeare's loving patron, to whom the poet dedicated *Venus and Adonis*, and *The Rape of Lucrece*. Previous to Southampton's time the Earls of Lincoln, who gave their name to the famous Inn of Court, resided there ; much of the ground upon which the old Temple stood must have been covered by this house. A noble and gallant young gentleman was this Henry Wriothesley, who stood by Essex in his mad revolt, not for the love of the treason but of the man.   He once gave Shakespeare £1000, a very large sum in those days, to complete the purchase, either of his share in the Blackfriars and Globe Company, or of New Place, Stratford.   And "Gentle Will" must have been as frequent a visitor at Southampton House as at Brooke House, and often walked in the garden of Staple's Inn, which adjoined that of his patron and friend, over that very ground, which, still uncumbered by bricks or stones, has felt the impress of his feet.

The house was demolished about 1657, in the time of the fourth earl, who, being an exiled royalist, probably had to sell the property to supply his needs, and private tenements were built upon the site.

William Hazlitt, the essayist, lived at No. 9 Southampton Buildings, where he wrote some of his best work, and fell frantically in love with a very commonplace young woman, his landlord's daughter, whom he has celebrated in the *Liber Amoris*.   Lamb for a time lived in apartments close by, and these two formed a tavern *coterie* at The Southampton, which then stood next to the Patent Office, at which Hone, Porson and George Cruickshank assisted.   Many of the great humorist's caricatures were designed there ; dipping a finger into his beer he would, with a few strokes of his wet digit, sketch his conceptions upon the table.   In Took's Court, Cursitor Street, stood Sloman's sponging house, to which the hero of Disraeli's *Henrietta Temple*, Captain Armine, and

Rawdon Crawley of *Vanity Fair* were taken ; and to those books I refer the reader for a description of the notorious den and its keeper.

Turning our faces eastward, the old Swan Distillery calls up yet another reminiscence of Dickens, as the house in which Mr. Haredale took refuge from the Gordon rioters in *Barnaby Rudge.* Vast changes were made in the topography of Holborn and its neighbourhood by the construction of the viaduct, and it is difficult to conjure up a picture of Holborn Hill, Snow Hill and Skinner Street as they stood previous to those improvements. As, for instance, Wren's Church, St. Andrew's, which is now in a hollow, was then approached by a flight of steps. Stillingfleet and Dr. Sacheverell, the famous High Church champion, are numbered among the rectors of St. Andrew's, and the latter is buried there : so is John Emery, the celebrated Yorkshire comedian, and Strutt, the author of the book on *Sports and Pastimes.* The tower is all that is left of the ancient church, destroyed by the zeal of Edward VI.'s reformers, the present building having been raised on its site in 1680. There is a tradition that John Webster, the author of the *Duchess of Malfi,* was parish clerk of St. Andrew's, but no record confirms it.

There are a couple of thoroughfares that claim some little attention before I pass on to the stories of Fleet Street—Shoe and Fetter Lanes. The quaint name of the former is at least as old as Stow's time: previous to the Holborn Valley improvements it was narrow

and ancient throughout.   In mediæval times the
bishops of Bangor had a town house there, a part of
which was standing in 1820, and is kept in remembrance by Bangor Court, a wretched collection of hovels,
strange successors to the splendours of papal bishops.

In Gunpowder Alley died, of actual want, that
sweet and noble cavalier-lyrist, Richard Lovelace,
who, in the poem *To Althea in Prison*, wrote the
world-famous couplet :—

> Stone walls do not a prison make,
> Nor iron bars a cage.

He lies in St. Bride's Church, close by.   In this alley
also lived Lilly, the astrologer, prophet, wizard and
almanac maker, much consulted during the Civil War
by royalists, including the king, as well as by the
Puritans, who likewise employed him as a spy.   The
houses in the alley are so ancient that the veritable
dwellings of these two men may yet survive.

Another curious survival of ancient times is Poppin
Court, originally Poppingay Alley.   It was the sign
of the Inn of the Abbots of Cirencester, who were
formerly housed there when they visited London.

In Fetter or Fewter [1] Lane resided for a while John
Dryden ; his reputed dwelling, opposite the Record
Office, has not been pulled down many years ; his
vis-à-vis was Otway, the dramatist ; Praise-God
Barebones was a leather seller at the corner of
Crane Court ; Lamb and his sister went to school in
a house in the passage which connects the lane with

[1] A Norman form of the French *foutre*, a vagabond, of which species
this thoroughfare was anciently a resort.

Bartlett's Buildings ; Hobbes wrote his famous *Leviathan* in Fetter Lane. No. 96 was, until very recently, a noted dissenting chapel, founded in 1660, and rebuilt in 1732. It was in the original building that the accession of George I. was first proclaimed. When Queen Anne was dying, that perfervid Whig, Bishop Burnet, was summoned on Sunday morning to her deathbed ; on his way to the palace he met Thomas Bradbury, the minister of this chapel, told him the news and arranged that as soon as all was over he would despatch a messenger to the conventicle with orders to place himself in the gallery exactly opposite the preacher and drop a handkerchief. The queen passed away as was anticipated, the signal was given, and Bradbury was not only the first to proclaim her decease but her successor as well.

A reminiscence of quite another kind is attached to a ruinous old house at the corner of Fleur de Lys Court ; it was there that the terrible Mrs. Brownrigg, a midwife to St. Dunstan's Workhouse, perpetrated those horrible cruelties upon two apprentice girls which have made her name notorious for ever, and for which she was executed at Newgate. I have often looked down through the gratings into the dismal cellar where the poor girls were flogged and cut with scissors, and otherwise tortured.

There were some notable old taverns in Fetter Lane : the Magpie and Stump, and the White Horse, once a well-known posting house, about which many memories clung, but they have all vanished.

CHAPTER VII.

FLEET STREET: ITS ANCIENT LIFE—TAVERNS—
COFFEE-HOUSES—RESIDENTS.

"LET us take a walk *up* Fleet Street." Not the
Fleet Street of to-day, nor of Dr. Johnson's day, but
of the days of "Good Queen Bess" and the first
Stuart. We might go back to the days of the
Plantagenets and still find it a busy, shop-lined
thoroughfare, when the Strand was only a grassy
highroad leading from the city to the village of
Charing. But at the opening of the seventeenth
century the world-famous street was in all its
glory.

There is ancient St. Dunstan's Church, thrusting
itself right across the roadway, and the bells are giving
forth a merry peal. The shops are only open, window-
less booths, like the stalls at a fair, and over each
gaily painted signboard hangs a flag, for every
tradesman has a sign ; men buy their hosiery at the
Lamb, their boots at the Jolly Tanners, and so on.
Pavement there is none ; road and footpath are not
divided, are full of ruts, and an open gutter or sewer
runs down the centre ; the gable ends of the picturesque
houses, which are entirely of wood, with their over-

(103)

ST. DUNSTAN'S-IN-THE-WEST.

hanging storeys, stand out against a bright blue sky.[1]
There is no dense throng of people, no vehicles,
yet the scene is full of animation ; splendidly dressed
cavaliers are riding to and fro between the city and
Whitehall, and every variety of costume is to be seen
among the pedestrians. Here comes an Alsatian of
Whitefriars, whom we have met at St. Paul's, his
ragged cloak fluttering in the breeze as he clanks along
fiercely twirling the ends of his moustache and glaring
at every peaceful citizen ; here are a party of Mercutios
and Gratianos, just come out of the Blackfriars Theatre,
and on their way to the Devil Tavern, where they
will meet Ben Jonson and Will Shakespeare and Dick
Burbage. In contrast to these splendid butterflies is
the sober cit. in sad-coloured suit, with perhaps a pretty
daughter in prim grey and with a neat little ruff
encircling her throat, who demurely gazes from under
her lowered eyelids at Mercutio or Gratiano as he
passes. Now and again the black shadow of an evil-
visaged Puritan falls like a blighting cloud upon the
sunshine. In front of every shop is a smart apprentice,
sometimes two, in close-fitting jerkin and flat cap,
who saucily assail every pedestrian with " What d'ye
lack ? What d'ye lack ? " with the same monotonous
iteration as a Clare Market butcher. They are satiri-
cal dogs too, who have a quip and a crank suitable

---

[1] The London atmosphere was little inferior in clearness to that of
continental cities; yet coals had been introduced, and in the next
reign came into general use. But then London had not many more
than 100,000 inhabitants in the reign of James I.

to every one. "What d'ye lack, noble sir?"—this
to the Alsatian—"A pair of scissors to clip your love-
locks, or a new cloak to cover your noble shoulders?
Your own has grown too thin for a blanket when you
sleep out at nights." "What d'ye lack, pretty miss?"—
to the cit.'s daughter—"A bunch of ribbons to catch a
sweetheart with? You've caught me without it."

All of a moment a distant cry of "Clubs, clubs!
'Prentices, 'prentices!" is heard coming from Ludgate,
and each moment nearer and nearer. It is a cry to
arms that no flat cap dare, if he desired, to disobey.
In an instant every 'prentice seizes upon his club,
which is always handy, abandons the shop to take
care of itself, and fleet as the wind rushes in the direction of the call. Certain apprentices for some offence
have been ordered to be whipped from Aldgate to
Temple Bar, and the fraternity have resolved to
rescue them. The halberds of the marshal men are
shivered by the rain of clubs, they themselves driven
back, and the liberated offenders, amidst a shouting,
singing crowd, are escorted to Temple Bar in triumph.[1]

Such scenes of turmoil are of almost daily occurrence. But the unruly 'prentices are not the only
offenders. The gentlemen students of the Temple
are equally addicted to rioting, especially at Christmas-
tide. Picture a cold, clear, winter's night, the hoar-
frost glistening in the moonlight, the tall houses standing out stark and grim against the glittering stars, but

[1] Every reader of Scott will perceive that I am partly indebted to
the *Fortunes of Nigel* for this description.

the street below in darkness. The shops are closed, the lights out in all the windows, and the good cits. are snoring upon their pillows. All is silent and dim as the grave. Suddenly there is a muffled din of voices that swells into clamour, then the gates of the Temple are swung open and a ruddy glare of smoky light dances on the grey and black fronts of the opposite houses, and out pours a throng of boisterous Templars who have been carousing pottle deep. At their head marches a student wearing a tinsel coronet ; he is the Lord of Misrule, and with drawn sword and unsteady gait he leads on his roistering crew. One of his henchmen raising a horn to his lips blows a blast that is heard from Cheapside to Charing. Stopping before a house, the horn is again wound. A light twinkles in one of the windows, it is thrown open and a voice demands, "Who is there?" "The Lord of Misrule, come to demand his rents," haughtily answers the leader. Then the door is opened and there is a chink of coins. And the procession passes on to another house. But here the summons is unheeded, though repeated thrice. "Fire upon the traitor!" cries the leader. A brawny blacksmith advances with a huge sledge-hammer, swings and brings it down upon the door with a crash that shivers the panels to splinters. An entrance is effected, and "My Lord" and his bacchanalian crew pour in and demand of the trembling inmates food and drink and double dues for not responding to his summons. His jurisdiction does not extend beyond Ram Alley (now Hare Place). Few

have the courage to resist these extortions, and all who
do have their doors and windows smashed, until the
riot becomes so alarming that messengers are sent to
the Lord Mayor calling for assistance. Soon the tramp
of horses and a flare of light announce the coming
of the magistrate and his officers,' all well armed.
Louder and louder are the blasts of the horn, warning
those within the Temple of danger, and summoning
them to the rescue. Far fiercer and more bloody than
the struggle with the flat caps is that which ensues :
blood flows like water, the 'prentices come to the help
of the city, the whole neighbourhood is up in arms, it
is a veritable town and gown row. Pressed by overwhelming numbers, the Lord of Misrule is, after a desperate resistance, captured, and his followers, put to
flight, take shelter within the gates of their Inn of
Court.

My next picture of Fleet Street dates a century later.
The great fire has wrought havoc with the houses
on the south side, and brick buildings are taking
the place of the wooden ; but on the north they are
still as quaint as ever, with their glittering signboards
projected over the pathway and looking very like the
flags in Henry the Seventh's chapel at Westminster.
A little to the west of Chancery Lane is the picturesque carved-fronted dwelling where the master of the
gentle art, Izaak Walton, carried on his millinery
business, and from which, many a time and oft, he has
started, humming one of his quaint, sweet ballads, upon
those piscatorial expeditions to the banks of the Lea,

immortalised in *The Compleat Angler.* Close against
St. Dunstan's Church is the shop of Edmund Curll

ST. DUNSTAN'S CLOCK, FROM FLEET STREET.
(Now at Lord Aldenham's Villa, Regent's Park.)

the bookseller, who has been gibbeted for all time by
the pens of Pope and Swift. Booksellers have always

affected the vicinity of this famous church. " Under the diall "[1] was first published *Hamlet*, and *Romeo and Juliet*, and *Hudibras*, Walton's book, and the first English tragedy, *Gordobuc*, and somewhere near, at the sign of the White Hart, was issued the *Midsummer Night's Dream*. At the south-west corner of Chancery Lane is a beautifully carved, five-storeyed house—which will remain intact until the close of the century—that in the reign of Henry V. was the residence of that notable, historical and dramatic personage, Sir John Oldcastle.

Looking across the road our eyes fall just between the two Temple gates, upon the shop of Bernard Lintot, from which Pope's *Homer* was issued, and to the west of it is a quaint building covered with the badges of Cardinal Wolsey,[2] erected for the great prelate by Sir Amyas Paulet, for an offence he had committed against Thomas Wolsey in the days when Wolsey was a parish priest. And there during six years Sir Amyas was kept close prisoner. It was an ingenious idea to make a man build his own prison, and the proud cardinal, from his house in Chancery Lane, must have daily passed it in all the pomp and magnificence of his gorgeous state. In times to come it will be known as Nando's Coffee-house, and afterwards as Mrs. Salmon's Waxwork Show. Jacob Tonson,

---

[1] A row of shops ran along the whole façade of the church, and above was the famous clock, with its giant figures that struck the hours, like that now in Cheapside.

[2] Now labelled " Henry the Eighth's Palace," but it never was so.

Dryden's publisher, carries on his business close to the Inner Temple.[1]

Within the shadow of Temple Bar hangs a device representing St. Dunstan tweaking Satan's nose with the traditional tongs—the sign of the immortalised Devil Tavern.[2] In the Apollo room, over the entrance of which, surmounted by a bust of the Sun God, on a black board, in letters of gold, are inscribed the well-known lines of Jonson, beginning :—

> Welcome all who lead or follow
> To the oracle of Apollo,

were celebrated those symposia, presided over by lusty Ben, of which Beaumont wrote, that after our revellers had quitted the room they—

> Left an air behind them which alone
> Was able to make the two next companies
> Right witty ; though but downright fools, mere wise.

Imagination may shadow forth the great president's herculean form, his rugged visage illumined by intellectual fire ; the noble, pensive face, now and again lit up by the merry humour of the moment, of the divine

---

[1] At the sign of the Crown, close by, Lieutenant John Murray, R.N., in 1768, purchased, for £400, the good-will of Sandby's publishing business, and there founded the famous house that still bears his name.   Butterworth's, which has just been demolished, was the site whereon another old publisher, Richard Tottell, carried on his business in the reign of Edward VI.   Gosling's old bank, established as a goldsmith's in the reign of Charles I., and rebuilt in 1667, has also gone the way of all bricks and mortar.

[2] Now incorporated in Child's Bank (Tellson's of *A Tale of Two Cities*), where Charles II. banked, in which are still preserved the bust of Apollo and " The Welcome ".

Shakespeare; that model of a fine, gallant gentleman, handsome Beaumont, and beside him his *fidus Achates* with whom his name is so inextricably associated, John Fletcher; Raleigh, bronzed on the Spanish main, to give a flavour of the sea and the camp to this rich, medley dish of wit; Dick Burbage, Will Kempe, and other famous players might be found among that goodly company. What flagons of Canary and clary and sack and sherris must those *bons vivants* have quaffed! Here, as well at the Mermaid, were fought those wit combats between Rare Ben and Gentle Will of which we have heard so much and know so little.

It is of the Devil one night in the reign of Queen Anne I was about to write, and have wandered back to the days of "Good Queen Bess". In a room—not the Apollo—are gathered the notorious Mohock Club.[1] At the head of the table, on a gilded throne, sits "the emperor," whose flushed and bloated face is rendered hideous by scars and a crescent engraved upon the centre of his forehead. His companions, who show

---

[1] Desperadoes, many of them men of birth, who under various names, Tityre Tuns, Scourers, Hectors, Muns, Mohocks, were the terror of the town from the days of Charles II., and committed atrocities well worthy of the savages from whom they took their titles. See *The Spectator*, 324, 347, and Swift's *Journal to Stella*. But they were all the descendants of Ben Jonson's "Roaring Boys" and "roisterers". There was a horrible custom among these of piercing their veins and drinking healths in their own blood (Greene's *Tu Quoque*). This was also done by "The Hectors". "And," says the author of *The Character of England* (1659), "they sometimes drank of it to that excess that they have died of the intemperance."

signs of the many bottles they have emptied, might
have done credit to Captain Kyd, or any pirate chief,
though they are dressed as gentlemen.   Swords and
knives and other weapons are laid upon the table in
front of them.   The emperor, who rejoices in the name
of Taw Waw Eben Tan Kaladar, is reading a mani- ·
festo, of which the following words form the last
paragraph : "And whereas we have nothing more at
our Imperial heart than the reformation of the cities of
London and Westminster, which to our unspeakable
satisfaction we have in some measure effected, we do
hereby earnestly exhort and pray all husbands and
fathers, housekeepers and masters of families, not only
to repair themselves to their respective habitations at
early and seasonable hours, but also to keep their
wives and daughters, sons, sisters and apprentices from
appearing in the streets at those times and seasons
which may expose them to military discipline, as it
is practised by our good subjects the Mohocks," etc.
"Given from our court at the Devil's Tavern, March
15th, 1712." "And now let us forth, each to his
respective work !" cries the emperor.

A few minutes later and the sleeping citizens of
Fleet Street are aroused by the war-whoop of the
savage. "The Mohocks are abroad," whispers a wife
to her husband, and securely barred as they are within their house they shudder at the sound. Belated
wayfarers fly before that yell ; the Mohocks give chase
and captures are soon effected ; a woman is seized
and thrust into a barrel, and, despite her screams, is

rolled down the street as far as the Fleet Bridge ;
another woman is set upon her head and her heels are
tied to a post ; a poor fellow has his nose flattened to
his face, while another division, who call themselves
" the Dancing Masters," prick a couple of victims with
their swords to make them cut grotesque capers for
the amusement of their torturers. No one dares to
oppose them ; the watchman sits trembling in his box,
fearing that he will be trundled down the street and
rolled into the river, and the authorities seem to be
equally timid. Later on the Devil was frequented
by Goldsmith and Johnson and their following. It
was pulled down and Child's Place built upon it in
1788.

Nearly opposite the Devil is Shire Lane, in which,
at the sign of the Cat and Fiddle, a pastry-cook shop
kept by one Christopher Kat, was held the famous
Whig Kit Kat Club, frequented by the Duke of Marlborough, the Earl of Dorset, Lord Halifax "the
trimmer," Sir Robert Walpole, Congreve the dramatist, Jacob Tonson the publisher, Sir Godfrey Kneller,
who painted the portraits of all the members, forty-
two in number, which for many years adorned the
walls of Tonson's house at Barn Elms. Addison and
Steele were Kit Kats, and many a night was inebriated
Dicky carried into a sedan chair and conveyed home
to his " darling Prue," to be shrewishly lectured when
his senses returned to him. The Kit Kats were hard
drinkers, and it was said of them that they learned
" to sleep away the days and drink away the nights ".

The pleasantest incident connected with the club was when the beautiful little daughter of the Duke of Kingston, then only eight years of age, thereafter to be known as Lady Mary Wortly Montagu, was brought in one night and made the toast of the evening, nominated a member, and her name graved with a diamond ring upon one of the glasses. She always protested it was the most delightful moment of her life.

No thoroughfare of London can boast of so many famous taverns as Fleet Street ; it was the very centre of that tavern life which was to the seventeenth and eighteenth centuries what club life is to the nineteenth. Most have vanished. Many of us remember the Cock, with its Jacobean fireplace, against which Pepys must often have stood ; for it was a favourite resort of his, and is several times mentioned in the *Diary ;* its sanded floor and wooden boxes, where many a lord chancellor, judge, and attorney-general have eaten their steaks and quaffed their pints of port ; its old-fashioned waiters, one of whom still lives in Tennyson's "Will Waterproof's Lyrical Monologue":—

> Oh plump head waiter at the Cock,
> To which I most resort.
>
> .   .   .   .   .   .
>
> He looks not like the common breed
> That with the napkin dally ;
> I think he came, like Ganymede,
> From some delightful valley.
>
> .   .   .   .   .   .

Thou battenest by the greasy gleam
In haunts of hungry sinners,
Old boxes larded with the steam
Of thirty thousand dinners.

Just opposite stood the scarcely less famous Dick's, now also only a memory of the past. Steele and his contemporaries enjoyed its cosy comforts ; so did Thackeray. It was there Mr. Bungay, the publisher, gave the little dinner preliminary to the inception of the *Pall Mall Gazette*, and it was haunted by the shadows of Pendennis and Warrington. Dick's retained to the last much of its original aspect. The frontispiece to a last century farce, entitled " The Coffee-house," pictures the interior of Dick's looking out upon the Temple, and might almost be taken for a representation of it at the time of its destruction.

The Rainbow, which still remains, was the second house in which coffee was drunk in England—the Old Jamaica, St. Michael's Alley, Cornhill, now a flaunting tavern, was the first, 1652.[1] The Rainbow

---

[1] Coffee, however, is described in Burton's *Anatomy of Melancholy*, first published in 1621. " The Turks have a drink called coffee (for they use no wine), as black as soot, and as bitter. . . . They spend much time in those coffee-houses, which are somewhat like our ale nouses or taverns, and there they sit chatting and drinking, to drive away the time and be merry together, because they find by experience that kind of drink, so used, helpeth digestion, and promoteth alacrity."

Tea was probably introduced into England about 1657, when it sold, to quote one of Garway's shop bills, " for six and sometimes ten pounds the pound weight ". Thomas Garway, of Exchange Alley, was the first who sold tea publicly in leaf and drink, retailing it at from 10s. to 50s. a pound. (See Disraeli's *Curiosities of Literature*.) Pepys writes (1667) : " Home and did there find my wife making of

was opened by a barber named Farr, in 1656, as a coffee-house—it was a tavern at a much earlier date. The Arabian berry was on its first introduction praised and denounced with equal extravagance : as many virtues were ascribed to the decoction as are now-a-days attributed to a quack pill ; it was a remedy for spleen and hypochondria ; it rendered the skin white, the steam was excellent for sore eyes ; it helped the digestion, quickened the spirits, cured dropsy, scurvy, gout, king's-evil, etc. Whilst its enemies villified it as devil's drink, " syrup of soot and essence of old shoes," under the influence of which the English would dwindle into a race of sterile apes and pigmies.

Let us pay a visit to the Rainbow in the first year of its inception as a coffee-house. The front, facing the street, is occupied by a bookseller. Entering the narrow passage that skirts the shop we find ourselves in a large room furnished with seats and small tables ; the walls are hung round with cases, containing popular pills, elixirs, perfumes, etc. The pungent odour given forth by the burning berries and the steaming beverage is overpowering. Seated about is a curiously mixed company of foreigners, London citizens, Temple beaux, some of whom have been persuaded by Barber Farr, while he was scraping their chins or dressing their locks in an adjoining room, to take their initial taste of the new drink. It is one of the rules that it shall be drunk scalding hot ; note the

tea, a drink which M. Pelling, the Potticary, tells me is good for the cold and defluxions ". It was in general use thirty years later.

face of that cit. who is enduring agony from tongue,
lips and throat as he gulps the liquid down ; another
feels his gorge rise at the flavour of the aromatic
beverage, which is softened neither by milk nor sugar,
and setting down the cup rushes into the Devil to
wash his mouth out with a cup of sack ; a Templar
sips it with the air of a connoisseur and pretends to
like it, because it will make him appear a man of
travel in the eyes of one or two men whose bronzed
faces tell of a sojourn in the East. A soldier, after
swallowing a mouthful, spits it out, swearing horribly,
at which Barber Farr cries "a fine, a fine!" and
points to a placard of rules hung against the wall,
by which the penalty of one shilling is exacted for
blasphemous language. The penalty is often resisted,
then swords are drawn and a *mêlée* ensues.

Of course the tavern keepers and vintners are up
in arms, and endeavour to get the coffee-house keeper
indicted as a public nuisance, on account of " the obnoxious smells and for the keeping of fires for the
most part of the day and night, whereby his chimney
and chamber hath been set on fire to the common
danger of his neighbours ". Old topers execrate
"this filthy potion," and pious Puritans, who love
the bottle, declare that it is an invention of the
evil one.

Shakespeare's and Dr. Johnson's Mitre Tavern was
absorbed in Hoare's Bank many years ago.[1]   Peele's

---

[1] Hoare's is one of the most ancient banks in London ; Lord
Clarendon kept money there in Charles II.'s time.

Coffee-house, so long celebrated for its files of newspaper, has entirely lost its original character, though above stairs much of the ancient house still remains.

The old Cheshire Cheese is still a model of what a Fleet Street tavern was in the days of Dr. Johnson, though it dates back to the previous century, and perhaps even to the sixteenth. And from the days of the ponderous lexicographer to those of George Augustus Sala, and the latest representatives of "the fourth estate," there has not been a literary bohemian unfamiliar with that old-world, dingy bar, and beamed and panelled dining-room, wherein the seats of the authors of *Rasselas* and *Vicar of Wakefield* are still preserved. The great Saturday institution of The Cheese is still that wonderful beef-steak pudding, so rich, so succulent, so savoury, so enticing to nose and palate, but, oh, so trying to town digestions !

"We are a close, conservative, inflexible body, we regular frequenters," wrote William Sawyer, some years ago. "No new-fangled notions, new usages, new customs or new customers for us. We have our history, our traditions and our observations, all sacred and inviolable. Look around! There is nothing new, gaudy, flippant, or effeminately luxurious here. A small room with heavily timbered windows, a low planked ceiling. A huge, projecting fireplace, with a great copper boiler always on the simmer. High, stiff-backed, inflexible 'settees,' hard and grainy in texture, box off the guests, half a dozen each to a table. Sawdust covers the floor, giving forth its peculiar faint odour. The only ornament in which we indulge is a solitary picture over the mantelpiece, a full length of a now departed waiter, whom in the long past we caused to be painted, by subscription of the whole room, to commemorate his virtues and our esteem. We sit bolt upright round our tables, waiting, but not impatient. A time-honoured solemnity is about to be observed, and we, the old stagers, is it for us to precipitate it? There are men in the room who have dined here every day for a quarter of a century—aye, the whisper goes round that one man did it on his wedding day."

It is curious that there is no mention of the Cheshire Cheese in Boswell's *Johnson;* but Percy Fitzgerald, in an article in *The Gentleman's Magazine*, says that when he first visited the house in the days of host Carlton, he met several very old gentlemen who had seen Dr. Johnson nightly there, "and they told me, what is not generally known, that the doctor, whilst living in the Temple, always went to the Mitre, or the Essex Head ; but when he removed to Gough Square and Bolt Court he was a constant visitor at the Cheshire Cheese, because nothing but a hurricane would have induced him to cross Fleet Street ". Cyrus Jay, who began his visits to the tavern about twenty years after the doctor's death, likewise records, in his book of anecdotes, that he met tradesmen there who well remembered both Johnson and Goldsmith as

DR. JOHNSON'S HOUSE, GOUGH SQUARE.

frequenters of the Cheshire Cheese. Goldsmith lived for a while in Wine Office Court.

The house in Gough Square, which the doctor some time inhabited, still survives, but in so dilapidated a condition that no long life can be predicted for it. It would be pleasant to dwell upon the doings in that more famous house in Bolt Court, where he passed his most prosperous days, received his most famous visitors, and breathed his last, the story has been so often told. Nor does it now exist, as it was burned down in 1819.

Never was a street so closely associated with one man's name as Fleet Street is with that of Samuel Johnson ; most of the anecdotes connected with him are too hackneyed to be repeated here. Not so well known, perhaps, is a story of the doctor's pugilistic prowess, how, being insulted by a burly drayman, he stripped off his coat and set to with the fellow in broad daylight, and drubbed him handsomely—such occurrences, even among the first gentlemen, were common enough in those days, and long, long afterwards. But Johnson had an uncle, who was a professional bruiser and stood in Lichfield market-place ready to take on all comers, from whom, perhaps, he inherited his pugnacity.

Note.—I omitted to mention, on p. 110, two ancient houses east of St. Dunstan's, only recently pulled down, one of which, a bookseller's, was said to have been the residence of the Elizabethan poet, Michael Drayton, author of the famous *Polyolbion*.

CHAPTER VIII.

FLEET STREET (*continued*)—SALISBURY SQUARE—
WHITEFRIARS—THE TEMPLE.

ON the eastern side of the narrow street leading
from Fleet Street into Salisbury Square is an old-
fashioned public-house known by the sign of the
Barley Mow, which was probably one of the notorious
" Mug Houses " of Charles II.'s time, so called
because all the drinking cups used in them were ornamented with the counterfeit presentment of the arch-
hypocrite Shaftesbury, Dryden's Achitophel, the idol
of the Whigs ; here assembled the supporters of that
party to drink destruction to Charles and his brother
James, and, when George of Hanover came to the
throne, to James's son and grandson. These taverns
were frequently the scene of riots ; the bibulous Whigs
would sit at the open windows and shout their toasts
to all the passers-by, and sometimes a party of irate
Tories would attack the houses and set fire to them.
This happened to a Mug House in Salisbury Square,
probably the one under notice.

The interior of the Barley Mow is quite ancient,
and in one of its quaintest rooms are held the meetings of that curious discussion society known as " The

Cogers ". And although it at one time migrated to

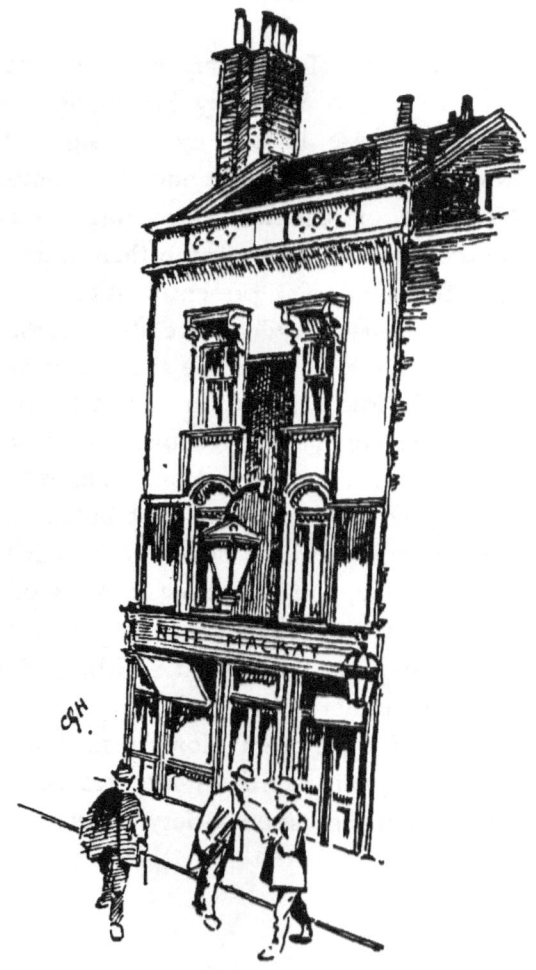

EXTERIOR OF COGERS' HALL.

Fetter Lane, the Barley Mow was its original quarters.

Here every shade of political faith, from the most staunch conservatism to the extremest radicalism, finds expression among the young barristers, lawyers' clerks, journalists, tradesmen who have adopted the venerable name. Many well-known orators have made their first essays in their art at Cogers' Hall, which has echoed with the voices of Johnson, Goldsmith, Wilkes, Dan O'Connell, and in our own days with those of Stewart Parnell, T. P. O'Connor, Sir Edward Clarke, Bradlaugh, and many another notoriety.

Down towards the river, in the time of James I., stood the Salisbury Court Theatre, a private house like the Blackfriars, and, after the Restoration, Dorset Gardens, so famous for its gorgeous " get ups," to use a present-day phrase. Previous to that time the noble mansion of the Earls of Dorset and its beautiful gardens sloping down to the river, occupied the ground. And hereabouts dwelt the renowned actor, Betterton ; Shadwell, the dramatist ; Woodfall, the publisher of *Junius's Letters*. Here, in the north-west corner of the square, was Samuel Richardson's printing office, in which Goldsmith was at one time a reader—in a dingy back room of this building were written *Pamela* and *Clarissa Harlowe*.

What a striking contrast Richardson presented to his great rival in the art of fiction, Harry Fielding. A fat, sleek, primly dressed, well-to-do man was the creator of Sir Charles Grandison ; vain, sentimental, kind-hearted, his pockets always full of sweetmeats for children ; very fond of women's society, but a

INTERIOR OF COGERS' HALL.

conventional moralist of the most pronounced type;
an indefatigable worker, always pen in hand, and
living more among the creations of his brain than
with people of flesh and blood. His office was the
rendezvous of most of the literati of the time. He
removed from Salisbury Court, as it was then called,
in 1755, to Parson's Green, where he died six years
afterwards. He is buried in St. Bride's.

And now it is but a step into Alsatia. Here in the
middle ages stood a Carmelite convent, which was
destroyed by Tudor Henry; but the area continued
to preserve those privileges of sanctuary, which though
much abused by scoundrelism, were a necessity in the
days of tyrant kings and nobles, and saved many
an innocent life, as well as many a guilty; but in the
time of James I. Whitefriars became a mere horde of
ruffians. Those who would realise what this den of
infamy was like should read Scott's *Fortunes of Nigel*
and Shadwell's play, *The Squire of Alsatia*, to which
the great novelist was indebted for much of his materials. The privileges of sanctuary were withdrawn
at the close of the seventeenth century. But in the
little known lanes and alleys lying behind Fleet Street
and about Whitefriars Street may still be found houses
of the Stuart days, relics of the ancient Alsatia. Only
a short time ago in a cellar in Britton's Court, in the
last-named thoroughfare, a crypt was unearthed which
antiquaries believe to be a portion of the old Carmelite
house, founded in the thirteenth century. One of the
romances of Alsatia was the murder of Turner, the

fencing-master. In a bout with sword and dagger
with young Lord Sanquhar, a Scotch gentleman of
ancient lineage, Turner had the misfortune to thrust
out one of his eyes. Sanquhar, burning for revenge,
as soon as he recovered, resolved upon Turner's death.
The fencing-master, in pursuance of his calling, was
continually changing his quarters ; his foe dogged him
from place to place, but by some accident always
failed in his design, until he employed two bravoes.
One May evening in 1612, as Turner was sitting at the
door of a tavern in Whitefriars, one of these fellows
came up to him, and drawing a pistol from beneath
his cloak, shot him dead. Sanquhar was hanged for
the crime in front of Westminster Hall, and his tools
shared his fate upon a gibbet raised at the Whitefriars
gate.

Passing through the postern, which alone divided
the lawless from the lawyers, we will stroll into the
Temple, than which there is no more haunted ground
in all this great metropolis. And yet how many
Londoners have I spoken with to whom the beautiful
church is as unknown as its prototype that covers the
Holy Sepulchre at Jerusalem. Standing before its
blackened walls in the dimness of an autumn night,
when the subdued roar of Fleet Street falls upon the
ear like the echoes of a distant torrent and all around
is solitary stillness, one might picture the ghosts of
those white-robed, red-crossed soldier-priests, who
founded this noble pile in the twelfth century, and
the bones of many of whom moulder beneath their

recumbent effigies within a few feet of us, gliding
through the solemn aisles. After the order was
abolished Edward II. bestowed the demesne upon the
Earl of Lancaster, who converted it into a hostelry
or inn for law students : these still preserved some
of the monkish customs and insignia of their predecessors, notably the coif, which was worn unto the
last by the now extinct sergeants-at-law.

Let us now enter the Middle Temple Hall. That
glorious carved screen, formed, it is said, out of some
wreckage of the Armada, has witnessed rare feastings
and pageantry. Memorable among which is the celebration of Twelfth Night, 1602, when Shakespeare's
comedy of that name is presented before the queen
and her splendid court ; among the illustrious visitors
are—the all-accomplished Raleigh, in his youth a
Temple student ; fiery Essex, who ere long will lay
his haughty head upon the block ; subtle, unscrupulous
Leicester, upon whom the ancient virgin now and
again casts amorous glances ; grave Burleigh, who,
with the weight of a kingdom upon his brow, is here
sore against his will, for he despises all poets and
players ; Robert Cecil, his son, a Templar, looking
demure enough under the paternal eye, but a notorious
roisterer, who scours the streets at night on mischief
bent. Heartily laughs the queen, who is too great
a woman to be prudish, at the quips and cranks of
the clown, at the conceits of Malvolio, at the humour
of Sir Toby and Sir Andrew. And after the play is
over, a gentleman, plainly but richly habited, with a

9

face of wondrous sweetness and intellectual calm, kneels to receive the gratulations, which his sovereign bestows upon her trusty and well-beloved servant, Master William Shakespeare. Having kissed the royal hand the poet draws back and is then surrounded by the courtiers, with many of whom he is on terms of intimate companionship, all eager to do him honour. When the feast is served, sixteen trumpeters, and two gentlemen bearing four torches of white wax, usher in the great dish, the boar's head, with a golden lemon in its huge mouth, which the servitors place upon the damask tablecloth, lighted up by wax tapers in twenty silver candlesticks, and glittering with gold and silver plate.

There were rare doings in the Old Hall at Christmas-tide when Chancellor Bacon presided; feasting, masking and mumming. During the reign of Charles I. some gorgeous "Masques" were performed, one of which is said to have cost £21,000! Charles II., William, Anne and the first and second Georges all held high jinks here. The Temple suffered much in the great fire of 1666, and most that was left of it perished in another conflagration twelve years later, which spared little or nothing except the church, as the dates over the doorways of the oldest buildings— 1678-9—inform us.

Stroll down into the gardens and you are again in the middle ages; seven hundred years ago the Red Cross knights there enjoyed the pleasant breezes wafted over the silver Thames from the Surrey meadows and

hills, that knew scarcely a human habitation ; and later
on that grave " Clerk of Oxenford," Geoffrey Chaucer
a member of the Inner Temple, meditated in its
sweet solitudes over his *Canterbury Tales*. It was
here that, tradition tells us, the followers of York and
Lancaster first plucked those fatal badges of their
factions, "the red rose and the white " that sent
" a thousand souls to death and endless night ". It
was the favourite promenade of the gallants of Elizabeth's and James's time, during the summer season ;
when heated by the canary and sack of the Devil
they strolled out into its greenery to take the air, and
amuse themselves by watching the busy scene upon
the river, Raleigh, Selden, Beaumont, Marston,
Ford, and, later, Dorset, Cooke, Clarendon, Congreve,
Wycherley, Burke, all of whom were Temple students.
While " the round " of the church was as frequented a
promenade as the middle aisle of St. Paul's.

For the Thames was the great highway. When
majesty passed from Whitehall to the Tower it was
in its gilded barge, and when the Lord Mayor journeyed from London to Westminster it was in no
rumbling carriage over rutty roads, but in a barge,
little inferior in splendour to royalty's ; and until
comparatively recent times the great Civic Show em-
barked at Blackfriars, and made the remainder of its
course by water. The shores swarmed with watermen
plying for hire, and both citizens and nobles preferred
to glide smoothly over the sweet, sunlit river to being
jolted through dark, tortuous and evil-smelling streets.

So while the Strand was almost deserted the river was all life and bustle, crowded with boats of all kinds, gay with laughing youth and brilliant state ; musical as the canals of Venice, with the fanfare of trumpets announcing the approach of some great personage, the songs of the boatmen, and the voices of the cavaliers chanting to the accompaniment of guitars or viols some light or sentimental French or Italian ditties to their mistresses. When Mr. Spectator took that grand old knight, Sir Roger de Coverley, to see Westminster Abbey, it was in a boat that he hailed at Temple Stairs.

Not long ago there was on the eastern side of the garden the decayed trunk of a tree, railed in ; it was all that remained of three, a seat beneath which was the favourite resting-place of Johnson and Goldsmith. On summer evenings the doctor would leave his garret chambers, that were just within Middle Temple Gate, clad in rusty-brown suit, his breeches unbuttoned at the knees, black worsted stockings wrinkling down the legs, scrubby wig, too small for his big head, white cravat soiled with the droppings of countless cups of tea, and there join Goldy, who had all day been engaged upon his Natural History in his chambers in Brick Court. And while the doctor is thundering forth his pompous aphorisms, his companion is trying to think where he can borrow a guinea, or how evade the writ his tailor has issued for that plum-coloured velvet suit which looks so incongruous upon his awkward figure.

A few years previously, when he was studying the law, another scapegrace, Henry Fielding, might have been absorbed by the same problem on that same spot, or in his dingy rooms close by ; where, after returning from the Rose, he would fall to upon his law books, or upon an article for *The Champion* to supply his daily needs, while his wife was living down at Salisbury waiting until he should be called to the Bar.

And so another generation passes away ; the doctor now a man well to do, has gone to live in Bolt Court, Harry Fielding is lying in his quiet grave on the hillside at Lisbon, and on a cold day in February, 1774, a modest funeral is passing from Brick Court to the Temple churchyard, followed by Sir Joshua Reynold, Edmund Burke and other famous men, and a gathering of poor waifs and strays from the streets are weeping for their benefactor, who, while he had a shilling in his pocket, was never deaf to their cry of distress ; and up in the trees close by, the wise rooks, whose doings it was his amusement to watch, are cawing what sounds like a monody upon the death of the gentle poet.

From the earliest times the Templars were riotous roisterers, very jealous of their privileges. When Lord Mayor Lyon, in 1553, came to dine with John Prideaux with his sword of state up, the weapon was snatched from the bearer and a free fight ensued ; when a hundred years later another Lord Mayor repeated the experiment his lordship had to hide himself

in a bencher's closet from the wrath of some fire-eating
students. Battles between the Alsatians and Templars
were of frequent occurrence, but the rogues usually
got the worst of it. William Murray, afterwards the
great Lord Mansfield, was frequently drinking at the
Cock while his clients were cooling their heels in his
chambers. He once kept shrew Sarah, Duchess of
Marlborough, waiting so long that when he arrived,
very seedy after a night's orgie, she swore at him as
lustily as did her duke's troopers in Flanders. Many
a time did Porson, greatest of Greek scholars, stagger
home from the Cyder Cellars, his favourite resort, to
his Temple chambers and wake up his neighbour
beneath by falling helpless upon the floor. Such was
his craving for alcohol that he would drink spirits of
wine and even embrocation in the lack of anything
better; Rogers, the poet banker, relates that after a
dinner-party he would steal back to the dining-room
to drain the bottles and glasses ; he would sometimes
go for days without food, living solely upon drink, and
made nothing of six pots of porter for his breakfast.
Poor Cowper spent some of the darkest hours of his
melancholy life in the Inner Temple.

Inner Temple Lane is reminiscent of dear delightful
Charles Lamb, as indeed is the whole of the Temple ;
and who has ever sketched it and its people so vividly
as he ? It was at No. 4 he gave those glorious but
frugal suppers, so graphically described by Talfourd,
at which some of the brightest wits and cleverest men
of the day assembled, Proctor, Coleridge, Wordsworth,

FOUNTAIN COURT.

Hazlitt, Haydon, Crabb Robinson, Talfourd himself; what talks there were anent those old dramatists whom Lamb had rescued from a couple of centuries of oblivion, about the poets of the day, the plays and players; what puns, what jokes, what Rabelasian laughter!

The annals of the Temple are singularly free of crime, but in Tanfield Court a murder was committed in 1732, that made a great sensation at the time. A young laundress named Sarah Malcolm strangled an old lady named Duncombe and her old servant, cut a young girl's throat, and plundered the chambers of money and plate. She was hanged opposite Mitre Court, Fleet Street.

Over the ancient home of the Templars Dickens and Thackeray have cast the halo of their genius; Ruth Pinch and John Westlock haunt Fountain Court, and in Garden Court, now no more, were Pip's chambers, where Magwitch, in one of the novelist's finest scenes, revealed his identity on that dreary winter's night to his horrified *protégé*, described in *Great Expectations*. Warrington in ragged dressing-gown, and dandy Pen, and little Fanny Bolton, and charming Laura, and the politic major meet us in "Lamb" Court and in the gardens, and are they not presences as real to us as any of its historical personages?

Rapidly the Temple of Lamb, of Dickens, of Thackeray, of our boyhood, is giving place to modern pretentiousness; the old courts were dingy, dull and

A STAIRCASE IN THE TEMPLE.

unpicturesque ; yet how interesting it was to peer
through those mouldy doorways, and up the dim
staircases, and speculate about the thousands of footsteps which shall never again be heard upon earth, that
have worn those oaken steps into hollows, upon the
vanished hands that have polished the rails of those
sturdy balusters to ebon smoothness, the great men
and little men, the heavy hearts and the light hearts
that have mounted them, and of the dreams of ambition fulfilled in success, or dying out in failure, that
those worm-eaten chambers wot of.

As the night closes in the passers-by grow fewer
and fewer ; the clerks have departed ; the Templars
have gone to dinner ; some of the windows are still
lighted up, and here and there you may catch sight
of busy fingers beneath a shaded lamp ; but the dim
and ghostly courts and the ancient church, which is
now quite nebulous, are pretty well " left to darkness
and to me".

Passing beneath the gateway into the vortex of life
on the other side what a transformation it is ! We
have been dreaming of the Fleet Street of Shakespeare, of the Mohocks, of Johnson and Lamb, but
no quaintly carved and gabled houses now meet our
eye, no wigged and buckle-shoed pedestrians leisurely sauntering to their favourite tavern, unruffled
by pushing crowd or noisy vehicle ; the street we
have been dreaming of was as placid and unhurried
as that of a remote country town of to-day. What
would the slow and sententious Doctor think of this

swarm of humanity that we are now mingled among? each unit of which seems as if life and death depended upon its speed; of these rushing, panting newspaper boys, with their shrill cries of "Special!" "Winner!" incomprehensible words to the eighteenth century man; this clatter of cabs and omnibuses, an endless procession; of the flood of light diffused by those huge globes of electric light that have taken the place of the dim oil lamps of his day and make the glaring gas, an illuminant of which he would be equally ignorant, look sick and pale in the shops? What would he say to the chatter, the noise, the scrambling drinking at the bars of those quiet and sedate taverns in which dead silence reigned when he rolled out his pompous sentences? Were he to attempt it now! Alack! Let him turn into the courts and alleys that live in his memory almost as peaceful as country lanes; they are humming with the thunderous din of the printing machine; and looking down through openings and gratings at his feet he will see interminable sheets of paper whirling over huge cylinders and hear a deafening, hissing and rushing of steam. Poor, bewildered Doctor, he would inevitably opine that he had strayed into a lower world than earth and hurry back to his tomb.[1]

---

[1] And yet, in running through the gossiping chronicles of past times, how frequently one finds that some of our own pet bugbears were quite as rampant generations ago as they are now. A curious instance of this is to be found in *The Spectator*, No. 251. In which there is a long letter upon street noises, and "Ralph Crotchet" complains

In and out the great newspaper offices reporters and telegraph boys are hurrying all through the night ; to the Central Press Offices messages are being flashed from every part of the globe, from nations unknown when our Doctor was in the flesh ; in editors' rooms the busy pens move to the accompaniment of the eternal click click of the tape

as bitterly as might any correspondent of a daily paper, of the shrill cry of the milkmaid, the bellowing of the chimney-sweeper, the small-coal man, the costermonger and the brick-dust vendor. "I must not omit one particular absurdity which runs through this whole vociferous generation, and which renders their cries, very often not only incommodious, but altogether useless to the public. I mean that idle accomplishment which they all aim at, of crying so as not to be understood." What a conservative race English hawkers must be! But in addition to these noises, the lieges of Queen Anne had to endure "for an hour together the twanking of a brass kettle or a frying-pan," the watchman's thump at midnight, and the sow-gelder's horn. But here is the most startling passage of all. "Our news should indeed be published in a very quick time, because it is a commodity that will not keep cold. It should not, however, be called with the same precipitation as *Fire*. Yet this is generally the case. A bloody battle alarms the town from one end to the other in an instant." So even the newspaper boy, O Solomon! is not new! It only wants the addition of a German band and a piano-organ to complete the resemblance between 1712 and 1899.

Yet another picture, from *The Spectator*, No. 87, the applicability of which, to our *fin de siècle*, will strike every reader. "I cannot but complain to you that there are, in six or seven places of this city, coffee-houses kept by persons of that sisterhood. These idols sit all day long, the adoration of the youth, within such and such districts; I know in particular goods are not entered at the Custom house, nor law reports perused in the Temple, by reason of one beauty who detains the young merchants too long near 'Change, and another fair one who keeps the students too long at her house when they should be at study." Then he goes on to describe how each adorer waits his turn for a glance "from these little thrones which all the company but

machine, which is adding its quota of " copy," to be
passed on to armies of compositors working silently
and swiftly on the floors above beneath a glare of
gas or electric light.   All night long the clatter and
click go on ; pale-faced, weary and perspiring " subs "
are feverishly scanning proofs or scrawling paragraphs,
or waiting anxiously for the last reporter's " flimsy "
from the Commons and the latest scrap of foreign
news.   Outside the bustle has not yet subsided ; late
omnibuses, crammed in and out, are rattling along,
and pedestrians are rushing to catch their last
train, which is puffing and panting in Ludgate
Station.

With the smallest hours comes a lull, though the
slaves of the lamp have not relaxed their toils, and
the thunderous hum of printing machines is louder
than ever.   Presently the street is all alive again ; the
compositors have finished their task and are hurrying out of the glare and heat into the cold morning
air.   A little while longer and the newsagents' carts
come clattering over the stones, and after being filled
with bales of newspapers dash off noisily for the railway stations.   And now from citywards great lum-
bering waggons, piled up with vegetables and baskets,

these lovers call the Bars," how one grew white as ashes because
his inamorata turned the sugar in his rival's tea-dish, and another was
going to drown himself because his idol would wash the dish in which
she had but just drank tea, before she would let him use it.

What a mortifying reflection it is for this up-to-date age to discover
that not even the pretty barmaid and her Johnny are originals!
There is no gainsaying that Solomon was the wisest of men.

drawn by slumberous horses, unguided by sleeping
drivers, slowly make their way to Covent Garden—
the one bit of repose in all this feverish turmoil.
And so the day life mingles with the night life, and
the eternal round of struggle and eager hurry goes
on unceasingly.

Note.—Four hundred years ago Wynkin de Worde opened the
first London bookseller's shop in " Flete Street at the sygne of the
sonne against the Condyth ". The printing offices of the *Standard*
in Shoe Lane now occupy the site.

Note to p. 125.—Since the context was written, Mr. Catling, the
editor of *Lloyd's Newspaper,* has informed me that their old office,
12 Salisbury Square, with an entrance through a court leading from
Fleet Street, was Richardson's printing office. The original lease is in
possession of the Lloyd's. I understand, also, that the dingy room in
which *Pamela* and *Clarissa Harlowe* were written still exists.

CHAPTER IX.

INSTEAD of making our way through Temple Bar
and along the Strand we will turn up Chancery Lane,
which has been completely transmogrified during
the last ten or dozen years. Of the Chancery Lane
of Dickens, haunted by the shadow of poor Miss Flite,
with its flat, soot-begrimed Georgian houses, little
remains except the grand old gateway of Lincoln's
Inn, which none of us wish to part with ; the imposing pile of the new Record Offices, and smart-looking
chambers have imparted to the old street a much
more cheerful and pleasant aspect—which, however,
the London atmosphere will soon tone down to its
previous sootiness.

Chancery Lane is a very ancient thoroughfare, and
Stow tells us that in the reign of Henry III. it was
known as New Street. Old Sergeant's Inn, founded
in the reign of Henry IV., and the ancient office,
Custos Rotulorum, the Rolls Court and its Chapel
have disappeared to make room for the buildings
of the Record Office. In demolishing the chapel,
built by Inigo Jones, remnants, including a beautifully

(143)

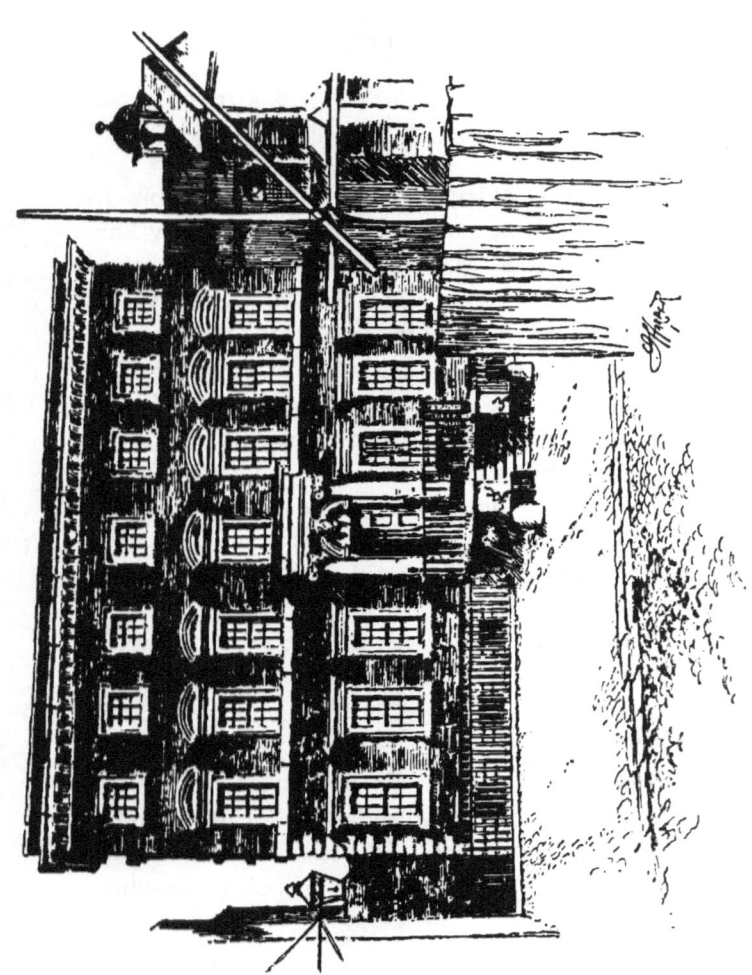

moulded chancel arch of the original structure, 1232, were discovered, that must have formed part of that Dormus Conversorum, or hospital for converted Jews, which originally occupied the site. Chichester Rents marks the site of the ancient town house of the Bishops of Chichester, which in the thirteenth century stood in spacious and beautiful gardens. Cursitor Street was originally the Coursitor's office, " built," says Stow, " with divers fair lodgings for gentlemen, all of brick and timber, by Sir Nicholas Bacon, late lord keeper of the Great Seal ". On the eastern side, near Holborn, stood one of the mansions of Cardinal Wolsey ; Thomas Wentworth, afterwards the great Earl of Strafford, was born in this street.

A narrow passage, on the eastern side of the lane, near Fleet Street, leads into that ancient house of the law, Clifford's Inn, originally the town house of the Lords de Clifford, which was given over to the students in the eighteenth year of Edward III. Of all the inns of court this wears the air of greatest antiquity, but it is the antiquity of decay that precedes dissolution. Harrison, Cromwell's lieutenant, was a lawyer's clerk here before he joined the Parliamentary army. Coke, that great lawyer but bitter advocate, who so ruthlessly crushed Raleigh, lived here for a time, but he is chiefly identified with the Middle Temple.

Passing beneath the great gateway of Lincoln's Inn, some of the bricks of which, it is said, were laid by Ben Jonson, whose stepfather was a mason, we note

10

CLIFFORD'S INN.

that ancient tower in the south-west corner, a plate upon which indicates to passers-by that my Lord Protector's secretary, Thurloe, had chambers there. And to think how often old Noll's burly form might have ascended those narrow winding stairs.

Timbs tells a romantic story in connection with these chambers. One evening Cromwell came there to talk with Thurloe over a plot which had been devised for seizing the persons of the Prince of Wales and the Dukes of York and Gloucester. In the dusk they had not perceived a young clerk with his head upon his desk, seemingly asleep. Cromwell drew his dagger and would have killed the man had not Thurloe interposed. The clerk, however, had only been shamming slumber, and found means to warn the princes of their danger.

Henry de Lacey, Earl of Lincoln, early in the fourteenth century, bestowed this noble domain upon the law students. In those days it was a rural garden filled with fruit trees and embowered in roses, with a fish pond in the centre. Previous to his time, in 1221, it was the first home of the Dominicans in London, where they continued to dwell until 1276, and then removed to their great house near Ludgate, thereafter called Blackfriars. With the exception of the gateway, hall and chapel, none of the buildings are older than the time of Charles II. The hall was built in the twenty-second year of Henry VII., and the chapel by Inigo Jones, 1623. Among the most famous men associated with this Inn are Sir Thomas More, Sir

Matthew Hale, Sir Robert Walpole, Lords Mansfield, Camden, Brougham. Although Lincoln's Inn was as famous for its revels and feasts as its great rivals, its traditions, apart from the law, would have little interest for the general reader, so I will leave it for the Fields.

During the seventeenth century, Digby, Newcastle, Somers, Sandwich and other nobles, erected mansions in Lincoln's Inn Fields—the Duchess of Portsmouth resided in one at the south-west corner, the *fleur de lys* may still be seen upon the walls of the remnant that yet remains of her house, which spans a passage leading to Clare Market casual ward. But the centre, which we now call the Square, was given over to swarms of loafers and beggars, who took their meals, played cards, quarrelled, fought, importuned every passer-by for alms, slept beneath the shadow of the trees, and under cover of night waylaid, robbed and sometimes murdered the belated wayfarer. A Lincoln's Inn mumper was a proverb. Mountebanks harangued, bears danced, bulls were baited by dogs, horses were exercised, and rubbish was shot everywhere.

The Fields were not infrequently used as a place of execution ; there Babington and his accomplices expiated their treason against Elizabeth, and there a far more illustrious personage, Lord William Russell, was beheaded for his alleged complicity in the Rye House Plot. On that July morning, 1683, a vast crowd fills the Square and looks down upon it from every window and roof and " coign of vantage ". Very slowly is the coach containing the victim and Bishops Burnet and Tillotson able to make its way through the dense human mass, and the Oxford Blues have much ado to keep back the mob, who make rushes to get near the carriage window. Some yell, some hiss and curse, others take off their hats and murmur prayers and blessings, and women sob; but all draw back with a momentary shudder as the headsman, clothed from head to foot in black, his face covered by a black mask, and the glittering axe upon his shoulder, stalks noiselessly, like Fate, in the rear. Singing a psalm and with a firm step, looking neither to right nor left, Russell mounts the black-draped scaffold, and, after protesting his innocence, kneels and prays; then strips off his coat and bares his neck, and when the executioner has cut off his hair, lays his noble head upon the block. An awful hush falls upon the riotous mob, the vilest among which are awed, for the shadow of the Angel of Death is over all. There is a flash in the sunlight, a silent thrill shivers through the multitude; the axe is raised; another flash and it descends; a third rise and fall of glittering steel, an awful shriek from the women and a cheering and groaning from the men, and the severed head falls upon the scaffold dyeing it with blood.

At the back of the Fields, in Portugal Street,[1] stood the famous Lincoln's Inn Fields Theatre, a fine house,

---

[1] Now covered by an extension of the College of Surgeons. Much of the theatre was preserved in a large china warehouse until 1848.

handsomely decorated and glittering with looking-glass : you will find plenty about it in Pepys' *Diary*. But that gossipy chronicler has long been laid at rest in St. Olave's Church, and the second George is on the throne when we pay our visit to it. The boxes are filled with beaux and belles, the pit with coffee-house wits from Covent Garden, the gallery with butchers from Clare Market ; on each side of the stage is a double row of seats, which the fops affect, as they did in the days of the Blackfriars. The play is *Macbeth*, and Mr. Quin, most pompous and stilted of actors, personates the Thane of Cawdor in a scarlet-velvet coat, knee breeches, silk stockings, buckled shoes, a huge powdered wig and a cocked hat ; while Lady Macbeth is in hooped skirt and stomacher, according to the fashion of the day, and all the other characters are costumed in the same mode. The beaux and belles on the stage are more interested in displaying their toilettes to the house and in their own conversation than in the business of the play, and freely exchange remarks. In the midst of the dagger soliloquy my Lord Sandwich deliberately crosses the actor to speak to some person on the opposite side. Cries of " Shame ! " " Throw him into the pit ! " come from the gallery, and John Rich, the manager—and most famous of harlequins—in great indignation, steps from the side scene and expostulates with the earl upon the unseemliness of his behaviour. My lord's reply is a blow in the face ; manager Rich draws his sword ; the beaux start to their feet ; the actors rush to the support of their chief, and the next moment there is a clash of steel and the players and their patrons are at cut and thrust ; gentlemen leap from the boxes to the succour of their friends ; ladies scream and faint.

The actors have the best of it, and drive their opponents off the stage and out of the building. But the hot-blooded beaux are not so easily got rid of. Rushing to the houses of the nobles close by for reinforcements, they soon return to the theatre in overwhelming numbers, cut down the door-keepers who oppose their entrance, and force their way in ; the more prudent among the audience have taken their departure, but some of the more fiery spirits, including the butchers, side with the actors. The beaux and their lacqueys, however, are too many for the defenders, who are put to the rout. Then the work of destruction commences, the mirrors are smashed, seats and scenery torn up, cast into a pile and set alight. But just at that moment there is a cry without of " The soldiers! The soldiers!" and in a few minutes a detachment of troops arrives, just in time to prevent a conflagration.

There will be no play at Lincoln's Inn Fields Theatre for many a day after this, and a custom, which has fallen into desuetude since the time of Charles II., will be revived—that is to say, a guard of soldiers will attend at both Lincoln's Inn and Drury Lane for every performance. And this regulation has always been observed at Drury Lane and Covent Garden, the latter being the successor to Lincoln's Inn, which was not used after about 1743.

Above that heavy stone archway leading into Duke Street is Sardinia Chapel, built in 1648, originally for the Sardinian Embassy, it will go for the new street. It has been partly destroyed more than once in no-popery riots, especially after the flight of James II., when every Romish church throughout London was sacked and burned, and again in Lord George Gordon's rising. That imposing-looking house, approached by a high flight of steps at the north-west corner, dates back to 1686; first known as Powis House from its builder, the Marquis of Powis; it was renamed Newcastle House when it came into the possession of that duke, whom Macaulay epigrammatically says, was "a living, moving, talking caricature". One of the most absurd and ignorant of men, the laughing-stock of every satirist of the day, was for thirty years a Secretary of State, and for ten, First Lord of the Treasury under George II. Foote said of him that he always appeared as if he had lost an hour in the morning and was all the rest of the day looking for it.[1]

As we turn round under the heavy stone arcade, where in days gone by footpads used to lurk at night for unwary pedestrians, our eye is caught by the name of "Whetstone Park". Why such a cramped-up bit of ground should be called a park I

---

[1] John Forster had chambers in Newcastle House. It was visiting him there that probably suggested to Dickens to make it, in *Bleak House*, the scene of Tulkinghorn's murder. [No. 57-58 Lincoln's Inn Fields, *not* Newcastle House, was the scene of the Tulkinghorn. The room is now the private office of Messrs. Soame, Edwards & Jones.]

cannot discover; in the time of Charles II. it was one of the most vicious spots in the metropolis. Yet Milton, on leaving Barbican, resided in it, or close by it, for several years.

Great Queen Street, notwithstanding its width, is a dull, depressing thoroughfare, yet with an air of faded gentility about it that tells of better days. And it has seen better days. Built by Inigo Jones, and named after Queen Henrietta Maria, its noble houses were early inhabited by the famous Lord Herbert of Cherbury, the author of one of the most interesting of autobiographies; by the Bristols, the Finches, the Conways and Paulets. Here lived the eccentric Dr. Radcliffe, as blunt and uncouth to his patients as was Abernethy after him. "I would not have two such legs as you have for your three kingdoms," he said to William III., to whom he was court physician. He frequently sent rude messages to Queen Anne when she summoned him. "Tell Her Majesty I shall not come; she's only got the vapours." When she was dying he sent a similar message, not believing in the gravity of her illness, and, after her death, would have been lynched by the mob, could they have got hold of him. He was the founder of the magnificent Radcliffe Library at Oxford.

Sir Godfrey Kneller, whom we shall meet again in Bow Street and Covent Garden, died in this street. Brinsley Sheridan lived at Nos. 55 and 56, south side, when he first became manager of Drury Lane Theatre in 1776, and it is probable that the *School for Scandal*

was written there.   Its vicinity to the great theatres
brought some notable actors and actresses to Great
Queen Street : " the airy " Lewis, most incomparable
of light comedians ; Kitty Clive, most humorous of
soubrettes ; and her successor, Miss Pope ; " Little "
Knight, and others.   Sir Robert Strange, the celebrated engraver, and Opie, the no less celebrated
painter, also resided here.   Most of these dwellings
were at the south-west end of the street, but little
remains of them now.

Lord Herbert of Cherbury's house was close to
Great Wild Street, down which we must now turn
on our way to Clare Market.   Wild Street marks
the site of Weld House, a fine mansion which
was destroyed in those terrible riots, when James
II. by his cowardly flight left London without head
or government to the mercy of a fanatical mob.

The last remnants of that once notorious haunt of
vice and misery, Clare Market, will soon have disappeared.   Until recently a bit of Dickens's Tom All
Alone's survived in a narrow lane of tall, toppling
houses, hideous with dirt and decay, and dark as pitch
at night.   It lay at the back of the south end of Portsmouth Street, and you reached it by passing through
an opening beneath a tumble-down house, upon which
were carved the arms of the Earls of Clare.

In the time of Charles I. the whole of this neighbourhood was covered by the mansion and gardens of
that noble family, who afterwards gave their names
and titles to the various streets.   A plate let into the

wall of one of the houses in Denzil Street, of which
an illustration is given, tells the story. A little before
the death of Cromwell, John Holles, a son of the earl,
created Marquis of Clare and Duke of Newcastle,
opened a market upon a portion of the grounds. It
was not until 1711, when the title became extinct, that

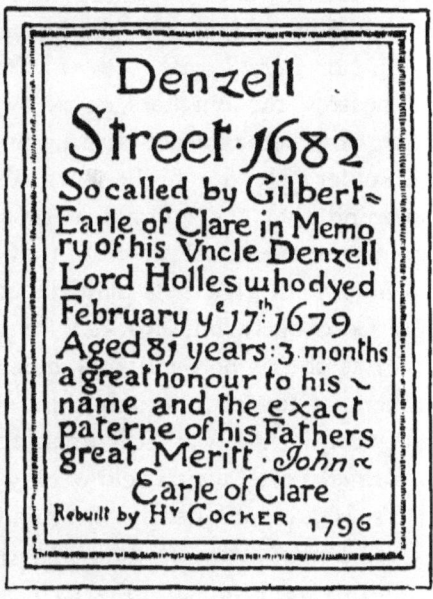

Denzell .
Street·1682
So called by Gilbert
Earle of Clare in Memo
ry of his Vncle Denzell
Lord Holles who dyed
February ye 17th 1679
Aged 81 years:3 months
a great honour to his
name and the exact
paterne of his Fathers
great Meritt · John
Earle of Clare
Rebuilt by Hy Cocker 1796

STREET TABLET, DENZIL STREET.

the family ceased to reside there. Picture to yourself
bright parterres of flowers, velvet lawns and blossom-
ing fruit trees flourishing in that now murky district!

While the eighteenth century was still young the
tide of poverty and crime was creeping closer and

closer up to this once aristocratic quarter. Clement's
Lane, however, was quite a fashionable lounge, and
beaux of the first water, with clouded canes, silver-
hilted rapiers and diamond buckled shoes, picked their
way among brawling butchers, squalid poverty and vice,
and along side-ways slippery with offal and garbage,
to the Spiller's Head, where an actors' club was held.
Spiller was a famous player who made his fame as
Mat o' the Mint in *The Beggar's Opera* at the Portugal Street Theatre ; the butchers swore by him and
changed the sign of their favourite tavern, the Butcher's
Head, to the Spiller's Head in his honour. And it must
be borne in mind that the knights of the shambles
were a power in the theatrical world of that day ; the
success of a new actor or a new play depending not
a little upon those burly blue-frocked frequenters of
Olympus. Thus their good-will was much courted
by the members of the sock and buskin.

So while Queen Anne was still upon the throne
some actors formed a club, which held weekly meetings
at the Spiller's Head until nearly the middle of the
century. Tom Durfey, who used to sing duets with
Charles II., and wrote novels and poems not *puerisque
virginibus*, a rakehelly cavalier, was the first president;
and that most famous of fops, off the stage and on,
whose Lord Foppington was to that age what Sothern's
Dundreary was to the last generation, though a member
of White's, was his successor. Can you not see him,
his broad, flat face half-hidden by a twenty-guinea
periwig, his stockings of spotless silk rolled high over

his velvet breeches, in his square-cut, buckram-skirted, embroidered silk coat and red-heeled shoes, groping his way up the dark staircase into the smoke-dimmed atmosphere of the low-ceiled room, where " King Colley " is hailed with a shout of welcome by those famous *confrères*, about whom, in old age, he will write so graphically in his *Apology* for his life. There is handsome Will Mountfort, with his musical voice, most irresistible of stage lovers, over whom hangs the shadow of a real tragedy, reminding one of poor Terriss's fate ; crooked saturnine Sandford, most incomparable of stage villains, who might have played Richard III. without any make up ; owlishly solemn-looking Nokes, who, however, cannot show his face upon the stage without provoking a roar ; droll Willy Pinkethman, who has come from his booth at Bartholomew Fair ; Dick Estcourt, *facile princeps* of mimics, about whom Steele writes so unctiously in *The Tatler;* the admired Tom Spiller himself, and others who are now *nomen preterœa nihil.* When Spiller died, a Clare Market poet wrote :—

> Down with your marrow bones and cleavers all,
> And on your marrow bones ye butchers fall ;
> For prayers from you who never prayed before,
> Perhaps poor Jemmy may to life restore.

Guy Fawkes day was celebrated with high jinks in Clare Market : a huge bonfire was always made in front of Newcastle House, in the Fields; but the butchers had one of their own, in the space near Bear Yard, and thrashed each other round about the fire

with the strongest sinews of bulls ; while large parties
of them from all the markets paraded the streets with
marrow bones and cleavers.   Indeed the whole of
London was so lit up by bonfires and fireworks, "that
from the suburbs," says Hone, " it looked in one red
heat," and such disorder reigned in the streets that
horses and carriages were sometimes overthrown by
the hustling, driving, fighting mobs.

Clare Market was noted for its taverns and sixpenny and shilling ordinaries, with " private rooms for
the nobility and gentry," who occasionally patronised
these houses ; they were mostly frequented, however,
by gentlemen in shabby scarlet coats, high jack-boots,
jingling spurs and fiercely cocked hats, their weather-
beaten faces showing them to be soldiers, most of whom
were proud of having fought under Marlborough.   Yet
these heroes of Ramilies, Blenheim and many another
bloody field, were glad of a sixpenny dinner—when
they could get it, and ogled and flattered buxom
landladies to shorten the reckoning, and sometimes
lived at free quarters with their Desdemonas.

How many ghosts flit across our memories of the
old place.   Here is a dainty one, quietly but exquisitely attired, a charming brunette, a pretty, demure
face half-hidden beneath a hood, upon which every
eye is turned ; the rough butchers check their free
talk and respectfully salute her ; she has a basket
upon her arm, and is making little purchases, and as
she buys her vegetables she talks to the poor women,
oh, so kindly, and asks them about their troubles, and

as she passes along drops coins in the hands of hungry shivering wretches huddled on doorsteps, and then hurries away, followed by showers of blessings from lips little used to such utterances. That is sweet Anne Bracegirdle—you walk over her tombstone in the abbey's cloisters; "the darling of the theatre," says Cibber in his *Apology*. "For it will be no extravagant thing to say, scarce an audience saw her that were less than half of them lovers, without a suspected favourite among them; and though she might be said to have been the universal passion and under the highest temptations, her constancy in resisting them served but to increase the number of her admirers."

> Would she could make of me a saint,
> Or I of her a sinner!

sighed Congreve, one of her most devoted admirers.

A later ghost that haunts the market is that of a young barrister, named John Scott, who not long ago ran off with beautiful Bessie Surtees from her home at Newcastle, flitted over the border and married her at Gretna Green, without a sixpence between them. It is hard times for the young couple who have to live upon love—and herrings, which the bridegroom cheapens in Clare Market. Bessie's parents are inexorable, little thinking that one day poor John Scott will sit upon the woolsack and be known as Lord Eldon. Only fancy such a romance being attached to the future ogre of the Tory party! Alas, for the end of a romance, in years to come my lord will be glad to steal into the George Coffee-house, at the top of the Haymarket, to drink his pint of wine, which his dear Bessie will not allow him to enjoy in peace at home!

A notable Clare Market tavern, which has only just disappeared, the Black Jack, was particularly associated with the names of Joe Miller and Jack Sheppard. In the low-ceiled, wainscotted room up-stairs—so well known to old medical students, and old lawyers' clerks of the Fields, who often took their dinner there before the days of the Holborn Restaurant—Joe Miller, an actor at Drury Lane, smoked many a pipe. Never was a reputation more curiously acquired than his. Joe was the most stolid of men, he could neither read nor write, and could learn his parts only by his wife reading them to him ; he seldom opened his mouth, except to put his knife or his pipe into it, and was never known to make a joke. So John Motley, a fellow-player, thought it would be capital fun to make a collection of jests and affix Joe Miller's name to them, little thinking that posterity would take him literally.

It is said that the Black Jack was at one time called the Jump, to celebrate one of Jack Sheppard's many escapes from the pursuit of Jonathan Wild. While Jack was lying *perdu* in the tavern, the word was passed that the thief-taker was at the door, and when he was mounting the stairs Jack leaped from the first-floor window into the street below and got clear off. This house was also the scene of "the Popgun

Plot," 1794, which aimed at assassinating the king with a poisoned arrow.

A peculiar-looking tavern at the corner of Portsmouth Street—to the south of the Black Jack—with the upper storey supported by slender pillars—known by the sign of the George the Fourth, which has also passed away, is generally believed to have been the Magpie and Stump of *The Pickwick Papers*, where Lowton, Mr. Perker's clerk, spent his evenings presiding over harmonic meetings, where Mr. Pickwick listened to the story of " The Queer Client," and where old Weller and his fellow-coachmen entertained Mr. Pell.[1] It would appear that several successive landlords of this house kept a register of the names of the different students attached to the hospital opposite, who used the tavern, and some late and present very famous doctors are to be found in the list.

Another notoriety of Clare Market, whom the butchers swore by, was the mad preacher, Orator Henley, satirized by Hogarth, Pope, and Foote, and in almost all the literature of the time.[2] He had a

---

[1] The Three Tons, or "Clock House" (now modernised), in Clement's Passage, seems to have a better right to be identified with the Magpie and Stump than the George the Fourth. Opinion is divided.

[2] "Preacher at once and Zany of thy age," wrote Pope in *The Dunciad*. His career is another illustration of the poor-devil author. Master of a Grammar School in Leicester, Henley came to London to try and make a living by his pen, endowed with a knowledge of *ten* languages; but he shared the fate of his brothers of the craft, both literate and illiterate, and fell to be a bookseller's hack. Soured by poverty and lack of appreciation, he resolved " to live by making one

chapel at the corner of Lincoln's Inn Fields, though he
frequently preached in the market, and he is described
as leaping, harlequin fashion, into the pulpit, which
Pope called his "gilt tub," through a spring door,
falling to work at once with hands, arms, legs, head,
and ranting and raving at the top of his voice.

Though greatly shrunken in its area Clare Market
still retains its characteristic features, and no more
graphic picture of how the poor of London live could
be gained than by mingling with the crowds that on
Saturday night gather about the stalls of stale and
much-watered vegetables, about the butchers and

half the world laugh at the other". He first opened his School of
Oratory in Newport Market, and then, at the invitation of the silly
Duke of Newcastle, removed to Clare Market. He proposed by his
lectures to supply the want of a universal school for all classes of the
community. But it was by preaching—always the best card for an
adventurer to play in cant-ridden England—in something after the
style afterwards so successfully adopted by Whitfield, Rowland Hill
and Spurgeon, a judicious mixture of brimstone and buffoonery, that
he made his mark. He advertised an oration on marriage, got
together an immense assemblage of women, and then coolly told
them he was afraid they oftener came to church in the hope of getting
husbands than to be instructed by the preacher, and wound up with
indecent jest. He announced a lecture on the most expeditious
method of making shoes, and attracted thereby all snobdom. Holding up a boot, he cut off the leg! Yet, says Pope :—

"'Twill break the benches, Henley, with thy strain,
While Sherlock, Hare and Gibson preach in vain".

All this time he was pursuing learned studies; he left behind him
6000 MSS., and 150 volumes of commonplaces, wit and memoranda,
all of which when sold realised less than £100, although for some
years the money had flowed galore into the oratory. Hurrah for
cant and buffoonery, they always appeal to John Bull's organ of
benevolence!

bacon shops, chaffering for uninviting-looking morsels of fly-blown meat and scraps of bacon that are heaped upon the boards. The flaring lights of paraffin jets throw up in grim relief this motley mob of buyers and sellers, while ears polite are outraged by the shouting costers and the riotous noise from densely packed public-houses. In all these things Clare Market is much the same as it was in the time of the Spiller's Head Club. But its days are numbered. Year by year, for a generation and more, this gruesome neighbourhood has been gradually vanishing before the march of improvement. The grand new thoroughfare which is shortly to pass through it will complete its demolition ; and though one cannot repress a sentimental regret at the disappearance of any historic landmarks, the most ardent antiquary must admit that in this case at least it was an urgent necessity.

CHAPTER X.

"THE JOYOUS NEIGHBOURHOOD OF COVENT GARDEN."

I. — *Drury Lane — Wych Street — Bow Street — Russell Street—Covent Garden Theatre—The Beef-steak Club.*

THE ancient name of Drury Lane was the Via de Aldwych—hence Wych Street; but in the reign of Elizabeth Sir Robert Drury built a mansion with gardens upon the spot where now stands the Olympic Theatre, and from that time it has been known by its present appellation. The gallant Earl Craven, who was supposed to have been secretly united to James I.'s daughter, the titular Queen of Bohemia, was the next tenant, and during the latter part of the eighteenth century the noble house was converted into a tavern, known by the sign of the Queen of Bohemia. By 1805 the structure had fallen into such decay that it was necessary to pull it down. The ground was taken by Philip Astley, of amphitheatre notoriety, who thereupon erected, chiefly out of the materials of an old French warship, a naval prize, " The Olymphic Pavilion," and opened it as a circus.

Drury Lane was quite an aristocratic quarter in

(164)

the Stuarts' days ; the Marquis of Argyle and the Earl
of Anglesey among others had mansions in it ; but
even in the time of Charles II. its inhabitants were

LAST OF THE BULK SHOPS, CLARE MARKET.

mixed. Pepys tells us that Nell Gwynne lodged
here when she was an actress, and some biographers
assert that Nelly was born in the Coal Yard, at

the Holborn end of the street, but this is very doubtful.   By the opening of the eighteenth century Drury
Lane had begun to be known as a harbour of vice
and squalor, and as such it has been notorious ever
since.   Goldsmith writes of "the drabs and bloods
of Drury Lane"; Pope, in *The Dunciad*, indicates
that it was the haunt of the hack writer who,

> Lulled by zephyrs through the broken panes,
> Rhymes ere he wakes,

and Gay, in *Trivia*, writes of

> Drury's mazy courts and dark abodes.

Hogarth here laid the scene of *The Harlot's
Progress*, and references to the peculiar vices of the
place will be found in *The Tatler*.

Drury Lane, from the time of James I., has been
closely associated with the stage.   The Cockpit,
burned down in a 'prentice riot, and rebuilt under
the name of The Phœnix, the first theatre erected
within its precincts, was, like the Blackfriars and
Salisbury Court, "a private house".   Its memory
was preserved until recently in Pitt Court, a noisome
cul-de-sac, now covered by the model lodging-houses
on the eastern side of the Lane.   It ceased to be
used soon after the Restoration.

Killigrew converted a tennis court in Vere Street,
Clare Market, into a temporary theatre, which he
opened on the 8th of November, 1660.   It had a brief
existence of less than three years, and it does not
appear to have been used again after the company was

transferred to their new house, of which I shall write directly. Vere Street would claim no notice here but for the fact that it was on its stage the first English actress made her *début*, 8th December, 1660, in the character of Desdemona. The name of the lady who inaugurated such a revolution in things theatrical, as the women's parts had hitherto been performed by boys, is unknown, though it might have been either of the beautiful sisters, Anne or Beck Marshall, so frequently mentioned by Pepys, or Prince Rupert's favourite, Mrs. Hughes, who figures in De Grammont's Memoirs.[1]

Charles II. granted Henry Killigrew, a groom of the chamber, a patent, still extant, for the erection of a theatre upon an old riding yard in Drury Lane. Four successive houses have stood there. The first, which cost only the modest sum of £1500, was opened on 8th April, 1663, and destroyed by fire nine years afterwards. The second, built from the designs of Sir Christopher Wren, was plain and unpretentious, and thereby offered a striking contrast to Davenant's splendid theatre in Salisbury Court. Its records were, however, unique ; it stood through six reigns, and was the scene of the triumphs of Betterton, Booth, Garrick, Mrs. Barry, Mrs. Oldfield, Mrs. Porter, Mrs. Pritchard,

---

[1] This was not the actual *début* of a woman upon the English stage. In 1656 a Mrs. Coleman took the part of Ianthe in the opera of *The Siege of Rhodes*. This was probably a private performance at the Cockpit, either in defiance of or by connivance of the law, for the stringent suppression of the theatres was beginning to be relaxed at that time.

Peg Woffington, Mrs. Abington, Mrs. Siddons, etc., etc. By 1791 the house had fallen into such decay that it had to be pulled down. A magnificent and colossal building, which could accommodate 3611 people, or nearly 600 more than the present theatre, was opened on 12th March, 1794, and perished in the flames on 24th February, 1809. The loss was so enormous that it was not until 10th October, 1812, that the Drury Lane of to-day was ready for the public. A host of delightful recollections are associated with this famous Temple of Thespis, but the exigencies of space forbid me even to glance at them.[1]

But as I have attempted a picture of the Blackfriars in the days of James I., I will now essay a companion sketch of Drury Lane in the days of his grandsons. The theatre is of moderate dimensions, and lit only by candles ; footlights are unknown, and will be until Garrick introduces them from Paris, and the stage is illumined only by a ring of candles dependent from " the flies ". The orchestra occupies a side balcony, as it did at the Blackfriars ; the deep proscenium projects in a semi-oval form to the front bench of the pit ; there are no stage boxes, but an entrance on each side for the actors. The auditorium consists of two tiers of boxes, divided into compartments ; at the sides are balconies, and a 12d. and 18d. gallery.

In the boxes, which are almost exclusive to the court,

---

[1] *See* the author's *Our Old Actors*, and *The London Stage from 1576 to 1888*.

with their heads affectedly posed on one side, lan-
guish the Sir Fopling Flutters and Sir Courtly Nices,
a raree-show of gaudy velvets and satins, slashed,
laced, spangled and covered with streaming ribbons.
Their inane faces, spotted with black patches of various
shapes, are half-hidden by huge periwigs, veritable
cascades of hair of every shade from flaxen to black.
Lounging back in their chairs, they languidly pass
silver or gold-mounted combs through their rippling
locks, to display the whiteness of their hands and their
jewelled fingers, and their ruffles of *point de Venise*,
while some wear gold-fringed and embroidered silk
gloves, buttoning up to the elbow, the cuff of the coat
or doublet not coming lower. Standing behind their
chairs lacqueys sprinkle their wigs and handkerchiefs
with delicate essences from gold and crystal *flaçons*,
while they themselves titillate their nostrils with
pulvilio from gold and jewelled snuff-boxes, lest the
odour from the groundlings should " nauseate " them.
A lady kisses her hand to one of these beaux from an
opposite box ; he rises, bows almost to his knees, and,
in doing so, contrives to jerk the whole mass of his
periwig over his face, and as he rises again throws it
back without ruffling a curl. To another enter *un bon
camarade*. With what effusiveness he greets him in a
jargon of French and Italian, and kisses him upon
both cheeks, amidst shouts of derision from " the
groundlings," whose choice sport it is to bait the
fops.

The male butterfly is so gorgeous that the female

is almost eclipsed by him. The faces of most of the
ladies are concealed by silk visors, a necessary reserve,
considering the *very free* dialogue of the play, though
here and there some Phryne braves the leers of men,
preferring to display her charms.

But what a hubbub of laughter, jesting, hissing,
quarrelling, jumping on seats, tumbling over seats,
scrambling and screaming rises from the half-crown
pit during the intervals. The more sober part of the
audience occupy the centre, while the sides are given
up to the gallants and the vizards. Ladies of quality,
hiding their identity beneath their masks, share the
licence of this Agapemone with the nymphs of Covent
Garden. In Fops' Corner, men of mode mingle
with the Temple beaux, threadbare wits, knights
of the post and adventurers of every description.
"Fine Chaney oranges! Fine Chaney oranges!" is
a cry that resounds on every side, and the buxom
vendors drive a thriving trade with their fruit at
sixpence each, while the gallants toy and flirt with
them.

Up in the galleries the fun is yet more fast and
furious. The Olympians pelt the boxes with apples
and oranges, and salute the Laises and Phrynes of
the court with epithets more truthful than decent.
Abigails, sempstresses from the New Exchange, and
Lindabrides from the Stews, better on the example
set by their superiors. When the curtain draws up,
another audience is revealed to the occupants of the
auditorium, which hem in the stage, much as I have

shown in my pictures of the Blackfriars and Lincoln's Inn Fields.[1]

During the last twenty years Drury Lane has undergone much purging, and many of its vilest slums have been cleared out. Not many years ago no fewer than three hundred professional thieves were located in Charles Street, which was equally notorious in the eighteenth century, when it was known as Lewkner Lane.

The clearing of the area to the south of Drury Lane Theatre has removed some plague spots and some interesting nooks as well.[2] Among them the burial ground in Russell Court, through the grated iron gate of which Jo showed Lady Dedlock her lover's grave, and against which on that bitter winter's night the erring woman was found dead. Apropos of that ghastly spot, less than half a century ago the coffins on Sundays, which was a general burial day, were often piled seven or eight deep beneath the back windows of the houses in Vinegar Yard, which looked out upon this Devil's acre, and even underneath the kitchen flags human remains were rotting. Another awful Golgotha was the Green Ground ; it was only one-third of an acre in extent, but in the twenty-five

---

[1] This most abominable privilege was supposed to have been abolished by Garrick, but it evidently survived long after his time, as is shown by the following paragraph from *The Times*, 9th May, 1796 : " The stage at the Opera is so crowded that Madame Rose, in throwing up her fine muscular arm into a graceful attitude, inadvertently levelled three men of the first quality at a stroke ".

[2] While preparing the ground for the new thoroughfare the Necropolis Company, it is said, cleared away the remains of 28,000 bodies from " Jo's Churchyard ".

years preceding 1848 over 5000 bodies were interred in
it.   Close to Clement's Inn was Clare Market Chapel,
beneath which interments were made until the coffins
touched the rafters of the floor.   When the place was
closed, in 1844, it was turned into a dancing room, and
continued to be used for that purpose during several
years !   The Green Ground is now covered by a portion of King's College Hospital, which at the same
time absorbed an ancient tavern, called the Grange,
much affected by the actors of Lincoln's Inn Fields.

Clement's Inn, which dates back to the fifteenth
century, and is associated with Sir Matthew Hale and
Justice Shallow, is being fast modernized out of all
recognition.   Many of us will remember that, before
the demolitions for the Law Courts began, it was
approached from the Strand by a spacious gateway,
enclosed at night by iron gates, which were there in
the days when Clement's Lane, as I have before
intimated, was the fashionable lounge of a fashionable
neighbourhood.   New Inn, of which Sir Thomas More
was a student, still retains its old-world appearance.
It is scheduled for the new street.   Upon the site of
Lyon's Inn, formerly an annexe of the Temple, now
stand the Globe Theatre and the Opera Comique,
opened in 1868 and 1870.

Bow Street—so called because its outline was in the
figure of a bent bow—was laid out in 1637, and for the
first seventy years of its existence was as aristocratic
a quarter as Drury Lane.   Here lived for a while the
libertine Earl of Rochester ; the poet Earl of Dorset,

Dryden's patron; Edmund Waller, William Wycherley
the dramatist, after his marriage with the Dowager
Countess of Drogheda, and here he died in 1715;
Edward Harley, afterwards Earl of Oxford, one of
Queen Anne's prime ministers, was born in this
street in 1660; Grinling Gibbons, the greatest of
wood carvers, lived in a house on the eastern side
from 1678 to the year of his death, 1721. Dr. Radcliffe felt pulses in Bow Street for some years, and
Kneller painted some of his best portraits here before
removing to Covent Garden piazza.

A notable Bow Street tavern was the Cock; it
frequently figures in the comedies of the Restoration
—in *The Country Wife*, *Plain Dealer*, and others. It
was the scene of that disgraceful frolic of Lord Buck-
hurst and Sir Charles Sedley, the wit and dramatist:
one day both of them stripped themselves naked,
and, going out on the balcony, harangued the passers-
by; an indignant crowd stoned the house, and the
jokers were heavily fined.

Edmund Waller's old house was converted into a
police court. And in 1749 Harry Fielding came to
reside in it as head magistrate. It was burned down
by the Gordon rioters in 1780.

Horace Walpole, in one of his letters, gives us a
curious, if ill-natured, glimpse of Fielding's *ménage*.
"Rigby and Peter Bathurst, the other night, carried a
servant of the latter's, who had attempted to shoot
him, before Fielding, who, to all his other avocations,
had, by the grace of Mr. Lyttleton, added that of

Middlesex Justice. He sent them word he was at supper and they must come next morning. They did not understand that freedom, and ran up, when they found him banqueting with a blind man, a w——, and three Irishmen on some cold mutton and a bone of ham, both in one dish, and the dirtiest cloth. He never stirred nor asked them to sit."[1] Nevertheless the great novelist was very zealous in his office, for he was able to boast, after he had held it five years, that during the last few months of 1753 there had not been a single robbery or murder in the metropolis. More than that Magistrate Fielding discountenanced the corrupt practices then common to his order. His office carried no salary, being paid in fees that had to be squeezed out of prisoners and prosecutors ; he used to say that his predecessor made £1000 a year, while he never gained more than £300, because he composed instead of inflaming the quarrels of porters and beggars, and refused to take a shilling from a man who would not have had another left.

The instruments used by Fielding for the suppression of crime, which had previously been rampant, were the men to whom this street is much indebted for its world-wide notoriety, the Bow Street Runners, who, until they were abolished by the institution of the New Police, in 1829, were as well known by their red waistcoats—from which they were nicknamed " Robin Redbreasts "—and silver-tipped staves, as the

[1] " The blind man " was his half-brother, Sir John Fielding, and the lady so opprobriously designated was Sir John's wife.

British soldier by his red coat and bayonet. A jovial crew were "the Runners," looking like what was formerly the type of the jolly farmer, and as dissimilar from the sphinx-like detective of our own time as the modern agriculturist is from the John Bull of our grandfathers. Most famous among the " Robin Redbreasts" was John Townshend, the special guardian and favourite of George III. After the death of that monarch Townshend used to say: "Why, bless you, his gracious majesty and myself were like brothers". And indeed " Farmer George" and his protector were frequently seen walking up and down the terrace at Windsor in familiar conversation; and John Townshend always dressed in exact imitation of his royal patron. In the performance of his duty this officer was as daring as he was expert; his very voice was a terror to evildoers. One night while he and Joe Manton, the gunmaker, were travelling in a chaise across Hounslow Heath they were attacked by footpads. Manton was about to fire upon them, when Townshend stopped him with "Wait a minute, Joe," and thrust his head out of the window. At the sound of that dread voice the thieves fled like the wind, but not before he had identified them. He acquired a great reputation by his captures of the notorious highwayman, Jerry Abershaw, and pickpocket George Barrington. He was usually selected for duty at all the royal *levées*, and at the routs and balls of the aristocracy.

George Ruthven, George Ledbitter, John and Daniel Forester were notable members of this formidable fraternity, which never numbered above forty, about whose doings some good stories might be told did space permit. The last of the Runners died only a short time ago at the age of eighty-five. These old-fashioned thief-catchers were much better rewarded than the modern detective ; they were paid from £40 to £100 for the conviction of every criminal they captured, and received besides handsome presents for private services. Townshend died worth £20,000. The " Robin Redbreast " played an important part in the fiction of his day. I think *Oliver Twist* is one of the last novels he appeared in, and it is curious that Dickens, with Inspector Bucket, was the first to exploit his successor. One may still be young and yet remember that dreadful old police court, at which Harry Fielding presided, in all its noxiousness. The chronicles of it would be tantamount to the history of criminal London during the last century and a half, since a very large percentage of the most notorious law-breakers have there undergone their preliminary examinations.

Among all the associations of Bow Street, however, those connected with its great theatre are the most world famous. Covent Garden playhouse was erected by John Rich, in 1731, to take the place of Lincoln's Inn Fields, which had then fallen into decay. Many curious scenes have been enacted without as well as within its walls. While it was building, the street became a fashionable lounge, and when the ladies had finished their shopping in Tavistock Street they drove round in their carriages with their cavaliers to watch the masons at work, and to flirt and chatter.

At the beginning of the present century there was the *furore* over the "Young Roscius" (1804), one of those unaccountable manias to which that most hysterical of bodies, the British public, is subject. A company of Foot Guards had to be sent to make a passage through the prodigious crowd that assembled round the theatre at one o'clock on the day of his *début;* when the doors were opened coats and gowns were torn to ribbons in the rush, and swooning people were dragged out of the press every few minutes. Duchesses contended for the honour of driving Master Betty in their carriages; William Pitt adjourned the House of Commons to see him act, and the University of Cambridge made him the subject of a prize medal. Yet he was only an ordinarily clever boy, after all, and when he reappeared the next season his whilom perfervid admirers found that out.

A very terrible scene was witnessed in Bow Street when, on the night of 30th September, 1808, the great theatre was discovered to be in flames. Twenty-three firemen perished in the conflagration. Kemble and his sister lost everything ; but the Duke of Northumberland sent him the munificent sum of £10,000, and burned the bond on the day the foundation stone was laid.

Never was Bow Street more lively than it was during the sixty-one nights of the O. P. riots. In consequence of the enormous sum, £150,000, expended upon th

new theatre, Kemble raised the prices of admission
—the boxes from 6s. to 7s., the pit from 3s. 6d. to 4s.
Instead of showing their disapproval by staying away,
theatregoers made the advanced tariff an excuse for one
of the most extraordinary riots on record. Night after
night not a word of the performance could be heard, the
voices of the actors being drowned by shouts of " old
prices!" groans, hisses, cat calls, dust bells, rattles, horns
and a kind of Carmagnole, called the O. P. dance. Men
went about with the letters O. P. stuck in their hats,
and ladies wore O. P. medals. The struggle ended in
the victory of the malcontents. It may be noted that
at this time the nightly expenses of the theatre were
£300. The new house went the way of its predecessor, on 4th March, 1856, during a masked ball given
by James Anderson, the conjuror.

Covent Garden Theatre was the original home of the
celebrated " Sublime Society of Beef-steaks," founded
in 1735.[1] The famous Earl of Peterborough, then an
old man—he who, for his daring and romantic exploits,
was called " the last of the knights errant," and who had
secretly espoused Anastasia Robinson, the singer—was
in the theatre one afternoon talking with Rich in his
room, while the manager was cooking a steak upon the
gridiron for his dinner ; my lord was invited to partake
of it, and, with the help of a bottle or two of good
wine, made such a hearty meal, and was so delighted

---

[1] This, however, was not the first club of that name. Reference
to a Beef-steak Club, of which Dick Estcourt was the first providore
is to be found in *The Tatler.*

with the novelty of the thing, that he proposed it should be repeated on the following Saturday. He kept his engagement and brought three or four friends with him. Everybody was charmed, and it was arranged that a select little club should be formed and meet every Saturday, the fare to be strictly confined to steaks, port and punch. This was the fortuitous commencement of a society, which, during the hundred and thirty-four years of its existence, numbered among its members the Prince of Wales and his brothers, the Dukes of Clarence and Sussex and York, Garrick, John Wilkes, George Colman, John Kemble, Sheridan, Brougham, and any number of peers.

Two of the most famous of its members were the gourmand Duke of Norfolk, Fox's great friend, and Captain Charles Morris, the poet laureate of the club, who celebrated its members in a ballad, of which the following is a specimen :—

First Rich, who this feast of the gridiron planned,
And formed with a touch of his harlequin's wand,
Out of mighty rude matter this brotherly band,
    The jolly old steakers of England.

   .   .   .   .

First George Prince of Wales, and York's royal Duke,
For the wit of this board other pleasures forsook,
And of good wine and punch they both freely partook
    With the jolly old steakers of England.

   .   .   .   .

And Norfolk's great Duke, who belonged to the band
Of sturdy old barons of famed Runnymede,
In the same cause of freedom delighted to feed
    With the jolly old steakers of England.

And his Grace certainly did feed, for after preparing his stomach by a fish dinner at a Covent Garden hotel, he would sometimes consume *six pounds* of steak at the club, and never less than four, with wine in proportion. A man of enormous proportions, such as we see in Rowlandson's and Bunbury's caricatures, he invariably dressed in a bright blue coat, which made him look even more unwieldy than he was.

Punctually at five "the jolly old steakers" sat down to table in a room set apart for them in Covent Garden Theatre. It was divided in two by a curtain, which, on the last stroke of the hour, was drawn aside and discovered the kitchen, partitioned off from the diners by an open grating, over which was this motto from *Macbeth* :—

> If it were done, when it is done, then 'twere well
> It were done quickly.

The Duke of Norfolk, with a small silver gridiron suspended round his neck by an orange ribbon, would take the chair. Captain Morris was the punchmaker, a very important office in those days, requiring great nicety of palate. When the cloth was removed the Steakers gave themselves up to conviviality, and the Captain was again in great request, for he had a good voice and trolled forth his own songs, sentimental and bacchanalian, with excellent effect.

The members were limited to twenty-four, and many notable persons were always on the list of candidates eager for election. Perfect equality among the Steakers was the rule of the club, and the last enrolled, though he were a prince of the blood, was made the fag for the rest. One night a somewhat pompous Liverpool merchant was among the guests, and perceiving the free and easy manners that obtained, communicated his suspicions to the friend who had brought him to the club that the royal and titled persons whom he had been told that he was among were all a flam. The friend informed his fellow-steakers of the bourgeois' incredulity, and to keep up the joke they pretended to be a society of tradesmen. The Duke of Sussex reproached Alderman Wood for the tough steaks he had sent in last Saturday. The alderman retorted upon his royal highness by complaining of the ill-fitting stays he had sent his wife, and so on. A leaf had to be withdrawn to shorten the table, and in closing it again the chair of the Duke of Leinster, who was presiding, was overturned, and his Grace was toppled into the grate. Nobody moved, everybody roared. This confirmed the Liverpudlian's scepticism. "Why, of course," he said, " if it had been a real duke everybody would have run to pick him up. It was a very good joke, but I saw through it from the first."

When Covent Garden was burned down in 1808 the Sublime Society took up its quarters for a time at the Bedford Coffee-house, in the north piazza, but very soon migrated to the Lyceum, where the club remained until its dissolution in 1869. Sir Henry Irving now uses the old beef-steak room for his receptions. A new Beef-steak Club, however, was

formed, and now holds its meetings in Charing Cross
Road, opposite the Garrick Theatre.

Among the chief glories of old Bow Street was
Will's Coffee-house, which stood at the south-west
corner. The earliest mention of it is in Pepys' *Diary*,
(2nd Oct., 1660). But it is with Dryden that it is chiefly
associated. " Under no roof," writes Macaulay, " was
a greater variety of figures to be seen ; earls in stars
and garters, clergymen in cassocks and bands, pert
Templars, sheepish lads from the universities, trans-
lators and index makers in ragged coats of frieze.
The great push was to get near the chair where John
Dryden sat. In winter that chair was always in the
warmest nook by the fire ; in summer it stood in the
balcony. To bow to him and hear his opinion of
Racine's last tragedy, or of Bossu's treatise on epic
poetry was thought a privilege. A pinch of snuff
from his box was an honour sufficient to turn the head
of an enthusiast." Pope, at his own request, was taken
to Will's when a mere child to see the great poet, and
at seventeen became himself a constant frequenter of
the house, but not until after the master's death.
Steele says in *The Tatler* that Will's declined after
Dryden's time, and that cards took the place of
conversation.

In Russell Street, nearly opposite to Will's, stood
Button's Coffee-house, which was of a much later date
than its celebrated rival. Button's was first opened
in 1712 by a servant of Addison's wife, the Countess
of Warwick, and it became the favourite resort of

Mr. Spectator and his colleague Steele, of Budgell
and Philips, Swift, Gay, Prior, and consequently of
"the Town". How charmingly Landor, in one
of *The Imaginary Conversations*, has sketched the
author of *Cato* as he appeared at Button's.

Servantur Magnus
isti cervicibus ungues
Nonnisi velecta Parcitur
III e Fera

THE LETTER-BOX AT BUTTON'S.

Addison. "There we have dined together some
hundred times."

Steele. "Aye, most days for many years. . . . Why,
cannot I see him again in his arm-chair, his right
hand upon his breast under the fawn-coloured waist-

coat, his brow erect and clear as his conscience, his
wit even and composed as his temper, with measurely
curls and antithetical top-knots, like his style; the
calmest poet, the most quiet patriot: dear Addison !
drunk, deliberate, moral, sentimental, foaming over
with truth and virtue, with tenderness and friendship,
and only worse in one ruffle for the wine."

At the entrance to Button's was the renowned
Lion's Head, into the mouth of which were dropped
contributions, by unknown hands, for *The Guardian*,
and so frequently referred to in that periodical. It is
preserved at Woburn Abbey.[1] Near Button's was the
no less famous Tom's, which survived until 1814; it
was during the eighteenth century the resort of " blue
and green ribbons and stars," of Garrick and Johnson,

---

[1] Steele writes in *The Guardian*, No. 98 (3rd July, 1713): " On the
twentieth instant it is my intention to erect a lion's head, in imitation of those in Venice, through which all the intelligence of that
commonwealth is to pass. This head is to open a most wide and
voracious mouth, which shall take in such letters and papers as are
conveyed to me by my correspondents. . . . Whatever the lion
swallows I shall digest for the use of the public. . . . It will be set
up at Button's Coffee-house, in Covent Garden, who is directed to
show the way to the lion's head, and to instruct any young author
how to convey his works into the mouth of it with safety and
secrecy."

In No. 114 Steele announces that the lion is set " for the reception
of such intelligence as shall be thrown into it. It is reckoned an excellent piece of workmanship, and was designed by a great hand in
imitation of an antique Egyptian lion, the face of it being compounded
out of that of a lion and a wizard. The features are strong and well
furrowed. The whiskers are admired by all that have seen them. It
is planted on the western side of the coffee-house, holding its paws
under the chin, upon a box which contains everything it swallows."

and Sir Joshua Reynolds, of Murphy, Sir Philip
Francis, etc., etc. The house, which was No. 17, was
pulled down in 1865. To the east, No. 8, was the
shop of Davies, actor and bookseller, the rendezvous
both of wits, players and literati. It was in Davies'
parlour that Johnson and Boswell first met. What
delights the reading world, past, present and to come,
owes and will owe to that encounter!

Notorious among taverns was the Rose ; it was
very near old Drury Lane Theatre, and in some of
Garrick's alterations was absorbed in it. It was
as old as the Stuarts' days, and there are frequent
allusions to it in the old dramatists as a haunt of
riotous *roués*. How many of us have supped at the
Old Albion after the play, and there met Ben
Webster, and Buckstone, and John Ryder, and
many another famous player of our young days. Nor
must I forget the Harp, close by, Edmund Kean's
favourite tavern, where I have seen a looking-glass
shivered by a tumbler he had hurled in one of his
mad freaks ; many a wild orgie had he assisted at in
that frowsy parlour, fresh from the delirious excitement of shouting and applauding audiences. It was
there he was at home, and he would abruptly leave a
nobleman's table to hurry back to his boon companions, and heartily damn all lords.

II.—*Covent Garden Market—Piazza—Coffee-houses —Taverns and surrounding Streets.*

The wanderer in the now dreary and depressing piazza of Covent Garden, where the squat market buildings loom ghostly through " the fog and filthy air," and the nostrils are assailed by every odour that foul mud and bruised and trampled vegetables can give forth, would require a very potent imagination to conjure up in its place such a picture as this. A pleasant garden all sweetness and greenery, shaded by umbrageous trees ; a sparkling stream of clear water that has come all the way from the northern heights, and, after eddying into a fish pond, overflows and pursues its way merrily into the brooks that run down to the river ; on the slope facing the sun is a vineyard clustered with ripening grapes ; above all a cloudless blue sky ; there is no sound to break the stillness save the songs of the birds, the soughing of the trees in the breeze, and now and again the chanting of the monks in their chapel. Mount those steps and glance over the south wall into Long Acre and your eyes will fall upon a delightful woodland, and over the mossy turf you will see citizens and their wives, and youths and maidens, taking their evening stroll and enjoying the fresh country air that is wafted over the golden meadows that stretch away to Hampstead. Less than four hundred years ago such a picture could have been realised in the Covent—it was always so spelled after the French *couvent*—Garden of the Abbot of Westminster.

At the confiscation of the monastery Edward VI. granted the lands to his uncle, the Duke of Somerset, and when that traitor was attainted they were transferred by patent to John, Earl of Bedford, who had so very interestedly served Henry VIII. in his appropriation of Church property. Upon the site now occupied by Bedford Street he built a half-wooden mansion, the garden of which skirted the Strand. But the greater part of the monastic domain was left a waste, where rubbish was shot and where football matches were played, a pastime that continued to be practised there even in the days of the first Georges.[1] From the reign of Elizabeth London had been rapidly extending, and in 1631 Francis, the fourth earl, having previously leased Long Acre to the builder, commissioned Inigo Jones to lay out a portion of the ground as a square.

[1] Gay thus describes the scene in *Trivia* :—
Where Covent Garden's famous temple stands,
That boasts the work of Jones' immortal hands,
Columns with plain magnificence appear,
And graceful porches lead along the square ;
Here oft my course I bend, when lo ! from far,
I spy the furies of the football war ;
The 'prentice quits his shop to join the crew,
Increasing crowds the flying game pursue.
Thus, as you roll the ball o'er snowy ground,
The gath'ring globe augments with ev'ry round.
But whither shall I run ? the throng draws nigh,
The ball now skims the street, now soars on high ;
The dext'rous glazier strong returns the bound,
And jingling sashes on the penthouse sound.

The plan prepared by the great architect was a model of the piazza at Leghorn ; on the northern and eastern sides were continuous porticoes—the south-eastern was destroyed by fire in 1769. On the west was built a church dedicated to St. Paul,[1] while the south side was bounded by the garden wall of Bedford House ; against this wall, beneath a row of trees, country people, from about Oxford Road and the village of Charing, obtained permission to vend fruit and vegetables from their gardens three times a week. The centre of the square was gravelled, and in the middle stood a column with a sun-dial. Stately houses were erected upon the lines of the porticoes, which soon found tenants among the chief nobility and other persons of consequence, and became the most fashionable quarter of London. The market rapidly increased and grew into a strange medley of shed and penthouse, rude stall and crazy tenement, coffee-house and gin-shop, intersected by narrow footways, where the shoeblacks kept up a din that would do credit to the modern newspaper boy, of " Black your honour's shoes ! "[2] Towards the end of the last century a portly woman, who stood at a fruit stall, appeared daily in a lace dress which was worth a hundred guineas. The market, however, continued to be a heterogeneous mass, without plan or definite

---

Burned down in 1795 and rebuilt on the same model as its predecessor.

[2] See *The Spectator*, No. 454, for a pleasant sketch of the market people in 1712.

arrangement, until the present buildings were erected in 1830.

Many remarkable people have been inhabitants of the Piazza.   In the mansion at the north-west corner lived that bitter Puritan, Sir Harry Vane, who, with Pym, compassed the destruction of the great Earl of Strafford.   To him succeeded the great scholar, mystic and man of action as well, Sir Kenelm Digby, who was accredited with the knowledge of twelve languages and with having discovered the philosopher's stone ; it was he who introduced into England the Greek " sympathetic powder," which, it was averred, healed a wound, not by its application to the injured part, but by anointing the weapon which had inflicted it.[1]   A more delightful presence than that of this learned pundit graced the mansion in the person of his wife, the lovely Venetia Stanley, so rapturously praised by the poets of the time ; one compared her hair to a stream of sunbeams made solid, and Ben Jonson composed an exquisite little poem upon her sudden and premature death.   Denzil Holles, a son of the Earl of Clare, and Admiral Russell, Earl of Oxford, the victor of La Hogue, were successive tenants of this house ; ultimately it was converted into an hotel, and at the beginning of the century Evans's Supper-rooms were

[1] It is worth noting that Francis Bacon in his *Natural History* says that such experiments, and the success of them, are " constantly received and avouched by men of credit," though he himself is not ." *yet fully* inclined to believe them ".   Yet the great philosopher presented to Prince Henry " *a sympathising stone*, made of several mixtures, to know the heart of man ".

built upon the site of Sir Kenelm's garden and labora-
tory.   Lately it has undergone rapid transformations
—it was the Falstaff Club and is now the New Club.

The Tavistock Hotel has a record equally illustrious,
as it was ·the abode of four celebrated artists, Lely,
Kneller, Thornhill and Richard Wilson.   Think of
the *illustrissimi* who flocked to the studios of Lely
and Kneller ; the Stuart kings, Charles and James ;
Dutch William and German George; all the princes
and   princesses ; the voluptuous beauties ; the fine
gentlemen, the wits and the philosophers, the literati
and the actors who still gaze at us out of the canvasses of those artists !   King James was sitting to
Kneller when the news came of the landing of the
Prince of Orange.   The painter naturally would have
retired but the king said : "No, I have promised Mr.
Pepys the picture and will finish the sitting ".   Sir
Godfrey charged only sixty guineas for a full length !
He was terribly egotistical.   " Don't you really think,
Sir Godfrey," said Pope to him one day, "that if your
advice could have been asked at the creation some
things would have been better shaped than they are ? "
" Foregad ! " retorted the painter, laying his hand upon
the poet's crooked shoulder, " I think they would."   It
is worthy of note, as a contrast between past and
present London, that Kneller's hobby, the cultivation
of flowers, was carried on in his garden that extended
to Bow Street.

Almost adjoining this house were the Piazza and
Shakespeare Coffee-houses—did not Major Pendennis,

and several other characters in Thackeray's immortal portrait gallery, sometimes dine at the Piazza ? At the latter end of the last century "the prince of auctioneers," George Robins, had his auction rooms at the Piazza; and here he once entertained no less a personage than George, Prince of Wales; the Piazza was afterwards incorporated with the Tavistock. Don't you remember that Harry Foker and that superfine snob, Arthur Pendennis, frequented the house ? It need scarcely be added that little or nothing of the original building, except the cellarage, is now left.

Among notable residents of the houses under the portico were the last Earl of Oxford, the Bishop of Durham, Lady Mary Wortley Montagu, John Rich, and Tom Killigrew.

At the corner of Russell Street stood the old "Hummums,"[1] another house used by Dr. Johnson, and with a ghost story scarcely worth relating; also the bar known as "Rockley's," the resort of generations of actors, especially on Saturday afternoons; both have disappeared to make room for the new hotel.

As I have attempted a sketch of Covent Garden in the sixteenth century, let me essay another, as a companion picture, of "the joyous neighbourhood" in the early decades of the eighteenth.

---

[1] Hummums is a corruption of the Turkish Homoum, a sweating bath, which was introduced into London in the reign of James I. But in course of time these "bagnios," which gave their name to houses of ill fame, were abolished as being haunts of immorality, to be revived in our own day as the Turkish bath.

The fruit and vegetable stalls have advanced from beneath the wall of Bedford House to the centre of the square, and are now presided over by buxom lasses from Fulham and Battersea ; fine ladies and city wives are cheapening the gifts of Pomona ; old and young beaux are loitering about, leering at the country girls, chucking them under the chin, snatching kisses, and proceeding even to greater freedoms.

But it is beneath the porticoes that the scene is most animated, for they vie with the Mall as a fashionable promenade ; the belles sweep backwards and forwards in their rustling silks and hoops and sacques, laughing over the latest scandal, and listening, with half-averted faces and fluttering fans, to hide the enjoyment in their sparkling eyes, to anecdotes from the lips of their cavaliers that would now be thought fit only for a bachelors' party. Yet much more salacious stories are exchanged among the beaux, as with mincing steps they follow behind, titillating their nostrils with pulvilio and interlarding their sentences with many a " Foregad " and " stap my vitals," the slang of that day. There are poets and statesmen, actors and painters, nobles and adventurers, actresses and ladies of title, just what you find now-a-days at an "afternoon" *à la mode*. That little, round, fat, sleepy-looking man is John Gay, the poet, whose *Beggar's Opera* is drawing all London to Drury Lane, and that charming girl, upon whom her somewhat staid but noble-looking cavalier is casting such doting glances, is Lavinia Fenton, the Polly Peachum, who will by-and-by be Duchess of

Bolton ; on the other side of my lord duke is a dark-eyed, vivacious, somewhat shrewish-looking lady, that is the eccentric, but good-hearted Kitty, Duchess of Queensberry, Gay's patroness, fearless in the defence of her friends and out of favour at court for her bold speaking.

Here come two gentlemen, evidently personages of importance from the attention they excite ; one is a handsome, well-made young fellow, very elegantly dressed, and with the swagger and self-satisfied smirk of a ladykiller, that is Tom Walker, the original Captain Macheath ; they say there is not a fine lady in the boxes who would not willingly play the part of Polly or Lucy in private life, while he is singing "How happy could I be with either". His companion, portly, stately, pompous, solemn and measured of tread, is Mr. Quin, the tragedian of Lincoln's Inn Fields, a man much esteemed, and received by the highest in the land, even by royalty.[1] A lady, handsome but somewhat raddled, superbly dressed, but somewhat slovenly—it is my Lady Mary Wortley Montagu, who has been both flattered and reviled by poet Pope—is evidently not a *persona grata* to the *canaille;* the basket women glower and the porters scowl upon her, and make uncomplimentary remarks; they have hissed and hooted her through

---

[1] Quin was elocution master to George III. when that monarch way Prince of Wales. "I taught the boy," said the old actor proudly, when he heard of the first speech that the king delivered from the throne.

13

the streets before to-day: for has not this Lady
Mary Wortley Montagu introduced a barbarous
practice from heathen Turkey, called inoculation, and
submitted her own child to the operation, for which
every mother feels that she should like to tear her eyes
out? We boast of our progress, and yet we have
returned to the same state of things! In the years to
come, a dapper little fellow, with eyes of fire, named
David Garrick, who carries on a wine business in
partnership with his brother in Adam Street, Adelphi,
and is terribly stage-struck, will walk up and down
here for hours, eagerly conversing upon his favourite
theme with Charles Macklin, who has just made a
great hit by playing Shylock as a serious character,
the Jew of Shakespeare having hitherto been presented as a low comedy part in a fiery-red wig.

The Piazza was almost as favourite a rendezvous
for duellists as Leicester Square or the fields behind
Montagu House, especially among the actors, who
were as sudden and quick in quarrel as the fine gentlemen. A dispute over stage business—as was the case
with Quin and a player called Bowen, who was killed
—and after the performance an adjournment to the
porticoes and a flashing of rapiers. Another actor, a
choleric little Welshman named Williams, who challenged the tragedian for deriding his pronunciation of
Cato—he called it " Keeto "—fell beneath Quin's sword.
But in both cases it was proved that the survivor
acted only in self-defence, and he was acquitted. Quin
had another affair with that rogue, Theophilus Cibber,

who well deserved pinking, but he was reserved for the
fishes of the Irish Channel. Pepys (29th July, 1667)
graphically describes the fatal duel between Tom
Porter and Sir H. Bellasses, the latter dying of his
wounds, that was fought here in Covent Garden.

The Bedford Coffee-house, under the eastern portico,
was to the second half of the eighteenth century what
Will's and Button's had been to the beginning of it,
the great resort of the actors and their following.
Here struts the Temple beau, a notable figure of the
day—a wit, a gallant—more versed in plays than
law books, who passes the hours, fondly believed by
parents to be engrossed by Blackstone and Coke, in
theatres, taverns, coffee-houses; here is the poor devil
author, shabby and humble, hoping to get a commission for a prologue or dedication, or to meet with some
one he can borrow a coin of; there is a sprinkling of
clergy in shabby cassocks; one or two country squires,
listening open mouthed to the discussions upon the
last new play or poem, or the repartee upon the
latest scandal, all of which is as Greek to them; a
young cit., supposed by his parents to be snug in bed
beneath the shop counter, in red-heeled shoes and
scarlet coat, is devouring the words of the wits and
actors that he may repeat them at a city tavern next
night. Every one is eager to listen to Foote's *bons
mots* and malicious quips, to Garrick's imitations of
the great French actors and actresses whom he has
seen during his visit to Paris. Although Garrick was
always his best and truest friend, Foote never spared

him. One night the famous actor, who was rather close-fisted, dropped a guinea at the Bedford, nor could the most diligent search recover it. "Where can it have gone to?" remarked some one. "To the devil, I think," answered Garrick irritably. "Trust Davey to make a guinea go farther than anybody else," retorted Foote.

Tavistock Row, now absorbed by the market, was in our time as dull and dreary a thoroughfare as any within the neighbourhood, but in the days of the first Georges it was the Bond Street, or Regent Street, of the town—the most fashionable shopping-place in London, and its narrow limits were crowded with carriages and sedans, and with lounging beaux dangling attendance upon the ladies, throughout the day.

In the year 1779 it was the scene of a notable tragedy. No. 4 was a hosier's and glover's, at which served a young girl, Miss Ray, who attracted the attention of that notorious libertine, Lord Sandwich— the inventor of the husky comestible which bears his name, one of "the monks of Medmenham," and familiarly known as "Jemmy Twitcher"—and she became his mistress. Miss Ray was the mother of several children when Captain Hackman, an officer in a foot regiment, conceived a mad passion for her. He proposed marriage, but Miss Ray had no taste for following the drum. So Hackman doffed his red coat for a black, entered holy orders and obtained a living at Wyverton, in Norfolk. But a country parsonage had no more temptation for the lady than a barracks.

Finding all hope gone and that Miss Ray was placed under the charge of a duenna, Hackman became desperate. On the night of 7th April she and her attendant went to Covent Garden Theatre ; as her carriage was skirting the northern portico on its way homeward, the door opened, a man thrust himself in and pressed the muzzle of a pistol against Miss Ray's forehead ; there was a report, a shriek, and the next moment the lady who sat next to her was deluged in blood. The murderer then tried to batter in his own brains with the butt end of his weapon, but was arrested before he could effect his purpose. This dastardly crime created a great sensation, and the letters and chronicles of the day abound in references to it. It is a curious trait of the time that the Earl of Carlisle and James Boswell rode in the carriage which conveyed the criminal to Tyburn.

There is not a foot of ground around Covent Garden that is not haunted by the memories of famous people. " Peter Pindar " (Dr. Wolcott), who so cleverly ridiculed the eccentric silliness of George III., and was himself so terribly and deservedly flayed by Gifford in *The Mæviad*, for he was a very black sheep, lived at one time in Tavistock Row. Wolcott was clever rogue enough even to do a publisher ! Putting on a dying air and a racking cough he sold him all his copyrights for an annuity of £250. " Barabbas " (I quote Byron) went away well satisfied that he had made a good bargain and would not be called upon for more than a quarter's payment. But " Peter

Pindar " rapidly recovered and enjoyed his stipend for many years. In a narrow passage, which joined Tavistock Street and Tavistock Row, stood, until the demolition of the Row, a public-house called the Salutation, at which, when bent upon some nocturnal ramble or a visit to Stunning Joe Banks's in "The Rookery," the Prince Regent, Sheridan and one or two others of that ilk, under assumed names, often dined, and witnessed a little sparring by " The Fancy," who used the house.

The improving of Maiden Lane, which, as it anciently formed a part of the convent grounds, was probably so called from an image of the Virgin that stood in it,[1] has swept away many interesting houses. Andrew Marvell, the republican poet and satirist, and Milton's Latin secretary, lived next door to the Bedford Head, and in the next century Voltaire, during his visit to London, lodged in the same domicile, then known by the sign of the White Peruke, and there wrote the greater part of *La Henriade*. At the west end of the north side was formerly a gloomy, tunnel-like place, approached by a low archway, called Hand Court, in the left-hand corner of which was a barber's shop, kept by William Turner, the father of the greatest of all English landscape painters, who first saw the light in that gloomy defile. It was demolished in 1861. The Bedford Head, just mentioned, was famous among Covent Garden taverns as a resort of the wits and

---

[1] Some authorities give a very different origin of the name by asserting that the true form of the word was Midden (Dunghill) Lane.

beaux, and was frequented by Voltaire, who dined there with Bolingbroke on his first introduction to the renowned statesman. There also M. Arouet met Pope, and Cibber, and Young, Arbuthnot and the literati of the day, and read portions of *La Henriade* to them. Pope celebrates the tavern in two couplets :—

> Let me extol a cat on oysters fed,
> I'll have a party at the Bedford Head.

Again :—

> When sharp with hunger, scorn you to be fed,
> Except on pea chicks at the Bedford Head ?

Here was held " the Shilling Rubber Club," of which Fielding, Hogarth, Wilkes, Garrick, Churchill, Goldsmith and others were members. The old house was not pulled down until 1870. On the south side of Maiden Lane, close to the spot where the stage entrance to the Adelphi now stands, was the notorious Cyder Cellar, first opened in 1730, a sort of *Café Chantant*, though no women ever sang there; its regular patrons seldom dropped in before midnight. As I have before mentioned,[1] it was the nightly resort of Porson, the great Greek scholar, whose power of memory surpassed even that of Macaulay, and whose learning was equally prodigious ; Porson was a most extraordinary combination of supreme intellect and gross bestiality. Somewhat late in life he married a widow ; on his marriage day he dined alone at the Bedford Head and afterwards repaired to the Cyder Cellar, where

[1] See " The Temple," p. 134.

he remained drinking until eight o'clock the next morning.

Round the corner, in Southampton Street, No. 27, now a gas office, Garrick spent the earlier years of his married life ; the house has been little altered since ; Caius Cibber, the father of Colley, who sculptured the designs on the base of the Monument, lived and died in this street, and the famous actress, Mrs. Oldfield, was also a resident in it. No. 3 Henrietta Street was Offley's Supper Rooms. The window of the large room looked out upon St. Paul's Churchyard, Covent Garden, and therein was buried the original of Thackeray's Captain Costigan ; out of this window, it is said, that some of his boon companions used to pour libations of punch upon his grave. In Henrietta Street lived the famous actress, Kitty Clive, the " Pivy " of Horace Walpole's *Letters*, and Garrick's " Joy and Plague ". It was in a room of the Castle Tavern in this street that Sheridan fought a duel with Captain Matthews for traducing the beautiful Maria Linley, "St. Cecilia," with whom Brinsley had made a runaway match, and forced the scoundrel to beg his life and publish an ample apology. King Street is equally rich in memories ; at No. 35, on the north side, the Garrick Club was first established, in 1834. At No. 38 lived Dr. Arne, the composer of the once famous opera, *Artaxerxes*, but now best remembered by his setting of Shakespeare's songs, and no musician, since his day, has succeeded so well in catching the spirit of the dramatist. His sister, Maria, afterwards the celebrated tragedienne, Mrs. Cibber, of whom Garrick said, hyperbolically, that tragedy died with her, passed her early years in this house. Coleridge the poet was for a time a resident of King Street. Readers of Richardson will remember that Clarissa Harlowe lay in hiding from Lovelace at a glove shop in this thoroughfare.

III.—*Covent Garden Elections—The Finish—Evans's Supper Rooms.*

In the pre-reform days Covent Garden had a lively time of it during the Westminster elections, especially when Sir Francis Burdett or Charles James Fox was the candidate. The poll was open three weeks, during which the whole neighbourhood was given over to riot and debauchery. The pencils of Hogarth and Bunbury have bequeathed us vivid representations of these scenes, but they are so unfamiliar to the present generation that a word-painting of the humours of an old-fashioned contest, in which Fox was the hero, may not be unacceptable.

The hustings are close against the east end of St. Paul's Church, and right away beneath the porticoes ; and overflowing into King Street, Tavistock Street, Henrietta Street is a turbulent, shouting, shrieking, scrambling, swearing, fighting crowd, almost every man and woman of which wears the candidates' colours, the blue and buff of Charles James being greatly favoured. Against the hustings is a phalanx of " bludgeon-men," a villainous-looking crew, chiefly selected from the prize ring, armed with heavy cudgels. A cry of " Here comes the duchess!" sends everybody wildly rushing in the direction of Henrietta Street, which is all of a roar as an open carriage drawn by four high-stepping horses, the panels and harness ornamented with a ducal coronet, slowly makes its way through the human billows. Seated within is a splendidly attired and very handsome woman, who smiles and bows and kisses her hand effusively in response to the cheers with which she is greeted. But, oh heavens! huddled on the satin and velvet seats, beside and opposite her, are three or four drunken, dirty creatures that her Grace of Devonshire has raked out of the slums of St. Giles's—"free and independent electors " who are going to vote for " Fox and liberty ". She has actually bribed one of them with a kiss! Faugh! It suggests Circe and her swine.

And now the shouts grow louder than ever as another carriage is seen making its way towards the market-place, the central figure in which is a very dark-complexioned man, very big, very slovenly in dress ; a frantic rush is made for the coach, men hang on behind, grip the horses' manes and harness, and a score of dirty hands are thrust out to be shaken by the hero of the hour, while a beery brass band brays out something intended for " See the Conquering Hero Comes!" It is with difficulty, and only by the interposition of the bludgeon-men, that his perfervid

admirers permit Fox to descend from his carriage and
mount the rostrum. As he bows to the seething mass,
"caps, hands and tongues applaud him to the sky,"
and quite drown the groans and hisses of the feeble
minority, who are little heeded until "the patriot" is
struck upon the breast by a well-directed dead cat.   In
a moment the bludgeon-men are in the thick of the
crowd, whirling their clubs and indiscriminately smash-
ing friend and foe ; there is a free fight, men pummel
one another, women scratch each other's faces and tear
out each other's hair by handfuls, while the spectators
from the windows shriek shouts of encouragement.

This is the last day of the poll, and when soon after
four o'clock Fox is declared to be elected by a substantial majority, there follows an indescribable saturnalia.
The taverns, which have been all full, are more crowded
than ever. Evoë Bacche! The friend of Fox who can
keep his feet under him that night is a skulker ; the
streets look as if London had been cannonaded ; they
are strewn with helpless wretches, but it is John Barley-
corn and not Mars who has put them *hors de combat !*
Then comes "the chairing" ; on a gorgeous throne,
covered with blue and buff, the successful candidate is
carried round the borough upon the stalwart shoulders
of bludgeon-men, who, however, have drunk his health
so frequently that they are in danger of breaking their
patron's neck.

In Hogarth's picture of " Morning " we see against
the north end of St. Paul's Church a wooden shebeen,
Tom King's Coffee-house, in his time a resort of the

market porters, of thieves, beaux, harlots. Half
a century later Tom King's was superseded by the
yet more notorious Carpenter's Coffee-house, nicknamed "The Finish". It was not demolished until
1829.

> Some place that's like the Finish, lads !
> Where all your high pedestrian pads
> That have been up and out all night,
> Running their rigs among the rattlers,
> At morning meet, and honour bright,
> Agree to share the blunt and taters,

wrote Tom Moore, in *Tom Cribb's Memorial to Con-
gress.* This tavern was supposed to be expressly for
the accommodation of the market people, but as it
was open all night, "the Corinthians" made it a house
of call in the early hours of the morning, and nicknamed it "The Finish". Here, at those unseemly
hours, in the long low sanded-floored room, with its
rough wooden benches and tables, its atmosphere reeking with fumes of stale tobacco, beer and unsnuffed
tallow candles, met footpads, highwaymen, cypri-
ennes, dandies, legislators, actors, literati ; Sheridan,
Fox, Tom Moore among others. Adolphus, in his
Recollections, gives us a glimpse of stately John Philip
Kemble coming into the Finish at five o'clock in the
morning, after a dinner-party, very drunk, and beginning to spout to an acquaintance some new part that
he was studying, at which the company, quite unawed
by the frown of Coriolanus, broke into a ribald chorus,
and the tragedian, who resented this insult, had to

be hurried into a hackney coach to save him from violence.

Kemble, like other men of his day, was a tremendous toper. When George Colman the younger had completed *The Iron Chest*, he invited John Philip to dinner and to hear it read. The reading progressed slowly, the bottle quickly ; the dawn found them both hard at it—the bottle, not the play. The butler was roused out of bed to get a fresh supply ; they drank all night and began again after breakfast, and, with dozes between, kept it up until dinner-time ; after that they made another night of it until they fell asleep. Both woke simultaneously in the grey light of the morning. " What are you staring at ? " cried Colman nervously. " By ——, Kemble, you look like the devil incarnate ! " Upon which Coriolanus took his departure in high dudgeon. And it might have been on that night that Adolphus met him at the Finish. Sir Walter Scott said that Kemble was the only man who, after he had attained middle life, could seduce him into deep potations, and more than once, when John Philip was playing at Edinburgh, did Sol's red face look in upon the pair as they sat with a half-emptied bowl of punch still between them.

Notable among dead and gone institutions of Covent Garden was the well-known " Evans's Supper Rooms ". Evans, an actor, who first opened the place at the beginning of the century, had long since quitted this world of chops, steaks and kidneys for another, where the eaters thereof are themselves eaten. When I knew

the rooms, famous " Paddy Green," rubicund of countenance and effusive of manner, who raised them to
the pinnacle of their glory, was the director.   And
there was the great star, Herr Von Joel, who whistled
like birds, imitated a farm-yard, sang Swiss moun-
tain melodies, and played tunes upon walking-sticks
borrowed from the company.

Ah, me ! What recollections of the halcyon days
of our youth, before we were on intimate terms with
our liver, before we troubled our heads about what to
eat, drink and avoid, and pessimism had taken the
savour out of life, what recollections that old familiar
name conjures up ! Why, Evans's was one of the
things to do, and a young man from the country
would now as soon omit a visit to the Empire or the
Alhambra as our provincial fathers and grandfathers
would have thought of returning home without supping at the famous Covent Garden rooms, where all
the lions of the day, actors, artists, literati were to be
seen after twelve.

Thackeray, spectacled, with nose in air, was at times
almost a nightly visitor ; he had his own particular
seat at the back of the room, against the wall, apart,
unsocial, wrapped in meditation ; it was an excellent
place for the study of character, and many a one in his
marvellous portrait gallery was mentally sketched over
his chop or kidney. What is more probable than that
the presence of some old Indian officer and his son
suggested, not only the scene at this " the Cave of
Harmony," but the immortal Colonel Newcome as

well? Many a time, after a midnight prowl about the neighbourhood of "Tom All Alone's," Dickens, keen of eye and restless of movement, might be seen at one of the tables ; but the *habitués* of Evans's were not in the way of " Boz's " pen. There you might see at one table Douglass Jerrold, a little body surmounted by a leonine head with a grey mane, with glowing eyes and a caustic sneer, not a pleasant person even to his intimates. Beside him is another little man, very thin, with the gentlest of faces and the merriest twinkle in his eye, dear Tom Hood, kindest and drollest of tender-hearted creatures, who has drawn tears from all the world by his " Song of the Shirt " and " The Bridge of Sighs "; thrilled it with " Eugene Aram's Dream," and shaken its sides with his puns and humour. A rotund little man, with a sly, moist eye, makes up a trio. It is Harry Lee, whose wit and drollery are second only to those of his companions. Talking with these, at an adjoining table, is the Falstaffian, Rabelaisian editor of *Punch*, genial Mark Lemon. A little apart sits a red-bearded man in seedy attire, gloomily discussing a chop, with a rejected play, called " Society," across which the Haymarket manager has contemptuously scribbled " Bosh," in his pocket. Yet some day not far distant that comedy will make the fortune of another theatre. But Tom Robertson's day has not yet come. He looks up savagely as he hears the well-known tones of " Buckey's " voice, which always sets the Haymarket in a roar before even his words are distinguishable, calling for a steak and punch. And at his heels follow a couple of the Broughs, who have just made a hit with one of their rollicking burlesques at the Strand. Albert Smith, fresh from the *descent* of Mount Blanc; cheery Planché, rippling with good-humour like one of his extravaganzas. And so I might pass in review the names of all the bohemians of the time, for they were all frequenters of Evans's after the play.

A happy-go-lucky, impecunious, spendthrift race! With a guinea in his pocket, dull care could find no place in the bohemian's heart; he made but little, and he spent that little merrily; he could not invite friends to an ostentatious banquet as his successors do, but he welcomed them to a cut of cold beef, a jug of ale and a jorum of punch, and pipes and tobacco after-wards; and on Sundays there were a knife and fork for any associate who liked to partake of a leg of mutton or a rib of beef, and pudding to follow; such was the hospitality offered by such men as Jerrold and Hood. Sometimes your Broughs and Robert-sons and Lees had not wherewithal to provide even this frugal meal, and then the bitterness of poverty fell heavily upon them. But, hey, presto! a guinea for a magazine or newspaper article, and all was forgotten. Off to the pit of some theatre—authors did not sit in the boxes half a century ago, and stalls were unknown—and a chop at Evans's, and all their troubles were dissipated.

And at Evans's we find them; little attention do

they pay to the glees and sentimental songs, though
these are admirably executed : but then they have
heard them so often, and they have so much to converse about. Presently there enters a performer whose
appearance is hailed with universal acclamation, a
performer whose terrible realism rivets the attention
of the most languid, and there is a dead hush. So
horribly but unconventionally repulsive is his make-
up that if you have not seen him before you instinc-
tively tighten your hold upon your walking-stick. He
slouches unto a stool upon the stage, casts a malignant
scowl around, and then, without any trick of manner,
without any attempt at effect, tells the story, just as
it would pass through his mind, of a convict in the
condemned cell the night before his execution ; no
maudlin, chaplain-humbugging criminal, but a callous,
ferocious, impenitent murderer, who ends every verse
of his chant with the refrain, " D——n your eyes ! "
Nothing so shudderingly gruesome as Bob Ross's song,
" Sam Hall," has been heard before or since.

After that there is a general movement, and William
the waiter comes with the reckoning ; he has a system
of arithmetic all his own. " Chop, potatoes, bread,
stout, sir—1s., 1s. 2d., 1s. 3d., 1s. 7d., and three brandies
are 3s. 1d., that's 3s. 6d.'" How 3s. 1d., without any
additional items, comes to 3s. 6d., nobody but William
can tell, but it always does. If we pass out under
the piazza the summer's dawn is breaking and the
market outside is all bustle and commotion.

The beaux and belles, the fine ladies and gentle-

14

men, the coffee-houses and taverns, the Finish, the
Cyder Cellar, and Evans's, and all their famous
and *in*famous frequenters, all the gaiety, fashion,
romance, wit, all the intellectual life of Covent
Garden have passed away, and nothing now is left but
a sordid emporium—in its squalor and ugliness a disgrace to the greatest capital in the world, and to the
magnate who owns it—to help feed the insatiable maw
of ever-ravening London; all that remains of old days
are the ashes of the famous dead, who lie interred in
St. Paul's—Lely, Hudibras Butler, Dick Estcourt,
Macklin, Robert Carr, Earl of Somerset, Sir Henry
Herbert, the famous master of the Revels; William
Wycherley, Kynaston, the celebrated actor of female
parts; Mrs. Centlivre, the authoress of *The Wonder;*
Robert Wilks, the renowned comedian of the Queen
Anne and the first George's days; Grinling Gibbons
Dr. Wolcott, Sir Robert Strong, and others who

> After life's fitful fever [there] sleep well.

CHAPTER XI.

ST. GILES'S — THE CHURCHYARD — THE ROAD TO
TYBURN—THE ROOKERY—THE SEVEN DIALS.

IT is a curious fact that the two London districts
which are invariably contrasted as the antithesis of
one another have a common origin, each having been
the site of a leper hospital ; the one was dedicated to
St. James the Less, a bishop of Jerusalem, the other
to St. Giles, the patron saint of beggars and lepers.
The latter was founded by Matilda, Queen of Henry I.,
and covered the ground between High Street and
two thoroughfares, Crown Street and Dudley Street,
now incorporated in Shaftesbury Avenue.   Both were
dissolved and their revenues confiscated by that rapacious robber, Henry VIII.   The land of St. Giles's
was granted to one of his myrmidons, John Dudley,
Viscount Lisle, who built a mansion on it.   In the
middle ages a village clustered round the church and
spital, and a stone cross in the centre made a halt-
ing-place on the country road that connected London
with Tyburn.   It was not until the reign of Elizabeth that it began to lose its rural aspect ; that is,
ceased to be divided from London by broad fields

At the opening of the seventeenth century buildings rapidly increased.

Of the original church, which as a portion of a small conventual establishment was very insignificant, there is nothing to record ; a second was erected in 1623, but the present edifice dates back only to 1730, though the " Resurrection" gate, which originally stood on the north-west side, and was removed to its present position in 1864, belongs to the previous century.

Nothing could be more hideously prosaic than the surroundings of St. Giles's Church, and yet what a world of romance is interred beneath those grimy tombstones and that soot-saturated soil! Here lies Richard Pendrell, who saved the life of Charles II. after the battle of Worcester, and whose extraordinary adventures form one of the most romantic episodes of that romantic period. Here, after his execution in 1715, were laid the remains of the heroic John Radcliffe, Earl of Derwentwater, so famous in Jacobite ballads ; the body was afterwards removed to Northumberland, and in 1874 was again translated, this time to Lord Petre's seat, Thorndon in Essex. Michael Mohun, the great actor of the Restoration days—he died in Brownlow Street close by—who fought in the king's army against the bitter enemies of his profession, lies here ; so does the gallant Lord Herbert of Cherbury ; and George Chapman, the dramatist and friend of Ben Jonson. Not far off reposes Shirley, the last of the "Elizabethan" dramatists ; Andrew Marvell, the satirist ; and that Countess of

Shrewsbury who, disguised as a page, held the horse of her paramour, the Duke of Buckingham, when he fought with and killed her husband in the grounds of Clifden.   Could a new Robert the Devil summon

PENDRELL'S TOMB.

them to rise from their tombs, how horrified these dainty shades would be at their surroundings !   There is no fear of their " walking " in that churchyard.

But St. Giles's is remarkable for quite another order
of humanity to that of the hero, the poet and lady of
fashion. Jemmy Catnach, for instance, from whose
press in Monmouth Court, Dudley Street, proceeded
those wonderful last speeches and dying confessions
of notorious criminals; those curious old ballads,
"Jemmy Dawson," "Jane Shore," "Barbara Allen,"
Christmas carols printed by the yard, and those wonderful broadsides, describing all kinds of marvels and
horrors, that used to be exposed for sale pinned upon
blankets, which in our grandfathers' time were the
principal literature of the working classes—collectors
pay high prices for them now. Catnach employed a
whole army of cadgers to hawk these delectable compositions about the town, and the frequent hoaxes
perpetrated by the unscrupulous vendors upon the
public gave rise to a new word, "catchpenny". What
these peripatetic Mercurys were like may be judged
from the fact that even the not over-particular trades-
people of St. Giles's in anything but particular days,
refused to take the mass of copper coins which were
brought into Monmouth Court every night, as it was
said fevers and all kinds of loathsome diseases had
been caught from handling them, so they had to be
boiled in vinegar and potash for disinfection before
being accepted.

Before the penny-paper days these broadsides were
the only vehicles of news within the means of the
poorer classes, and their sale was enormous. The
death of George III., the Cato Street conspiracy,

the trial of Queen Caroline, kept the press going
night and day. But there was nothing comparable
to a good murder ; by the Thurtell and Weare case
Catnach, it is said, realised £500 from the sale of
250,000 copies, and that the block from which the
"likeness of the murderer" was taken, served for the
likeness of all the other popular murderers for the
next forty years. Yet the above number was quite
put in the shade by the Greenacre murder, of which
1,650,000 broadsides were issued ; while the Red Barn
tragedy broke even this record by some thousands.

The gala days of old St. Giles's were the hanging
days, and they were frequent enough for a Popish
calendar. As I have said, it was the high road to
Tyburn, and at an ancient tavern called the Bowl,
or Crown, that stood within a door or two of the
eastern end of the churchyard, where the Angel
now stands, the procession always stopped and the
doomed man was given his last drink. Just outside
the leper hospital, in the middle ages, was a gallows,
and it was an ancient custom for a bowl of ale to
be sent out from there to every criminal who was
executed. When the spital was demolished and all
executions removed to Tyburn, a public-house was
built on the spot and named the Bowl, the hosts of
which kept up the old tradition.

Let me endeavour to piece together a picture of one
of those gala days, and for the purpose I will select
a notable one, in November, 1724. Although it is a
dreary, foggy morning, the house tops, the windows

and the wooden balconies erected in front of the houses of the High Street are crowded with spectators, many of them beaux and fine ladies of St. James's, while the sideways and road beneath are a seething mass of filth, squalor and blackguardism, a riotous, swearing, hideous mob of men and women, that extends from the church and beyond to the gates of Newgate. Now, along this line of route, the sound of shouts, distant at first, then growing nearer and nearer, swell above the clamour of the crowd, and the cry is raised: " he's coming! he's coming!" the pushing, swaying and scrambling of that human sea of darkness grow fiercer, so do the shrieks and oaths and fighting, as each unit endeavours to secure a coign of vantage. Then, with a clatter of horses' hoofs, a clank of sabres, and tramp of heavy feet, through the grey gloom is seen advancing a detachment of cavalry, cleaving their way through the human ant-hill that divides with howls and imprecations.

In an open cart, with a coffin in front of it, sits a man, still young, with dare-devil defiance upon his pale and vice-ploughed face ; beside him is a bibulous-looking clergyman, reading prayers from a great prayer-book ; mounted troopers ride beside and behind the cart, while the rear is brought up by a *posse* of constables and javelin men. The crowd, men and women, salute the doomed man with cheers and cries of encouragement. The procession stops at the Bowl, for which there is a horrible rush, the weaker being knocked down and trampled upon ; soldiers and con-

stables fall to drinking, and forth comes Boniface
with the fatal bowl, which he smilingly hands to the
criminal, who raises it and drinks to the health of
the ladies that crowd a small balcony, raised over the
entrance of the tavern, whose velvet masks and costly
cloaks proclaim them to be people of quality ; they
respond by waving their handkerchiefs, one kisses
her hand to him, one or two sob hysterically.   Then
our Jailbird turns to the mob and calls out : " Here's
your health, my noble pals, and when your turn
comes may you all die as game as I shall !" A
mighty roar answers the wish ; everybody who can
get a drink is hobnobbing with his neighbour, and
even the parson is as jolly and mirthful as though it
were a party of pleasure ; nothing indicates the terrible
meaning of it all, except that ghastly box of black
boards.   At last the commanding officer gives the
word to fall in ; again the cavalcade moves forward,
followed by the wild, screaming mob, increased from
every street and alley that it passes, rolling on like
an ever-gathering torrent of Stygian blackness, until
it beats and surges, a dammed-up flood, against the
gallows-tree, upon which swings the lifeless body of
Jack Sheppard.

Between the High Street, St. Giles's, now High
Street, Holborn, and Bloomsbury, upon the ground
covered by New Oxford Street, within the last half-
century was a labyrinth of courts, alleys and streets,
inhabited by the most vicious classes of the metropolis, and known by the appropriate name of " The

Rookery ". Once upon a time, however, it had been
a fashionable quarter of the town, and in those hideous
lanes were to be seen the carved doorways and the oak-
panelled apartments of tall mansions that had been
the home of riches and fashion in the Stuarts' days.

But even one hundred years ago the Rookery was
the cadger's paradise, where the maimed became
whole again, the blind were restored to sight, the
paralysed regained vigour and the starved feasted
on the fat of the land. Almost every house was a
cadger's crib, wherein thief and beggar spent their ill-
got earnings in nightly orgies; the most infamous of
these, the Hare and Hounds, had once upon a time
been one of the noble mansions afore-mentioned, and
was kept by a man named Joe Banks, who from his
popularity among his customers won the sobriquet
of "Stunning Joe Banks". Over the door was inscribed the legend, "Here you can get drunk for a
penny; dead drunk for twopence and have straw for
nothing ". Perhaps the reader who has just assisted
at a procession to Tyburn will not be too fastidious,
to pay a visit with me to the Hare and Hounds.

Your handkerchief to your nose, for the odours from
these open sewers and unscavengered lanes are vil-
lainous. Yes, it is that house with the dim oil-lamp
over the door, which announces it to be a public one.
It is a ramshackle place grimed with the dirt of generations; yet red-heeled, diamond-buckled shoes have
tripped over that threshold, and silks and satins rustled
in that now gulf-like hall. The scraping of a fiddle,.

snatches of song, coarse laughter, and all kinds of
riotous noises salute our ears as we enter a large apartment, in which are the remains of a finely carved fireplace, and of a painted ceiling almost obliterated by
smoke.   In a raised arm-chair, covered with red cloth,
at the head of a long table, sits a good-looking, strapping
wench in a gaudy-coloured gown and mob cap ; she
is " the queen of beauty " for the week, after which she
will have to give place to some other Blowsabella.
As motley a crew as ever Burns sang the story of in
" The Jolly Beggars " are gathered on each side the
board, and mingled with the tatterdemalions are burly
cracksmen, prize fighters, Minions of the moon, in
scarlet and gold lace ; at the end of the table is
Stunning Joe himself, with a paunch like Falstaff's
and a nose fiery as Bardolph's.   The company have
just despatched a dinner, as Joe said, " fit for the
king ".

In the midst of the orgie the door opens and enter
four dandies.   The company, accustomed to such visitors, evince no surprise ; Joe bids the strangers welcome,
and the queen of beauty, who rejoices in the sobriquet
of " Blooming Sal," beckons one of the four, a handsome, full-faced, fleshly gentleman, to take a seat
beside her ; the other three make for the best-looking
" blowens ".   Joe waddles out to bring in a big supply
of drinks, including bottles of wine.   Does the host
know who his guests are ?   Does " Blooming Sal " know
that her arms are round the neck of George, Prince of
Wales, or do her companions recognise in his friends

his Grace the Duke of Norfolk, Major Hanger and Mr.
Brinsley Sheridan, lessee of Drury Lane? Very probably. "I call on that 'ere gem'man in a shirt for a
song!" hiccoughs a fellow, pointing to his Royal Highness. But the Prince, though a fine singer, probably
thinks that it is playing a little too low to oblige such a
company, so the Major undertakes to be the substitute
of his friend, "who has a cold," and trolls forth "The
Beggar's Wedding," which evokes rapturous applause.
Presently a call is raised for a dance; table and seats
are pushed aside; the Major leads off with "the queen
of beauty". But heads and legs are too unsteady for
such exercise, and in a few moments the floor is covered
with sprawlers; the women scream and scratch, the
men punch one another's heads, and in the midst of
the hubbub the dandies slip out, and grope their
way through the dark alleys with many a stumble into
unsavoury gutters, and at last emerge into the High
Street.

It was as much the fashion for "Corinthians,"[1] as the
dandies were called, to visit the beggars' haunts of St.
Giles's in the Regency days as it was a few years ago
for swells, under the protection of a policeman, to
explore the opium dens of Whitechapel. In one of the
autobiographical books of Lord William Lennox there

---

[1] The term "Corinthian," as applied to the fast young man, is as
old as the days of Shakespeare. "I am no proud Jack, like Falstaff,
but a Corinthian, a lad of mettle," says Prince Henry in *Henry IV*.
It was a term borrowed from Greece and Rome, in which Corinth was
a by-word for every species of immorality.

is a reminiscence of an orgie at the Hampshire Hog
in St. Giles's, very similar to the above.

That great Whig *bon vivant*, his Grace of Norfolk,
must have been perfectly at home among the lazza-
roni of the Rookery, since his habits so closely resembled their own, for certainly none among them
had a greater contempt for soap and water than the
Lord of Arundel, as he seldom voluntarily performed
any ablutions. After leaving a tavern or a club, where
perhaps he had been drinking for days and nights
together, he would lie down in the streets and go to
sleep on a heap of garbage. Discovered by the watch
or some one who knew him, and carried to his mansion, his servants would take away his filthy clothes
and put him into a much-needed bath. One day he
complained to Lord North of rheumatism—doubtless
incurred by those *al fresco* slumbers. " I have tried
everything," he said. " Have you tried a clean shirt?"
was the query.

Hanger was one of the prince's private equerries,
and a most amusing blackguard. One day after he
had dined at Carlton House the prince said, half-
jestingly, " I am going to impose upon your hospitality
and dine with you; but you must not provide anything extravagant ". The major promised that all
should be plain. Being without money or credit, when
the day came Hanger was at his wit's end how to
procure anything at all. It was court etiquette that
an officer should be sent in advance to any house at
which royalty was to be a guest, to ascertain that

everything was in proper order for the reception of the
august personage.   When this functionary arrived at
the major's quarters, which were on a third floor somewhere about Drury Lane, he found that gallant gentleman in his shirt sleeves, with a scullion for aide-de-
camp, basting a leg of mutton that was cooking in
front of the fire ; beneath the joint was a pan full of
simmering potatoes, and on the table some foaming
jugs of ale, just fetched from the neighbouring tavern.
This was the banquet which was to be served on anything but a snowy cloth, and with very primitive
crockery and cutlery.   Need it be added that royalty
did not dine with Major Hanger that day?   At the
death of his father the major became Baron Coleraine.
His *Life and Adventures*, written by himself, is a
frank confession of a disreputable career.

About half a century ago the Rookery was destroyed for the construction of New Oxford Street,
but fragments of it, notably Church Lane, remained
until the clearances for Shaftesbury Avenue finally
swept away the last vestiges.

Within a few more years the once notorious Seven
Dials will be a quarter as much of the past as the
Rookery is now.   The first mention of it is to be found
in Evelyn's *Diary* (5th Oct., 1694) : " I went to see the
building beginning near St. Giles's, where seven streets
make a star from a *Doric pillar* placed in the middle
of a circular area, said to be built by Mr. Neale, intro-
ducer of the late *Lotteries*, in imitation of those at
Venice ".   These streets covered what was known as

the Cock-and-Pie-Fields, which were surrounded by a fetid ditch. The houses, considered to be quite triumphs of architecture, were inhabited by people of position and even of fashion. The column, with its dial of six faces, was removed in 1774, on account of a report that a treasure was buried beneath it. It may still be seen on Weybridge Green, where it was set up as a memorial to the Duchess of York.

CHAPTER XII.

A WAYFARER, in the earliest decades of the eighteenth century, after passing St. Giles's Church, and Round-house—the station-house of that day—would have found himself at the junction of two country roads ; the one, on the left, leading to Uxbridge, the other, straight before him, to Hampstead. A little to the north-east, where now stands the British Museum, he would have caught sight of stately Montagu House, and to the east of that the less conspicuous pile of Bedford House, both encompassed by extensive grounds ; north of these mansions all would be open meadows, much frequented by hot-blooded gentlemen, among whom, as with Mercutio, it was a word and a blow. Many bloody duels were fought in those fields.[1]

[1] Bloomsbury is named after the ancient manor of the De Blemontes or De Blemunds, which in the reign of Henry VIII. fell into the hands of the Wriothesleys, Earls of Southampton (see p. 98). Hence Southampton Row, and it was through the marriage of Lady Rachel Wriothesley, heiress of the house, to Lord William Russell that the estate came to the Bedfords. Bloomsbury Square was built in the reign of Charles II., and there was little building north of this and Great Russell Street until the end of the century. Bedford House was not pulled down until 1800.

Close to where Woburn Square now stands was the noted Field of

At the corner of the northern road our wayfarer's eye might have rested upon a wooden booth, where-in the redoubtable James Figg, whose pictorial card was engraved by Hogarth, challenged all comers with fists, broadsword, quarter-staff, or any other weapon, to try conclusions with him. A few years later his pupil, John Broughton, the first of the champion pugilists, opened a much larger booth on the ground, where Hanway Street now stands, and was patronised by the *élite* of fashion ; for while the area was crowned with the ruffianism of St. Giles, mingled with citizens and professional men, the galleries were filled with lords and ladies, headed by Frederick Prince of Wales on one side, and his Royal Highness of Cumberland —deadly rivals—on the other, with their respective sultanas, all of whom took as much delight in seeing Broughton and Slack, the butcher, beat one another into a red jelly, as did the groundlings below.

While, as I have said, all to the north was open country, on the south the town, even in the time of Charles II., extended some little distance west of the church. Indeed, building between Leicester Fields and Tyburn Road (now Oxford Street) must have commenced in the reign of his father, as in the parish books of St. Martin's-in-the-Fields, Peter Cunningham

Forty Footsteps, where, as the legend goes, two brothers, about 1680, fought a duel to the death—about a woman, of course—and left the impress of their feet stamped indelibly upon the earth. Many veracious witnesses, Southey and "Rainy Day Smith" among the number, attest to have seen these impressions, on which the grass never grew, as late as the year 1800.

found an entry, under date 1636, referring to persons who lived at the brick kilns near " So Hoe ! "

The origin of that curious name has been always a puzzle to antiquaries. As everybody knows, it is a hunting cry, and in the sixteenth century, curiously as it sounds to us, the neighbourhood afforded good sport, and on certain days the Lord Mayor and aldermen there hunted the hare and the fox, that could then find thyme-scented herbage and bosky coverts upon the ground over which Dean Street and Wardour Street now run their unsavoury lengths, and many a puss has been bagged, and many a brush secured round about St. Giles's Church.[1] Thus it might have been the cry of the huntsmen that suggested " So Hoe ! "

Years afterwards that cry led thousands to death on the bloody field of Sedgemoor, where it was the watchword of the unfortunate Duke of Monmouth, who had a noble mansion on the south side of King's Square, afterwards renamed Soho. At that time, and many years afterwards, Soho Square was one of the handsomest parts of the metropolis ; it had a railed-in grass-plotted centre, with a fountain in the middle. The imposing pile of Monmouth House dominated all the neighbouring domiciles ; standing within a large courtyard, its gardens extended to Compton Street. Monmouth Street, afterwards Dudley Street, so notorious as an emporium of " Ole Clo," was built

[1] Pepys notes the running down and killing of a buck in St. James's Park in 1664.

over a part of them. Monmouth House was demolished more than a century ago ; the Women's Hospital occupies a portion of the site.

Another famous resident of the Square was Madame Corneleys, who, about 1770, was giving her splendid masquerade balls at Carlisle House, formerly the residence of the Earls of Carlisle, which stood at the corner of Carlisle Street, then Merry Andrew Street. Madame Corneleys was a German singer who came over to England to follow her vocation, lost her voice, and was only rescued from utter destitution by a prize in the lottery of £20,000. Her garret in St. Giles's was quickly exchanged for fashionable apartments ; Madame became a *lionne ;* the best-dressed woman in London, drove the smartest of equipages, and gave little card parties, which proved so lucrative that she was able to spend £11,000 on furnishing Carlisle House for her reception. It was at the suggestion of his Grace of Queensberry that she added *bals masqués* to her other entertainments, and the town went "horn mad" over them.

Not since the days of "King Monmouth" had the Square presented such scenes of gaiety. From nine at night until six in the morning one continuous stream of gilded and emblazoned carriages, with gorgeous coachmen and footmen, made their way through an evil-smelling mass of rags, filth and ruffianism, assembled to jeer, applaud, insult and rob. Hither came dukes and duchesses and princes of the blood, some in very eccentric costumes ; the

Countess of Pomfret one night made a sensation as the White of Endor, the Duchess of Kingston—the heroine of a most notorious trial for bigamy ; she who hounded Sam Foote to death for satirizing her and her myrmidons in his *Trip to Calais*—created a yet greater, when she appeared as Iphigenia, her beautiful and voluptuous figure only veiled by gauzes; the admired of all observers was a noble lady, every seam of whose dress of cloth of gold was encrusted with precious stones, and who carried upon her head, neck, and arms diamonds worth £100,000. But the climax was reached when a captain in the Guards presented himself as Adam, with the addition only of fleshcoloured tights to the biblical costume. Might the gentleman who, made up as a corpse, alighted from a coffin and danced in a winding-sheet, afford a hint to some one competing for a prize at the Covent Garden balls ? A Roman Catholic chapel now occupies the site of Carlisle House.

The White House, upon the scenes of which Messrs. Cross & Blackwell now stew jams and pickles, was no more reputable, even less so, than Madame Corneleys' ; it was a gambling hell, bagnio, assembly house, under the immediate patronage of George Regent, the Marquis of Hertford (my " Lord Steyne "), " Old Q," and others of that ilk. The Soho Bazaar is the house in which that illustrious naturalist, Sir Joseph Banks, lived and died.

Readers of *The Confessions of an English Opium Eater* may remember that big, lonely, unfurnished

house at the north-west corner of Greek Street
(originally Grig Street), in which De Quincey, then
little more than a boy, took up his quarters on his
first arrival in London, sleeping upon the floor with
a bundle of law papers for a pillow, and a horseman's
cloak for sole covering : they may also remember that
·night when he sat down upon the steps of a house
in the Square in company with "noble-minded Ann
————," a poor outcast whom he had met in his
eternal perambulations of Oxford Street, that "stony-
hearted stepmother," and how he would have died of
inanition had not that good Magdalene run and got
him some hot spiced wine. I know nothing more
sadly impressive in biography than De Quincey's
story of that episode in his strange life.

Building went on so fast in the fields about So
Hoe in the days of Old Rowley that the king considered it necessary to issue a proclamation forbidding
the erection of any more cottages in Windmill and
Dog Fields, as they choked up the air of his Majesty's
palaces and parks, and threatened to draw away water
which was conveyed thither in aqueducts for royalty's
especial convenience ! In 1688, however, after the
revocation of the Edict of Nantes, the French Huguenots poured into London ; while a great part took
up their abode in Spitalfields, a number equal to
filling 800 houses flocked into Soho, which from
that time became a French quarter.

There is much history and anecdote connected with
the dim and dingy streets of Soho : Crown Street,

now Charing Cross Road, originally Hog Lane, is
the scene of Hogarth's picture, " Noon," and the old
almshouses on the western side are supposed to have
been founded by Nell Gwynne. Dean Street is chiefly
notable for the little theatre, built some sixty years
ago by Fanny Kelly. William Hazlitt died in Frith
Street, and was interred in the churchyard of that·
odd, depressing specimen of ecclesiastical architecture,
St. Ann's ; wherein also lie the notorious duellist
Lord Camelford, and Theodore, titular King of Corsica, whose tomb is marked by a somewhat pompous
tablet.

The story of this crownless monarch is one of the
romances of history. Born in 1696, of a noble Prussian
family, he served under Charles XII. of Sweden, and
so distinguished himself that the people of Corsica,
then under the heavy yoke of Genoa, at that time
an independent republic, invited him to become their
king. His reign was brief ; the Genoese set a price
upon his head, his own subjects conspired against
him, and he was obliged to fly to escape assassination.
After that he wandered from country to country,
imploring, but in vain, the monarchs to assist him
to recover his crown. At last he arrived in London,
utterly destitute, took up his abode in Soho, found
means, probably at the gambling table, to make an
appearance, and nearly persuaded Lady Lucy Stanhope to share with him his kingdom *en l'air*. By-and-
by his old foes, the Genoese, employed agents to buy
up his debts, threw him into prison, and made the

price of his release a formal renunciation of all claim upon the Corsican throne. Worry, want, and loss of liberty, however, had done their worst ; when released from jail he was penniless ; he took a Sedan chair to the house of the Portuguese ambassador, hoping to borrow a little money. Not finding the gentleman at home he had not wherewithal to pay the chairmen, and desired the man to carry him to a tailor's, in Greek Street, who had worked for him, and of whom he begged a shelter. Three days afterwards the phantom monarch was no more.

In a curious and indirect way King Theodore is associated with a notorious scandal of English royalty. He left behind him an illegitimate son, who bore the name of Frederick and became a colonel in the British army. By an amour with a young girl, Frederick had a daughter, but as the girl afterwards married a man named Thompson, the child was brought up as Mary Anne Thompson. Mary Anne was very pretty and fascinating, and when quite young a builder's son, named Clarke, fell in love with her and married her. But he was a worthless, dissipated fellow, who treated her so badly that she left him. Mrs. Clarke then became the *chère amie* of more than one gentleman of fortune, and while living at Blackheath accidentally attracted the attention of a distinguished-looking person who turned out to be the Duke of York. His Royal Highness was madly infatuated, and settled her in a sumptuous house in Gloucester Place. As every one knows, the duke was the commander-in-chief, and

consequently the military were very strongly represented at Mrs. Clarke's receptions. It now occurred
to the lady that she might make an addition to her
income by disposing of the duke's patronage—that is
to say, selling commissions below the Horse Guards
price : for instance, a captaincy worth £1500 and a
majority, which would have fetched £2600, could be
obtained at Gloucester Place for £700 and £900.
How the inevitable discovery was brought about is
not the least curious part, of the story. Among her
morning visitors was Colonel Wardle, M.P., a most
notorious Radical, who was so bitterly opposed to the
court that Mrs. Clarke never informed the duke of
this acquaintance. One day when Wardle was with
her the royal carriage drove up to the door. Unable
to get the colonel out of the room, she thrust him
beneath a sofa. It was not her lover, however, but
an aide-de-camp, who had come about the purchase
of a commission for a friend, and a conversation
ensued which opened Wardle's eyes to the iniquity
that was going on. Being a red-hot reformer, he made
no scruple of using this information against the duke.
The exposure made a tremendous sensation, and
although there was no vestige of proof that the
duke knew anything about his mistress's doings, he
naturally resigned his post and his inamorata. Nevertheless Mrs. Clarke was cute enough to get £7000
down and an annuity of £400 a year settled upon her
in exchange for his Royal Highness's love letters,
which she had threatened to publish, on condition

that she left the country and never returned to it. She died at Boulogne in 1852.

The most notable thoroughfare of Soho is Gerard Street. Until Shaftesbury Avenue played such havoc with the old neighbourhood and let in the light of modernity, Gerard Street still wore an air of respectable if decayed dignity, quite different to the frowsy squalor of Wardour and Greek Streets, and the faint echoes of the feet of the illustrious dead who had once inhabited it still seemed to linger in its drowsy atmosphere. At No. 43, which is the veritable house, in a room on the ground floor, "glorious" John Dryden wrote some of his best plays and later poems. Can we not fancy his plump figure, clad in a well-fitting suit of black, his fresh-coloured face, shaded by his own wavy, grey hair, issuing from that pedimented doorway for his daily visit to Wills', and returning in the small hours of the morning not quite so steady of step or precise of mien as when he departed? On a May day, in the year 1700, the great poet here passed away. His remains were escorted to Westminster Abbey by a procession on foot, on horse and in carriages, headed by a band of music.

Lord Mohun, whom we shall meet in the next chapter, lived in a house which, after being partly consumed by fire, was pulled down to build the Pelican Club. And after him an equally notorious *roué*, Lord Lyttleton, of ghost-story fame—a story which has been told too often for me to venture upon its repetition—made it his abode. Early in the nineteenth century Charles Kemble resided there ; and it was from that house that his daughter Fanny issued on the memorable night when she made her *début* as Juliet at Covent Garden, created a *furore*, and saved her father from bankruptcy. Edmund Burke resided in Gerard Street, and "Rainy Day" Smith,[1] in his *Recollections*, tells us that he had often watched the great orator in his drawing-room, after his return from the Commons, dictating to an amanuensis during the greater part of the night. And to turn from fact to fiction, do you not remember that Mr. Jaggers of *Great Expectations* lived in *Gerrard Street*, and there entertained Pip at dinner ?

Close by, at the junction of Compton with Greek Street, stood the famous Turk's Head Tavern, at which, in 1763, Johnson first started The Club—after Garrick's death, in 1779, known as the Literary Club—which included amongst its members Burke, Fox, Reynolds, Sheridan, Lord Spencer, Goldsmith and other celebrated men of the time. Its members were at first strictly limited to nine, a number soon afterwards extended to thirty. It met at the Turk's Head until 1783, when in consequence of the landlord's death it was removed to St. James's Street.

Passing through what is left of that once unsavoury emporium, Newport Market, and turning into Cranbourne Street, which was only a narrow alley sixty years ago, we find ourselves in Leicester Square.

[1] So nicknamed from a work he wrote called *A Book for a Rainy Day*.

CHAPTER XIII.

EVERY one knows the Leicester Square of to-day, with its trim garden and statues, and swarms of dirty loafers and ragged Arabs, its shops and sale-rooms, its two huge theatres, glittering like fairy palaces through the foggy night air ; its grimy foreigners, its flaunting vice, its pushing crowds and Babel of many tongues. Let me put beside this bustling picture another of Leicester Fields in the days of Shakespeare.

A wild, desolate waste, as much in the country as Hampstead Heath is now, an expanse of grass, bush and bramble; there is the old church of St. Martin's —not the classic building of to-day—standing literally in the Fields, its western front opening on a muddy lane fenced in by hedges and broken banks, on the other side of which is a line of low buildings, the King's Mews, the present site of Trafalgar Square ; to the west the sails of a windmill move lazily in the breeze ; to the south clusters the little village of Charing, backed by the fretted towers of Westminster ; the great mansions of the nobility, marshaled along the Strand on either side, conceal " the silver winding

(235)

Thames," save where they divide ; but to the north all is open country.

Here in 1632 the Earl of Leicester, Algernon Sidney's father, built a mansion upon a piece of ground then known as Swan's Close, surrounded it with extensive gardens, and gave his name to the district. Soon other houses were erected in the vicinity, and a square was formed, the centre of which was after a while laid out with grass plots and paths, and railed in. The readers of *Esmond* will be reminded of that wonderfully graphic scene, the duel between Mohun and Lord Castlewood, an incident that was suggested, no doubt, by an historical encounter as bloody as the fictitious, in which Mohun, one of the greatest scoundrels of his time, was also a principal.

Soon after midnight, on the 29th of October, 1698, when most of the inhabitants had retired to rest, and the watchman was slumbering in his box, a sudden glare reddened the moonlight, a confusion of voices agitated the silence, and from the direction of St. Martin's Lane, six sedan chairs, illumined by the smoky light of as many torches, were borne towards the Fields. A company of roisterers, all men of note, the Earl of Warwick, Lord Mohun and Mr. Coote, an Irish gentleman, on one side, and Captains James and France and Mr. Dockwra on the other, who had been drinking together at the Greyhound in the Strand, and having quarrelled over their cups, were coming thither to settle their differences at the point of the rapier. Finding the enclosure locked, they mounted upon the roofs of the sedans and leaped over the railings. Eager for the fray, the six coats and waistcoats were soon cast off and six blades were flashing like lightning in the moonlight. After a while there was a sharp cry followed by another, Coote and France were pinked by their noble opponents. The fight ceased ; the wounded men were raised, but the chairmen, who had been lounging against the railings, refused to have them put into the sedans, as the blood would spoil the silk linings. "A hundred pounds if you will take them to the nearest surgeon," cried the earl. The bribe was more persuasive than humanity, and they were conveyed to a bagnio close by. Coote died almost immediately, Captain France soon afterwards. Warwick and Mohun were tried by their peers at Westminster for murder, but both were acquitted.

Such scenes were common enough in Leicester Fields, and indeed all kinds of violence, and its inhabitants were so accustomed to cries of " murder " that they paid no more heed to them than did the Charleys snoring in their boxes ; so duellists and footpads, with which the place was infested, were seldom interrupted in their work.

References to Leicester House will be found in the pages of Pepys and Evelyn. It was there that the latter, after dining with Lady Sunderland, witnessed the extraordinary feats of Richardson the fire-eater (8th Oct., 1672), who " devoured brimstone on hot coals, and melted glass and roasted an oyster in its shell on a red-hot coal placed upon his tongue and blown by a bellows ; drank melted pitch, wax and sulphur, and performed divers other prodigious feats". After the death of the earl, in 1677, the mansion fell into other hands ; it was for a time the residence of the German ambassador, and afterwards of Colbert, the envoy of Louis XIV. Prince Eugene, the hero of Cremona and Turin, when he came to London to plead against the Peace of Utrecht, in 1712, took up his abode at Leicester House. It is curious to contrast the different estimate of the great General given by Tory Swift, who was of course in favour of peace, with that of Whig Steele, who advocated the continuance of the war. " He is plaguy yellow, and literally ugly besides," writes the dean. " He who beholds him will easily expect from him anything that is to be imagined or executed by the wit or force of man," writes Isaac Bickerstaff.

In 1718 the Prince of Wales, having been kicked out of St. James's by his amiable father, George I., for rebellious conduct, purchased Leicester House and resided there until his accession to the throne. And here butcher Cumberland, his son, was born. It has been the tradition of the Hanoverian sovereigns that the *de facto* and the *in futuro* representative of the dynasty could never get on together, and when Frederick, Prince of Wales was expelled from St. James's, as his father had been before him, and for a similar offence, he also took up his abode in Leicester House. Mother and father both hated Frederick, and the young man returned the compliment with equal ardour. "My eldest born," said the queen, "is the greatest ass, the greatest liar, the greatest *canaille* and the greatest beast in the whole world, and I wish he was out of it." "Fred," however, though a most contemptible creature, a common cheat, was much more popular than his dapper, lobster-eyed father; he frequented all places of public resort, would talk with the humblest people, and even sit down at their tables; he was to be seen among the Norwood Gipsies, at Hockley in the Hole, at Bartholomew Fair, as well as at Ranelagh, the opera, the masquerades and ridottos.

Yet he surrounded himself with quite an intellectual *coterie*, to which all the clever men of the Tory party were welcomed—he was Tory because the king was Whig, as the Prince Regent was a Whig because his father was a Tory; it was always the way with the Guelphs.

Walpole, in a letter to Mann (11th March, 1750), writes: "The Middlesex election is carried on against the court; the prince, in a green frock (and I won't swear but in a Scotch plaid waistcoat), sat under the park wall in his chair, and hallooed the rioters on to Brentford. The Jacobites are so transported that they are opening subscriptions for all boroughs that shall be vacant."

It was the time of the deadly feud between Handel and Bunoncini, and all the town took sides, the Duchess of Marlborough spent £12,000 to ruin the composer of *The Messiah* at the King's Theatre.

The princesses espoused the cause of the Italian, but Fred was " on the side of the angels ". He had a great taste for music himself, and gave musical evenings at Leicester House, where he entertained his guests by scraping upon his 'cello, while his wife accompanied him upon a spinet. Of course everybody went into raptures before his face and ridiculed him behind his back. And there were all kinds of splendid entertainments which quite eclipsed the bourgeois court at St. James's Palace.

On the 20th of March, 1751, Leicester House was draped with black for the death of its owner. When the news was carried to St. James's, his royal father was playing at cards with one of his fraus. He turned pale and whispered to her, " He is dead," and then continued the game as if nothing had happened. I will quote one of the numerous epitaphs written upon the Prince to show the estimation in which the House of Hanover was held by all the nation—only excepting the bigoted Whigs :—

Here lies Fred,
Who was alive and is dead !
Had it been his father
·I had much rather ;
Had it been his brother
Much better than another ;
Had it been his sister
No one would have missed her ;
Had it been the whole generation,
Still better for the nation ;
But since it was Fred,
Who was alive and is dead
There is no more to be said.

George III. was born in Leicester House and passed all his youth there under the tutelage of his mother and her *cher ami*, Lord Bute, and was proclaimed king in front of it. At the death of the princess, 1766, who, though hard, domineering and narrow-minded, had had between her husband, father-in-law *and* " the Boot,"[1] a sorry life, the mansion fell into other hands, and was pulled down in 1790. The site of it is indicated by Leicester Place ; Lisle Street was run through the grounds.

Savile House, which stood on the western side of Leicester House, was built about the same time as its neighbour. In 1698 Peter the Great lodged there ; it was afterwards annexed to the royal residence. In the Gordon riots it was gutted and half-burned because its owner, Sir George Savile, had brought the Catholic Bill into Parliament. When rebuilt Savile House was opened as a museum ; and then as the " Linwood Gallery," a famous exhibition of needlework, which was to country cousins what Madame Tussaud's is now. Here were to be seen sixty copies of some of the finest pictures in Europe, executed by the needle. After the exhibition was sold off in 1844, all kinds of shows, including Madame Wharton's notorious *Posés Plastiques*, occupied the premises, until the fire of 1865 demolished them. The establishments of Messrs. Bickers & Bush and of Messrs. Stagg & Mantle and the Empire Theatre now cover the site.

When Sir James Thornhill became reconciled to

[1] The nickname of the obnoxious Marquis of Bute.

16

William Hogarth, after that young man's elopement
with the knight's daughter, he set up the couple in
Leicester Fields ; a tablet on a modern red brick
façade marks the site of the house, the last remnant
of which disappeared in 1870, wherein the immortal
" Mariage à la Mode," "The Rake's Progress " and
other famous works were conceived and painted. This
was Hogarth's home from 1733 until his death in 1764.
There is nothing anecdotical or romantic in the life of
the burly little àrtist, with the exception of that runaway match with pretty Jane Thornhill ; with all his
great genius Hogarth was a bourgeois, body and soul ;
he mixed little in artistic society, or any other ; he
seldom wandered beyond the little London of his day,
wherein he found all the materials for his pictorial
Comédie Humaine ; he lived only in his pictures.

Of quite another order was the famous painter, who,
little more than three years before the death of the
incomparable satirist, came to live at No. 47, on the
opposite side of the square.   In Messrs. Puttick &
Simpson's auction rooms much yet remains of Sir
Joshua Reynolds' old house—the sale-room was
his studio ; the broad staircase, likewise is, I believe,
the original one.   What a procession of ghosts one
might imagine gliding up those dusty stairs, and passing into the whilom studio; ghosts of the celebrated
people, the lords and ladies, statesmen, literati, artistes,
actors, notorieties who have sat there and upon whose
" counterfeit presentments," given us by the hand of
the great master, the world has been gazing admiringly

through so many generations, and will continue to
gaze until the canvasses have perished ; to mention
only pretty Angelica Kaufman, stately Siddons, pro-
vokingly saucy Abington, demure Fanny Burney.
And then those symposia[1] at which yet more illustrious
sitters assisted—Johnson, Garrick, Goldsmith, Burke,
Boswell ; should we ever know them so familiarly as
we do had not that Promethean pencil given their
forms and features immortality? Do we know the
face of our own father better than the ponderous
dogmatic visage of the lexicographer? Does not
Garrick still fascinate us with those wondrous eyes of
his? and is not the first of the Lady Teazles as vivid
to us as Ellen Terry? They have all, and hundreds
more of those days, foregathered within these walls,
and though their bodies have long since fallen into
dust and ashes, yet, thanks to Sir Joshua, they will

---

[1] These little dinners, which were served precisely at five, and no
person was ever waited for, were not, to use the phraseology of the
age, "elegant repasts"; there was a great deal of the freedom of
bohemia about them, though the word was not coined, and the race
not born just then. Prepared for seven or eight, the table had often
to accommodate fifteen or sixteen; seats were sometimes short—
knives, forks, plates and glasses often ; the attendance was confusion, and the cookery not blameless. Beauclerc once suggested
that a dish of peas should be sent to Hammersmith, because that was
the way to *Turnham Green*. And the host sat quite calm, leaving
every one at liberty to scramble for himself, and call for what he
wanted. It was not the crockery, the food, the drink that constituted
the charm of those dinners, but the brilliant people who sat around
the board, and the brilliant talk of poets, physicians, lawyers, divines,
historians, actors, peers, members of parliament, artists, musicians,
scientists and dilettanti meeting on a ground of hearty ease, good-
humour and sociability.

still be, in their habits as they lived, the cherished companions of unborn generations as they are of our own, and have been of our fathers and grandfathers and great-grandfathers.

In our homage to these Oracles of Art, however, we must not overlook a great scientist, to whom our poor frail bodies owe a deep debt of gratitude. John Hunter's house and anatomical museum stood upon the site of the Alhambra. Here in the closing years of the last century the celebrated surgeon held on Sunday evenings his receptions, to which all the medical profession was invited.

The greatest name of all those associated with Leicester Fields, however, is that of Sir Isaac Newton, whose battered old house in St. Martin's Street, on the south side of the square, is marked by a plate. But the heyday of his life was past and he was an old man when he came to live here, in 1710, and the observatory, which tradition says was his, there is reason to believe was erected after his death by a Frenchman. Few are the recollections associated with the great philosopher's fifteen years' tenancy, but somewhere in the sixties of the last century Dr. Burney, the historian of music, took up his abode there, and, "few nobles," says Macaulay, "could assemble in the most stately mansions of Grosvenor Square or St. James's Square a society so various and so brilliant as was sometimes to be found in Dr. Burney's cabin". Hither came the greatest Italian singers of the day—Paccheorotti, Agujari, Gabrielli—all ready to display their talents for the delight of his guests. One evening it was all lords, including the Russian ambassador, the gigantic Count Orloff, one of the lovers of the Empress Elizabeth ; on another actors and literati—Colman, Barry, Harris, Barretti, Hawkesworth ; Garrick came often and played with the children, now raving like a maniac, now imitating an auctioneer, a chimney-sweep, an old woman, to their huge delight. All the sensations of the season, African travellers, Indian savages, anything in the shape of a lion, were to be found at Dr. Burney's evenings. It was in this house that demure Miss Fanny Burney secretly wrote her *Evelina*, about which everybody raved, including Aristarchus Johnson, before they knew the author ; her second novel, *Cecilia*, was also brought into the world in one of its rooms. She tells you all about these things in her delightful *Memoirs*. Who could suppose, to look at that tumble-down, faded old house, that it was the resort of nearly all the celebrities of the second half of the eighteenth century ?

But there is a dark side to Leicester Square reminiscences which has yet to be touched upon. In the old gambling days it was notorious for its "hells". Let me put back the clock a hundred years or more and try to call up a picture of these dens of infamy. The outer door of a sinister-looking house stands open, but there is an inner one closely guarded by a human Cerberus, who jealously surveys every arrival through a wicket, lest among the flies who are desirous to enter the spider's web there should be an inimical

bluebottle. Having satisfied the scrutiny of the door-
keeper, the portal is unbarred, we enter a dark passage
and thence into a large, low-ceiled, dingy apartment; the
atmosphere is close and fetid with human exhalations,
no ventilation being admitted from year's end to year's
end. The smoke-blackened ceiling, the dark-panelled
walls are all in deepest shadow ; the light of the gut-
tering tallow candles, which the players snuff with
their fingers, such as it is, being concentrated on the
green tables. To those not infected by the vice the
pictures that may still be seen in the great gaming
establishments of the Continent, in the midst of blazing
light and every adjunct of luxury, are ghastly enough ;
but this dimness and squalor, the yellow, flickering flare
of the smoky dips wavering over the eager, cadaverous
faces render the tableau yet more awful.

Every stage and nearly every grade of manhood is
represented. There is the young fellow who has just
come into a fortune, every farthing of which he has lost
this night. He cannot quite realise yet all the horror of
it, but sits blank, white, staring, benumbed, paralysed.
Most probably this time to-morrow he will be em-
bedded in the Thames' mud ; and there is an old man,
blear-eyed and toothless, clutching the dice-box with
trembling fingers, chuckling with delight when he
claws up the gold the croupier pushes towards him ;
watching him with fiendish envy is a grizzled-haired
man still in the prime of life, who has just staked and
lost his last guinea, his livid features dank with sweat,
his eyes bloodshot and glaring with incipient madness ;

a few hours hence the old man will be found dead in the street, robbed of all his winnings. But even here all is not lurid, there are neutral tints : placid, sphinx-like men, quite imperturbable through good and bad luck ; there are winners and losers that can still afford to treat the chances with indifference, though a time may come when they also will be numbered with the Volpones and the Ugolinos.[1]

At last the croupiers, utterly overwhelmed by exhaustion, close the bank. Now out into the cold light of the morning stream forth the ghoulish crew, shivering at the touch of the crisp air, and blinking

[1] Gambling was no hole-and-corner vice in the eighteenth century; gaming-houses were as public and frankly avowed as theatres and taverns. In 1770 the Moorish ambassador kept a common gaming-table at his house in the Strand ; in Golden Square the ambassador from Bavaria, and in Suffolk Street, Haymarket, the representative of Hesse Darmstadt turned their establishments to the same use. The privileges of these ministers safeguarded them from the law. Hannah More relates in one of her letters that at the opening of the Savoir Vivre, in St. James's Street, £60,000 were lost in one night. Young men of fashion sometimes lost £15,000 to £20,000 at a sitting. There is a story told of a young nobleman, who, after losing £11,000, won it back at a single hand at Hazard, upon which he exclaimed with an oath : " Now, if I had been playing *deep*, I might have won millions ! " Here is a good story from Horace Walpole : " Within the week (1780) there has been a cast at Hazard at the Cocoa Tree, the difference of which amounted to one hundred and four-score thousand pounds. Mr. O'Brien, an Irish gamester, had won £100,000 of young Harvey of Chigwell, just started from a midshipman into an estate by his elder brother's death. O'Brien said, ' You can never pay me '. ' I can,' said the youth, ' my estate will sell for the debts.' ' No,' said O'Brien, ' I will win £10,000, and you shall throw for the odd £90,000.' They did, and Harvey won."

More anecdotes of this terrible mania will be found in chapters xx. and xxi.

like surprised owls at the first gleam of sunshine ; the milkmaids, going their rounds, cast terrified glances upon them, for they look more like spectres who have overstayed their appointed time and are hurrying back to the graveyards than living beings.

And now we must retrace our steps to Temple Bar, and thence continue our course westward, until we arrive at the end of our pilgrimage.

CHAPTER XIV.

TEMPLE BAR—THE STRAND : ITS HISTORY, MANSIONS, CHURCHES AND STORIES.

TEMPLE BAR is now but a memory of the past ; a
line as imaginary as the equator. But in olden times
it was a very real boundary between city and court,
between the privileges of London and " the liberties "
of Westminster. When the sovereign approached in
state the gates were closed ; a herald sounded a
trumpet ; a second herald knocked ; a parley ensued,
which ended in the portals being flung open ; the
Lord Mayor then advanced and presented the city's
sword to the monarch, who graciously returned it,
after which royalty and its attendants were free to
pass. Even in the reign of Queen Victoria this custom was religiously preserved, though it was then a
ceremony, a survival and nothing more. But when
Elizabeth halted at the Bar, on her way to give
thanks for the victory over the Spanish armada, it
indicated that the city fathers were so jealous of their
rights that they would not have them infringed by a
hair's-breadth, as they never knew how soon they
might be called upon to defend them against the
encroachments of the regal power. Everybody,

(249)

however, is not aware that Temple Bar was not a city gate, but belonged to Westminster.

Anciently the two cities were divided only by chains and posts, and Edward, afterwards first of that name, punished the London citizens for aiding Simon de Montfort by destroying these barriers. The earliest gate was erected in the reign of Henry VII. ; it was entirely of wood. The funeral procession of his queen, Elizabeth of York, was the first pageant that passed beneath the archway. Then came the coronation procession of Anne Boleyn, of Edward VI., not long afterwards that of Mary Tudor, his sister ; and then of Elizabeth. But all these were inferior in splendour to the entrance of Charles II. Evelyn stood close by and witnessed it. " A triumph of 20,000 horse and foote, brandishing their swords and shouting with inexpressible joy ; the wayes strewed with flowers, the bells ringing, the streets hung with tapistry, fountaines running with wine ; the Mayor, Aldermen and all the Companies in their liveries, chaines of gold, and banners ; Lords and Nobles clad in cloth of silver, gold and velvet ; the windows and balconies well set with ladies ; trumpets, music, and myriads of people flocking even so far as from Rochester, so as they were seven hours in passing the city, even from 2 in the afternoon till 9 at night." The gloomy nightmare of Puritanism had been lifted from the soul of London. But, alas ! that so splendid a promise should not have been fulfilled.

In 1670 a new stone gateway, designed by Wren,

took the place of the old.   Fourteen years later it
was surmounted by the ghastly heads of some of the
Rye House Plot conspirators, and in the next century
it bristled with the heads of the victims of the '45.
Walpole says that men used to make a living by
lending spy-glasses at a halfpenny a time to people
who wished to have a good view of these horrible
relics.   Few regretted the disappearance of the grim,
dingy old gateway, which had long been an anach-
ronism ; but could we have anticipated the griffin we
might not have been so ready to part with it.

The Strand is one of the streets of the world : it is
the representative street of London.   According to
metropolitan boundaries it begins at Temple Bar ; but
the atmosphere of the Law Courts is more congenial
to the City than to Westminster ; thus I hold that
the true Londoner's Strand starts from St. Mary's
Church, and that it is only from that point you enter
upon that region of theatres, clubs, taverns and famous
restaurants, the genial influences of which have per-
meated the whole neighbourhood through so many
generations.   Coming from the east you find yourself in a new phase of London life the moment you
pass Somerset House : you have left behind the
feverish hurry, the terrible tension, the haggard eager-
ness of the Ixions and Sisyphuses of the great Temple
of Mammon—the city ; the pace is slackened ; men
loiter about book and picture shops, their minutes are
not so precious ; they lounge at their favourite bars,
and sip instead of bolting their drinks ; actors and

actresses, artists, journalists, men about town stroll and chat and laugh, or gather in knots, and the nobodies linger to observe them. Whatever there is of business is the business of pleasure.

The Strand is the pleasantest street promenade in all London ; and the only one of which, perhaps, a Londoner does not sometimes weary. Yet, from the point I have started, it has not one single architectural feature to recommend it ; nay, in its perversity of tall houses, short houses, narrow houses, broad houses, flat houses, and bulgy houses, dingy brick and glaring stucco, grimness and tawdriness, it is a positive offence to an artistic eye, and would not be tolerated in any other land than England. Yet so potent and delightful are its associations, that one not only forgives its faults and shortcomings but almost loves them : to the *passé* man about town it recalls some of the pleasantest hours of life ; its very air is rejuvenescent ; those old nights at the play, before satiety and the development of the critical faculty robbed us of half the power of enjoyment ; those nights at the club, when " the lions " were still lions to us, and the good stories were not chestnuts, and the wit and repartee were fresh ; those dinners at —— (let each fill up the blank for himself), when we did not shirk the bottle or the *menu*. A saunter up and down the Strand recalls these memories, and many others to the old and middle aged ; while to the young—for the old order, though it changeth in detail, varieth but little in form—the pleasures are in progress.

To the man who may contemplate vast crowds from the same point of view as Xerxes gazed upon his army, and think how soon all will be as if they had never been, the Strand is a weird spectacle when theatre and music hall are pouring forth their thousands into the semi-darkness of the night; a veritable human ant-hill swarms over the pavements; while along the roadway an endless procession of vehicles, cabs, carriages, omnibuses, packed as densely as the crowd, is moving east and west. Every diversity of London life is interwoven as inextricably as the threads of a many-coloured fabric: the peer and millionaire, looking for their carriages, jostle the coster dodging his way among the horses; my lady in sables and jewels is pushed aside by a city work girl; and the club man leisurely strolling towards the Savage or Garrick is nearly overturned by some suburban dweller frantically rushing after a fast-filling bus or to catch a last train. All sorts and conditions of men rub shoulders.

But it is yet more remarkable that all these heterogeneous individualities, as differentiated at all other times as though they were separate orders of creation, have, for a few brief hours, been united in community of thought and feeling, have been absorbed in the same ideas, moved by the same emotions, whether of laughter or of tears,—in fine, have been one common humanity. But now once more they are sundered as the poles: isolated atoms, each struggling for himself and his own in the great ocean of life; some return to their garrets and crust, heavy with thoughts of the morrow, which the illusions of the stage have faded for a brief while ; suburban snobbery retires to its jerry-built villa ; Crœsus to his luxurious mansion or club ; and so on through all the grades and varieties of grades of the social scale. Night after night the Strand witnesses the same scene : this rush of the mighty river of London life, sudden, overwhelming as a torrent, then fast flowing away until it is lost in the midnight. A brief lull, with only a fitful ripple now and again passing over the silent stones ; but as the strokes of the clock increase, the ripples come faster and faster with a murmurous sound of the approaching flood ; then swell into waves and break into cross currents, growing, and swirling and roaring, ebbing and flowing until another day is ended. And each day some drops sink into the quicksands and are seen no more, but fresh fountains ever growing in volume, pour their streams into the tide and few miss the lost waters.

Mr. Loftie, in his *Memorials of the Savoy*, tells us that in the tenth century much of the Strand now covered by buildings was non-existent ; that the Thames extended up to what is now Covent Garden, and even to Lincoln's Inn at high water, and was fed by streams from the northern hills that ran across the roadway. Little by little the foreshore was reclaimed and fell to the crown. In the reign of Edward III. three bridges were thrown across the Strand: two were known as Ivy and Strand Bridges ; the name

of the third has not come down to us, but its remains
were discovered near St. Clement Danes at the beginning of this century, buried deep in the soil. In
1315 a petition was presented to Edward II., in which
it was set forth that the road from Temple Bar to
Westminster was so overgrown with thickets and
bushes, and in such bad condition, that it was ruinous
to the feet both of horses and men. Imagine such
a picture of the Strand, such a picture of desolation:
the scrubby thickets and bushes, the rushing streams,
the swampy, rutty ground, the broad, silent river, the
almost houseless waste, across which a solitary horseman gingerly picks his way, or a few wayfarers plod,
now the dwelling-place of thousands, traversed by
countless human footsteps, and ringing with a cease-
less din and clatter of wheels and horses' hoofs day
and night.

Even in the reign of Henry VIII., although the
great nobles were building rapidly on both sides of
the road, the Strand was still described as full of pits
and sloughs and very noisome. Yet long before the
close of the sixteenth century it must have been a
stately thoroughfare, with its double line of imposing mansions, within courtyards or encompassed by
pleasant gardens sloping down to the silver, winding
Thames, with a vista of green meadows and the
Surrey hills, while retinues of splendidly liveried
lacqueys, passing in and out, would have imparted
a colour and picturesqueness to the scene scarcely
realizable in this dull, grey age. But, as I have

previously noted, in consequence of the badness of the
roads, the Thames was the great highway, and each
house had its water-gate and boats and sumptuous
barges.

Less than a century ago the Strand between Temple
Bar and the Church of St. Clement Danes was divided
by a narrow thoroughfare of ancient, overhanging
houses called Butcher's Row, which much resembled
Holywell Street as it was five and twenty years ago ;
on the north side of it was a maze of courts and alleys,
a refuge of vice and misery, that was not demolished
until the ground was cleared for the new Law Courts.

It is nearly a thousand years since the first St.
Clement Danes was built, a little to the north of the
present church, marking the spot where, according to
legend, lie the bodies of Harold Harefoot, the Danish
king, and some of his followers. The St. Clement
Danes of to-day is by Wren, and dates back to
1682. It is associated with memories of Dr. Johnson,
who worshipped here in the pew now marked by a
brass tablet ; of poor Otway and Lee, the dramatists,
both of whom perished so miserably and sleep their
last sleep in the churchyard, not far from Bishop
Berkeley, who anticipated the transcendental philosophy.

Essex Street was built just two years later than
Wren's Church, over the ruins of that great mansion
which had been inhabited in turns by the Norfolk,
who died in the cause of Mary Stuart, by Elizabeth's
favourite Dudley, Earl of Leicester, and by her other

less fortunate lover, Robert Devereux, Earl of Essex, who gave his name to the house, and about whose brief career so much romance has gathered. Here the gentle Spencer was a frequent visitor. In his *Prothalamion*, after describing the Temple, he says :—

> Next whereunto there stands a stately place
> Whereof I gayned giftes and goodly grace
> Of that great lord which therein wont to dwell.

The last of Essex House did not disappear until the middle of the eighteenth century.

THE EARL OF ESSEX, DEVEREUX COURT.

In Devereux Court we have another memento of the hot-headed lord. There also stood the Grecian Coffee-house, celebrated in *The Spectator* as a chief resort of the wits of Queen Anne's days. Grim, ugly Essex Street has interesting memories. One of its old houses sheltered for a while the devoted Flora Macdonald, and Charles Edward was concealed

17

there during his brief visit to London in 1750. Dr. Johnson made the Essex Head, little altered interiorally since his time, the home of one of his many clubs.

Milford Lane—the ford by the mill (a mill stood there in the time of James I.)—divided the boundaries of Essex and Arundel Houses. The latter was the residence of the Howards, Earls of Arundel and Dukes of Norfolk. The Princess Elizabeth was for some time an inmate of Arundel House, then in possession of Admiral Lord Seymour, who had married the widow of the late king, Catherine Parr; and it was there my lord carried on his schemes against the person of the princess, which might have succeeded had not the headsman interposed in the nick of time. Probably she never re-entered the house until she was summoned, only a fortnight before her own death, to the death-bed of the countess of Nottingham, who was born a Howard, to hear the wretched woman confess that she had withheld the ring, the queen's pledge of pardon, which Essex, just before his execution, had entrusted her with to deliver to his royal mistress. "God may forgive you, but I never can!" cried the heart-broken Elizabeth. And from that hour she laid in no bed nor took any sustenance.

Old Parr was a guest in Arundel House when he came to London from his native Shropshire, to die of good living at the age of 152 (?). It was one of these Earls of Arundel that here housed the famous marbles. Arundel, Howard, Surrey and

Norfolk Streets now cover the ground of the great historic mansion.

Congreve, the dramatist, passed his last years in Surrey Street. Will Mountford and his clever wife, of whose acting Cibber has left us so vivid a picture in *The Apology*, lived in Norfolk Street, and Mrs. Bracegirdle and the great tragedienne Mrs. Barry in Howard Street.

On the 9th December, 1692, Norfolk Street was the scene of a tragedy, the counterpart of which was acted not long since in Maiden Lane. No actress was ever more pestered by importunate admirers than was Anne Bracegirdle.[1] One of the most persistent of these suitors was Captain Richard Hill, who, finding that persuasions were useless, conspired with another villain, Lord Mohun,[2] to achieve his conquest by force. Hearing that his proposed victim was to sup with a friend in Drury Lane, he hired a carriage and six ruffians to carry her off that night. Just as she was passing Craven House they rushed upon her, but, thanks to the courage of her brother and a friend and her shrieks, which brought a crowd to her rescue, the attempt was baffled. Then my lord and the captain insisted on escorting her home. For some

[1] Dryden's epilogue to *King Arthur*, spoken by this actress, begins :—

> I've had to-day a dozen *billets doux*
> From fops and wits and cits and Bow-street beaux ;
> Some from Whitehall, but from the Temple more,
> A Covent Garden porter brought me four.

She then proceeds to read the supposed contents of some of them.

[2] For more about Lord Mohun see the chapter on " Leicester Square "; for Mountford and Mrs. Bracegirdle, " Clare Market ".

reason, probably because they played lovers together
upon the stage, Hill chose to suspect, though without
the least foundation, that Mountford enjoyed the lady's
favour, and all the way along uttered the most violent
threats against him.   As soon as Mrs. Bracegirdle
reached her lodgings she sent a messenger round to
Mrs. Mountford to warn her of her husband's danger.
In the meantime the two ruffians, having procured a
bottle of wine from a neighbouring tavern, walked up
and down before the house with their swords drawn,
and after some time Mountford was seen coming up
the street.   He had heard of what had passed, and came
to ask an explanation of Hill's language and behaviour.
Lord Mohun embraced him, and Mountford said that
he hoped his lordship would not assist Captain Hill
in his designs against Mrs. Bracegirdle.   Upon which
Hill struck the actor in the face, and before Mountford could draw his sword ran him through the body.
He expired on the next morning.   He was only thirty-
three.   The assassin fled the country, and there is no
further record of him.   Mohun was tried by his peers
and acquitted—to do more villainy.

Mrs. Bracegirdle resided in the same house until her
death at the age of eighty-five.   A curious story is told
by Cibber in connection with this lady, which shows
the respect that could be won by chastity even in that
dissolute age.   One day, while sitting over their wine,
my Lords Dorset, Devonshire, Halifax and other gentlemen were eulogising her virtue, which had withstood
all their importunities, when Halifax remarked that

they might show their appreciation in a better form than words, and put down 200 guineas. Six hundred more were quickly added. And then my lords proceeded in a body to Howard Street and laid their offering at the feet of the fair actress. Walpole relates that my Lord Burlington sent her a love-letter and a present of splendid china. " You have made a mistake," said the lady to the servant who brought them ; " the letter is indeed for me, but the china must be for your lady, the countess ; take it to her at once."

What a transformation from the stately dignity of the House of the Howards, and even the quiet seclusion which formerly marked the streets that took its place, to the feverish bustle of the gigantic news emporium of Smith & Son. It is these wonderful contrasts, the unbroken continuity, the flawless links that connect the past with the present by the preservation of ancient names and landmarks, that render London so uniquely interesting, so superior to Paris, where every fresh revolution makes a *tabula rasa* of tradition. Over this same ground that now rattles with the perpetual din of the newspaper carts, carrying their countless reams of newspapers night and day for distribution through the length and breadth of the land, have paced Elizabeth " in virgin meditation fancy free," the dark plotter Seymour, injured Catherine Parr, and how many more illustrious ones whose doings are chronicled for all time. Nay, close at hand, in Strand Lane, is a memento of times to which those are but yesterday ; for there in its entirety, still fed by the pellucid waters

of the " Holy Well,"[1] is a Roman bath, in which men
who gazed upon the face of Augustus or Nero, or may
have talked with Pontius Pilate about the crucifixion
of " the King of the Jews," have bathed.

Where the new Church of St. Mary-le-Strand now
stands—the ancient church occupied a portion of the
site of Somerset House—rose the famous Maypole,
which at the Rebellion was destroyed by those bitter
kill-joys, the Puritans. It was 100 feet high. But
after the Restoration another, thirty-four feet longer,
was raised in the same place, with much ceremony and
drum and pipes and tabours and morris dancing, the
Duke of York superintending its erection by twelve of
his sailors. It was paid for by the subscriptions of the
inhabitants round about, at the head of whom was one
John Clarges, a farrier in the Savoy, whose daughter,
Anne, became the wife of General Monk, and so
Duchess of Albemarle; she was a coarse, ill-looking
woman who never rose above her origin. Newcastle
Street was then known as Maypole Alley. This
Puritan's horror was finally taken down early in the
next century, as it interfered with the new church.
At the Maypole, in 1634, four hackney coaches plied
for hire ; this was the earliest coach-stand in the
metropolis.

Much history gathered about Old Somerset House,
built by that rapacious tyrant, Protector Somerset, out
of the spoils of houses, Inns of Court, and the ancient
Church of St. Mary. He never inhabited it himself,

---

[1] It is beneath a book shop in Holywell Street. The water is still
of the purest, and about ten tons daily pass through the bath.

for ere it was completed he was sent to the Tower
for high treason.   But Elizabeth, Anne of Denmark,
Henrietta Maria—it was here the disputes raged over
her papist household—and Catherine of Braganza in
turns held their court within its walls.

Evelyn describes two notable funeral processions
that he saw start from Somerset House.   On 6th
March, 1652, that of Ireton, Cromwell's son-in-law
and the most implacable of his lieutenants ; the body
in a chariot canopied with black velvet and drawn by
six horses, attended by four heralds and regiments
of soldiers, and followed by my Lord Protector,
parliament men and officers.   Less than seven years
afterwards (22nd October, 1658) he witnessed the
obsequies of a far mightier man.

Though he died at Whitehall, it was in Somerset
House that the body of Oliver Cromwell lay in state,
and was carried thence on a velvet bed, lying in effigy
in royal robes with crown and sceptre and globe, like
a king, and drawn by six horses to the abbey.   And
there were imperial banners, a horse in housings covered
with gold, a knight of honour, armed *cap-à-pie*, guards,
soldiers, and innumerable mourners following.   " It
was," adds Evelyn, " the joyfullest funeral I ever saw,
for there were none that cried but dogs, which the
soldiers hooted away with a barbarous noise, drinking
and taking tobacco in the streets as they went."   The
old house was pulled down in 1776, and the *chef
d'œuvre* of Sir William Chambers took its place.

The mansion of the Earls of Worcester, which was
called Beaufort House, is kept in remembrance by

Beaufort Buildings. And the old house of the Cecils, formerly marked by Salisbury and Cecil Street, is covered by the huge hotel, which has swallowed up the last-named thoroughfare, the date of which was marked by a stone, as seen in the illustration above. It was from lodgings in Cecil Street that, hungry and almost shoeless, on a rainy, miserable winter's night,

STREET TABLET, CECIL STREET, STRAND.

the poor stroller, Edmund Kean, started to make his first appearance at Drury Lane as Shylock. " The pit rose at me ! " he cried, when he returned home after the performance, almost delirious with his triumph. " You shall ride in your carriage, Mary ; you shall go to Eton, Charles."

Both prophecies were fulfilled to the letter.

Most famous among Strand palaces was that erected by Peter, Earl of Savoy, the uncle of Henry III., in 1245. John, the French king, taken prisoner at Poitiers, was lodged in the Savoy. Chaucer lived there, and drew an annuity from the revenues of the manor. ˌStow tells us that "in 1381 the rebels of Kent and Essex [this was the Wat Tyler and Jack Straw rebellion] burnt this house, unto the which there was none in the realm to be compared in beauty and stateliness. They set fire on it round about, and made proclamation that none, on pain to lose his head, should convert to his own use anything that there was, but that they should break such plate and vessels of gold and silver as was found in that house, which was in great plenty, into small pieces, and throw the same into the river Thames. Precious stones they should bruise in mortars, that the same might be of no use, and so it was done by them. One of their companions they burnt in the fire because he minded to have reserved one goodly piece of plate." (Verily a mediæval mob was more virtuous and disinterested than a modern would be.) " They found there certain barrels of gunpowder, which they thought had been gold, or silver, and, throwing them into the fire, more suddenly than they thought, the hall was blown up, the house destroyed, and themselves very hardly escaped away.

" The house being thus defaced, and almost overthrown by these rebels for the malice they bore John of Gaunt, Duke of Lancaster, of latter time came to the king's hands, and was again raised and beautifully

built for an hospital of St. John the Baptist, by King
Henry VII., about the year 1509, for the which hospital, retaining still the old name of Savoy, he purchased
lands to be employed upon the relieving of a hundred
· poor people."

This was no other than an ancient casual ward,
where the said hundred were received nightly, and
the master and chaplain were obliged to take the
first who came and not to choose "the most clean".
The charity was suppressed by Edward VI., but revived by Mary. It soon afterwards, however, fell into
decay ; the hospital was let out in rooms to fashionable
people and the revenues malappropriated. In Queen
Anne's time its inhabitants were utterly disreputable
and no bailiff dared enter it. The chapel is supposed
to have been built in the reign of Henry VII. The
interior was burned in 1860 ; and was restored in
accordance with the ancient model. After the revocation of the Edict of Nantes, William III. allowed
many French Huguenots to settle there. In 1755
Strype described Savoy House as "a very ruinous
dwelling," and adds that a cooper used a part of it
as a storehouse for his hoops, and another part was
converted into a prison. The last of the old Savoy
was demolished in 1806 to make an approach to the
new bridge, now known as Waterloo.

The Savoy was as notorious for illegal marriages,
before the passing of the Marriage Act of 1755, as
the Fleet, and in that year the Rev. Dr. John Wilkinson, chaplain of the Savoy, and father of the noted

Tate Wilkinson, the actor, was condemned to fourteen years' penal servitude for these practices.

The nomenclature of the Strand streets is an unerring index to their history. Exeter Street indicates that thereabout stood the house of the Exeters. But it was originally known as Burleigh House, the residence of Elizabeth's great minister, who died within its walls. Being a great lover of gardening, he had in this garden the finest collection of plants in the kingdom! It was one of his sons who was created Earl of Exeter, and so we get the name of two thoroughfares. The house extended over the site of Wellington Street, and thereupon, after its demolition at the end of the seventeenth century, was built the Exeter 'Change. In Strype it is described as containing two walks below stairs, and as many above, with shops on each side for milliners, sempstresses, hosiers. There were upper apartments beside for general purposes, in one of which the body of Gay, the poet, lay previous to its interment in the abbey. During the earlier part of the nineteenth century it was chiefly famous for its menagerie. It bulked over the Strand in a most ungainly fashion, and was pulled down in 1830 for the new thoroughfare to Waterloo Bridge. The Lyceum Theatre stands upon a portion of the ground of the Cecils. It was originally built in 1765 for the Society

Note.—Terry's Theatre stands on the site of the notorious "Coal Hole," first opened by John Rhodes, a bass singer, as a sing song for the coal-heavers of the Thames wharves. In 1851 " Lord Chief Baron Nicholson " brought " the Judge and Jury Society " there from the Garrick's Head, now the Opera Hotel, Bow Street, where it was first started.

of Artists.   Here, in 1802, Madame Tussaud first
exhibited her waxworks in London.   It was first
used as a theatre by the burned-out company of
Drury Lane in 1809.

Such was the volume of water that ran down the
declivity, now known as Catherine Street, in olden
times, that, as I have before noted, it was found necessary to throw a bridge across the roadway, which was
called emphatically the Strand Bridge.   Steele relates
in *The Spectator*, No. 454, how he landed with " ten
sail of Apricock boats " at Strand Bridge.   This was
in 1712.   A little farther west was Ivy Bridge, at
which commenced " the Liberties " of Westminster,
and just beyond rose the great London palace of
the Bishops of Durham.

Stow has bequeathed us a sumptuous picture of
doings there in 1540, when Henry VIII. held at Westminster one of those splendid jousts for which his
reign was famous.   It had been formally proclaimed
in France, Flanders, Scotland and Spain for all comers
that would undertake the challengers of England and
continued through six days ; and at this mansion
the king, queen and court held feast and open house,
on the last day entertaining the Lord Mayor, the
aldermen and their wives, knights and burgesses.   The
pale shadow of gentle Lady Jane Grey falls upon the
memories of Durham House, for it was from those
portals she was conducted to the Tower for her mock
coronation.   And the brilliant Raleigh, at the time
when neighbour Cecil was spying upon him to

compass his destruction, was amongst its many dwellers.

When, in the reign of James I., a portion of Durham House facing the Strand was pulled down, a fashionable mart, called the New Exchange, frequently referred to by Restoration dramatists, was built on the site. The shops were raised upon a gallery, approached by an outside staircase, beneath which the gallants lounged attendance on their ladies. Here gathered milliners, dressmakers, perfumers, sempstresses, booksellers, jewellers. It was the Bond Street of its time, and at the back, overlooking the river, with a special water-gate, was a sheltered promenade, shaded by trees, as notorious for amorous assignations as a West-end modiste's is at the present day.[1] Anne Clarges, thereafter Duchess of Albemarle, and her first husband, Ratford, sold wash-balls, powder and gloves, and did sempstress work here ; and another duchess, the widow of that rapscallion, Tyrconnel, Viceroy of Ireland under James II., had a stall. She always wore a white mask to conceal her personality, and was known as the White Milliner. Coutts' Bank now stands upon the site of this once famous Vanity Fair. When Durham House fell into ruin, about 1768, the ground was bought by the brothers Adam, who, to celebrate the fraternal arrangement, christened the district the Adelphi.

[1] " For close walks the New Exchange," says Alithea to Mrs. Pincknife, in *The Country Wife*, one of the scenes of which, where Margery eludes her husband's jealous vigilance, takes place there.

CHAPTER XV.

THE STRAND (*continued*)—THE ADELPHI AND ITS PRECINCTS — CHARING CROSS — HUNGERFORD MARKET — TRAFALGAR SQUARE — SCOTLAND YARD.

TURNING out of the noise and bustle of the Strand into the quiet precincts of the Adelphi, we breathe an eighteenth-century air; much as it was when David Garrick and his brother Peter carried on their wine business in Durham Yard, as when the mortal remains of the great actor, whose death Johnson said finely, if hyperbolically, "eclipsed the gaiety of nations," were carried with all pomp and ceremony from his house in Adelphi Terrace to their last resting place in the abbey. The stones of the terrace still seem to echo to the footsteps of Johnson and Garrick and Beauclerk, and Goldsmith and Burke and Reynolds, and the very house in which they foregathered, nay, the very rooms, in which "Little Davey" received his guests, are still there.

It is the fashion now-a-days to sneer at the eighteenth century and the men thereof, and to depreciate its influence; but, in London at least, its footsteps have sunk deeper into the soil than those of any other era.

(270)

The seventeenth-century men, with all their superior genius, have left no such clearly cut impress upon their haunts and associations ; we know them only by their pictures and effigies, at least out of their works. But Johnson and his group still live and breathe about Fleet Street, the Strand, Leicester Square, Covent Garden ; the powdered wigs, velvet coats, silk stockings and red-heeled shoes are still more vivid to us even than the high stocks, strapped trousers and curled hair of our grandfathers' days.

Buckingham Street is as dreary and Villiers Street as commonplace thoroughfares as any about the Strand, though the plates on a couple of houses, bearing the names of Peter the Great and Samuel Pepys, give interest to the former. Yet the locality abounds in reminiscences of the great dead. Here stood York House, sometime the abode of the archbishops ; afterwards of Charles Brandon, Duke of Suffolk ; then of Sir Nicholas Bacon, and later of his illustrious son, Francis, who had a great love for the place. It was at York House that he dwelt during his chancellorship, and it was there he was deprived with degradation of the Great Seal, the privileges of which he had so unhappily abused. It is one of the darkest pages in the history of genius.

York House was rebuilt by that brilliant and superb favourite of two sovereigns—George Villiers, Duke of Buckingham, the records of whose magnificence read like stories of Haroun al Raschid. His coach was drawn by six horses, an extravagance in which no

sovereign had as then indulged, and he first brought
the sedan chair into fashion, though it had been
known in London before his time. He would in his
house shake diamonds off his clothes for his guests
to pick up. His cloaks were trimmed with great
diamond buttons, and he wore diamond hat-bands,
cockades and earrings, yoked with knots of pearl. He
had twenty-seven suits of clothes, the richest that
embroidery, lace, silk, velvet, silver, gold and gems
could make ; one of these was a white, uncut velvet,
set all over, both suit and cloak, with diamonds valued
at fourscore thousand pounds, besides a great feather,
stuck all over with diamonds, as were also his sword,
girdle, hat and spurs.

Bassompierre, the French ambassador, in his *Memoirs*, relates how the king took him in his barge to
York House, where the duke gave "the most magnificent entertainment I ever saw in my life. The king
supped at one table with the queen and me, which was
served in complete ballet [1] at each course with sundry
representations—changes of scenery, tables and music ;
the duke waited on the king at table, the Earl of Carlisle on the queen, and the Earl of Holland on me.
After supper the king and we were led into another
room, where the assembly was, and one entered it by a
kind of turnstile as in convents without any confusion,
where there was a magnificent ballet, in which the duke
danced ; and afterwards we set to and danced country
dances (*contre-danse*) till four in the morning ; thence

[1] Served by persons in fancy dresses with music and dancing.

we were shown into vaulted apartments, where there were five different collations." In a letter of the period, published in Disraeli's *Curiosities of Literature*, also describing this *fête*, it is stated "that all things came down in clouds," and that the cost of the entertainment was £5000.

Gerbier, the duke's painter, once gave an entertainment to the king and queen that cost £1000. The costumes on these occasions were equally extravagant : the gentlemen dressed in crimson or white velvet covered with precious stones, the ladies in white with herons' plumes, jewelled head-dresses and ropes of pearls.

Imagine, then, something of the splendour that must have passed beneath Inigo Jones's old water-gate, that now looks so grim and desolate beneath the shadow of the embankment trees, as though brooding, melancholy, and alone, in its grey, colourless surroundings, upon the wonders it has witnessed. Contrast the gorgeous state of York House with the present aspect of the streets that have taken its place. What a text for a preacher upon the well-worn "*Sic transit*". Transitory indeed was the splendour of which the knife of the assassin made so tragical an end.

The next notable figure in the annals of York House is that of the great Commonwealth general, Lord Fairfax, the marriage of whose daughter with the son of the late duke restored the old mansion to the second George Villiers, lavish, extravagant and brilliant as his father, but very much his inferior in dignity, who is so

18

YORK GATE.

conspicuous a personality in the chronicles of Charles
II.'s reign ; here he "played chemist, fiddler, statesman
and buffoon "; painted, rhymed, drank, wrote satires,
and squandered his wealth until he was beggared,
and died in obscurity and almost actual want. Some
time before his death need compelled him to dispose
of the historic house and grounds, which were then
demolished and laid out in streets.

Scarcely less interesting are the associations connected with the new departure. Among the inhabitants of Buckingham Street were gossip Pepys, and
the Czar Peter the Great, who indulged in many an
orgie, and consumed many gallons of brandy and
cayenne, his favourite tipple, in that shabby house
overlooking the Thames. Here also lived the poet
Earl of Dorset, one of the most brilliant wits of the
Restoration; Harley, Earl of Oxford ; Clarkson Stans-
field and Etty, the painters; while Villiers Street was
for a time the abode of Evelyn and of Steele.

The Strand, however, even in its palmy days, was
not all grand mansions. In the time of Charles I.
fish and other stalls were set in front of the noble
houses, and increased to such an extent that, in 1630,
an edict had to be issued for their clearance.

As everybody knows, Charing Cross marks the last
resting-place of the body of Edward I.'s beloved
queen, Eleanor, previous to her interment in the
abbey. The cross erected by the great king cost
nearly £600, an enormous sum for those days ; it was
of Caen stone with Purbeck marble steps, and contained

eight gilt metal figures. The derivation of the name
Charing from *chère reine*, however, is less acceptable
than that of *cerre-ing*, two Anglo-Saxon words which
mean "bend" and "meadow," so that it was the
meadow at the bend of the river. The brutal bigotry
of the Puritans destroyed this beautiful relic of antiquity. But it was well avenged, for Hugh Peters, the
zealot Harrison and others of less note were executed
in front of its site.

Behind the Cross stood the mansion of the Hungerford family. Its destruction by fire is noted by Pepys
(April, 1669). It was not rebuilt, but Sir Edward
Hungerford obtained permission from the king to
establish a market upon the ground. This same
Sir Edward was a notorious spendthrift; he is said
to have once spent £500 upon a wig for a court ball!
No wonder he died a poor knight of Windsor; but
it is wonderful that he attained the age of 115.

It was at Old Hungerford Stairs, "in a crazy, tumble-
down old house, abutting on the river, and literally
overrun with rats," that the boy Dickens had his dole-
ful experiences in the blacking warehouse. Whence
he wandered about those coal-sheds and mouldering
old taverns—notably the Fox Under the Hill, which
covered the foreshore previous to the formation of the
Thames Embankment and for some time afterwards.
"Until Old Hungerford Market was pulled down," he
wrote, "until Old Hungerford Stairs were destroyed,
and the very nature of the ground changed, I never
had the courage to go back to the place where

my servitude began. I never saw it." Hungerford
Market was cleared away in 1862 for the Railway
Station.

Twelve years later the last of the noble mansions
which had adorned the Strand, Northumberland House,
built in 1605, on the site of the hospital of Ste. Marie
Rouncevalles, was demolished to form the new avenue
to the Thames Embankment. Exteriorally it had no
architectural beauty to recommend it ; but, with its
noble terrace overlooking the river, its magnificent
galleries and suites of apartments—it contained 150
private rooms—with their columns, statuary and
pictures by the great masters, its painted ballroom,
vestibules and wonderful spiral staircase, it was worthy
of the Howards, the Somersets, the Percys who had
in turns inhabited it ; and it was an act of vandalism
to destroy so interesting an edifice when the avenue
could have been formed just as conveniently a little
further to the west.

Only during the later decades of its existence
did Northumberland House command so pleasant a
prospect as Trafalgar Square, which was not formed
until 1830; and even the pepper-castors of the National
Gallery were preferable to the mass of dull, mean
buildings that covered the site from the time of Richard
II. Here, in the hawking days, the king's falcons
were kept in moulting time, this being the royal
mews ;[1] and from the reign of Henry VIII. to that of

---

[1] From the Anglo-Saxon word *mew*, to moult.

George III. here were the king's chief stables. Hence
the origin of the term "mews" as applied to stables.

A little further to the east it looked upon the tower
of old St. Martin's Church, which dated back to the
Norman kings, the lower part being hidden among a
maze of courts and alleys that, from the days of Ben
Jonson until well into the present century, was known
as "The Holy Land," "Bermudas Straits," "The
Caribbee Islands," and "Porridge Island," noted for
its cook-shops. Here again we encounter the shadow
of the boy Dickens, his little figure clad in a short
jacket and corduroy trousers, looking in longingly at
the window of that "special pudding shop," hesitating
between quality and quantity, for two penn'orth there
was not more than one penn'orth at ordinary shops—
but then it was made with currants. When, in 1721,
the present handsome church took the place of the
ancient, it was still obscured by these squalid dens of
vice and poverty, which were not removed until after
the square was formed.

And Northumberland House had looked upon some
strange scenes as well as strange places. To go no
further back than 1678, when the murder of Sir Edmund Berrie Godfrey [1] threatened London with riot, if

---

[1] Sir Edmund Berrie Godfrey was the magistrate before whom Titus
Oates, first a beneficed clergyman, then a Roman Catholic, lastly a
Protestant zealot, laid his information of the existence of a popish
plot, which aimed at the subjugation of the kingdom and the massacre
of all the Protestants. Godfrey, a few nights afterwards, was enticed
from his home by a false message, and four days from then his body
was discovered with the neck broken and a sword passed through it

not revolution. He was buried in St. Martin's Church, and the wildest excitement marked the funeral. Thousands followed the bier of the murdered magistrate, and a crowd equally dense flowed towards it from the opposite direction. At the Cross the bier was set down, and Titus Oates, standing beside it, delivered a fierce oration, in which he called upon every citizen to avenge "the Protestant martyr". Then went up a tremendous shout, "We will! Burn all the papists!" And but for the troops there would have been a terrible massacre of the Romanists.

Seven years later Northumberland House beheld an equally turbulent and ferocious crowd surging about the pillory, which had risen opposite it for many generations, pelting, with every missile they could lay hands upon, a creature who looked more like a satyr than a human being, as he stood there with his head thrust through a throttling hole, a helpless victim to the pitiless wrath of those who but a brief time before had looked upon him as a saviour, and cheered him to the echo. He was removed from the pillory to Tyburn, thence scourged through the streets to Newgate, and then sentenced to be imprisoned for life. Even Macaulay says that, terrible as were the sufferings of Titus Oates, they were not equal to his crimes.

It was at Charing Cross that the first Punch and

on Primrose Hill. The mystery of the murder has never been solved; whether indeed it was committed by some fanatical papist, or, what is more likely, by Oates himself to confirm a story which was afterwards proved to be a fabrication, will never be known. The name is usually spelled " Edmondbury," but the form here given is the correct one.

Judy show was set up by an Italian, in 1666, and at once became the rage. Three years afterwards Pepys notes that everything short and thick was nicknamed " Punch ". Of course this puppet play differed greatly from the itinerant show that we are familiar with.

Of all that old time only the statue of King Charles —one of the very few statues for which a Londoner does not blush—remains. A curious history is attached to it. Though cast as early as 1633, it was not put up until after the Civil War broke out. Then the Puritans seized upon it, as they did upon the sign of the Golden Cross hostelry opposite, and ordered both to be destroyed as accursed things. The brazier to whom the statue was handed over was a secret Royalist, and concealed it until the Restoration, but, in consequence of a dispute, it was not set upon its pedestal until 1674.

Where Drummond's Bank now stands was Locket's Ordinary, a noted resort of the wits and fine gentlemen of the last century. " I go to dinner at Locket's," says Lord Foppington, in Vanbrugh's, *The Relapse*, " where you are so nicely and delicately served that, stap my vitals ! they shall compose you a dish no bigger than a saucer, shall come to fifty shillings."

A palace, standing in large gardens, was assigned to the Scottish kings at Charing Cross by Saxon Edgar, and continued to be their dwelling when they came to London to do homage for their kingdom and certain lands, which were held under the suzerainty of England, until the union of the two crowns by James

I. But ere this the palace, known as " Scotland," had fallen into ruin, and the site was used for Government offices. John Milton lived here for a time, when he served Cromwell; it was also the residence of Inigo Jones, Sir Christopher Wren and Sir John Vanburgh, architect and dramatist; from which we gather that it was used as the Board of Works of the period. " Scotland " became the headquarters of the new police in 1829, and continued to be so until the removal of the principal offices to the abandoned Opera House on the Embankment.

CHAPTER XVI.

BUT for the reign of the Saints, Whitehall would have been the noblest palace in Europe. The Banqueting House is still unrivalled in the domestic architecture of London ; how beautiful it is may be judged by comparing it with the abortive imitation that now shoulders Inigo Jones's masterpiece on the southern side. In the original plan, which was never finished, there were four of these structures; five courts, the largest 245 feet square; an embankment, with flights of steps down to the water, faced the river, while towards the street were beautiful gardens and a lake. The entire façade would have been 1152 feet long.

In the reign of Henry III. one of the great barons, Hubert de Burgh, Chief Justice of England, erected a castle upon this site, and bequeathed it to the Dominicans. It was afterwards sold to the archbishopric of York, and was thereafter known as York Place. Its history begins with Cardinal Wolsey, who enlarged the building and kept regal state in it. Cavendish, his biographer, writes : " The banquets were set forth with masques and mummeries, in so gorgeous a sort and costly a manner, that it was heaven to behold. . . .

(282)

I have seen the king suddenly come hither in a mask,
with a dozen other maskers, all in garments like
shepherds, made of fine cloth of gold, and fine crimson satin paned, and caps of the same ; their hair
and beards either of fine gold wire or else of silver,
and some being of black silk ; having sixteen torch-
bearers, besides their drums, and other persons attend-
ing upon them with visors, and clothed all in satin of
the same colours." Then, in a passage too long for
quotation, the writer goes on to recount all the forms
and ceremonies, and how the table was laid with " 200
dishes or above of wondrous costly meats and devices,
subtlely devised ". Some readers will be able to recall
the splendid realization of this picture in the Lyceum
revival of Shakespeare's *King Henry VIII.*

At the fall of the great Cardinal his royal master
took possession of York House, added some grand
apartments, and rechristened it Whitehall. It was at
a masque at the cardinal's house that Henry first
met Anne Boleyn ; the grand *fêtes* that followed his
marriage with that lady, those given to celebrate the
notable events of his reign, and at the receptions of
foreign princes, surpassed in magnificence even
Wolsey's time. Within those walls the tyrant Blue
Beard breathed his last. Under puritan Edward
and bigot Mary, Whitehall had no history outside
preachers and priests, both being equally priest-
ridden ; the first by perfervid Reformers, the second
by persecuting Romanists.

Elizabeth revived the glories of the court ; and there

were tournaments and maskings and revels as in the days of her father, and a galaxy of great men to give them lustre, such as no other sovereign of the world was ever surrounded by. Here foregathered the superb figures of Essex, Leicester, Sidney, Raleigh ; that greatest of buccaneers, Drake ; wise Bacon, Burleigh and Cecil.

Probably the splendours of the court were little, if at all, diminished by her successor ; but whereas under the great Tudor queen all was high bred and orderly, coarseness and drunkenness tarnished the state of the first Stuart, whereof some very unsavoury pictures may be found in the secret history of the reign : of ladies so intoxicated that they could not keep their legs under them, and of His Majesty dancing while in the same condition. The most brilliant and decorous period in the history of Whitehall is that of Charles I. Drunkenness and open profligacy were banished, while gorgeous show was chastened by artistic taste. Charles was not only the patron of Rubens, Vandyke and Ben Jonson, but of all men of art and letters that came within his sphere. His collections of paintings and articles of *vertu* were matchless ; the catalogue of them when dispersed by the Roundheads filled over 1000 pages. His court was the most polished in Europe, and its magnificence and "exquisite order" excited the admiration of Bassompierre, who was familiar with all the courts of Europe. The famous *fêtes* of Louis XIV. were modelled on those of England. Never before or since has this country held such a supreme position in the world of culture.

Foremost among the entertainments of the court of the first Stuarts was " The Masque ". It was in vogue in Henry VIII.'s time, but was then little better than mummery ; nor did it make much progress in grace and refinement under the *régime* of his great daughter.   James and Charles had the good fortune to have these entertainments written by such men as Jonson, Middleton, Heywood, Shirley, and illustrated by such fine artists as Inigo Jones and Gerbier. The queens both of James and Charles, as well as the great ladies of the court, frequently danced and took part in them.   This was one of the severest accusations brought by the Puritans against Henrietta Maria.   All that has been achieved in our time in the way of stage splendour and illusion, after allowing for the absence of lime-light and electricity, was quite equalled in these exquisite productions.[1]

For the benefit of those who may not have the original to refer to, I will give some brief account of Shirley's " Triumph of Peace," which was presented by the gentlemen of the Inns of Court before Charles I. and his queen, in 1633.   It was the most magnificent of all the masques, and cost over £20,000.

At Ely and Hatton Houses the gentlemen of the four Inns met, and thence went in procession to Whitehall. First, to the music of hautboys or clarionets,

[1] See Ben Jonson's " Masques," and the article on " Masques " in Disraeli's *Curiosities of Literature.*

started the Ante-masque, a crowd of grotesque figures
in showy dresses attended by torch-bearers; then a
number of allegorical personages, Fancy, Opinion,
Confidence, Jollity, Laughter, etc., suitably attired ;
others, dressed as beggars, mastiffs, all kinds of
birds, jays, kites, owls, satyrs, Don Quixote, Sancho
Panza and the windmill; then a drummer and fourteen trumpeters, in crimson satin, followed by the
marshal and ten horse and forty foot, in scarlet and
silver ; to these succeeded 100 gentlemen splendidly
mounted, each attended by two pages and a groom in
rich liveries. Then came two chariots, each drawn by
four horses, adorned with gold and silver, and containing musicians dressed as priests and sibyls, playing
upon lutes, each attended by footmen in blue and
silver bearing flambeaux ; four chariots after the
Roman form : the first, silver and orange ; the second,
silver and pale blue ; the third, silver and crimson ; the
fourth, silver and white, all surmounted by canopies
of feathers and silver fringe, contained the grand
masquers, and between each rode four musicians in
robes and garlands, attended by torch-bearers and
crowds of splendid lacqueys.

This is but a very condensed description of the
procession. Within the Banqueting House the scene
was yet more picturesque : the king and queen under
a canopy of state, attended by their superb court, and
opposite them the raised stage enclosed in arbour-work
of loose branches and leaves, festooned with draperies,
fruits and flowers ; children with silver wings blowing

golden trumpets, and on each side of the proscenium two figures in Roman habits representing Minos and Numa.

When the curtain was drawn up the stage represented a large street with sumptuous palaces, porticoes, pleasant trees and grounds ; a spacious place adorned with public and private buildings, among which was the forum of Peace.   Over all was a clear sky with transparent clouds which enlightened all the scene.   The stage direction marks " From one of the 'sides of the street enter Opinion and Confidence," which shows that this was not a mere flat canvas but a " set ". In another scene " there appeared in the highest and foremost part of the heaven, by little and little to break forth, a whitish cloud, bearing a chariot feigned of goldsmith's work, and in it sat Irene or Peace, in a flowery vesture like the Spring," etc.   Again : " Out of the highest part of the opposite side came softly descending another cloud, of an orient colour, bearing a silver chariot curiously wrought, and differing in all things from the first; in which sat Eunomia, or Law, in a purple satin robe, adorned with golden stars, a mantle of carnation, laced and fringed with gold, a coronet of light upon her head," and so on.   " A third cloud of various colour from the other two begins to descend towards the middle of the scene with somewhat a swifter motion, and in it sat a person representing Justice, in a white robe and mantle of shining satin, fair long hair circled with a coronet of silver fishes, white wings and buskins, a crown imperial in her hand."

Passing over other transformations we come to this
exquisite finale : " The Revels being passed the scene
is changed into a plain champaign country, which
terminates with the horizon, and above a darkish sky,
with dusky clouds, through which appeared the new
moon, but with a faint light by the approach of morning ; from the farthest point of the ground arose by
little and little a great vapour, which being about the
middle of the scene, it slackens its motion, and begins
to fall downwards to the earth, from whence it came ;
and out of this rose another cloud of a strange shape
and colour, on which sat a young maid with a dim torch
in her hand ; her face was an olive colour, so were her
arms and breast, her garment was transparent, the
ground dark blue and sprinkled with silver spangles,"
etc.   This is the forerunner of the morning, "and is
that glimpse of light which is seen when the night is
past and the day not yet appearing ".

Such a combination of regal splendour, of poetry,
music, painting, dancing, enshrined within those noble
walls, vaulted with pictures by Rubens, and hung with
rare tapestries, formed a *coup d'œil* that is scarcely
realizable by imagination.   What a contrast to that
dark January morning, when the Master of all this
magnificence passed through this same apartment
to the black draped scaffold without, to be brought
back a headless trunk.

Changed indeed was Whitehall when Protector
Cromwell reigned there, though the transformation
was not quite as complete as the more zealous of the

saints would have desired; Milton and Waller and Marvell gave a flavour of culture to the surroundings, and Oliver, who was very fond of music, had a concert as often as he dared, though some smite-the-devil-hip-and-thigh preacher denounced it from the pulpit. And after solemn feasts, at which the grace was longer than the feeding, my Lord Protector would exercise his superfluous exuberance by such horseplay as bedaubing the faces of the ladies with sweetmeats, and pelting his companions with cushions, which they failed not to return, so that presently the chamber rather resembled a boys' dormitory than the room of a palace. And, if the *Chroniques Scandaleuses* tell the truth, there were other diversions much less decorous, smacking rather of the court of James than that of his son. There is little doubt but that Lady Dysert, afterwards Duchess of Lauderdale, and General Lambert's wife were Cromwell's mistresses; the former, however, was too lively for the godly, and had to be put aside; but they held that there could be no hurt in his " holding heavenly meditations with Mrs. Lambert," who was a very prayerful woman.

There was a strange scene when the death-warrant of the king was signed. When it came to Cromwell's turn to affix his signature he wrote his name hastily, and then, in a nervous burst of mirth, smeared the ink in his pen across the face of Henry Martin, who after signing returned the compliment.

A yet stranger scene was that when Cromwell visited alone the room in Whitehall, where lay the headless

19

trunk of the king, which had been put into a coffin, covered with black velvet, and carried thither through the snow. Unshrouding the corpse and gazing long upon it he muttered, " Cruel necessity ! "

The latter days of the great Protector were scarcely less gloomy than those of the King whom he had doomed. Haunted by remorse, by the shadow of the dead, by the reproaches of his favourite daughter on her deathbed, in hourly dread of assassination from fanatical republicans, as well as over-zealous royalists, not daring to sleep three successive nights in the same chamber, or to employ the services of a barber lest his enemies should bribe the man to cut his throat ; even his gloomy faith in being one of the elect failing him at times, and plunging him into the terrors of hell ; diseased in body, diseased in mind, all his glory, all his ambition, all his successes were withered into dust and ashes. While he lay tossing *in extremis* in his chamber in Whitehall on that September night, the last of his life, an awful storm arose, such a storm of wind and rain as there was no record of in England. It was impossible even for horses to make their way through the streets. All next day, the anniversary of Dunbar and Worcester, the storm raged with the same fury, and about four o'clock my Lord Protector's dark and daring spirit passed away, amidst the crash of the thunder, upon the wings of the lightning. A curiously appropriate finale to so tempestuous a career. Charles was happier in his death than his doomsman.

Brilliant and gay once more is the Whitehall of

Charles II., but as destitute of nobleness as it is
of refinement and morality. There are feastings,
and balls and music and concerts, but the poetical
" Masque" would be too slow for the Rochesters and
Sedleys and the second Buckingham, for my Lady
Castlemaine, Nell Gwynne, Louise de la Querouaille,
La Mazarin and the other ladies of that ilk ; they care
for no poetry beyond a love song, for no wit that is
not salacious, for no dramatic work that keeps within
the bounds of decency ; there is no restraint, moral
or ceremonious ; courtiers flout at the king, and his
mistresses treat him with no more respect than a
fish-woman does her husband ; all is unbridled licence
and self-indulgence. Pepys has rendered every detail
of this joyous, godless life as familiar to us as our
personal experiences. We see the maids of honour
strolling in the galleries, in their riding garbs of coats
and doublets with deep shirts, " just for all the world
like mine, and buttoned their doublets up to the
breast, with periwigs and with hats ; so that only for
the long petticoats dragging under their men's coats,
nobody would take them for women in any point
whatever". May I not write 1666—1899? We watch
with the dear old gossip the maids of honour in their
velvet gowns playing cards with the Duke of Monmouth ;[1] and stand beside him at the ball while the

---

[1] Pepys writes (14th February, 1667-8) : " I was told to-night that
Lady Castlemaine is so great a gamester as to have won £15,000 in
one night, and lost £25,000 in another night at play, and hath played
£1000 and £1500 at a cast ".

king leads a lady a single coranto, all the lords and
ladies following. " Then to country dances, the King
leading the first, ' cuckolds all awry,' the old dance of
England."

The rule of life at Whitehall is—let us eat, drink
and be merry, for to-morrow we may die. And this
gospel of hedonism is fulfilled to the letter. In the
midst of his toyings and revellings the English Sar-
danapalus is struck down. Always good natured,
the man " who never said a stupid thing nor ever did
a wise one " is true to himself to the last. He earnestly
recommends the Duchess of Portsmouth and her son to
his brother, and begs him "not to let poor Nelly starve ".
When the queen implores his pardon for any offence
she may unwillingly have given, he cries : " She asks
my pardon, poor woman ; I ask hers with all my
heart ". On the last night of his life he apologises to
those about him for the trouble he has caused them,
and almost his last words are—that he has been an
unconscionable time dying, but he hopes they will
excuse it !

The advent of James II. wrought another change
in the ways of the palace. A gloomy seclusion marked
his brief *régime ;* outward decorum was restored, but
true-blue Protestants were frightened away by the
sight of brown-frocked friars ; and saturnine priests
and haughty monseigneurs were not to the taste of
the courtiers. On a bleak, rainy December night the
queen and the infant prince, the last of the Stuarts
born in the purple, were secretly conveyed out of the

palace, placed in a boat under the care of Lauzun and rowed across the black river to Lambeth; horses carried them to Gravesend, where a vessel was waiting for their reception.   A few nights afterwards James himself fled in the darkness from the home of his ancestors.   He was captured and brought back.   But on the morning of 18th December, 1688, through grey gloom and beating rain he took his last sight of the grand old palace.[1]   Ten years after the flight of James it perished in a great conflagration, not without suspicion of incendiarism.   The Banqueting House alone escaped destruction, and was converted by George I. into a chapel royal.   It is now incorporated with the United Service Museum.

The Whitehall of the Tudor and Stuart days was a collection of heterogeneous buildings, ranging from the Tudor period through the Jacobean and Carolian, some handsome, some mean, some shabby and decayed.   These various piles were separated into blocks by courtyards or gardens, and included, besides the sovereign's state and private apartments, residences for court officials and favourites, quarters for officers and soldiers, and dwellings for the vast swarm of servants and dependants attached to the palace.   The area of the entire demesne extended from the Thames to St. James's Park, the road from London to Westminster dividing it into two unequal

---

[1] Charles lost his head for refusing to renounce the Church of England, his son lost his crown for attempting to subvert it.   What a strange fatality hung over the Stuart race!

parts. This road followed the same line as the present thoroughfare; between Scotland Yard and the Banqueting House it was tolerably wide; but to the west of the latter it narrowed and passed through Holbein's gateway, a handsome structure of two-coloured glazed bricks, designed by the great painter whose name it bore, and finally it debouched into King Street, through another massive gateway.

On the western side of the road were the Tennis Court, Tilt Yard, Bowling Alleys and Cockpit, etc. On the Tilt Yard Charles II. built the first Horse Guards, the present building dates from 1751; the Cockpit was also covered with buildings, in which were General Monk's apartments; likewise a theatre, frequently referred to in Pepys' *Diary;* Downing Street now occupies the site. Wallingford House, also within the precincts, which William III. converted into the Admiralty Offices, was built early in the reign of Charles I.

Spring Garden, so called from one of those *jets d'eau* which did not act until pressed by some unwary foot, and then deluged the victim, originally a part of the private grounds of Whitehall, became in the time of Charles I. and his sons the Vauxhall of the seventeenth century. In 1634 we read in Garrard's *Strafford's Letters*, that the bowling was put down in Spring Garden[1] for one day, "but by the intercession of the queen, it was reprieved for this year; but here-

[1] There were two or three other Spring Gardens in other parts of London.

after it shall be no common bowling-place. There
was kept in it an ordinary for six shillings a meal,
when the king's proclamation allows but two elsewhere : continual bibbing and drinking wine all day
long under the trees, two or three quarrels every
week. It was grown scandalous and unsufferable ;
besides my Lord Digby being reprehended for
striking in the king's garden, he answered that he
took it for a common bowling-place, where all paid
money for their coming in."

A little farther west was the notorious Mulberry
Garden. Evelyn refers to it in 1654 : " My Lady
Gerrard treated us at Mulberry Garden, the only
place of refreshment about the town for persons of the
best quality to be exceedingly cheated at ; Cromwell
and his partisans have shut up and seized upon
Spring Garden, which till now had been the usual
rendezvous for the ladys and gallants at this season ".
One of Sedley's comedies is called *The Mulberry
Garden* : the action takes place under the Commonwealth, but the manners depicted are as gross as they
were under Charles. The Restoration and Revolution
dramatists abound in references to this place as the
favourite rendezvous of lovers. Buckingham Palace
is supposed to stand upon the site, though some
say Arlington Street covers it.

The most extensive and important division of
Whitehall was on the Thames side ; the royal and
state apartments, the famous galleries, the privy
gardens, over three acres in extent, set out formally

in sixteen grass plots with a statue in the centre of
each, and the royal seraglio, which far surpassed all
the rest in splendour.

King Street, which has just been pulled down, could
boast of illustrious residents. Edmund Spenser died
there in almost actual want, though his remains were
carried to the abbey in great state. There lived Lord
Howard of Effingham, High Admiral of the Fleet sent
against the Spanish Armada ; the brilliant Earl of
Dorset so frequently mentioned in these pages ; that
delightful lyrist, Thomas Carew. Oliver Cromwell
resided here in 1648, and his mother died in that same
house—it was at the north-west end—after her son had
attained almost regal power. The Bell Tavern was the
headquarters of " The October Club," the members
of which were 150 High Church Tory country gentlemen, who drank "old October" to "the king over
the water"; it was established in opposition to the
Mug Houses and Calves' Head Club, but was broken
up after the death of Queen Anne.

CHAPTER XVII.

WESTMINSTER ABBEY AND PALACE, AND THEIR
ASSOCIATIONS—THE THAMES AND ITS ASPECTS.

BEYOND King Street was anciently a network of
narrow streets and alleys, and the Broad Sanctuary
still marks the site of the "Alsatia" and "Old Mint"
of Westminster, a refuge alike for the criminal and
the persecuted.   In this maze, not far from the western
door of the abbey, was Caxton's house, wherein the
first book was printed in England.   On the ground
now covered by Vine Street, near Rochester Row,
was the abbey vineyard.

Gazing upon that noble pile, dedicated to St.
Peter, it is difficult for imagination to carry us back to
the days when Thorney Island was a desolate swamp,
the haunt of the heron and the bittern, divided from
the adjacent ground by the creeping sinuosities of
the river.   From the earliest days of Christianity in
England the Cross had been rooted here, and when
the Confessor laid the foundations of the abbey two
churches had already preceded it.   Something, but
not much, remains of the saintly Edward's edifice,
in which the last of the Saxon and the first of the
Norman kings were crowned.   Henry III. fashioned

what is to us the more ancient portion into its present form ; and Henry VII. completed the beautiful temple in which Plantagenets, Tudors, Stuarts and Hanoverians have been enthroned—and many buried ;. and in which rest all that is mortal of so many mighty Englishmen.

On the ground now known as Old and New Palace Yards stood the ancient Palace of Westminster, in which Cnut, the Danish usurper, resided, in which the Confessor died, in which Edward I. was born, and the walls of which were shadowed by the presence of all succeeding monarchs to Henry VIII. After that time Whitehall usurped its place. In the ancient palace sat all the ancient parliaments, and on its site have deliberated all the modern. In the burning of old St. Stephen's, in 1834, much that remained of the mediæval structure was destroyed. Fortunately the flames spared the crypt, and the glorious hall, founded by Rufus and rebuilt by Richard II. And in that same hall the unhappy son of the Black Prince was arraigned, and centuries afterwards another unhappy monarch. Here, also, Stafford, Duke of Buckingham, Protector Somerset, Sir Thomas Wyatt, Sir Thomas More, the Duke of Norfolk, the Earl of Essex, the Gunpowder Plot conspirators, the great Strafford, the seven bishops, the Jacobite lords of '45, Warren Hastings—to mention only a few—have stood as culprits.

But more pleasant memories are associated with Westminster Hall. It was the scene of many a

coronation banquet ; kings sometimes kept Christmas there. There Henry V. received the congratula-
tions of the citizens on the victory of Agincourt ;
and Anne Boleyn came thither in great pomp.
The particulars of all which you will find in Stow.
All the kings and queens, soldiers, statesmen, lawyers,
orators, all the makers of England's glory for centuries have stood beneath that roof, world-famous for
its beauty.

No spot in Europe, at least out of Rome, is so
crowded with historic interest, so haunted by the
mighty shadows of the past as that small area that
lies between Dean's Yard and the Thames. In the
ancient school generations of great Englishmen
have been educated : among others Ben Jonson,
Cowley, Dryden, George Herbert, Giles Fletcher,
Prior, Cowper, Southey, Sir Christopher Wren,
Earl Russell, Gibbon, Froude, Locke, Warren Hastings. On the beams of the old schoolroom, that
almost vies with that of Eton in fame, are carved
in autograph the names of Dryden, Hakluyt,
Cowper, Wren, Locke, and many another known
to fame. Four years ago the bicentenary of the
death of the renowned master, Dr. Busby, as
notable for flogging as for imparting learning, was
duly honoured.

At the hour of evening prayer there is preserved,
in the great hall, a custom that goes back to the
monastic days. A boy called the " Monos " cries the
hour in Latin, in a high clear voice, that presently

subsides into a whisper, like the muezzin of the Mahomedan. At the summons the scholars hurry in, and when all is silent a voice calls "Oremus!" and the Latin prayers are repeated, much as they were by the Benedictine monks, who once reigned supreme here.

It is difficult to tear oneself away from so fascinating a spot, so replete with stories, but their very abundance renders selection almost impossible, and with one more glance at the Thames I must bend my pilgrim's steps in another direction.

Standing upon Westminster Bridge, one thinks of Wordsworth's fine sonnet, and especially of the lines :—

> Dull would he be of soul who could pass by
> A sight so touching in its majesty.

The stories of the river might rival the stories of the streets in interest ; they go back to the time when, unconfined by any artificial bank, the silver Thames flowed in, north and south, over meadow and morass that have now for centuries been covered with buildings, and so on to the days when patrician mansions and fair gardens lined the Middlesex side, and the Surrey shore was all grassy meads, rising into wooded hills, with one little cluster of town on the bankside ; when the river was alive with gilded barges and stately processions of court and city state, and with boats conveying gallants and ladies to the Globe or the Blackfriars, or to Paris Garden, to see the bear baiting.[1] There was only one bridge across the Thames in those days and for long afterwards. Westminster Bridge was not built until past the middle of the eighteenth century; the only means of crossing the river between Westminster and London Bridge being by the Horseferry, still kept in remembrance by Horseferry Road.

It was not such scenes as these that Wordsworth gazed upon; mansions and gardens and meads had long since given place to hideous tumble - down wharves, and mud banks, to all the wretched sordidness that then marked the river's bank and still offends the eye on the Surrey side. What would he say now to our splendid Embankment, with its background of stately buildings, its beautiful gardens, its umbrageous boulevard and broad roadway? But it must be remembered that the grandeur and beauty that the great poet saw was not an outward but an inward vision, the " ships, towers, domes, theatres and temples " were but symbols of the mighty city's life, and even the dirt and ugliness of the river's side was to his vision but the soiled garment of that

[1] John Taylor, " the water poet," in his petition to King James (1615) for the suppression of all theatres on the Middlesex side of the Thames, states that such was the number of watermen who plied for hire between Windsor and Gravesend, half of whom had been called into existence by the bankside theatres (of which there were several) and other places of amusement, which visitors always approached by the Thames, that he estimated that, including the families of the breadwinners, some 40,000 persons were dependent upon these sources. for a living.

commerce to which London owes so much of its greatness.

The grand old river has many aspects, mostly sombre, yet mostly picturesque. Passing over London Bridge on a spring or autumn evening, towards sunset, I have often been struck by Rembrandtish effects of massive shadows and subdued lights. To the east land, water and sky have been blended indistinguishably in one grey gloom, through which the Tower and Tower Bridge and the wharves and buildings loomed ghostly, like faded silhouettes or faint pictures in sepia. To the west a lurid crimson, blurred sun, framed in a sulphurous halo, flecked with smoky red, has glared from purplish - black clouds, and cast shafts of sullen fire upon the dome of St. Paul's, upon the roofs of buildings, upon the water, upon boat and bridge and barge, veiled in shrouding grey, through which more distant objects appeared as seen through a glass darkly.

On summer evenings the light is brighter, and a saffron glow suffuses the west ; yet always subdued by that gauzy film, never absent from the London atmosphere, and which causes such varied refractions of light. But to see London in its most beautiful aspects you should stroll along the length of the Embankment, when, through a clear air the full moon glitters and shimmers upon the rippling water, when the long rows of light blend in the distance into a line of white fire which, by the windings of the banks and the lamps on the bridges, seems to cross and re-cross the river in chains of luminous points, while the cold electric blue from the hotels and railway stations falls upon tree and turf and roadway with a lustre as brilliant as that of Luna herself.

Had he looked upon this scene Wordsworth might indeed have exclaimed :—

Earth has not anything to show more fair.

CHAPTER XVIII.

THE HAYMARKET—ST. JAMES'S SQUARE—PALL MALL—ALMACK'S.

WHEN Sir John Vanbrugh, in 1704, proposed to build a theatre at the bottom of the Haymarket, all to the north of it was pasture land, and it was argued that the city, the Inns of Court, and the middle part of the town, from which came the chief supporters of the theatre, would be beyond the reach of an easy walk, and coach hire would be too hard a tax upon the pit and gallery. Houses, however, had been erected close by in Charles II.'s time, and in 1692 the roadway was formed on its present lines, but the air was still so pure that laundresses bleached their linen upon the hedges of Hedge Lane, which stretched from what is now Pall Mall East to Tyburn Road; and the farmers of Kensington and Chelsea sold their hay there three times a week, as they had done since the days of the Tudors.

The Queen's Theatre, however, as it was called until the accession of George I., when it became The King's, was built and opened in 1705. But it proved such a disastrous failure at first that it was let to Owen Swiney for £5 a night! After oscillating for a while

(304)

between drama and opera, in spite of the ridicule and opposition of such potent publications as *The Spectator* against this exotic species of entertainment, it finally settled down to an opera-house.

Vanbrugh's great theatre was burned down in 1739, set on fire, it was believed, by the leader of the orchestra out of revenge. It was a dull, heavy building of red brick, roofed with black glazed tiles, and with a frontage only thirty-five feet wide, in which were three circular-headed doors and windows. Upon its site rose the building which many of us remember, first opened in 1791, to fall a prey to the flames in 1867. It was rebuilt two years later; but the history of the third house was one of disaster and finally of degradation until its demolition. A handsome new theatre, bearing the old name, now occupies its site.

No spot in Europe can show a grander record of lyric genius than that south-west corner of the Haymarket; every great singer from Nicolini, the male soprano, to Tamberlik and Mario, from Faustina and Cuzzoni to Christine Nillson and Titiens, has sung there; the operas of every celebrated composer, from Handel to Verdi and Gounod, have been heard there; every famous ballerina from Mlle. Sallé, who first introduced the opera ballet into London in 1734, to Taglioni, Ellsler and Rosati have pirouetted there. That spot has echoed to the notes of the wonderful Farinelli, for whose powers of execution no composer could write passages difficult enough, for whom, while he was singing, the orchestra forgot to play, over-

20

whelmed by his genius; to the *bravura* and *fioturi* of
Catalani, who could leap two octaves ; to the voice
of that transcendent artiste, Pasta, of whom in her
decay Viardot said : "She is like the *Cenacolo* of Da
Vinci at Milan, a wreck of a picture—but that picture
is the greatest in the world ; " to the wonderful B
flat of the incomparable Rubini, which he once gave
forth with such vigour that he fractured his collar-bone ;
to the thunderous bass of Lablache. Here was the scene
of the Jenny Lind *furore ;* and have not many of us the
glorious notes of Titiens and the dulcet, silvery ring
of Nillson's voice still echoing in our ears? Who in
the present day can realise that dancing, vulgarised
as it is now, was ever the poetry of motion? Yet
what could have been more poetical than the ethereal
grace of Taglioni, the intoxicating sorcery of the
divine Ellsler, the ideality of Lucille Grahn, the
dazzling brilliancy of Carlotta Grisi, the fascinating
verve of Cerito.

When Lumley announced that Taglioni, Grahn,
Grisi and Cerito would appear together in a *pas-de-
quatre,* all fashionable Europe was in a flutter. But,
oh, what a team of fillies for any man to control! At
the final rehearsal they all but broke away. The last
pas was ceded to Taglioni, but the crux was the first,
each of the other three flatly refused to begin, and each
desired to come immediately before Taglioni. Perrot,
the ballet master, rushed to Lumley's room in despair;
it was all over, the thing was impossible. The
manager pondered until a happy thought flashed

across his mind. " Let the *oldest* take her unquestion-
able right to the envied position," he said. Perrot
chuckled with delight, and bounded back to the stage.
Lumley's judgment was as subtle as that of Solomon,
no one of the three was inclined to accept the position
on that count, and left it to the ballet master. The
pas-de-quatre was performed ; every night the house
was crowded to suffocation ; it was the one absorbing
topic of conversation, and foreign newspapers teemed
with stories of its wonders.

In 1720 a small, wooden theatre, which with all
appliances cost only £1500, was built on the eastern
side of the street and came to be known as "the
little theatre in the Haymarket". First opened by a
French company, it passed into the hands of mountebanks and rope-dancers, until Harry Fielding under-
took it, in 1730, and produced his own comedies,
burlesques and farces, one of which, for holding Sir
Robert Walpole up to ridicule, brought about, in 1737,
the stringent Theatrical Licensing Act, by which the
London theatres were restricted to two, Drury Lane
and Covent Garden. From that time until 1766, when
Samuel Foote obtained a patent to open the house
during the summer months,[1] the little theatre led only

[1] How Foote obtained the licence is a curious story. At a country
house at which he and the Duke of York were staying, His Royal Highness for a practical joke mounted the comedian, who could not ride,
upon a spirited horse, with the result that he was thrown and his leg
broken. Foote at that time rented the Haymarket, and was driving
the proverbial coach and four through the Act of Parliament ; as a
compensation for the injury, the duke got him a patent legally to keep
open the house six months in the year.

a vagabond existence, its managers and actors being
more than once arrested for breaking the law.

After being repaired, patched, renovated, the original
building, or rather all that remained of it, was pulled
down in 1820, and the theatre of Webster and Buckstone took its place, which, though greatly altered by
the Bancrofts, remains practically the same. It is
probably a unique circumstance in the history of
theatres that the Haymarket, during the hundred and
seventy-eight years of its existence has never suffered
from fire, and only once from any serious accident—
on the occasion of the visit of George III. to the
house, February, 1794, when the crush at the pit
door was so great that fifteen people were killed and
twenty seriously injured.

But theatrical riots have been by no means uncommon at the little theatre. The most curious of these
occurred in 1805. Dowton announced for his benefit an old burlesque, " The Tailors," which had been
brought out by Foote ; it was a satire upon the sartorial
craft, who convened an indignation meeting of its
members, and resolved to oppose the performance with
might and main. A letter was sent to the *bénéficiaire*
signed DEATH, warning him that 17,000 tailors would
attend to hiss the piece, and that 10,000 more could
be found if wanted. The actors laughed. But on the
evening the knights of the needle contrived to secure,
with few exceptions, every seat in the house, while a
mob of tailors clamoured round the doors. When
Dowton appeared, some one threw a pair of shears at

him, then the whole audience bellowed and roared, and the crowd outside answered with bellows and roars and attempted to storm the house. Magistrates were summoned, special constables called out, but all were helpless against the overwhelming odds ; so formidable did the riot become that it was only quelled by a detachment of the Life Guards, who after taking sixteen prisoners put the rest of the mob to flight. The Haymarket was the last theatre which was lit by candles, gas not being introduced there until 1837, the first year of Webster's tenancy.

The Haymarket, in addition to its two theatres, was always noted for exhibitions, notorious among which was Mother Midnight's Oratory (1750), a sort of Barnum's show of monstrosities and trained animals.[1] Monkeys and dogs did acrobatic performances and danced a minuet ; a bear beat a drum ; birds spelled names and told the time by the clock ; turkeys executed a country dance ; there was a cats' concert, to ridicule the opera, by which the inventor cleared thousands ; a man who smoked out of a red-hot pipe and ate burning sulphur; giants, dwarfs, ventriloquists, dancing bears.

At the Cock Tavern, in Suffolk Street, the notorious Calves' Head Club held many of its meetings, on the 30th of January, to insult the memory of Charles I. According to Ned Ward the club was founded by Milton, and consisted of Independents and Anabaptists.

[1] See " Horace Walpole to George Montagu," 9th January, 1752, for a full account of the oratory.

They dined on a dish of calves' heads, to typify the late king and his friends; a copy of the *Icon Basilike* was burned; a calves' skull was filled with wine and passed round for the guests to drink to the pious memory of "those worthy patriots who had killed the tyrant".

Even forty years ago, and less, the Haymarket, after midnight, was considered by fast young men to be one of the sights of London, though by day it was one of the shabbiest and drowsiest of thoroughfares. Until noon most of its inhabitants slumbered : and until night the half-awake attendants in the shops and taverns regarded a stray customer with heavy-eyed surprise and indifference ; some of the proprietors did not trouble to take down their shutters before the shades of evening began to fall. Then the young ladies behind counters and bars rouse themselves and go away to take their hair out of curl papers, and change their "frocks," to reappear as transformed as the fairy of the footlights is from the fairy of the stage door ; while slovenly waiters, who have been crawling and yawning all day, suddenly develop spotless shirt fronts and become as brisk as harlequins. Twelve o'clock ! The opera ballet is just over ; Ellsler has performed her last pirouette, or Taglioni her last *pas*, or graceful Cerito has brought down the curtain with thunders of applause ; out rush the swells and every bar is quickly crammed with them clamouring for drinks, and in a great hurry to get into the Haymarket Theatre to see Ned Wright in a farce—he is paid £50 a week to appear after midnight. And a very good bargain Buckstone makes of it, as he frequently takes £150 a week after the witching hour. The little theatre gives you plenty for your money ; it begins at 7 P.M. and closes about 1 A.M. Sometimes you have a good long comedy and a drama and about three farces. After roaring at the irresistible Wright for three-quarters of an hour or so—Edmund Yates used to say that Wright made him laugh until he was a helpless mass— the swells again crowd oyster and restaurant bar, or perform wild gallops with their lady friends up and down roadway and pavement, or order a keg of gin to be brought into the open and serve the liquor out to their friends and every passer-by, beggar or loafer, that chooses to partake of it. It is a veritable pandemonium of shrieks and laughter, and language unfit for ears polite. And the demons scarcely relax their fury until daylight dims the gas and the traffic of a new day commences.

Pall Mall when first formed was named after Charles II.'s Queen, Catherine Street. But as early as 1666 Pepys writes of it as " Pell Mell ". At this time only a few houses were dotted here and there, in open country. Nell Gwynne lived for a time on the north side, but later on removed to the south. Evelyn relates in one of the entries of his *Diary*, 1671, how, while walking through St. James's Park, he saw and heard a very familiar discourse between (the king) and Mrs. Nellie, she looking out of her garden on the top of the wall and (the king) standing on the green walk under it. "Thence the king walked to the Duchess of Cleveland's"—who also lodged in Pell Mell. In the house just referred to, now No. 79, "poor Nelly," the best of a bad lot, died in 1687, and was buried in St. Martin's-in-the-Fields. The Army and Navy Club stands upon the site of her first dwelling, and I understand that a looking-glass that must have often reflected her saucy face, taken with the old house, is still preserved there.

Schomberg House, the eastern wing of which was rebuilt for the War Office, is associated with many notable people. Originally inhabited by William of Orange's famous general, it passed to Culloden Cumberland. After his death it was divided into tenements and became a haunt of artists; here lived John Astley, a noted portrait painter; Conway, the miniature painter, and Gainsborough, who died here. On the western side of Schomberg House lived Mrs. Fitzherbert, the wife of George IV., of whom I shall have much to say anon.

Notable among the residents of Pall Mall was that charming, delightful *comédienne* of the Garrick period, Mrs. Abington, the original Lady Teazle. Like all theatrical managers Garrick was a martyr to the ladies of his company, but Fanny Abington was the greatest plague of all, the most capricious and unreasonable. How full of mischief and *espièglerie* is the face that still peeps at you out of Sir Joshua's canvas; it is Miss Prue herself, just as Congreve conceived her. Mrs. Abington associated with ladies of the highest

rank, and her devotion to cards in her old age was
worthy of the time in which she lived. Not even in
the summer months could she tear herself away from
the pasteboard; to keep up appearances she shut up
her house, pretended to leave London, but was really
in lodgings in the immediate neighbourhood, where
she kept up her nightly rubbers. Yet in spite of this
sedentary life she attained the age of eighty-four.

Two celebrated houses, Marlborough and Carlton,
the one still flourishing, the other a thing of the past,
remain to be mentioned. The first was built for the
conqueror of Blenheim, by Sir Christopher Wren, in
1709, on the site of a religious house, the Friary. To
economise expense the parsimonious hero had the
bricks brought over from Holland as ballast and un-
loaded at Westminster, Dutch bricks being smaller
and much cheaper than English; six large mirrors
being required for its adornment, his careful Grace
petitioned the States-General of Holland that these
might be exported free of charge from that country,
and the petitioner was too powerful to be refused.
Though he died worth a million and a half of
money, he would in his old age walk through the
most inclement night to save a sedan hire. Before
his death Marlborough fell into a state of dotage,
and the mighty victor of Ramillies, Malplaquet, Blenheim became a whimpering old man who could walk
only by the support of two servants. Marlborough
House remembers him in his greatness, when crowds
gathered about its walls to applaud the conquering

hero; remembers him senile, tottering, crying, in
second childhood ; remembers that grand lying in
state of the dead soldier, that splendid funeral *cortège*,
than which, for solemn grandeur and military pomp,
England has seen the like but once since, when as
great a Captain—and a far nobler man—was carried
to the tomb,

> To the noise of the mourning of a mighty nation.

The Duchess, a woman who was as destitute of all
goodness as her lord, and without his genius to com-
pensate, survived the duke twenty years. Avaricious
to the last, though her income was £40,000 a year,
she was always heaping acre upon acre, and wearied
the Treasury by petitions for a few hundreds per
annum that she believed herself entitled to as Ranger
of Windsor Park. She lived to the age of eighty-four.

Marlborough House was leased from the crown, and
when the lease expired, between sixty and seventy
years ago, it was greatly enlarged for the Princess
Charlotte on her marriage. And there her widowed
husband continued to reside until he was called to
the throne of Belgium. Queen Adelaide was its next
occupant, and after her death the Vernon Gallery
pictures were exhibited there. At the marriage of
the Prince of Wales it again became a royal residence.

Carlton House was erected in the same year as
Marlborough, 1709, by the Earl of Burlington.
Twenty-one years afterwards it was purchased for
the father of George III. But Frederick preferred
Leicester House, and it is with the last of the Georges

SARAH, DUCHESS OF MARLBOROUGH.

that the former is more especially identified. Old Carlton House was but a mean building, and it was practically reconstructed for George of Wales in the classical style popular at the time. The centre was adorned by six Corinthian pillars, which now support the portico of the National Gallery, and this was flanked by two wings. Carlton House has furnished as much material, true and false, for the *Chroniques Scandaleuses* of the regency as *Le Parc aux Cerfs* did for those of Louis XV.

Sir Nathaniel Wraxall, in *Memoirs of My Own Time*, describes the banquets that were given here to celebrate Fox's victory in the Westminster election, 1784 —for the Prince of Wales was as noted a radical as George IV. was an unbending Tory—one of which lasted from the noon of one day to the morning of the next. A separate repast was served for the ladies : " On whom, in the spirit of chivalry, His Royal Highness and the gentlemen present waited while they were seated at table. It must be owned that on these occasions, for which he seemed peculiarly formed, the Prince appeared to great advantage. Louis XIV. himself could scarcely have eclipsed the son of George III. in a ballroom, or when doing the honours of his palace, surrounded by the pomps and attributes of luxury and royal state."

At Carlton House the Prince gathered about him all the men identified with the days of the Regency— Fox, Brummell, Moore, Sheridan, Colman, Kelly. Here the Princess Charlotte was born, apropos of whom the

Hon. Amelia Murray tells a good story. The engagement of the heiress presumptive to the English throne with the Prince of Orange was so disagreeable to Russia, that the Grand Duchess of Oldenburg made a journey to London to break it off, not by any direct means but by the usual Muscovite weapons, treachery and intrigue. Taking a house in Piccadilly the duchess gave a grand dinner party and ball; to the first the Prince of Orange was invited, to the second his *fiancée*. The duchess set the young man next to herself at table, and continually plied him with champagne, which it was impossible for a gentleman to decline under the circumstances; so that when he entered the ballroom, and solicited the princess's hand for a dance, he was very drunk indeed, and not being by any means good-looking or *distingué* was rather a disgusting spectacle in the eyes of a young girl of seventeen. Close at hand our *intriguante* had the handsomest and most fascinating young prince in Europe, Prince Leopold of Saxe-Coburg, to whom the princess was introduced, and who made such good use of his chance that soon afterwards the Orange was sent packing—and was secured by our grand duchess for her own sister. And that was how the Princess Charlotte became the wife of Prince Leopold. It was rather a curious coincidence that her present majesty should also marry a Saxe-Coburg, a nephew of Leopold, both princesses being likewise cousins and heiresses to the throne of England.

Gronow describes the Princess Charlotte as a young

lady of more than ordinary personal attractions, with
regular features and a fine complexion; blue eyes,
abundant hair, "such as the middle-age Italian painters
associate with their conceptions of the Madonna ". She
was over the ordinary height, well developed and
well proportioned, while her manners were remarkable for simplicity and good nature. The story of
her early death is extremely pathetic.

The York column, the Athenæum, the United Service Club and Carlton Terrace were erected upon the
land left vacant by the demolition of Carlton House
in 1828. The Carlton Club was built upon the site
of a famous tavern, the Star and Garter, wherein took
place that duel to the death between Lord Byron of
Newstead and Squire Chaworth of Nottinghamshire,
which arose out of a trivial dispute over dinner.
It was fought by the flickering flame of a fire, in a
room only twelve feet by six. Byron ran his opponent clean through the body. At nine o'clock the
next morning the unhappy gentleman breathed his
last. Lord Byron surrendered and took his trial in
Westminster Hall, but there was no shadow of proof of
malice prepense; Mr. Chaworth had been the challenger,
and furthermore was noted for his superior skill in the
use of the sword. Byron was acquitted. At his
death, in 1798, his grand-nephew, George Gordon
Byron, succeeded to the title and estates. Does
it not read like some old Greek story of Fate that
the heir should fall in love with Mary Chaworth,
whose grandfather his uncle had slain?

Although Golden Lane was lit by gas in 1807, Pall Mall was the first thoroughfare in the more central part of the town in which the new illuminant was used (1809). As a matter of course everybody jeered at the innovation, while some prophesied that all London would one night be sent flying up to the clouds. Even such scientists as Sir Humphrey Davey averred that it would be as easy to bring a bit of the moon down to light London with as to illuminate it with coal smoke.[1]

At the Restoration those of the nobles who had not mansions in the Strand were still living in the City, or in St. Clement's Lane, or Drury Lane, or Clare Market. Henry Jermyn, Earl of St. Albans, was the first to draw the aristocracy westward, by obtaining a piece of ground known as Pell Mell Field, where the king and his courtiers played the game so called— which was much the same as croquet—and building thereon a square, which from its vicinity to the palace was named St. James's.

We are greatly shocked in these days of sanitation to hear of a refuse heap outside an Irish cabin, but the ancestors even of blue-blooded English were almost as indifferent to noxious sights and smells at their very threshold as is a hibernian peasant. Macaulay thus describes the condition of St. James's Square,

[1] Until the last year of the reign of Charles II. no attempt was made to light the streets of London at night, but, in 1684, a projector, named Heminge, was granted letters patent to place a lantern before every tenth door on moonless nights from Michaelmas to Lady-day.

then recently built, in 1685 : " It was a receptacle for
all the offal and cinders and for all the dead cats and
dogs of Westminster. At one time a cudgel player
kept the ring there. At another time an impudent
squatter settled himself there, and built a shed for
rubbish under the windows of the gilded saloons in
which the first magnates of the realm—Norfolk, Ormond, Kent and Pembroke—gave banquets and balls.
It was not until these nuisances had lasted through a
whole generation, and till much had been written about
them, that the inhabitants applied to Parliament to
put up rails and plant trees." But although a pond
was subsequently sunk in the centre, and a fountain
squirted a stream of water, dead cats and all kinds
of rubbish continued to be shot there, even at the
time when Samuel Johnson and Richard Savage, the
poet, paced round and round the square on summer
nights, for lack of a lodging, inveighing against
ministers, making patriotic speeches and building
castles in the air.

The town house of all the Dukes of Norfolk, since
the time of Charles II., has been in this square (the
south-eastern corner) ; next door to it is the " official "
residence of the Bishops of London. It was in the
house two doors west of the London Library, then
tenanted by Mrs. Bohm, that the Prince Regent
received the first news of the victory of Waterloo; he
was dining there in company with Castlereagh and
other ministers. " It is a glorious victory," said the
Prince, after reading the despatch, "and we must

rejoice at it; but the loss has been fearful, and *I* have lost many friends." And while he spoke the tears ran down his cheeks. The great bibliophile, who has bequeathed his name to a club and that most famous collection of old ballads, the Duke of Roxburghe, resided at No. 20. The sale of his library, in 1812 occupied forty-two days.

Previous to his time the house had been the residence of the celebrated Right Hon. William Windham, statesman and scholar, in honour of whose memory the Windham Club, now held there, was instituted. It was of Windham that Dr. Johnson wrote: "Such conversation I shall not have again until I come back to the regions of literature,[1] and there Windham is, *inter stellas luna minores*". Yet Windham was a great upholder of the Prize Ring and warmly defended it in the newspapers. He seldom missed being present at a fight, and when a match was fought between two noted gladiators, Gully and "the Game Chicken," being detained in London by State affairs, so eager was he to know the result that he secretly employed a Government courier to bring him the news in a Government despatch box.

Castlereagh lived for a time at No. 18; Arabella Churchill, the sister of John and mistress of James II., at 21, and after her this same house was tenanted by Charles Montagu, Earl of Halifax, who, with Paterson, founded the Bank of England. The Sunderlands, Clarendons, Churchills, Oxfords have had their town

[1] He wrote this in Derbyshire.

houses here at different times.[1] Of one Lady Oxford
a good story is told. After leading a life of pleasure
as long as she was able to enjoy it, her ladyship was
" converted ". One day the Duchess of Buckingham
was telling how " her lord " was doing this, and " her
lord " was doing that, when Lady Oxford interrupted
her with the severe remark that she knew " no lord
but the Lord Jehovah ". " Oh dear, who is that ? "
inquired the duchess. " I suppose it is one of the
new titles, for I never heard of him before."

From St. James's Square it was but a step to
Almack's, that most renowned and most exclusive
arcanum of fashion that has ever existed in Europe.
" There is a new institution that begins to make, and
if it proceeds, will make a considerable noise," writes
Walpole to George Montagu, 6th May, 1770. " It is
a club of both sexes to be erected at Almac's, on the
mode of that of the men at White's. Mrs. Fitzroy,
Lady Pembroke, Mrs. Meynel, Lady Molyneux, Miss
Pelham and Miss Lloyd are the foundresses." The
club had been started about eighteen months previously ; but the rooms were built and opened for
balls and assemblies in 1765 by a tavern-keeper named
Almack. As it was impossible for two or three to
gather together without gambling, Almack's was no
exception to the rule, and indeed gaming was conducted there on an even more extravagant scale than
elsewhere. No stake less than fifty guinea *rouleaux*

[1] In 1676 the rates of one of the largest houses amounted to £10
per annum, while others were under £2 !

was permitted, and £10,000 would frequently be piled upon the table at one time.

Probably Almack's did not attain its highest glories until the days of Ladies Jersey, Castlereagh, Cowper, and the Princesses Esterhazy and Lieven, who ruled it with such despotic exclusiveness that to be admitted to its balls and assemblies was a greater honour than to be presented at court.

Captain Gronow tells us that out of 300 officers of the Foot Guards only half a dozen were admitted ; " very often persons whose rank entitled them to the *entré* anywhere were excluded by the cliqueism of the lady patronesses ". The Duke of Wellington was once refused admittance because he was not dressed *en règle.*

Here the first waltz (1813) was danced, and it is very suggestive to read of the horror it excited, not only among goody people, but in such moral censors as George Gordon Byron, who in " The Waltz " denounces the woman who indulges in its gyrations with all the fervour of a male prude.

> If such thou lovest—love her then no more,
> Or give, like her, caresses to a score,
> Her mind with these is gone, and with it go
> The little left behind it to bestow.

It reads yet stranger, however, to hear that the quadrille, introduced about the same time at Almack's, was quite as much objected to on the score of modesty by women—who never practised that virtue. Almack's was afterwards known as Willis's. There are two other institutions in King Street I would love to gossip about, the St. James's Theatre and Christie and Manson's, but space will not permit.

After Queen Anne's reign fashion entirely deserted the neighbourhood of Covent Garden and took up its permanent quarters to the west of Charing Cross, and "the sweet shady side of Pall Mall" was the place where most did congregate, the beaux, fops, dandies, bucks, bloods and swells, while those varieties of one species existed. The first who affected the region were the Macaronis, so called because it was they who introduced that favourite Italian dish into London, and Almack's. Can we not see them as they appeared in 1772, in an extremely close-cut jacket, waistcoat and breeches, an immense knot of artificial hair behind, like a chignon, a very small cocked hat, red-heeled shoes, and carrying an enormous walking cane, with long tassels, in their hands? Or a year afterwards in a very lofty head-dress, and a nosegay as big as a cabbage at their breast, talking a jargon of French-Italian-English, their faces painted and patched, their eyebrows pencilled, simpering and mincing like monkeys treading upon hot bricks, in winter time, their hands thrust into muffs?[1] Watch them at the gaming table. They begin by pulling off their

---

[1] Muffs, however, were in general use among men. "I send you a decent small muff, that you may put in your pocket; it cost fourteen shillings," wrote Walpole to George Montagu, Christmas, 1764. The beaux of Charles II. and James II.'s reign greatly affected the muff; it was small, lined with down and covered with satin, with a bow in front, and suspended by a ribbon round the neck.

embroidered clothes and putting on frieze greatcoats, or turning their coats inside out for luck. Then they put over their sleeves pieces of leather, such as are worn by footmen when they clean the knives, to save their laced ruffles, don high-crowned, broad-brimmed straw hats, trimmed with flowers and ribbons, to guard their eyes from the light and to preserve their hair from being tumbled, while they cover their faces with masks, in order that no change of expression, occasioned by gain or loss, may be visible, imperturbability being the correct form on these occasions.

Carlton House was the focus of the dandies during the Regency. How familiar the caricatures of Bunbury and Rowlandson, and other satirists of the end of the eighteenth and the beginning of the nineteenth centuries have made us with those English *Incroyables*, in extraordinary striped trousers, which had taken the place of breeches and skin-tight pantaloons, fulled very much at the hips and strapped tightly over the boots; in blue swallow-tailed coats, or braided frocks with collars half-way up the head, tight sleeves and brass buttons; buff or striped vests; huge cravats, bell-crowned beaver hats of enormous expansion, with only the narrowest border of a brim, promenading with a pompous or simpering air that would now be considered exaggerated in burlesque. And their fair companions, fat as cooks, in short dresses, so skimping that they could not step over a gutter, waists under the arm-pits, no petticoats beneath, sandalled shoes, huge bonnets with gigantic plumes of feathers, the *ensemble* of all the colours of the rainbow.

We are always fond of a fling at fashion, even in the present day ; but we do not make apes and dolls and monsters of ourselves as did our great-grand-fathers and great-grandmothers.

Note to p. 317.—As a curious contrast to Lady Amelia Murray's picture of Prince Leopold I subjoin another of the Princess Charlotte's widower, taken from the memoirs of Karoline Bauer, the celebrated German actress. It is her first impression of her future lover.

"He wore an unusually long surtout of black cloth, tightly buttoned from top to bottom. His short black hair, glossy with pomatum, turned out by daylight to be a very ingeniously made wig. Add to this his pale, languid complexion, his weary, weary expression, his stooping, relaxed gait, his slow, deliberate, subdued way of speak-ing—all this reminded one more of a pedantic, recluse professor and old bachelor of upwards of fifty than of a gay prince of eight-and-thirty. Only his finely shaped mouth, with its pleasing smile, and his large, dark, melancholy eyes were exceedingly interesting and attractive."

CHAPTER XIX.

THE GHOSTS OF ST. JAMES'S PALACE.

COULD a spiritualist summon up from their graves the *genii loci* of that gloomy pile of smoke-stained bricks called St. James's Palace, what a curious dance of death it would be. On all Mudie's shelves there are not so much *real* romance, so much of love and hate, of pomp and sordidness, of satire, absurdity and thrilling sensations as those walls have witnessed.

The early associations of the spot are gruesome enough. As I have already noted in my chapter on St. Giles's, a leper hospital was founded here. It was in the days of the Norman kings, when the terrible scourge of leprosy was almost as prevalent among the western as it was among eastern nations, that some pious soul endowed this house of refuge for " maidens that were leprous" and dedicated it to St. James the Less.

Think of the generations of ghastly faces that, through hundreds of years, gazed drearily across the desolate swamps which lay between them and the river! Loathed, abhorred, dreaded, a touch of their garments pollution, for ever cut off from the world outside their living tomb. No hope but death!

(327)

Could all the pessimism, the agonies, the terrors of
all the psychological novels ever written descend to
the depths of those isolated, despairing souls when
from the windows of their oubliettes they looked
out upon the beauty of summer, heard the birds
warbling, the joyous song of the lark and laughter
of happy children, watched young lovers, and husbands and wives strolling about the pastures that
stretched away from the gates of the hospital? All
the world seemed full of love and happiness save
that one God-accursed spot which they must never
leave. Not even these wretched lepers, however, could
escape the savage greed of Bluebeard Henry, who
seized upon the revenues of the hospital, converted
the land into a hunting park and game preserve,
pulled down the house and erected thereon a palace,
of which only the old gateway and a part of the
chapel remain.

What a transformation from that gruesome charnel-
house with its living corpses to the gayest and most
superb court of Europe! Kennington had hitherto
been the rural palace of our kings, and it was just
after his marriage with Anne Boleyn that Henry
came to St. James's. Health and beauty now laughed
and romped and danced and sang and disported
themselves, where those living ghosts had groaned
and sobbed and prayed and dirged and rotted. Forth
at dawn from the gateway, to the jocund sounds of
horns and the barking of the hounds, issue a splendid
cavalcade of hunters and lords and ladies, with the

king and queen at their head, glittering in green and
gold, to hunt the stag, which, after a glorious chase
over the frosted grass of St. James's Fields, right away

PRINCESS CHARLOTTE.

to Edgeware and Harrow, will be brought home in
triumph. Then the banquet, and afterwards the dance
to the strains of the harp and viol and sackbut. What

a kaleidoscope of gorgeous colours and jewelled splendour where but a short time before there were only ashen grey and funereal black! On a May morning the royalties and a joyous retinue of knights and squires and dames and demoiselles, all arrayed in white and silver, ride into the fields and return laden with hawthorn branches and sweet wild flowers.[1] Many a time might Henry and beautiful Anne have stood against the mantelpiece—which may still be seen in the old presence chamber, with the initials " H. and A." entwined in a true loveknot—hand clasped in hand, eyes gazing into eyes, unconscious of the red spectre and the gleaming axe that lurked in the shadows of the coming time.

Those were the palmy days of St. James's ; it has known nothing like them since. Mary and long-chinned Philip of Spain, not then a gloomy bigot but quite a preux chevalier, have many a time been shadowed by that frowning archway ; and in this palace the wretched woman, who deserves our pity as much as our execration, passed out of a world that had never been much more than a lone dungeon to her. Among the crowd of ghosts we catch

[1] Stow tells us how Henry and his queen, Catherine, from the Palace at Greenwich, accompanied by the court, went Maying over Shooter's Hill, and met a company of archers dressed as Robin Hood and his merry men. Elizabeth followed the same old custom. Pepys notes (1667) meeting, on his way to Westminster, many milkmaids, with their garlands upon their pails, dancing with a fiddler before. The old lyrists, especially Herrick, are full of allusions to " Maying ". It need scarcely be added that it is a survival of Beltane, or sun worship.

a glimpse of the sharp features of " the virgin queen," but St. James's was never a favourite abode of hers, and her successor preferred the more gorgeous White-hall.   But it was here that his son Henry, Prince of Wales, a noble youth of great promise, breathed his last.   Had he lived to succeed to the throne instead of his brother Charles, the whole future history of England might have been different.   A notable ghost, not to be overlooked, is that of beautiful and stately Marie de Medicis, the consort of the great Henri and mother of Henrietta Maria—was she privy to her husband's assassination?   God knows, and only He.   She held a little court in St. James's for three years, and then went away to die in a garret in Cologne.   What an end to so much greatness!   The Stuart and Medici blood was a fatal combination; each was a doomed race, and all that sprang from it died miserably.   The fateful visage of Charles the Martyr reminds us that within those walls he and his queen passed some of the happiest hours of their lives; and, terrible contrast, it was there that he took the last agonising leave of his younger children, and slept his last living sleep on that sombre January night that preceded his execution.   And so like "the blood-bolter'd Banquo" the shadow of the pale king fades away.

Hey, presto!   " Hence, loathed melancholy!" Here is a new troupe of ghosts bringing with them—

> Jest and youthful jollity,
> Quips and cranks and wanton wiles,

Nods and becks and wreathèd smiles,
Such as hang on Hebe's cheek,
And love to live in dimple sleek ;
Sport that wrinkled care derides
And laughter holding both his sides.

It is "the merry monarch" and his Comus crew, the
Rochesters, Buckinghams, Dorsets, Sedleys, Ethereges,
De Grammonts in their flowing periwigs, plumed
beavers, laces, and be-ribboned velvets ; laughing-
eyed Nell Gwynne, voluptuous Castlemaine, baby-
faced Louise de la Querouaille, La belle Stuart, that
white dove among the soiled ones, immortalized on
our coinage as Britannia, and in the midst of them
" Old Rowley " himself, gay and *sans souci* as though
there were no cares of state, and life was one perpetual
holiday.   And so it is for him.   And with peals of
laughter they fade away towards the Mall.   In the
wake of the jovial rout plods saturnine James and
haggard Mary of Modena, who within those walls has
given birth to the last prince of the Stuart line born
within his kingdom.   A hacking cough announces the
presence of Dutch William ; he and his beloved Mary
were married in the chapel.

Now comes the unwieldy figure of plethoric, heavy-
eyed Anne, who, with ever-watchful Sarah Churchill
on one side, and Mrs. Masham on the other, the two
tyrants of the poor queen, who hate each other like
poison, is about to go through, for the last time in
history, a ceremony which has been performed by
English sovereigns since the days of Edward the
Confessor—touching for the king's-evil.   A crowd of

people is assembled round the gateway, men, women, children, infants in arms, all more or less disfigured by scrofulous blotches and sores. Among them is a masculine woman of about fifty, with a hydrocephalic-looking boy in her arms, much scarred. It is the wife of a Lichfield bookseller, named Johnson, who, on the recommendation of a great physician, has brought her son Samuel to essay the healing powers of the royal hand. At the approach of the queen all kneel ; then at a signal the people one by one approach the chair, on which the sovereign has seated herself, and upon each sufferer she lays her hand while a prayer is offered up. Then each is presented with a small gold coin, or " touch piece," and goes away devoutly believing that a cure is effected. Thereafter little boy Johnson will describe it all and how he remembers the queen as a stout, florid-faced lady, attired in black, that sparkled with diamonds, and wearing also a long black hood. Some of those touch pieces, too, will be treasured up for generations.

And so fades away the last of the Stuarts, and enter heavy-jowled, potato-digging George of Hanover, who looks more fitted to handle a spade than a sceptre, and on each side of him a German frau, Madame Kielmensegge, Countess of Darlington, tall and scraggy, nicknamed "the Maypole"; and Madame Schulenberg, Duchess of Kendal, fat and flabby, rejoicing or not rejoicing in the sobriquet of " the Elephant," but quite to the taste of the man who hates " blays and boetry " and England and the English ; who never speaks their language, never associates with them, but only with his Hanoverians, whom he has brought over to help him plunder the nation—and they do that work bravely.

Close at his heels is a dapper, strutting, lobster-eyed little man, upon whom the ghost casts a hateful scowl : it is his son and heir. And yet he is worthy of such a parent, for he also loves a fat frau, he too rages like a bull at the sight of a book or a work of art, detests everything and everybody not German, and but for the plunder would soon shake every particle of English dust from his shoes and go back to beloved Hanover, which he visits so frequently that one day the following placard is affixed by some wag against the gateway of St. James's : " Lost, stole or strayed out of his house a man who has left a wife and six children on the parish. Whoever will give any tidings of him to the churchwardens of St. James's Parish, so he may be got again, shall receive four shillings and sixpence reward. This reward will not be increased, nobody judging him to be worth a crown." Another time a wretched worn-out horse, blind and lame, is driven through St. James's Court ; he has a broken saddle and a ragged pillion upon his back, and this inscription is affixed to his forehead : " Let no one stop me, I am the king's Hanover equipage going to fetch his majesty and his harlots to England ".

Beside this little red-heeled ghost stands stately and beautiful Caroline of Anspach, his consort, a woman of culture and keen intellect, who actually loves

this ridiculous fantoccino—but did not Titania love
Bottom ?—even to the toleration of his amours ; and
when tow-haired, stupid but kindly Lady Suffolk,
thinking herself neglected by her royal lover, threatens
to quit St. James's, Her Majesty is complaisant
enough to write and say how much she would regret
her loss and to beg her to remain. When George brings
fat frau Walmoden from Hanover he presents her to
the queen with this recommendation : " I am sure you
will love her because she loves me ! "   Was ever anything so delicious !   But Caroline, with the aid of Sir
Robert Walpole, rules the court in state affairs, and
dapper George is the only person who is unconscious
of it, for he snubs his wife and then struts and crows
like a bantam cock.   " Governed by my wife, oh, oh !
ah, ah ! "

That very shadowy, foppish-looking figure, pale even
for a ghost, is Lord Hervey—Pope called him "that
white curd of ass's milk," but the great satirist was
unjust to the English St. Simon, who is making notes
for his famous *Memoirs*, in which he will show us
some wonderful pictures of the domestic life of this
curious court.   Here is an evening piece :—

A gloomy apartment in the palace lit up by a few
tallow candles sparsely distributed ; at a table sits the
queen, knitting and yawning, while her spouse, his
little figure clad *à la militaire* and his plethoric visage
framed in powdered peruke, is walking up and down,
soundly rating her for giving vails to the servants at
the houses she visits.   " My fader was never fool

enough to give away his money," he growls. Caroline says no more, snuffs her solitary dip and knits placidly, until the coming in of the Count de Roncy and his sister; then the king talks of military matters and genealogies, Caroline dozes, presently snores; the company depart and Darby and Joan go to bed.[1]

Another night picture. George and Lady Deloraine—one of the harem—are seated at a table playing cards, when one of the princesses, who hate the sultanas, pulls the chair from beneath her ladyship and down goes La Deloraine in a conceivably ungraceful position. Little George laughs until his eyes almost start from their sockets, and everybody joins in. The sultana picks herself up and, livid with fury, clutches savagely at the royal seat and down comes the cachinnating king with a sounding thump. Awful consternation! There is a wild rush to help the fallen monarch, who, struggling to his feet and rubbing the injured part, shrieks out such furious imprecations in

[1] The life of his grandson, George III., and his household at Buckingham Palace was equally dreary; every day was precisely the same as the one that preceded it, and every act—eating, walking, riding, sleeping—never varied by the clock. George was mediocrity personified and he liked only mediocre people; he had no liking for great ministers, great painters or great poets. He did not like Burke nor Nelson, Reynolds nor Shakespeare. When he went to the theatre he loved plenty of buffoonery, at which he laughed till he was purple in the face. He was as ignorant and as stupid as his grandfather, but he was impeccably respectable — alas! stupidity and respectability are usually synonymous: " 'Tis true, and pity 'tis, 'tis true ". But the second George had a very clever queen, the third of that name had one as narrow and obtuse as himself; if he had had a Caroline he might not have lost the American colonies.

high Dutch that La Deloraine flies terror-struck and is seen no more.

When this crowned Simon Tappertit is in Hanover, the queen, who has a taste for art and literature, holds *levée*, according to the fashion of her time, at her toilette, and while her maids are assisting her to dress, the ante-chamber is crowded with gentlemen ; the brilliant costumes of the courtiers mingling with the black cassocks of the clergy and the shabby slovenliness of the literati.

The conversation is very mixed ; the sententious lip morality of Dr. Young, who is then writing *Night Thoughts*, and who, between ourselves, is as destitute of morals and religion as—well, any of the company, is shot by the *piquant* scandal or *double entendres* of a Mirabel, or the polished worldly aphorisms of Chesterfield ; and the playful wit of Gay is pointed by the wicked sneer of the owner of Strawberry Hill, while a little, deformed, withered-up man in black, named Alexander Pope, is gathering hints for those *Satires* in which he will gibbet some of the assembly for all time.   Now and again, when some more delicate operation of the royal toilette is being performed, the chamber door is closed, and some of the more complaisant will kneel down and talk to the queen through the keyhole.   George hates " bictures " as much as he does books ; the only one that he will tolerate is a gross, ugly German Venus.   When he is away the queen has this filthy thing removed, and some works of art hung round the private apartments.

22

But he would storm and rage were he to miss the hideous daub, which has to be replaced at the first warning of his coming, and the other pictures have to be hidden away.

The women of such a court, as may be imagined, are worthy of it. Licentious as was the age of the second Charles, it was far exceeded in gross brutalism by that of the two first Hanoverian kings. A couple of exceptions may be made in favour of beautiful Molly Lepell, afterwards Lady Hervey, and saucy, enchanting Mary Bellenden, who was made a colonel of infantry in her second year—could the ambition of the most advanced women go beyond that! And she was brave enough to throw the infamous gold that Prince Frederick tendered her in the royal satyr's face.

Another picture of this noble king. Caroline is dying, and M. le mari, with a white nightcap drawn over his dumpling head, in nightgown and slippers his feet upon the fender, is keeping watch. "You look like a calf with his throat cut!" he cries, as she stares vacantly with fast-glazing eyes. The next minute he breaks out into a blubber; that passed he begins to expatiate upon his own virtues and wonderful bravery. One of his daughters is in the room and pretends to be asleep, but when her royal dad has gone bursts out: "I have been bored to death by his stories: I believe they are all lies; his bravery exists only in his imagination, and I believe he is as frightened in a battle as I should be!" But there she was unjust to papa ; dapper George was brave ; when his horse ran away with him at Dettingen he dismounted and went into the thick of the fight on foot. He was the last king of England who led his army on the field of battle. " You must marry again," are almost the last words of the queen. " No, no ; I will only have mistresses," blubbers George. " Oh, that will do as well," she answers complacently.

Last scene of all—25th October, 1760. On that morning, when the royal valet enters the royal chamber with the royal chocolate, he finds his royal master lying upon the floor—dead.

George III. little affected St. James's, but it was during his reign that the most mysterious tragedy in its annals—as far as we know—was enacted. Here resided the Duke of Cumberland, the most unpopular of the king's sons—perhaps on account of his repulsive ugliness. On the morning of 31st March, 1810, Neale, the duke's page, who sleeps in a closet adjoining his master's bed-chamber, is startled out of his sleep by a cry of "murder!" and sees the duke standing beside him pale and trembling, his nightgown stained with blood ; he stammers out that his Corsican valet, Sellis, has entered his room and attacked him in his sleep, and that when he jumped out of bed, the assassin pursued him and wounded him in the thigh with a knife. The cries of the page and the duke rouse the palace ; some rush off to Sellis's room ; the door is locked inside and no answer is returned to their summons, but there is *another entrance*

by which they gain admittance. The morning is just
breaking, and by the dim grey light they perceive a
figure in a semi-erect position upon the bed ; it is
bathed in blood and the head is almost severed from
the body. The theory is that, after failing in his attempt upon his master's life, he has committed suicide.
It is curious, however, that some severe wounds are
found on the back of his neck, and that though a
left-handed man he must have cut his throat with his
right hand. Some say he was jealous of his wife with
the duke ; others that it was to avenge the coarse abuse
that his master was in the habit of using against the
Romish religion. But a few darkly hint that Sellis
knew too many of His Royal Highness's secrets, that
the duke's wounds were self-inflicted to throw off
suspicion, but ——

The ghosts have vanished. Looming through the
foggy night is the old gateway upon which all those
living eyes have rested, hugging its dark secrets ;
and beating upon the dull ear of the night is the
tramp of the sentry that has never ceased night or
day through all the centuries. It was heard by Henry
and Anne Boleyn, it is heard by Victoria, and will be
heard perhaps by generations of her successors.

CHAPTER XX.

IN the days when this great centre of fashionable,
political and club life was not, and its lines were indicated only by a by-way leading to the leper hospital,
there was a quiet roadside inn on the western side,
near the gates of the spital, covered with roses and
woodbine, called the Thatched House, a common
sign in those days. At this time it was mostly used
by the rustics who tilled the land round about, or by
persons who came to and from that ghastly house of
refuge. But when the court was brought to its doors,
the humble tavern rose in importance, and, in the
reign of Queen Anne, it became a favourite resort of
the wits and beaux and politicians. Yet few changes
had been made in it since the Tudor days, when
humble labourers were almost its sole guests: the
floor was sanded, the furniture rough and uncouth,
and so limited were its resources that Dean Swift, after
dining there with people of fashion, noted in his
Journal to Stella that the company had to send out
for their wine. But gentlemen were content with the
humblest accommodation in those days, and lords dined

(341)

in rooms which a clerk would scorn in this sybaritish
era.[1]   In the middle of the century it became the headquarters of a number of literary and artistic societies.
Here, after its removal from the Turk's Head, where
we visited it in our wanderings about Soho, met the
Literary Club.   Here was established the no less
celebrated Dilettanti Society.   Horace Walpole said
that the nominal qualification for being a dilettanti
was having been in Italy, "and the real one being
drunk ".   But this was mere cynicism, as some of the
most distinguished of the nobility and men of taste
and learning belonged to it between 1734 and 1835.
The old Thatched House was not pulled down until
1843.

Quite as famous was the Cocoa Tree Chocolate-
house, now No. 64 ; it was the great Tory resort, as
the St. James's Coffee-house, the last house but one
at the west corner of the street, was the rendezvous of
the Whigs in the reign of Queen Anne and long afterwards.   The latter survived until 1806, but Brooks's,
started in the middle of the last century, had long
superseded it as a rallying place of the party.

Of those early clubs, associated with the wits of
Queen Anne's time, only White's remains.   And indeed White's, which was originally a Chocolate-house,
was founded in the reign of Charles II.   During the

---

[1] Some of the Chocolate-houses, however, seem to have been fitted
up in a modern manner.   Lord Foppington says : " If it be nasty
weather I take a turn in the chocolate-house, where, as you walk,
madam, you have the prettiest prospect in the world ; you have
looking-glasses all round you ".

last 200 years it has numbered among its members some of the most famous names in English political and social history. How many immortals have gazed through that famous bow window, not only the immortals of history, but those very much more real immortals, the immortals of fiction. Can lovers of Thackeray pass it without the figures of Major Pendennis and those whom the great novelist has associated with him rising upon their imagination?

White's has always been the most exclusive of clubs; neither rank, nor fame, nor genius was ever an infallible "open sesame!" to its doors; indeed, "pilling" has sometimes been resorted to upon no other grounds than mere whim. Even in our own time the Prince of Wales was not potent enough to obtain permission to smoke in the drawing-room ; the question was put to the committee and vetoed, a refusal which lec to the founding of the Marlborough.

Apropos of the number of years even the most eligible candidate has to wait for election to White's, a good story is told. When the heir to a certain Tory dukedom was born the butler first registered the infant's birth then left a nomination paper at the club, so that by the time the young gentleman came of age he might have a chance of admission to the charmed circle. One actor, and only one, ever obtained the privilege of membership, and that was Colley Cibber. Disraeli regarded it as the highest of social distinctions. Both Louis Napoleon and Count D'Orsay were blackballed.

In pre-reform days there were always pocket-boroughs to be bought, or had for the asking, at White's. The head waiter was once presented with one. But then the head waiter at White's was a personage of importance who made a big income. M. le garçon, just referred to, married the proprietor's daughter, and was made a knight as well as an M.P. Although never so notorious for gambling as Brooks's, play ran very high at White's in the old days. The first Lord Mountford, after supping and playing there one night, sent for his lawyer, made his will, invited some friends to dine with him next day, played the host to perfection, and then went into another room and shot himself.

White's, however, was most famous for extraordinary wagers. Mr. Algernon Bourke, in his History of the Club, gives the betting-book from 1743 to 1848, a most curious record of the Englishman's mania for making anything and everything the excuse for a bet. Politics, private affairs, matrimonial prospects figure largely in the list of subjects. Noble lords and gentlemen staked their guineas upon every movement of Buonaparte, the duration of ministries, and whether so and so would be married within a certain time.

But even more curious are the bets of the moment, to be found in the gossip of the last century; two drops of rain trickling down the window-panes excite the idlers to wager as to which will first reach the bottom; a woman is coming up the street with a basket of crockery-ware very lightly poised upon her head; " It will drop before she is opposite this window ! " cries

one ; " I'll lay you five guineas it doesn't," cries another.
" Done ! " half a dozen others join in. Just as the
hawker reaches the club, down goes the basket with a
crash. There is great rejoicing with the winners who,
however, give her a handsome solatium. Horace
Walpole relates how a man dropped down lifeless at
the door of the club, and when the body was brought
inside the members fell to betting as to whether he was
dead or not. Upon the doctor preparing to use the
lancet the " ayes " interposed and said it would be unfair
to them to attempt to revive him. As late as 1856
Lord F. Cavendish bet Mr. H. Brownrigg that he
would not kill a bluebottle fly before he went to bed.

Famous, or rather infamous, among St. James's
Street Clubs was "Crockford's". William Crockford
was originally a fishmonger, a speculator in trade and a
Turf sharp ; a lucky hit on the Derby laid the foundation of his fortunes. In 1816 he took the ground
floor of a house in King Street, St. James's, and, while
still pursuing his old calling, opened it as a gambling
saloon. Crockford was a second Midas ; whatever
he touched turned to gold ; two more houses were
soon added to enlarge the establishment. And in
1827 he erected a palatial building, for that period,
and named it Crockford's Clubhouse (now the Devonshire). Magnificent rooms, *à la Louis Quatorze*, gilded
pillars, painted ceilings, ormolu, *marqueterie*, were a
marvellous advance upon the dingy "hells" of Leicester
Square.

There were 800 members ; each one paid fifty

guineas entrance fee, and a subscription of ten guineas. "Morning play" began at 4 P.M. and lasted until 7 P.M., during which the stakes were from half a guinea to fifty, the bank standing at £2500. But this was mere bagatelle. The real gambling commenced at eleven with a bank at £10,000, while the stakes were practically unlimited. Men who one day had been surrounded by all the luxuries that fortune could provide were often reduced to beggary by one night's play. The proprietor, never interfering with the business of the tables, sat at his desk in a far corner of the room watching his croupiers rake up the stakes, like some bloated spider gloating over the flies entangled in his net, unmoved by the sight of the wrecked bodies and souls he fattened upon. It was a face white, flabby and fishlike, heavy and expressionless, except for the small, cunning eyes; when he laughed he showed a large, loose mouth filled with aggressive white teeth; his bald head was covered by a brown wig; his hands were quite destitute of knuckles and so pallid that they resembled raw veal.

Yet Lord Leamington, in *The Days of the Dandies*, tells us that Crockford's was the *beau idéal* of a club. "The notion that any man of large fortune was at once elected a member to pluck and pigeon him was absurd. It was very difficult for any one, however well known or highly considered, to be elected a member of Crockford's. . . . During the parliamentary season supper was provided from twelve o'clock to five in the morning—and such a supper! Francatelli

was the *chef*. I rather think he received £800 a year.
But there was every dish and drink that could gratify
the most fastidious taste ; and night after night were
met there all those who were noted for any superiority,
intellectual or personal. Politics, literature, art, fashion,
rank ; the wit, the courtier, the poet, the historian, the
politician were found at the table. It was frequently
a tilt of freshest wit and clever repartee." This other
picture, however, by no means invalidates the previous
one, the club was kept distinct from "the hell," which
was situated at the end of a long suite of magnificent
apartments.

There was a Nemesis in the end of " the father of hell
and hazard," as he was nicknamed. His horse, Ratan,
which was regarded a certainty for the Derby, had been
hocussed, as it was supposed through the instrumenta-
lity of a brother hell-keeper, Goody Levi, who had
sworn his destruction. This loss and disappointment
brought on a paralytic seizure, of which Crockford
died on the night after the Epsom event. Large sums
of money, however, depended upon his living over the
Oaks day ; his death was known only to his associates,
who hit upon a daring and ghastly idea to save their
stakes : they sat the corpse in its ordinary attire with
the usual white hat upon its head, at one of the
windows and made it wave one of its dead hands at
the people returning from the race, thereby establish-
ing an alibi. A few hours afterwards it was all over
London that William Crockford had dropped down
dead. The story is told by Serjeant Ballantyne.

Among the notabilities who have dwelt in St.
James's Street were Edmund Waller, the poet; Alexander Pope; Gibbon, who died in No. 76; Sir Christopher Wren, whose funeral *cortège* started from one
of these houses for St. Paul's; and Charles James
Fox. Thackeray wrote *Barry Lyndon* at No. 88.

Nor must I omit from the list a person who would
have considered himself quite equal to any just named,
and certainly superior to a mere author. I allude to
Hoby, bootmaker to George III., the royal princes,
and dukes and marquises galore, to all of whom he
was both pompous and impertinent. To Sir John
Shelley's complaint that his topboots had split in
several places when he was walking to the stables, " I
made the boots for riding, not walking," sneered Hoby.
While this superfine disciple of St. Crispin was with
the Duke of Kent trying on a pair of boots on his
Royal Highness, the news arrived of the great battle
of Vittoria. "If Lord Wellington," remarked Hoby
coolly, " had had any other bootmaker than myself, he
would never have had his great and constant successes ;
for my boots and prayers bring his lordship out of all
his difficulties!" Hoby had had "a call," he was a
Methodist preacher, he employed 300 workmen, and
died worth £120,000. His shop was at the Piccadilly
corner, next to the Old Guard's Club.

A curious story of fatality attaches to the rest at
the top of St. James's Street. Mr. Pierrepoint, a
member of White's, had long been haunted by the
danger of the crossing just there, and after appealing

to the vestry in vain, he, with their permission, had a refuge made at his own expense. One day he was showing it to a friend when in stepping on one side he was knocked down by a passing cab and killed.

Passing into that quiet nook, St. James's Place, we are surrounded by memories of famous people who have lived within its precincts. Henry St. John ; Lord Bolingbroke, the famous statesman ; Addison ; John Wilkes; Secretary Craggs; Parnell, the poet; "the beautiful Molly Lepell," whom we met at St. James's Palace; Sir Francis Burdett, who died there in 1844. Quite a romance is the story of " Old Glory's " death. He and his wife had just completed their half-century of married life when her ladyship passed away ; utterly prostrated by his bereavement Sir Francis from that hour refused all nourishment, and within ten days rejoined her in the land of spirits. So this new Baucis and Philemon were on the same day interred in the same vault.

In St. James's Place lived Samuel Rogers, poet and banker. He resided at No. 22 from 1808 until his death in 1855. The house is best known by the old-fashioned bow-windowed back, which looks out upon the Green Park. Here were given those famous literary breakfasts, which became world-famous. The *déjeuner* was at ten, the number of the invited never exceeded six, and often was limited to three ; the repast did not finish before noon, and sometimes not until an hour later. During that half-century there was scarcely a literary, artistic, political or social celebrity who had

not sat at Rogers' table, and it was one of the greatest
privileges of aspiring young men to obtain an entrance
to that charmed circle. Not an amiable man was
the author of *Pleasures of Memory;* witty, though
many of the good things attributed to him were the
offspring of others ; nor was his appearance by any
means attractive, indeed it was said that he was the
ugliest man in England :—

> Eyes of lead-like hue and gummy,
> Carcass picked out from some mummy :
> Vampire, ghoul or ghost, which is it ?

wrote Byron, who conceived an enmity against him.
Rogers' poems are now almost forgotten. So slowly
did he write that Sidney Smith said of him : " When
Rogers produces a couplet he goes to bed, the knocker
is tied, the straw is laid down, and the caudle is made,
and the answer to inquiries is that Mr. Rogers is
as well as can be expected ". The conversation at
these gatherings was always upon literary and artistic subjects, and when carried on by such people
as Moore, Campbell, Coleridge, Shelley, Haydon,
Wordsworth, the host himself, Caroline Norton—for
ladies were not excluded—it must indeed have been
an intellectual feast.

To individualise all the famous people who have
been associated with St. James's Street from the
days of Charles II. would be impossible. We can
picture the belles and beaux of the Stuart days in
gilded sedan chairs, borne by gorgeous footmen, or in
emblazoned carriages drawn by six Flanders mares,

and attended by half a dozen gold-laced lacqueys,
or swaggering and sauntering on foot to the palace,
and when night fell escorted by a procession of torch-
bearers—a very necessary precaution, as the precincts
of the court in those days were no more exempt
from ruffianism than was the rest of the metropolis.

As an instance : one night Colonel Blood, he who
stole the crown jewels from the Tower, with a party
of scoundrels, to avenge some real or reputed wrong,
attacked the carriage of the great Ormond, dragged
out the duke, in spite of his resistance and that of his
servants, bound him hand and foot, and would have
carried their prisoner to Tyburn, and there hanged
him, had not some of his retinue, who contrived to
escape, raised a rescue party at Clarendon House.

Can we not picture Dean Swift, in rusty cassock,
on his way to the Cocoa Tree ; and prim Addison,
and careless, swaggering Dicky Steele strolling towards the St. James's Coffee-house to plan the next
Spectator ? Bovine Sir Robert Walpole, after a night
of drunken debauch, dirty and unkempt, is being
carried in a sedan to a council at the palace ; while
from a window of White's the distinguished figure of
his great rival, Bolingbroke, is watching him with the
curled lip of contempt. That gaunt, eagle-eyed man
with the Roman nose is the great Mr. Pitt, whose
mighty genius has in so brief a time raised England
from the lowest depth of degradation to be the all-
conquering nation of Europe. Ponderous Dr. Johnson,

peach-blossomed Goldsmith, brilliant Edmund Burke, quick-eyed Garrick, placid-faced Reynolds are passing into the Thatched House—it is the Literary Club night. Not far behind are the burly, buff and blue figure of Fox, and debonair George of Wales, garnishing his talk with as many expletives as a cabman would now, arm in arm with dun-hunted Brinsley Sheridan ; they are making their way to Brooks's, where they will gamble all through the night, and perhaps until the House meets the next day.[1] Coming out of Duke Street, where he lives,

[1] In the recently published *Letters of George Selwyn* we have some vivid pictures of Fox and his doings. Selwyn tells how heavily taxed Lord Holland's wealth was by the gambling debts of this scapegrace son. Charles James was as thoroughly unprincipled as Sheridan himself, and great abilities, social amenities, and a fascinating *bonhomie* have cast a false glamour over two men who, had they been less distinguished, would have been dubbed heartless rogues. Fox entangled Lord Carlisle into signing bonds in almost precisely the same manner as did the scion of a great house just lately, but was more fortunate in escaping the just penalty. In 1781 he started a common faro table. "This faro bank," writes Selwyn, "is held in a manner which, being so exposed to public view, bids defiance to all decency and police. The whole town, as it passes, views the dealer and punters by means of the candles, and the windows being level with the ground. The opposition, who have Charles for their ablest advocate, is quite ashamed of the proceeding, and hates to hear it mentioned."

Here is a suggestive sketch of the Whig leader : "I saw Charles to-day in a new hat, frock, waistcoat, shirt, and stockings; he was as clean and smug as a gentleman ; his old clothes, I suppose, have been burned, like the paupers', at Salt Hill ". A fortnight after this date, however, our letter-writer paints quite another scene : "The passers-by in St. James's Street were much amused with seeing two carts at Charles's door filled by the Jews with his goods, clothes, books, pictures. Such dirty furniture I never saw."

is broad-faced, beaming Tom Moore, in blue frock coat and buff waistcoat, humming, in a dulcet voice, one of his own " Melodies". Here comes William Pitt, the younger, with nose in air ; every hat is doffed to "the heaven-born minister," who does not look in the least like a three-bottle man, but he is. There is George Canning, with his bright, humorous face concocting a poem for the *Anti-Jacobin ;* Peel, looking cold and *gêné;* rollicking " Pam," with his hat on one side, and his thoughts divided between " The Trent " and the coming Derby ; little Johnny Russell, so small and fragile that he looks as if even his hat were crushing him ; a pair of broad plaid trousers and a face like an old-fashioned door-knocker can belong to no other than Lord Brougham.

Here comes a gentleman of the dandy class ; not that there is anything *outré* in his closely buttoned-up frock coat and faultlessly-cut trousers, except that his black silk neckerchief is fastened by a diamond eagle with spread wings, clutching in its claws a thunderbolt of rubies ; his face is handsome, and remarkable from the circumstance that he wears a moustache and imperial, uncommon adjuncts in those days, and from its immobile and fatalistic expression. That is Prince Louis Napoleon, who lives in Arlington Street. He is not held in very high esteem ; he has been blackballed at White's, as we have seen, and is regarded as little better than an adventurer ; an opinion which will be confirmed a few days hence, for to-morrow he will make his mad descent upon Boulogne.

23

LOUIS NAPOLEON.

A sphinx-like face, its cadaverous pallor heightened by clots of black ringlets shot with grey, heavy eyed, heavy lipped, with a little bunch of hair on the chin ; the fragile figure, which stoops at the shoulders, wrapped in a fur-lined coat. He is leaning heavily on the arm of a gentleman, and passers-by respectfully salute Lord Beaconsfield, who has just brought back with him to England "peace with honour". What a contrast to the next ghost that comes stalking on with vigorous gait, sinewy of hand and body, eagle-eyed, aggressive of nose, bitterly stern of lip, masterful of look ; a very high, old-fashioned shirt collar, frayed at the edges, a spotted blue neckerchief, frock coat rather seedy, check trousers very baggy and worn. There is much doffing of hats, for that is William Ewart Gladstone ; but whether that concentration of brow is occasioned by the Irish problem, by Homeric theories, by Englishing a couplet of Horace, or by the next tree that he has picked out for his axe at Hawarden it would be difficult to guess.

And so I might stretch out the line to the crack of doom. But the charm is wound up, the vision is dissolved. Yet these shadows were men and women once like ourselves, dear reader. "We are such stuff as dreams are made of, and our little life is rounded by a sleep."

Of the St. James's Street of the seventeenth or eighteenth century little or nothing survives. But that old smoke-grimed brick gateway of the palace that is now staring at you, has frowned upon all these people in the flesh, and will, in all probability, look down upon new generations of houses and people when all of this age have gone to join the procession of ghosts that has just passed before us.

CHAPTER XXI.

PICCADILLY: ITS TRADITIONS, GREAT HOUSES AND CELEBRATED RESIDENTS.

THE word Piccadilly[1] has had several meanings assigned to it. But it seems to have originated in a peculiar ruff with stiff points, like spear heads, that was named " piccadilla," the diminutive of " picca," the Italian for pike. The place where the ruffs were sold was a large, solitary house of entertainment and gambling, with extensive recreation grounds, called Pickadilly Hall, built in St. James's Fields. That there were other houses round about is evident from a decree issued by the Star Chamber in 1637, which ordered all houses about Pickadilly, that had stood since the thirteenth of King James, to be pulled down as they were found to be great nuisances and fouled the springs of water which passed by those houses to Whitehall and the city. (Garrard in *Strafford's Letters.*)

---

[1] This place name occurs 300 years ago in Gerard's *Herbal*, wherein the old botanist records finding bugloss in the dry ditches about " Pickadilla ". Cotgrave defines " Piccadilles " as several divisions, or pieces fastened about the brim of the collar of a doublet. A "pickadel " is mentioned in the old comedy of *Northward Ho !* as part of a woman's dress.

(357)

In 1664, the Earl of St. Albans, who was then forming St. James's Square, built a market, which he also called after the patron saint of the locality, in St. James's Fields for the sale of provisions on Mondays, Wednesdays and Saturdays. Later on, within the boundaries of the market, somewhere close to the spot on which the Criterion now stands, was the Mitre Tavern, which in 1699 was kept by one Mrs. Voss, the widow of an officer in the Guards.

Let us peep into the hostess's private room on a certain summer's evening in the year just named: Seated in an arm-chair is buxom Mrs. Voss, and by her side is a beautiful girl of fifteen, her niece, who assists her in the house. She is reading aloud Beaumont and Fletcher's comedy, " The Scornful Lady ". And with such spirit and rare appreciation of its wit and dramatic power that a young gentleman, who has been listening at the half-closed door, presently starts applauding, and, running into the room, seizes both hands of the blushing reader and declares that she has the making of a great actress. Mr. Farquhar, though a very young man, does not speak without warranty, for he has just produced his first comedy, " Love and a Bottle," at Drury Lane, and will thereafter write two of the sprightliest comedies of the century, " The Recruiting Officer " and " The Beaux Strategem ". He has also figured upon the stage as an actor. He offers to get her an introduction, through Vanburgh, to the managers of Drury Lane, a proposal which she is eager enough to accept.

Never did anticipations prove more prophetic : Miss Nancy, under the name of Mrs. Oldfield, became one of the most brilliant actresses in the annals of the English stage, incomparable in comedy, admirable in tragedy ; she created the characters of Lady Betty Modish, of Lady Townley, and of Jane Shore ; she was received on terms of perfect equality by ladies of the highest nobility ; at her death she lay in state in the Jerusalem Chamber, lords were pall-bearers at her funeral, and Pope immortalized her under the name of Narcissa, in his *Moral Essays*.[1]

If we pay another visit to St. James's Market about sixty years later we shall light upon another romance. It is much changed, shops have been built, and among these is a glover's and draper's kept by one Mr. Wheeler, who has a pretty shopwoman of Quaker parents, named Hannah Lightfoot. A very young gentleman is so smitten by her charms that he comes every day to buy articles, of which he has no need, for the pleasure of talking with her. Smirking Mr. Wheeler, who is of course delighted with such a profitable customer, little imagines that he is helping to weave an historical romance, and would be thunderstruck if he were told that this lad is the heir to the throne of England. Yes, it is no less a personage

---

[1] Odious ! in woollen ! 'twould a saint provoke
(Were the last words that poor Narcissa spoke) ;
No, let a chintz and charming Brussels lace
Wrap my cold limbs and shade my lifeless face ;
One would not, sure, be frightful when one's dead,
And—Betty—give this cheek a little red.

than George, Prince of Wales, who is living with his
widowed mother at Leicester House close by. The
youth does not plead in vain. His intentions are
honourable, and one day, in 1759, in Curzon Street
Chapel, George marries the pretty Quakeress.

Alas, two years later he is forced to forsake his
charming wife for " the ugliest woman in Europe,"
Charlotte of Mecklenberg-Strelitz. Hannah afterwards
married a Mr. Axford, and resided for some years at
Hampstead. But in her will she signed herself
" Hannah Regina," and commended her children " to
the kind protection of their royal father, my husband,
his Majesty King George the Third ". One of her
two sons became demented and committed suicide ;
the other, who took the name of George Rex, emi-
grated to the Cape of Good Hope, where he held
a high official position, and was said to be the
very image of his royal father. When the Duke of
Edinburgh visited the Cape he was entertained by
Mr. John Rex, the son of George! Probably the
remembrance of this youthful folly had, among other
considerations, something to do with the framing of
the Royal Marriage Act, by which all the good things
of royalty have ever since been secured for German
princes and princesses.[1]

---

[1] So runs the popular legend, of which there are several other
versions. In one it is asserted that Hannah was married to Axford,
who was a man in her own station of life, previous to her connection
with the prince, and was conveyed from the church door to the arms
of her royal lover; in another she is called Whitefoot ; Mr. Thoms
denied that such a person ever existed and was of opinion that the

In the middle of the last century that once famous hostelry, the Old White Bear, was erected upon a portion of the Market ground ; but the Market did not wholly disappear until Waterloo Place was run through it, in the second decade of the present century. The Criterion marks the spot where once stood that notorious gambling saloon, the Piccadilly Casino.

The great houses of the nobility, for which Piccadilly was once so famous, have nearly disappeared, but the ghosts of the past must ever haunt the ground. Let me invoke them. To begin with the Albany which marks the site of the mansion of the infamous Earl of Sunderland, one of James II.'s favourite ministers ; gambler, traitor, *roué*, who here entertained all the famous men of the age, and plotted against the too trusting master, whom he had led to ruin by his vile counsels. The Albany dates back to 1770, though it did not assume its present appearance until 1804. That cloister-like corridor, which traverses it from end to end, has echoed to the daily footsteps of

whole story was an invention (see *Notes and Queries*, 1863-7), but Mr. Thoms was an universal sceptic, and was equally positive that no human being ever attained a hundredth birthday. Some say she died of a broken heart ; others that she lived happily with Axford after the marriage of the king. In the *Proceedings of the Quakers' Society of the City of Westminster* at the time in question, there is an entry referring to one Hannah Lightfoot, who was summoned before it to answer for the heinous sin of having been married by a clergyman. There is also a passage in *The Gentleman's Magazine* of about a century back, to which I have lost the reference, which indicates that the story was generally accepted. As there is never smoke without fire, romances so circumstantial must have their foundation in fact.

many famous men : Lord Byron (at No. 2, in 1814), Lord Brougham, in his early days, and George Canning were at different times residents of those bachelor's chambers. But the Albany is the most intimately associated with memories of Lord Macaulay, who

THE ALBANY.

made his abode in F. 3 during fifteen years (1841-1856). It was here that he wrote his later Essays, and the greater part of his History. He loved the place, and left it with much regret.

"After fifteen happy years passed in the Albany I am going to leave it thrice as rich a man as when I entered it, and far more famous. . . . To-morrow I take my final leave of this room where I have spent most of the waking hours of so many years. Already its aspect is changed. It is the corpse of what it was on Sunday. I hate partings. To-day, even while I climbed the endless steps, panting and weary, I thought that it was for the last time, and the tears would come into my eyes."

In St. James's Church many illustrious dead sleep their last sleep: Charles Cotton, the companion and colleague of Izaak Walton in "The Gentle Art," and the translator of Montaigne; Mark Akenside, the author of the almost forgotten *Pleasures of the Imagination*, who was so ridiculously caricatured by Smollett as the "Doctor" in *Peregrine Pickle;* Mrs. Delaney, whose autobiography, edited by Dr. Doran, affords such vivid pictures of the society of the last century; Robert Dodsley, one of the most famous of booksellers, the publisher of *Tristram Shandy;* and brilliant Mrs. Abington, whom we met in Pall Mall. Wren was very proud of St. James's, and with its Grinling Gibbons carvings and beautiful altar, which Evelyn, with much exaggeration, pronounced to be equal to any at home or abroad, is a very fine building.

Albemarle Street marks the site of that splendid mansion of the great Earl of Clarendon, which his opponents nicknamed "Dunkirk House," because they averred that it was built out of a part of the money that Louis XIV. paid to Charles II. for the sale of the old Flemish town, which Cromwell had taken from the Spaniards.

"Hatchett's" and the White Horse Cellars conjure up pictures of the coaching days of the Regency. See here are the bucks of the Driving Club, clad in light drab-coloured coats, the full skirts reaching to their heels, with three tiers of pockets and mother-of-pearl buttons, each the size of a crown piece; waistcoats with stripes of blue and yellow, an inch wide; breeches of yellow plush with sixteen strings and a rosette to each knee (it was by imitating this fashion that the dandy highwayman, Jack Rann, obtained his sobriquet of Sixteen String Jack); buff-topped boots, wrinkled down to the ankles; a bell-shaped white beaver hat, three and a half inches deep in the crown and of the same width in the brim; and, to complete the picture, an enormous bouquet at the breast.

One of the most famous of these Jehus is Sir John Lade. He was once under the guardianship of Thrale the brewer, and if you turn to your Boswell's *Johnson* you will find some very severe verses, written by the sage of Fleet Street, upon the occasion of this young gentleman's birthday, in which is very accurately fore-shadowed Sir John's future career. Lade took for wife the mistress of the aforementioned Jack Rann, and, as the story goes, won her from the gentleman highway-man in fair fight at "Stunning Joe Banks's," in St. Giles's Rookery, where he was in the habit of carousing with certain illustrious persons, whom we have met there. Many anecdotes are told of his marvellous feats as a whip. He could drive the two off wheels of a phaeton over a sixpence at a start of a hundred yards ; and once drove backwards and forwards through a gate, just wide enough to admit a carriage, with lightning-like speed, twenty-two times, scarcely allowing himself room enough to turn. And it was said that his " lady" almost surpassed him in tooling a coach and four. Between them they soon passed the patrimonial acres into the hands of the Jews, Sir John took to the box professionally, and was glad to pocket tips such as he had once lavished upon others. Nevertheless he lived to see eighty years. Another notable member of the club is Tom Akers, he with the white beaver turned up with green, who is so determined to look a "professional" to the minutest point that he has had his front teeth filed so that he may spit in the orthodox style. And there is "golden" Ball Hughes, one of the most languid exquisites of the Regency, doing his best to run through his £40,000 a year. It will be a lucky day for him when he runs off with beautiful Mercandotti, the opera danseuse, said, by-the-bye, to be a daughter of the Earl of Fife ; she will make him a brilliant wife and save him from ruin.

> The fair damsel is gone, and no wonder at all,
> That bred to the dance, she is gone to the ball,

wrote a wag.

I might fill pages with sketches of the members of the Driving Club and the no less famous Four-in-

Hand, reminiscent of the Marquis of Worcester, Lord Sefton, Sir St. Vincent Cotton, Harry Stevenson and many another, but the coaches, red, blue, green and yellow, with their horses groomed until their coats look like polished glass, are crowding up to the blowing of horns; the windows at Hatchett's are filled with fair demoiselles, who nod and laugh and kiss their hands as their favourite whips mount the boxes; and there is a confusion of Jew hawkers thrusting oranges and cakes and pencils through the coach windows to tempt the passengers, and—the vision fades.

I have before me a picture of Burlington House as it looked two hundred years ago. It was built in the reign of Charles II., and was then said to be the western boundary of the metropolis. In this picture it lies back in its own grounds and gardens, and all behind it is open country. Here Rochester and Buckingham recited their erotics, Pope spat venom upon his rivals, and Dean Swift exercised his savage wit upon friends and foes alike; for Richard Boyle, Lord Burlington, was a Mæcenas in his patronage of men of letters, and so were some of his successors. A famous memory associated with the old mansion was the *fête* given to the allied sovereigns in 1814, when the gardens were splendidly illuminated. And since it has been pushed into the background by a more superb structure, celebrated men and women have certainly not ceased to haunt it.

Little less notable than Burlington is Devonshire

House. The present building was erected in the middle
of the last century ; but there was an elder one which,
like its neighbour, had echoed to the voices of Waller
and Rochester, as well as to those of Pope and Swift.
The most famous reminiscences connected with the
new house are of the time when "the beautiful
Duchess" reigned here, the idol of the great Whig
leaders, Fox, Burke, Windham, Fitzpatrick, Sheridan,
Tom Moore. It was curious that while all the world
was in love with her whom even carping Horace
Walpole declared to be " a beautiful girl, full of grace,"
her husband alone was indifferent to her charms. She
was married at seventeen, but even during their
betrothal, when she was the loveliest star of London
society, the duke was cold and distant. Their marriage was an extraordinary one. On a certain Sunday
morning, by her mother's instructions, she went to
Wimbledon. His Grace was awaiting her at the parish
church, and there the ceremony was performed, the
only persons present being the Duchess of Portland
and the bride's grandmother, Lady Cowper—for she
was a Spencer. The new duchess at once became the
leader of fashion at court. And a nice dance she led
her devotees ; beginning by abolishing the hoop and
high head-gears in favour of Quaker-like aprons and
flat caps, she suddenly started a head-dress of feathers
six in number, black, white and pink, an ell and three
inches high. The difficulty of obtaining a plumage
of this height was so great among those who desired
to emulate their leader, that one aspiring wight in

desperation sent to an undertaker, who provided her
with hearse plumes ! So, when going to assemblies in
their carriages, the ladies had either to sit upon the
floor or have openings made in the roofs of them.
But our duchess condoned these monstrosities by that
incomparable hat of Gainsborough's portrait. How her
canvassing in the slums of Seven Dials won the Westminster election for Charles James Fox, has been
already alluded to in the chapter on " Covent Garden ".

"Lord, it was a fine sight," said an old elector,
fifty years afterwards, " to see a grand lady come
smack up to you with, ' Master, how d'ye do ? ' and
laugh so loud and talk so kind, and shake us by the
hand, and say, ' Give us your vote, worthy sir ; a
plumper for the people's friend, our friend, everybody's friend '. And then if we hummed and ha'd she
would ask after our wives and children, and if that
didn't do she'd think nothing of giving us a kiss, aye,
or a dozen or so. Kissing was nothing at all to her, it
came so natural." As the polling lasted twenty-three
days the task of canvassing in this style must have
been an onerous one.

By these political intrigues, by leading the follies
of fashion, and by gambling, which was her mania,
the neglected wife tried to console herself for the loss
of domestic happiness. But at a terrible cost.

With our duchess the taint was hereditary ; her
father, Earl Spencer, who once boasted that he could
spend £30,000 a year without feeling it, left his widow
in poverty. The gaming at Devonshire House was

appalling, it was the *raison d'être* of every party there, and her Grace was frequently driven to pawn her diamonds, the family plate, and even borrow privately from the duke's man of business to pay her losses at cards.[1]

But with all her faults Georgina, Duchess of Devonshire, had much of the better angel in her nature ; she was a devoted daughter, mother and sister, her heart was always tender, her purse ever open to distress, and even her bitterest enemy said of her : " Never did holy nun carry to a vestal grave a heart more true to her vows than did the duchess to those she had made at the altar ! " Considering that the Prince Regent and Charles James Fox were her most intimate friends she must indeed have been a miracle. She died at Devonshire House in 1806, when only in her fiftieth year. Hazlitt gives us a last glimpse of her, calling over the banisters for her servant. " If she had been

---

[1] Such difficulties were common enough to ladies at this period. To obtain funds for the gaming table they frequently not only beggared their fortune, but their honour as well. Some women of noble family even went so far as to start a faro bank—they were nicknamed " Pharaoh's daughters "—and convert their houses into gambling hells. The Duchess of Cumberland and Lady Elizabeth Luttrell were guilty of like practices, and the latter had to fly the country. Being convicted .of cheating in Germany, she was chained to a barrow and condemned to draw it through the streets. Ladies have been known to lose £3000 at a sitting. Here is a curious paragraph from *The London Chronicle*, 13th August, 1775 : " On Wednesday morning two ladies of distinction, having a dispute at a party at cards, repaired in their carriage to a field near Pancrass, and fought a duel with pistols, when one of them being shot in the left arm, the affair terminated ".

as she once was a thousand admirers would have flown
to her assistance. But her face was painted over like
a mask, and there was hardly any appearance of life
left, but the restless motion of her eyes." *Sic transit
pulchritudo mundi!*

It is but a stone's throw from Devonshire to Cambridge House, now the Naval and Military Club, where
another queen of society, Lady Palmerston, presided
over the Whig cabals of the early Victorian era, as
the duchess had manœuvred those of the Regency.
Lady Palmerston's dinners and receptions, Lord Lamington considered, probably did more for the party
than her husband's talents. She was the most frank and
genial of hostesses; and the geniality came from her
heart; she was really grateful to her husband's supporters. "Many a difficult crisis has been averted
by Lady Palmerston entering the room at the right
moment, and in her charming manner insisting on
the discontented and disappointed one accepting her
gracious hospitality. She possessed the power of
making each visitor feel that he was the guest she
delighted to honour; and thus her receptions were
highly appreciated and were of incalculable benefit to
the party."

Palmerston himself was equally clever in disarm-
ing the wrath of an indignant complainant. An old
friend had been recalled from an important post to
fill an inferior one; in a towering rage he rushed off to
the minister and afterwards related the result to Lord
Lamington. "Plague confound the fellow I couldn't

get in a word! I sent in my card and was kept in the
dining-room, while he was, of course, arranging the
scene; for no sooner was I shown into his study than
before I could utter a word, he rushed up, seized me
by both hands. 'My dear, dear friend,' he said, ' I
rejoice to have you back among us; you exchange
barbaric life for civilisation; all your friends are so
glad to welcome you.' 'My lord, I am surprised,' I
struggled to say. 'Not a word, not a word; here is
Lady Palmerston. My dear, welcome your old friend
home; he is one of us again. He will dine with us to-
day—won't you? We must keep you now we've got
you back. I'm off to a Cabinet. Lady Palmerston,
get our friend to tell you some of those anecdotes which
used to delight us; I leave him in your care, good-bye,
au revoir, at eight o'clock '—and he rushed out. I am
engaged to dine and so have lost my chance!"

Close by is dingy, bow-windowed Stratton House,
now the town residence of the Baroness Burdett-Coutts,
which is reminiscent of another famous duchess, *née*
Harriett Mellon, who, starting in life as a strolling
actress, became first the wife of the richest banker in
London, and then the consort of a duke. Quite a
romance of old age was the marriage of the great
banker with the poor player. Sheridan having seen
her act at Stafford engaged her for Drury Lane (1797)
to play soubrettes at thirty shillings a week! Hear
that, ye modern actors! Thomas Coutts, who was a
great frequenter of the theatre, conceived an affection
for the buxom, though neither handsome, refined, nor

particularly clever actress, and did her many kindnesses
That all was purely platonic between them is evident
from the fact that his two daughters received her most

HARRIET MELLON (MRS. COUTTS).

cordially.   Eighteen years afterwards Mrs. Coutts, who
had long been in a state of imbecility, died.   Mr. Coutts,
who was then eighty, fell ill, and, on what he believed

to be his deathbed, asked Miss Mellon to be his wife in order that he might be able to make ample provision for her without scandal. Hymen's torch, however, seems to have put new life into the old man, for he survived during another seven years. He wrote beneath an engraved portrait of her : " When she became my wife she proved the greatest blessing of my life, and made me the happiest of men ". He left her the whole of his vast wealth. Some four years afterwards the widow married the Duke of St. Albans ; he was twenty-three, she fifty. But the duchess was faithful to the memory of him who had been so devoted to her. She died (1837) in Stratton House, and, by her wish, in the same bed in which Mr. Coutts had expired. To his granddaughter, now the Baroness Burdett-Coutts, the daughter of Sir Francis Burdett, she left £1,800,000 ; thus fully justifying the great trust Mr. Coutts had reposed in her. Under the present owner the old house has been the resort of all that is artistic in London society, and the baroness has never forgotten that she owes her wealth to an actress.

The mention of Sir Francis Burdett conjures up a reminiscence of No. 80 Piccadilly, which was the residence of " Old Glory," as he was nicknamed by his admirers. In *Cobbett's Political Register*, 1810, he denounced the House of Commons as a set of borough-mongers and violators of Magna Charta. Parliament was more jealous of its honour then than now, perhaps it had more honour to be jealous of, and an order was issued for his committal to the

Tower. As soon as the news spread abroad a vast concourse filled Piccadilly from Hyde Park Corner to the Haymarket, and every person who came that way was compelled to take off his hat and shout for the idol of the hour, or—take the consequences. The Life Guards were called out, the Riot Act read. Nevertheless the mob commanded every householder to illuminate his windows on pain of having them smashed, those who obeyed were raided by the military and their lights were extinguished ; thereupon the logical crowd battered in all glass within stone's throw and wounded and even killed several innocent people. On the morning of the third day of the riot the Serjeant-at-Arms with a *posse* of constables forced his way to the house, followed by a carriage and a detachment of soldiers; upon entering the drawing-room they found themselves in the presence of a very strikingly arranged dramatic tableau. Sir Francis was posed in the centre of a group which consisted of his wife, his three sisters, his brother-in-law, Mr. Coutts the banker, and Mr. O'Connor, while his son, a boy of fourteen, was reading aloud Magna Charta.

When the arrest was discovered, it is said that only a tremendous storm, which flooded the streets, saved London from a revolution. On the 21st of June, when Sir Francis was released, every dwelling in Piccadilly, willy nilly, was hung with blue, the Burdett colour, and illuminated at night.

It was at the south-west corner of Bolton Street

that Wattier's Club stood. It was the dandies' club.
" They made me a member of Wattier's," writes
Byron " [a superb club at that time], being, I take
it, the only literary man except two others [both men
of the world], Moore and Spencer, in it. Our masquerade was a grand one; so was the dandy ball
too." The gambling there, at a game called macao,
was terrible; the number of men of fortune ruined
incredible; at last the suicides—Lord Lamington
knew personally of six or seven—were so frequent that
the club was closed. A story is told of Brummell, who
lost the greater part of his fortune at Wattier's, finding
there Tom Sheridan, Brinsley's son, who had been
playing all night, watching in the grey dawn of the
morning his last stake being swept away. The
beau, having been lucky, offered to take " the box "
for him and share the winnings. In a short time
he gathered up a thousand and handing poor Tom
half the amount bade him go home and never touch
dice again. He might as well have told him never
to eat again. Brummell attached all his luck and ill
luck at the green cloth to a crooked sixpence he
picked up one night while crossing Berkeley Square.
As long as it remained in his possession Fortune
smiled upon him; at last he lost his talisman, and
from that hour the fickle goddess deserted him.
Wattier was a cook of the Prince Regent's, who, by
his royal master's desire, started the establishment for
providing more *recherchés* dinners than the monotonous
joint, poultry and apple tart which was the almost

unvarying club bill of fare. The dinners were as superlative as the play was after them.

It was somewhere about ten years ago that the mansion of the notorious Marquis of Queensberry, better known as "old Q.," which stood between Hamilton Terrace and Park Lane, was pulled down to make room for the more spacious building that now occupies the site. After his death the mansion was divided into two houses numbered 138 and 139. Here the ancient rake, the Lord March of Thackeray's *Virginians*, the most famous whip, amateur jockey and voluptuary of his day, lived—and died at the age of eighty-six—in a luxury worthy of Lucullus. Waxen tapers in silver sconces cast subdued and many-coloured lights over costly hangings, priceless pictures, eastern carpets, Venetian mirrors, buhl and *marqueterie* that had furnished the palaces of Italian princes and French kings, upon dinners that might have tempted Apicius; the dishes, the handles of the knives and forks were of gold; the hand of Pompadour had painted the exquisite Sèvres, and that of Cellini had modelled the noble epergne; from the ruby-tinted glasses Doges had sipped the wines of Cyprus, and had the crystal decanters been filled with distilled gold their contents could scarcely have been more costly. (After his death the Tokay fetched a hundred guineas a dozen.) At the head of the table sits the host, a little weazened old man attired in the court dress of the *ancien régime*. Sometimes after these banquets there is an entertainment, or tableau, realising

the Judgment of Paris.   Three of the most beautiful
women to be found in London, with no more costume
than Rubens has given the Graces in his famous
picture, represent the three immortals, while the
duke poses for Paris, his shrunk shanks encased in
flesh-coloured hose, over which hangs a tunic of blue
silk, a laurel wreath is upon his head, his withered
cheeks are well rouged and the golden apple is in
his hand.

Every morning he bathed in a silver bath filled
with milk.   In summer time he sat upon his balcony
with a parasol over his head, ogling every pretty
woman that passed, and when one particularly took
his fancy he would send his groom, who stood beneath
waiting his orders, to follow and if possible lure her
into the spider's web.   Country cousins were taken
to have a peep at this wicked old ogre who devoured
innocent virgins, as a sort of moral lesson upon the
awful depravity of London.   True to himself to the
last, when he lay dying, his bed was covered with
seventy letters from women of all grades, from ladies
of title to courtesans, soliciting money and favours,
for he had a pitiful heart for the fair sex ; they came
by every post and he had them laid upon the silken
coverlet, and so he died shrouded in *billets doux !*
Old Q. was a good friend to the French *émigrés*, many
of whom might have died of want but for his generous
hospitality, and to spare their delicacy he would purchase boxes at the theatres for their use, pretending
that they were sent to them free by the managers.

It may be noted that he was the last of the nobility who kept running footmen.[1] He died in 1810.

It is not, however, the ghost of old *roué* Queensberry that alone haunts the spot, it is associated with far more interesting shadows. As I have noted before the house after its noble owner's death was divided into two, and in one of these, No. 139, Lord Byron spent the greater part of his brief married life. It was here that that icy precisian, his wife, left him with smiling, hypocritical face, but intending never to return. The moment was well chosen by such a model of propriety as she posed before the world. " At the time when he had to stand this unexpected shock," writes Moore, " his pecuniary embarrassments, which had been fast gathering around him during the whole of the last year (there having been no less than eight or nine executions in his house within that period), had arrived at their utmost ; and at a moment when, to use his own strong expression, he was ' standing alone on his hearth with his household gods shivered around him,' he was also doomed to receive the startling

[1] The running footmen was no doubt a survival of the middle ages, when it was necessary for great persons while travelling to send out scouts in advance to guard against ambuscades. The running footman was usually dressed in white, carried a wand and ran before his master's carriage, crying out, " Make way for my Lord So-and-So ". Many anecdotes, that sound almost incredible, are told of their powers of endurance and the distances they could cover in one heat. An old public-house in Charles Street, Berkeley Square, has the sign of " The Running Footman," and represents a tall fellow in the costume of his calling, a long staff with a metal ball at the top in his hand, and underneath the legend, " I am the only Running Footman ".

intelligence that the wife who had just parted with
him in kindness had parted with him for ever." In
this house were written *Parisina* and *The Siege of
Corinth.*

Upon the ground now occupied by Apsley House
and the mansions of the Rothschilds, in the middle of
the last century, stood some tumble-down dwellings
and a couple of taverns. The Hercules Pillars, which
Fielding has immortalised in *Tom Jones*, and the
Triumphant Chariot, that was much affected by the
military. A portion of this site was given by George
II. to an old soldier named Allen, who had fought
with him at Dettingen, with permission to put up a
hut on it for the sale of apples and cakes. Being
close to the entrance to the park he drove a thriving
trade; at his death, however, the hut was deserted,
and Lord Apsley, obtaining a grant of the land from
the crown, erected a mansion thereon. But Allen had
a son whom he had articled to an attorney, and this
young man, like a true disciple of the Law, lay *perdu*
until the building was finished, and then, to the
astonishment of everybody, the transaction having
been forgotten or perhaps unknown, he presented
his claim and had to be compensated with a ground
rent of £450 per annum. This was afterwards compounded for a round sum. Apsley House was originally an ugly red brick building in the tasteless style
that prevailed at the period. As most people know it
was presented to the duke by the nation in 1820, but
it was not until eight years later that the front was

encased in Bathstone, and so converted into what was then called the classic style; this has been the only alteration effected in the original building.

One of the greatest functions of the London season was the Waterloo banquet, given in the great gallery, at which the officers who had helped him to gain that mighty victory, that had decided the destiny of the world, were present as long as death spared them. On those occasions the sideboard was ornamented by the Golden Shield that the city of London had given to the duke; upon this trophy were embossed representations of the hero's most celebrated victories, after designs by Stothard; it was worth £15,000.

Heroic figures frequently fade after being long exposed to the fierce light that beats upon them; how smudged and tarnished is that of the mighty Napoleon! But every fresh fact and trait that is added to our better knowledge of his conqueror sheds a brighter lustre upon the stainless marble of the grand old warrior. Even crabbed Carlyle, who usually could see only the seamy side of greatness, had nothing but praise and reverence for the hero of Waterloo. He met him at one of the great houses, and after caustically epigrammatising every one present, he writes : " By far the most interesting person present was the old Duke of Wellington—truly a beautiful old man. I had never seen till now how beautiful, and what an expression of graceful simplicity, veracity and nobleness there is about the old hero when you see him close at hand. . . . Eyes beautiful light blue, full of mild valour, with infinitely more faculty and geniality than I had fancied before ; the face wholly gentle, wise, valiant and venerable. . . . He glided along slightly saluting this and that other, clear, clean, fresh as this June evening itself, till the silver buckle of his stock vanished into the door of the next room and I saw him no more."

No man ever had a fuller opportunity of testing the value of popular applause. After Waterloo he could not leave his house without being mobbed *ad nauseam ;* but the moment he opposed the passion of the hour demos thirsted for his blood and smashed his windows, until he was obliged to have them covered with iron shutters. After a while the many-headed turned again and shouted and ran after the hero as in the pre-reform agitation days. But he treated them with the most stoical indifference, and one day, when demos followed him to the gates of Apsley House, he turned round with a smile, pointed to the still closed windows, made a sarcastic bow and entered the court without a word. " I owe all I have achieved,": he once said, " to being ready a quarter of an hour before it was deemed necessary to be so." " All the business of war, and indeed all the business of life," he remarked on another occasion, " is to find out what you don't know by what you do."

CHAPTER XXII.

LONDON was anciently noted for its fairs ; it had Bartholomew's in its central district, Southwark and Greenwich in its southern and Mayfair in the western. It was Edward I. who conferred upon the hospital of St. James's the privilege to hold a fair in St. James's Fields during six days in May, in honour of its patron saint.

Let me picture this patrician quarter in the days of George II. : a tract of waste ground lying behind the demesnes of Piccadilly, bounded on the west by a muddy country lane which divides it from Hyde Park, and then straggling away to Oxford Road. In the centre is Shepherd's Market, which is crowded with stalls for the sale of the usual fair commodities, while all around are booths for prize fighters, with swords and cudgels as well as fists, wild beasts, jugglers, fire-eaters, mountebanks of all kinds, bull baiting and dog fighting. To the north, just upon the spot where Hertford Street now stands, is an enclosure containing a duck pond, in which the cruel amusement of duck hunting by dogs is being sarried on with great zest. The great attraction,

for it is just after the rebellion of 1745, is "the
beheading of the puppets". Three puppets, nearly
as large as life, are made up to resemble the Lords
Lovat, Balmerino and Kilmarnock, while a fourth
represents the headsman ; the figures lay their heads
upon the block, down comes the axe, and the loyal
spectators shout lustily. Not even the strong young
Frenchwoman, who has an anvil set upon her breast
and a horse shoe forged thereupon, lifts an enormous
weight by twisting her long hair round it, and walks
upon red-hot iron, can draw the crowd from those
mimic executions. Neither can the boy on the stage
of another booth attract much attention, though the
few gathered round are convulsed by his comical
antics. This is young Harry Woodward, who will
by-and-by be one of the most celebrated members
of David Garrick's company at Drury Lane, the
greatest of speaking harlequins, the most dashing
of Petruchios and Mercutios.

But Mayfair at this time was also a metropolitan
Gretna Green ; it was as notorious for clandestine
marriages as was the Fleet, and Dr. Keith, who had
a chapel there, was as celebrated for rivetting matrimonial fetters as thereafter was the blacksmith of the
Scotch border. All charges, inclusive, were only a
guinea. The doctor was a kind friend to all ladies
in distress ; if sued for debt they could hire a husband
who would leave them at the door of the chapel for a
five shilling fee, so that they could plead coverture ;
if they had loved not wisely but too well. they could

obtain a marriage certificate for the same fee, and by doubling it have the marriage that had never taken place entered in the books. A daughter of an Earl of Berkeley escaped from marrying a man of her father's choice by the last-mentioned device. At St. George's, Hanover Square, are some of Dr. Keith's registers in which are entered many noble names. One entry has a curious history attached to it. It is as follows : " 1752, February 14, James, Duke of Hamilton, and Elizabeth Gunning ". Horace Walpole thus tells the story of this entry in a letter to Horace Mann : " About a fortnight since, at an immense assembly at my Lord Chesterfield's, made to show the house, which is really magnificent, Duke Hamilton made violent love at one end of the room while he was playing pharaoh at the other end ; that is, he saw neither the bank nor his own cards, which were of £300 each ; he soon lost £1000. I own that I thought that this parade looked ill for the poor girl [Miss Gunning]. . . . However, two nights afterwards, being left alone with her while her mother and sister were at Bedford House, he found himself so impatient that he sent for a parson. The doctor refused to perform the ceremony without licence or ring ; the duke swore he would send for the archbishop ; at last they were married with a ring of the bed curtain, at half an hour after twelve at night, at Mayfair Chapel."

The Misses Gunning, two portionless Irish ladies, were the most beautiful women of the day. " They

can't walk in the park or go to Vauxhall but such
mobs follow them that they are generally driven
away," says Walpole.

It was their mother's shrewdness that obtained for
these young ladies their first introduction into high
society. Some scoundrel, who had evil designs upon
them, sent them a forged invitation to a great assembly
at the Duchess of Bedford's. Mrs. Gunning detected
the fraud, and resolved to turn it to her own account.
Although unacquainted with her Grace, she went with
one of her daughters to Bedford House, obtained
an interview and showed the false invitation. The
duchess was so struck by the girl's beauty, as well as
by the infamy of the hoax, that she presented her with
a genuine invitation for herself and sister. The Misses
Gunning came and saw and conquered, and from
that night every drawing-room was opened to them.
" May the luck of the Gunnings attend you ! " became an Irish blessing.

Mobs waited about to see them get into their chairs,
rushed to the theatre when it was known they would
be there ; and mounted chairs and tables in drawing-
rooms wherever they were present to get a good
look at them. When the new-made duchess was
travelling with her lord to his Scotch castle, the same
pen tells us that " 700 people sat up all night in and
about an inn in Yorkshire to see her get into her
chaise next morning ". The elder was married to the
Earl of Coventry. At Worcester a shoemaker made
two guineas and a half by showing a shoe he was

making for the countess, at the charge of a penny to each person.[1]

The Bishop of London excommunicated Dr. Keith, who was sent to prison; but his clerk carried on the business just as usual. The Marriage Act of 1754 put an end to it at last; on the day before the Act became law, this high priest of Hymen united no fewer than sixty-one couples! During his reign at Mayfair Chapel he married 7000 people. That the life of this notable parson was in accordance with his practices may be easily imagined; nevertheless he attained to the age of ninety, and wrote a very pious treatise entitled *The Guide; or, the Christian Pathway to Everlasting Life*. Was his chapel the pathway?

When Lord Chesterfield built his grand mansion in South Audley Street in 1747, it stood in the midst of green fields, and had beautiful grounds attached to it, upon which Chesterfield's Gardens have risen. In the glorious library which is, I believe, still preserved, he wrote those famous letters to his son, which, to the good people who have never read them, are a kind of Mephistophelian catechism. Probably if they did read them they would be very disappointed. The letters are immoral only from

---

[1] That any beauty, however remarkable, should excite such a sensation seems incomprehensible, but the explanation is not far to seek. It was so great a rarity at that time to meet with a woman not deeply pitted by small-pox that a smooth skin combined with good features was quite a phenomenon. "Conscientious" people are bidding fair to bring us back to the same condition within the next few years.

an English point of view—a Frenchman or a German
regards them in quite a different light—because certain
inevitabilities of youth, which we ignore with most
disastrous results, are recognised by a father. Yet
they are full of admirable wisdom, and at times even
noble and lofty sentiments are not lacking. Up that
magnificent marble staircase all the famous men and
women of the second half of the eighteenth century
have passed, all the fashion, all the beauty, all the
intellect. What a crowd of ghosts the thought
conjures up!

Among others, we see the ponderous person of
Samuel Johnson, on a certain occasion when he
came to solicit the earl's patronage for his projected
dictionary, departed in a huff and wrote his well-
known letter. Much ink has been spattered over
the incident, and it has been made the subject of a
well-known picture; but Boswell's explanation puts
quite a different complexion upon the event. Colley
Cibber, who had entered the house by a private staircase, was closeted with the earl while Mr. Johnson
was waiting in the anteroom; the modern Aristarchus always looked down upon actors with lofty
contempt, not excepting David Garrick, and when
the poet laureate came out he was so indignant that
he would not wait to see the earl. But, in the first
place, my lord did not know he was there, and Mr.
Colley Cibber, one of the managers of Drury Lane,
one of the finest comedians of his day, the author
of "The Careless Husband" and other excellent

comedies, was, after all, a far more important personage at that time than Mr. Samuel Johnson, who was
then little more than a literary hack.

No. 72 in the same street was the residence of
Alderman Wood, and there "the injured queen"
Caroline stayed while her trial was pending. Popular
idols are usually of clay, and Caroline of Brunswick
was a poor specimen even of that material. In *The
Paget Papers*, recently published, there is a letter
written by Mr. Paget to Lord St. Helens, concerning
the then pending marriage of the Prince Regent, in
which he states that it was well known in diplomatic
circles that the Princess had already lost her character,
and implores him to use his influence to prevent so
undesirable a union. This "well-known" fact was,
no doubt, the notorious scandal of the Princess and
her chamberlain, Bergami, the Neapolitan. To which
warning St. Helens replied, that "the engagement is
too far advanced now to be dissoluble, and therefore
we must make the best of it and hush up all bad
stories". Lady Maria Stuart, in some reminiscences,
describes the wedding. "He [the Prince] was so
agitated during the ceremony that it was expected he
would burst into tears. . . ." When they passed out
of the chapel, "the Prince looked like death, and full
of confusion, as if he wished to hide himself from the
looks of the whole world. I think he is much to be
pitied." George loathed her from the beginning—
after their first salute he had to take brandy—
and further acquaintance could not modify that

impression. Can we not see her trapesing through the
streets, all satin and tinsel, more like a queen of the
maypole than a queen of England, with soiled, daggled
petticoats, clothes and skin alike testifying to her
dislike for soap and water; then the rabble rout of
dingy foreigners, with the same hydrophobic ten-
dencies as herself, that she foregathered with !

If we step into Park Lane we may find there an
explanation of the prince's death-like looks at his wedding. It was in the drawing-room of her house in that
thoroughfare that George of Wales was married to Mrs
Fitzherbert. He had long raved, stormed and wept at
the feet of the adorable Maria, who, at the age of
twenty-four, in the zenith of her beauty, was a second
time a widow. But she was not to be won on the
same terms as poor Perdita Robinson. When he first
offered her marriage, knowing what a royal marriage
meant, she firmly refused, and forbade him her house.
This sent the sweet youth—he was only twenty at the
time—into a frenzy. One day a surgeon, Lord Onslow,
Lord Southampton and others drove up in haste to
Park Lane with terror-struck faces. "The prince has
stabbed himself, and you alone, madam, can save his
life," was their cry. But even then Mrs. Fitzherbert
would not be induced to go with them to Carlton
House unless escorted by a lady. So on the way they
took up the Duchess of Devonshire. The prince had
really stabbed himself—more or less, and raved like a
bedlamite, and swore he would stab himself to the heart
if she did not relent. Terrified at the sight of the blood

and by her lover's frenzy, the young widow faltered. The duchess lent a ring, and a form of betrothal was gone through. But in the calm self-commune of the night the lady repented of her compliance; wrote a letter next morning saying that she could not abide by the arrangement, and fled to Aix-la-Chapelle. George, upon hearing that she had escaped him, tore his hair, gnashed his teeth, rolled upon the floor, and then got up and wrote a burning love-letter of thirty-seven pages and despatched it to the fair Atalanta by courier. But this fiery cross did not bring her back ; nor another, nor another ; indeed for eighteen months Cupid was ever on the wing. The genuineness of the prince's passion cannot be doubted, only a very big fire can be rendered more ardent by constant douches of cold water.

Could any woman resist for ever such importunities from a frantic lover, more especially when that lover was a prince, young, handsome, fascinating?[1] So at

[1] That George IV., in his youth, was gifted with a remarkable fascination is testified to by contemporaries who were superior to the arts of flattery, and by men who even disliked him. The prince was highly accomplished, well read in ancient and modern literature, a fine musician, with a taste in music far beyond his time. He was one of the first to appreciate Weber, and was an enthusiastic admirer of that composer's compositions when the management of Covent Garden had to omit some of the finest concerted pieces from *Oberon*, and were doubtful even of the delicious " Mermaid's Song " because they feared that " the public would not stand them ". Sensual by nature, condemned to idleness and uselessness, and finally united to a woman he loathed, one can scarcely wonder that George finally sank into a mere gross voluptuary. No one would attempt to palliate much of his conduct, but we must remember the age in which he lived, its

last she returned to London, and on the 21st December, 1785, the ceremony was performed in her drawing-room in Park Lane. But by whom ? Aye, there's the rub ! A roistering cleric, named Rosenhagen, had been asked to officiate, but got frightened at the thought of farmer George and grim Charlotte. It is said that the Rev. Mr. Burt of Twickenham confessed upon his death-bed that he had done the deed for a consideration of £500, that Mr. Orlando Bridgman, afterwards the Earl of Bradford, and General Keppel were present, and that, when the storm arose, they induced Mrs. Fitzherbert to cut their names from the certificate.

"I never committed adultery in my life, unless it was with *Mrs. Fitzherbert's husband.* That is the Prince's true wife," said Queen Caroline in answer to the king's accusations against her. That is pretty strong evidence. After his brother's death it is said that William IV. gave her back all the documents which proved her true relations with the late king, and offered to make her a duchess ; but her answer was, "I have never disgraced the name of Fitzherbert, and I will never change it".

When Charles James Fox, who had been induced to declare in the House of Commons that no marriage ceremony had been celebrated between the prince and Mrs. Fitzherbert, discovered that he had been made the cat's-paw of a lie, he did not speak to the royal liar for many months. As the Duke of Clarence

manners, usages and standard of morality. George IV. was not quite so black as he has been painted.

lived upon Mrs. Jordan's salary, so did his brother
of Wales live upon his wife's income. She was once
arrested for debt through his extravagance. "We
were very poor, but very happy," she said. It was a
disgraceful business, but "the good king and queen,"
those divinities of Mrs. Grundy, refused to pay George's
debts or give him any supplies unless he married
Caroline of Brunswick. Really, I think these goody
people do more mischief and make more unhappiness
in the world than the wicked folks do. George never
ceased to love his true wife ; her miniature, when he
lay dead, was found next his heart, and lies with him
in the tomb.

On 6th May, 1840, all London was thrown into
consternation by the news that Lord William Russell
had been found in his house in Norfolk Street, Park
Lane, with his head nearly severed from his body.
Lord William's household consisted of two women
servants and a Swiss valet named Courvoisier. Bank
notes and rings being found hidden in the butler's
pantry, suspicion fell upon the valet. He was
arrested, tried, condemned, and afterwards confessed
the crime. Courvoisier had intended to rob the
house and fly the country ; he was found at midnight
in the dining-room by his master under circumstances
that left little doubt of his intentions. When Lord
William had retired to his room the Swiss, knowing that
his character was gone if Lord William discharged him,
resolved upon murder. In the small hours of the
morning he crept upstairs to his master's chamber,

found him sleeping, and cut the old man's throat—he was seventy-three—with a carving knife. Death was instantaneous, a slight movement of the hand was all. Twenty thousand people witnessed Courvoisier's execution at Newgate.

There are two highly interesting houses in Hertford Street, No. 10 and No. 35 (A). In the first Sheridan passed eight years of his life, 1797-1801. It was while living here that being found one night, or rather early morn, in the gutter by a guardian of the night —he had just come from Wattier's—he was asked his name, " Wilberforce," he hiccoughed, which would be about equal in these days for a bacchanalian to aver that he was the Archbishop of Canterbury! In this house died his first wife,the once beautiful Maria Linley, " St. Cecilia"; she of whom the Bishop of Norwich said that she seemed to him the connecting link between woman and angel. She was indeed a ministering angel to her husband, who was totally unworthy of such a treasure. But her loss was a blow from which he never recovered, the *descensus Averni* was indeed rapid after that. " I never saw more poignant grief," says Michael Kelly, " than that which Mr. Sheridan felt for the loss of his beloved wife. I have seen him sit night after night and cry like a child."

The widower's affections were now centred in his child, a little girl. One night when a large party was assembled in Hertford Street a pale-faced servant whispered to his master that she was dying. In the silence of the night the distracted father was hanging

over his dead child, who, as she lay in the calm beauty
of her last sleep, was the image of her mother, as he
remembered her in those early days at Bath, so pure,
so fresh, so lovely. How his thoughts would have
travelled back in that vigil to the time of their
passionate love ; to his duels with Captain Matthews ;
their elopement ; her short-lived happiness—and his
own brilliant youth marred by vice and folly. And
all that remained of that beloved past was this dead
child, soon to be hidden away for ever in the darkness
of the grave.

The other Hertford Street house referred to, No. 35
(A), is that in which Lord Lytton, then Sir Edward
Bulwer Lytton, went to live in 1835. Here he wrote
Rienzi, *Ernest Maltravers*, *Alice*, and his great dramatic successes, *The Lady of Lyons*, *Richelieu*, and
Money. He was a fop of the first water, could not
pronounce the letter " r," was self-conscious and vain-
glorious ; but he was a brilliant all-round man, and
his novels, albeit their grandiose, high-falutin style
render them impossible at the present day, are perhaps
nearer akin to genius than those of either of his great
rivals, Dickens and Thackeray. Willis, the American,
in his *Pencillings*, describes him as rushing into a
drawing-room joyous as a boy just let out of school,
" gay, quick, various, half-satirical," talking because
he could not help it, and infecting everybody with
his high spirits. Here is Charles Reade's vivid thumb-
nail portrait of him taken at a later date : " He is
comic beyond the power of pen to describe, goes off

mentally into the House of Commons and harangues
with an arm stretched out straight as a line. Puts
on an artificial manner, 'Yaw, yaw, yaw,' and every
moment exposes the artifice by exploding a laugh—
loud, sudden, clear, fresh, naïve, and catching as a
ploughboy's."

We *fin-de-siècle* people are always patting each
other's backs over our superior education, culture and
refinement; but what have we to compare with the
society that gathered in the salons of Lady Holland,
Lady Blessington and of Lansdowne House? What
brilliant assemblies have gathered in that plain-look-
ing house, No. 8 Seamore Place, between 1830 and
1836, when the Countess of Blessington held her court
there. What a lovely woman she was in those days,
with something of Juno blended with Aphrodite, with
a grace of manner that was irresistible, and a ringing
laugh that rivalled Jordan's or Nisbett's, a tact that set
every guest at his ease however obscure he might be.
Then the wonderful manner in which she would draw
out clever people, and afford even the humblest an
opportunity of saying something that would bring
them into notice, while she herself would utter a smart
sentence, throw off a *bon mot*, but would never for five
minutes together monopolise the conversation. And
her patronage of literature and art was not confined
to mere pleasant receptions, for her purse and her
interest were ever at the service of struggling talent.
She herself made from £2000 to £3000 a year by her
pen.

D'Orsay, who was then living with his wife—they were a most ill-assorted pair—in Curzon Street, was seldom absent from these *réunions*. If Lady Blessington was a Juno or an Aphrodite, he was as handsome as Apollo Belvidere ; above six feet in height, modelled like a statue, and the dandy of all dandies. " When I used to see him driving in his tilbury through the Park," writes Gronow, " I fancied that he looked like some gorgeous dragon-fly skimming through the air, and, though all was dazzling and showy, yet there was a kind of harmony which precluded any idea or accusation of bad taste." His costume in the Park was a high-collared blue coat, with gilt buttons, thrown well back to show the wide expanse of shirt front and buff waistcoat; tight leathers and polished boots, wide-brimmed hat, white gloves, curled hair and whiskers. He was as careful in his toilette as a woman. It required two men to carry his gold dressing-case, and when he fought a duel he stipulated that his opponent should not aim higher than his breast. Though a dandy he was not a dude, but a man of brilliant wit, who could pen an epigram or utter a *bon mot ;* a clever sculptor, a cleverer draughtsman, a masterly swordsman, horseman, whip, and one of the kindest-hearted and most generous of men. Disraeli has sketched him admirably under the name of Count Mirabel in *Henrietta Temple.*

Gathered about these central orbs was a galaxy not inferior to themselves. There was the author of *Vivian Grey*, as great a dandy as the count himself,

glorious in gold-brocaded waistcoat, his eyes black as
night, hair black as his eyes and massed in ringlets
upon his left cheek, his complexion lividly pale ; a
wonderful talker, with a power of description that
held his hearers spellbound. Bulwer, bright and
joyous, as I have just described him ; Landor, burly
aggressive, but an intellectual giant ; Tom Moore
singing his own Irish melodies with a pathos and
tenderness that no other singer of them ever
approached. And there was conversation in those
days,—the art was declining, perhaps, but was not yet
lost ; men and women talked about books and art
and on intellectual subjects of all kinds, brightly,
cleverly, in well-chosen language, not in thieves'
kitchen slang. In the parallel society of to-day there
is nothing worth speaking about except "biking" :
some idiotic book, or academy picture with a history
to it ; an inane " musical comedy " may obtain a few
remarks, but literature and art are voted bores even
among their professors. " There are some wits
among us still," writes Shirley, " but no one cares to
listen to their *bons mots* ; the gay wisdom of Sidney
Smith himself would fall flat in circles where a rude
practical joke is treated with imbecile laughter."

No. 4 Chesterfield Street is haunted by the shade
of another dandy, the founder of the race, for it was
here that Beau Brummell passed the better part of
his butterfly existence. " These are our failures," said
the valet, showing a basketful of unworn cravats, the
tying of which had fallen short of the perfection

required by the beau. It was he who first hit upon
the felicitous idea of starching the limp bandage with
which men had previously encircled their throats.
Brummell was never *outré*; there was an exquisite
propriety in his dressing that no other male leader of
fashion ever quite attained, not even D'Orsay. And
like him, Brummell was a man of brains; he was
keen, shrewd, and associated with the cleverest men
of the time.

But in the earlier decades of the present century all
notable men were more or less dandies; men of the
highest intellect did not disdain to give serious attention
to the cut of their coats; they took great pains with
themselves—they did not slouch and moon through
life, and they were highly appreciated by all classes.
"I will take the men I have personally known of a far
later date," says Lord Lamington. "Count D'Orsay,
Lord Cantilupe, Lord Chesterfield, Lord Alvanley,
Sir George Wombwell, Sir Henry Mildmay, Ridley
Colborne, and others. They were all men of excellent
accomplishments, and dress was the least part of their
merit."

It is a mere platitude to say that the tailor does not
make the gentleman; neither is it essential to a gentleman to dress like a groom; there is a subtle influence
in outward form and ceremony, more potent than
most people are able to conceive. Slovenly in one
thing, slovenly in all; rough in dress, unrefined in
manner. The disappearance of the genus gentleman
during this century has been considerably hastened

by the hideous garb which our youth has adopted for athletics as well as for ordinary wear.

Listen to the words of the immortal Teufelsdröch : " From the soberest drab to the high flaming scarlet spiritual idiosyncrasies unfold themselves in choice of colour ; if the cut betoken intellect and talent, so does the colour betoken temper and heart. In all which, among nations as among individuals, there is an incessant, indubitable, though infinitely complex working of cause and effect ; every snip of the scissors has been regulated and prescribed by ever-active influences, which, doubtless, to intelligences of a superior order, are neither invisible nor illegible."

The dandies were a power ; it was feared that there would be disturbances at the coronation of George IV. ; so the king sent for Lord Gwydyr, one of the leaders, and very anxiously inquired what the feelings of the dandies were. " I care nothing for the mob, but I do for the dandies," he said. And the dandy was a very muscular Christian, who could use his fists, and if he were molested did not shelter himself behind a policeman's staff, but gave his insulter a good thrashing or took one without flinching—and did not think it " vulgar," an epithet most frequently upon the lips of underbred people, struggling against heredity.

In this same Chesterfield Street, No. 3, Mrs. Norton, one of the three beautiful Sheridan girls, though the least lovely of the trio, passed thirty years of her life. Hers was an Italian type of beauty, with blue-black hair, and framed in gold-coloured silk, shaded and

softened by black lace draperies, head, neck and
arms adorned with Etruscan gold ornaments, her usual
toilette, it was a queen-like type. Caroline Norton inherited much of her grandsire's brilliancy, combined
with a fine touch of poetical genius all her own. Tom
Sheridan, her father, was as great a scapegrace as his
awful dad, and like him a gambler and a spendthrift,
while her mother was meek and lymphatic ; Tom
never had a guinea, was always in debt, and perpetually shadowed by bumbailiffs. Two of the girls,
by their marriages with the Duke of Somerset and
Lord Dufferin, escaped from this harassing degradation ; but poor Caroline was less fortunate, for she
married a brute. A year or two ago her name was
brought up rather prominently in a discussion as to
whether she really betrayed the secret of Sir Robert
Peel's Cabinet—his intention to propose the repeal of
the corn laws—confided to her by Sidney Herbert,
her devoted admirer, and sold it to *The Times*. But
Lord Dufferin distinctly denies it, and proofs are on
his side. Lord Melbourne was another attached
friend, and his attentions brought about divorce
proceedings, but they came to nothing.

Many a pleasant little dinner, that might have
delighted Lucullus by the choiceness of its viands,
and Horace by the flavour of its wit, not to forget
its Falernian, was given by Sidney Smith at No. 33
Clarges Street, between 1836 and 1839. The Church
has always loved good eating and drinking, and no
old Benedictine ever more enjoyed the pleasures of

the table than did Canon Smith. When Luttrell
spoke lightly of veal soup he took him aside and
gravely reasoned with him upon his levity, but in
vain. " To speak the truth," he says, " Luttrell is not
steady in his judgment on dishes. A person of more
calm judgment thinks not only of what he is consum-
ing at the moment, but of the soups of a like kind
he has met with in a long course of dining, and which
have gradually and justly elevated the species. I
am perhaps making too much of this, but the failures
of a man of sense are painful." He loved to draw
his figures of speech from the *menu*. Speaking to
Tom Moore of the excellent way in which a certain
host mixed his guests, " That is the use of a good
conversational cook who says to his company, ' I'll
make a good pudding of you ; it's no use what you
came into the bowl as, you must come out a pudding '.
' Dear me,' says one of the ingredients, ' wasn't I an
egg just now ? ' But he feels the batter sticking to
him." " Give him melted butter with his turbot for
a twelvemonth instead of lobster sauce," was his
proposed punishment for an offending alderman. It
was Sydney Smith who christened Monckton Milnes,
when the poet was young, " the cool of the evening ".

Stanhope Street calls up many memories of Lord
Brougham, who resided at No. 4. Those who are
familiar with the old cartoons of *Punch* will recall
that gruesome face, ugly as a gargoyle, and those
inevitable plaid trousers. Greville considered him to
be the most remarkable man whom he had ever met,

full of gaiety, humour, animal spirits. Rogers said
of him after he had left one day : " This morning
Solon, Lycurgus, Demosthenes, Archimedes, Sir Isaac
Newton, Lord Chesterfield, and a great many more
went away in a post-chaise". Brougham once told Lord

LORD BROUGHAM.

Lamington, " if I were sentenced to be guillotined at
ten o'clock, I would not think of it until eight o'clock.
On the occasion of my speech on the queen's trial,
when all my reputation depended upon it, I deter-

mined to banish it from my mind. I slept so sound
the night before that I awoke in the morning only
in time to get into court."

Sir Robert Peel resided for some years at No. 12
and married Miss Floyd in the drawing-room. He
was curiously reserved and shy in his manner, which
gave him an appearance of coldness; but he was
warm-hearted and generous for all that. Witness
his tenderness to poor Tom Hood on his deathbed.
Not knowing of his danger he wrote the poet a noble
and touching letter announcing that a pension had
been conferred upon him and ending with : " One
return, indeed, I shall ask of you—that you will give
me the opportunity of making your personal acquaintance". "Sir R. Peel came from Burleigh on
Tuesday night," wrote Hood to a friend, " and went
down to Brighton on Saturday. If he had written
by post I should not have had it till to-day. so he
sent on a servant with the enclosed on *Saturday night*.
Another mark of his considerate attention." And the
great statesman kept his word and came to the bedside
of the dying humorist and poet, as Thackeray says,
" speaking noble words of respect and sympathy, and
soothing the last throbs of that tender honest heart".
On that fatal day on which Peel was thrown from his
horse, the Duke of Wellington, hearing of the accident,
hurried to Whitehall Gardens. When told that Sir
Robert's condition was desperate the old man said
with a husky voice : " He was the soul of truth ".

Edmund Kean passed the early days of his delirious

success at No. 12 Clarges Street, gave his little son guineas and bank notes to play with—a few months before he had scarcely ever known what it was to possess one—and drove backwards and forwards to Drury Lane in a coach and four ; dined at the Marquis of Hertford's or Holland House, and supped with Tom Cribb or perhaps at Stunning Joe Banks's in the Rookery, though in that respect he might have excused himself behind such illustrious examples as the Prince Regent and Brinsley Sheridan.

Bourdon Manor House, which stands at the corner of Bourdon and Davies Streets, is closely connected with the fortunes of the Westminsters. On that spot stood Bourdon Farm, the owner of which was a man named Davies. In 1676 Sir Thomas Grosvenor married Davies' daughter, Mary, who inherited the farm and lands. A century and a half before William conquered England the ancestors of Sir Thomas held the high post of *Le Grosveneur*, or head huntsman, to the Dukes of Normandy, but the few acres of meadow and swamp and ditch which Sir Thomas inherited with his wife did more for the Grosvenors than all they had gained or acquired in all the previous eight centuries of their existence, for on that ground his descendants built the whole of Belgravia and Eatonia.

A dark memory attaches to No. 45 Berkeley Square, in which the great Lord Clive, the founder of our Indian Empire, tortured by enemies and the ingratitude of the nation he had by his genius enriched with a priceless treasure, put an end to his

LORD CLIVE.

life at the age of forty-nine. Such was the reward
of the man who had saved India from the French,
and had raised a mere trading company, living upon
suffrage in a remote land, to be masters of a mighty
empire. England in the past was rarely grateful to
her great men, but never so ungrateful as to those
who won for-her the brightest jewel in the English
crown. She drove Clive to suicide, and she persecuted Warren Hastings with a malignancy as diabolical
as recent researches have proved to have been unjust.
When the Britisher has one of his awful sentimentally
virtuous fits upon him he is as dangerous as a mad
dog, and invariably turns upon his best friends.

No. 11 was the town house of Horace Walpole
from 1779 until his death.

Lady Jersey, one of the most noted leaders of *bon
ton* in the reign of George IV., and a royal favourite,
resided in Berkeley Square, and entertained there all
the most brilliant people of her time. Byron was her
frequent visitor, and she used to relate that one
evening, just after his separation from his wife, when
he left the seat he had occupied next to her, the
ladies lifted their dresses that they might not be
polluted by touching the floor he had passed over!
No wonder Childe Harold anathematized society.

" The haunted house in Berkeley Square," which, I
think, stood on the western side, was much talked
about years ago. More than once tenants quitted it
in all haste. It was asserted that one gentleman was
driven raving mad by something he had seen in the

haunted room. But what that something was never seems to have transpired. Among the stories told was one to the effect that a policeman who had been put in as caretaker cut his throat when delirious, and

THE HAUNTED HOUSE, BERKELEY SQUARE.

that it was his apparition that was supposed "to walk".

The last of the old aristocratic mansions of London that stands within its own grounds is Lansdowne

House, which forms one side of Berkeley Square. It
was built by that much-hated minister, Lord Bute,
scandal said with the money he drew from France
for bringing about the shameful Peace of Paris, by
which we forfeited so much that the splendid genius
of the elder Pitt had won for us. In his own fortunes
he was as poor as a church mouse ; and though the
cher ami of the Princess of Wales and the despotic
governor of the weak young king, he could not have
made the money out of *them*. Before long he sold
the mansion to the Earl of Shelburne, afterwards
Marquis of Lansdowne.

It was under the third marquis that Lansdowne
House became so celebrated as a centre of literary
society and Whig politics ; it was equally renowned
for its splendid collection of works of art. Rush, in
his *Residence at the Court of London*, writes : " In the
dining-room were ancient statues, standing in niches.
These time-honoured masterpieces of genius and art
had been obtained from Rome. As we walked into
dinner through a suite of apartments, the entire aspect
was of classic beauty."

Lansdowne House was likewise one of the chief
rallying-places of the Young England party, who
believed that by improving and brightening the social
condition of the peasantry and reviving old games
and pastimes there could be brought back something
of " the Merrie England " of our ancestors. At the
head of it was the ardent and dreamy George Sydney
Smythe, supported by such choice spirits as Lord

John Manners, Baillie Cochrane, Beresford Hope,
Mr. Peter Borthwick, and Benjamin Disraeli. But
it was "Ben Dizzy" who, by his brilliant novel,
Coningsby, of which Sydney Smythe was the hero,
became the animating spirit of the movement. In
those last days, when the veteran statesman passed
the great house on the way to his home in Curzon
Street, how often he must have recalled the dreams
of that band of young enthusiasts, who, like all other
enthusiasts, past, present, and to come, were convinced that in them and in their ideas alone lay
the regeneration of humanity. He must often have
pictured himself as he appears in that well-known
sketch of Maclise's—the handsome dandy, cynical,
daring, insolent—"Vivian Grey". But beneath that
foppish mask was concealed an inflexible purpose.
"What do you intend to be?" inquired Lord Melbourne of the boy "Dizzy". "Prime Minister of
England," was the quick reply. And to attain that
object was the purpose of his life. Equally prompt
was his answer to a supercilious opponent on the
hustings at High Wycombe. "What does this gentleman stand upon?" was the sneering query. "On
my head," was the retort. "*Audace, audace, toujours
audace*," was his motto. But in those last days, when
Azriel was already shadowing him, he had realized
that all human ambitions crumble into dust in the
grasping, and the truth of his own axiom : "Youth is
a blunder, manhood a struggle, old age a regret".

It was in Curzon Street, No. 19, that Lord Beaconsfield died. Sir William Fraser in his *Recollections* gives us a striking picture of "Dizzy" in his closing days : "During his last premiership I dined with him in Downing Street ; on entering he replied to my hope that he was no worse for the bitter weather with a feeble groan. I ventured to say that I found him surrounded by his illustrious predecessors ; he groaned again. 'Sir Robert Walpole over the mantelpiece ?' He feebly bleated the word 'Walpole'. At first I thought he must be dying. I waited for a minute or two and then was followed by the Duke of Buckingham and Chandos, his intimate personal friend from boyhood ; his words bore resemblance to my own ; to my relief he replied in the same ghastly manner. I felt that he could not survive the night. Within a quarter of an hour, all being seated at dinner, I observed him talking to the Austrian Ambassador, Count Apponyi, with extreme vivacity. During the whole of dinner their conversation was kept up ; I saw no sign of flagging. . . . One theory has been that Disraeli took carefully measured doses of opium, these being calculated to work at a given time, that the effect of the subtle drug was as I have described. I never saw the phenomena in any other person." Another anecdote, which would help to confirm Sir William's theory, is to be found in Mr. Raikes's recently published *Reminiscences*. On the day that Disraeli, then in opposition, made his great speech at the Free Trade Hall, Manchester, he requested a friend to get him three bottles of *white* brandy ; it was only after much searching that two could be procured. They were taken to the hall and put under the table, and Disraeli told his friend to keep the tumbler constantly filled with brandy and water in equal proportions. " Stronger, stronger !" muttered Dizzy as he continually drank ; and by the time the speech was ended both bottles were emptied. But no one else knew that he had taken anything but water.

Horace Walpole's great friends, the two Misses Berry, resided at No. 8 Curzon Street, where they gave most brilliant receptions. The female element, however, frequently preponderated to such an extent as to embarrass the hostesses, much as it does their successors. When enough and to spare of the sex had arrived, Miss Berry would call out, " No more petticoats !" upon which the footman extinguished the lamp over the door and not another woman was admitted. This exclusion, however, did not extend to the men. As every reader of the great letter writer knows, the Misses Berry lived for many years at Twickenham, and were great favourites with the master of Strawberry Hill, who offered his hand and coronet to one, but was refused. One of the sisters survived until 1852, dying at the age of ninety, thus forming an extraordinary link between the eighteenth and nineteenth centuries.

CHAPTER XXIII. AND LAST.

BROOK STREET—HILL STREET—BOND STREET—
CONDUIT STREET—" LIMMERS' "—REGENT STREET.

EVERY passer-by along Brook Street will be arrested by the plate against No. 25, which states that in that house George Frederick Handel resided for thirty years. Ye gods, what echoes of heavenly harmony may yet linger about that roof-tree! I think it must have been there that he composed "The Messiah," when, as he said : "I did think I did see all heaven before me, and the great God Himself". It was a curious coincidence that he always expressed a wish to die on Good Friday, "in the hope of meeting my good God, my sweet Lord and Saviour on the day of His crucifixion". And it was on Good Friday, 1759, that he breathed his last. The double life that so frequently exists in men of genius was remarkably exemplified in Handel. The spiritual soul was the tenant of a very gross body. He was a man of enormous appetite ; when he dined at a tavern he always ordered dinner for three, and his habits were no more refined than those of his friend Dr. Johnson, whom in ponderosity of build and movement he greatly resembled. No man was ever more violently abused by rivals and know-nothings than the great Hanoverian.

The goody people called him swindler, drunkard, *blasphemer*, to whom Scripture was not sacred, in allusion to his sublime oratorios !   May we not slightly alter the words of Madame Roland and exclaim, "O religion, how many crimes are committed in thy name ! "

Two curious facts connected with Grosvenor Square are worth noting : it was the last thoroughfare in London to be lit by gas ; it did not give up its oil lamps until 1842.   Mount Street owes its name to the Civil Wars : during the great rebellion the parliamentarians threw up a line of earthworks for defence, and upon that line Mount Street was afterwards built.

When the celebrated Mrs. Montagu, of whom Cowper wrote—

> The birds put off their every hue
> To dess a room for Montagu,

first initiated the "Blue-Stocking Society" in Hill Street, about 1750, that thoroughfare was an unpaved, unlighted suburb, dangerous after dusk, as the neighbourhood was infested by footpads and highwaymen.[1]   The Bas-Bleu was started as a protest against that universal card playing, which entirely banished all conversation at fashionable assemblies. Lord Lyttleton, Walpole, Johnson, Burke, Fanny

---

[1] And it had not improved thirty years later, for one night Lord Lyndedoch's carriage, when on the way to Mrs. Montagu's, was stopped on Hay Hill by masked men, and soon afterwards the Prince of Wales and his brother of York when riding there in a hackney coach were robbed of money, jewellery, and everything portable.

Burney, Mason, Garrick, were among its earliest supporters. Many explanations have been offered of the
term "Blue Stocking". Perhaps the most feasible is that
given by Hayward in his *Life and Correspondence of
Mrs. Thrale.* When these assemblies were in their
infancy Mde. De Polignac was invited to one of them,
and came in a pair of blue stockings, then all the rage
in Paris. The fashion was so greatly admired by the
ladies present that they forthwith adopted it, and it
became a badge of the society.

Bond Street is one of the world's thoroughfares,
and its name is familiar wherever civilisation exists.
Old Bond Street was built in 1686 ; New Bond Street
about a quarter of a century later. I never pass
through the former without thinking of the lonely
deathbed of that fine genius, Lawrence Sterne. Peter
Cunningham was of opinion that the house in which
he died is now No. 41. Only a hired nurse and a
footman, who had been sent by his master to inquire
after the sick man's health, were by his side. The
latter has left a record of those last sad moments.
" I went into the room, he was just a-dying. I waited
ten minutes, but in five he said : ' Now it is come '.
He put up his hand as if to stop a blow and died in a
minute." It is said that those who performed the last
offices for the dead stole some of his jewellery. Strange
to say he had written in *Tristram Shandy* that
he would prefer to die at an inn, untroubled by the
spectacle of the concern of friends and the last service
of wiping his brow and smoothing his pillow. His

desire was almost literally fulfilled. The funeral of
this man, whose fame had filled two kingdoms, was
as lonely as had been his death ; only his publisher
and that same footman, James Macdonald, followed
him to the burying ground near Tyburn, now a
squalid and long decayed graveyard, in which his
lichen-stained tombstone is still to be seen.

For several generations after the middle of the
eighteenth century Bond Street shared with Pall Mall
the distinction of being the fashionable lounge of the
"bucks" and "Corinthians". A great resort of the
latter was the boxing rooms of John Jackson, known
as "Gentleman Jackson," pugilist and professor of " the
noble art of self-defence ". Readers of Moore's *Life of
Byron* will be familiar with the name. The great poet
entertained a sincere respect and regard for Jackson,
and, after he had been away from England several
years, spoke of him as " my old friend and corporeal
pastor and master, John Jackson, Esq., professor of
pugilism, who, I trust, still retains the strength and
symmetry of his model form, together with his good
humour and athletic as well as mental accomplishments ".

Pugilism was as much a part of a gentleman's education in those days as Latin or dancing, and Jackson
was instructor to half the nobility. It was quite the
thing for the dandies when tired of promenading Bond
Street to turn into No. 13, where Jackson, in white silk
stockings and buckled shoes, was ready to receive
them ; some put on the gloves, while others watched

them set to. The professor was one of the Prince
Regent's bodyguard, and at the coronation of his
royal master was present in the livery of a royal
page. Jackson was a man of herculean yet perfect
form. You see his figure in the well-known picture of
Kemble as Rolla, for which he posed, the head alone
being that of the great actor.

But the pugilist a hundred years ago, and less, was
not the disreputable personage he is at present. I
have noted in a previous chapter the Right Hon.
William Windham's passion for pugilism, a *penchant*
for which Mrs. Windham expressed the greatest dis-
gust. One day Mr. Windham brought home with
him to dinner a gentleman whom he introduced to her
as General Jackson. The lady was delighted with her
guest, whose ease of manner, perfect *ton* and evident
personal familiarity with the great world, assured her
that he was a man of breeding. When he had gone
she was loud in his praise. "A charming man ; you
must ask him again, my dear," she said. "Certainly,"
replied her husband with a wicked look, "but the next
time he comes you must receive him not as General
Jackson but as Mr. John Jackson, the pugilist!"

The maze of fashionable streets that lie between
Bond Street and Regent Street abound in reminis-
cences of celebrated people. The brilliant George
Canning lived at No. 37 Conduit Street.

> And on that turtle I saw a rider
> A goodly man with an eye so merry—
> I know 'twas our foreign secretary—

> Who there at his ease did sit and smile
> Like Waterton on his crocodile ;
> Cracking such jokes at every motion
> As made the turtle squeak with glee,

wrote Tom Moore in *A Dream of a Turtle*.

Canning was indeed an inveterate joker. Fancy some member of the awfully serious and unjokable division in the House of Commons of to-day hearing that Lord Salisbury had been guilty of the following : the embassy at the Hague was in high dispute with the King of Holland, and in the midst of it a despatch arrived for the ambassador, Sir Charles Bagot, from the Foreign Secretary, written in cypher. The attachés at once set to work to *de*-cypher it. Could they believe their senses, it was a quatrain in rhyme :—

> Dear Bagot, in commerce the fault of the Dutch
> Is giving too little and asking too much ;
> So, since on this policy Mynheer's so bent,
> We'll clap on his vessel full 20 per cent.

The O's and Ap's and Mac's and Joneses would now call for the impeachment of a minister capable of such frivolity. We are sadder : are we wiser ? There was an abundance of fools in the old House, but they kept their secret by being silent ; in the new they are always blabbing it.

Canning was famous for his *mots.* Lord Londonderry was describing a Dutch picture of the animals coming out of Noah's ark, "and last of all," said my lord, "was the elephant". " Certainly," remarked Canning quickly, "he had been packing up his trunk."

His aptness of quotation was marvellous. Lord Lyndhurst had delivered a speech, the substance of which
was almost entirely taken from a pamphlet of Dr.
Phillpotts, afterwards the well-known Bishop of
Exeter. When Canning rose to reply, he began—

> Dear Tom, this brown jug that now foams with mild ale,
> Out of which I now drink to sweet Nan of the dale,
> Was once—*Toby Phillpotts.*

There was no need to say any more ; my lord was
put out of court with roars of laughter.

In the celebrated *Anti-Jacobin* Canning, with
the assistance of Frere, was almost as successful in
extinguishing the would-be imitators of Danton and
Robespierre as he had been with Lord Lyndhurst, and
the political squibs, which wrecked the noted ministry
of "All the Talents" by sheer ridicule, were chiefly
from his pen.

Conduit Field, upon which Conduit Street is built,
was anciently a place of much importance. Stow
tells us that, on the 18th of September, 1562, "the
Lord Mayor, Harper, the aldermen, and divers other
worshipful persons, rid to Conduit Head before
dinner. They hunted the hare and killed her, and
thence to Conduit Head to dinner. A man who was
living in 1780 shot woodcocks in this field when he
was a boy."

But the most notable of all the memories connected
with Conduit Street are those of Limmers'. It was
in the old days—it is now rebuilt—one of the dingiest,
not to say dirtiest hostelries in London, yet one

of the most exclusively aristocratic. Limmers' was really a sporting club, a sort of residentiary Tattersalls. It was in that house, then known as the Prince Regent's Tavern, that Sheridan and Beau Brummell cracked their first bottle of wine together. All the Corinthians, all the young Jerry Hawthorns and the old Jerry Hawthorns, and even the sedate country squires—don't you remember that Squire Hazeldean (*My Novel*) put up there?—were fond of Limmers', perhaps because the old-fashioned English dinner *and* the port were super-excellent. But the floor of the coffee-rooms was sanded after the night on which the Marquis of Waterford shovelled the red-hot coals out of the grate on to the carpet. If an unknown man intruded within the sacred precincts he would be charged half a crown for a brandy and soda, or anything else he might call for, and would be treated with supercilious disdain by John Collins, the waiter—whom Frank Sheridan celebrated in verse[1]—because he was not "one of *hus*". John was the inventor of the famous drink known by his name.

Limmers' was in the height of its glory between 1830 and 1860, and on the night before the Derby you would find most of the sporting aristocracy in the coffee-rooms. Conspicuous figures on that occasion would be the Hon. Charles Greville of Diary

---

[1] Which began—
  My name is John Collins, head waiter at Limmers',
    In Conduit Street, Hanover Square;
  My chief occupation is filling up brimmers
    For the gentlemen frequenting there.

fame, in bright blue coat and brass buttons, with the knob of his gold-headed walking-stick pressed against his lips, his invariable habit. Perhaps beside him is that other buck and wit Lord Alvanley who gives the best little dinners in London, but is always hopelessly involved. Greville has been trying to arrange his affairs, but after having a full statement of his liabilities made out, Alvanley suddenly remembers that a "trifling debt of £55,000 has been omitted !" There is Lord George Bentinck, in stiff white cravat and faultlessly cut green Newmarket coat, from top to toe a patrician ; guardsmen, bookmakers, pugilists. This tavern is also the favourite resort of the Marquis of Waterford, whose extraordinary pranks furnish the newspapers with endless "copy". It was he who one night emptied "the Rookery" of its denizens and took them all round the town in a procession of hackney coaches that stopped at every public-house until the whole crew, men and women, engaged in a general *mêlée* on Pentonville Hill. It is more than suspected that the marquis, assisted by some of his companions, is the notorious " Spring-heeled Jack," who for months has kept the town in almost as much terror as did the Mohocks in the previous century.[1]

[1] Spring-heeled Jack was ubiquitous, and assumed as many forms as Proteus ; now he appeared in the shape of a white bull or bear ; then in brass armour with great claws, at another time as a baboon with saucer eyes, then with huge horns, and gleaming with phosphorescence. He could spring over a man's head; his leaps and

My lord's great friend, the Hon. William Duff
—one of the Fifes—better known as "Billy Duff,"
in outrageous devilry and vile practical jokes is
quite abreast of "the mad Marquis". These were
the men who carried off and made collections of
door knockers, barbers' poles, signs ; Douglass Jerrold
has described some of their doings in *John Applejohn*
(*Men of Character*) under the names of Lord Slap and
the Hon. Tom Rumpus. They once painted a policeman pea green and dropped him, bound hand and
foot, down an area. Sala, in *Things I Have Seen*,
relates how the Hon. Billy once went into a fashionable milliner's show-room in Regent Street when all
the attendants were at tea, and sat down upon twenty-
two bonnets. Limmers' was the scene of many of his
extraordinary freaks and fancies. John Collins used
to tell a story how one night he brought a Highland
piper, whom he had picked up in the street, into the

somersaults were prodigious, effected, no doubt, by some machinery
attached to the feet, and these added not a little to the terror this
apparition inspired. Women feared to walk out at night, as several
had been frightened into an illness by the goblin, and men were
attacked and severely beaten by it ! All London was roused : in
January, 1838, a committee was formed at the Mansion House, and a
subscription was raised to assist the police in capturing the monster.
But without any result. After the April of that year Jack was seen
no more ; his identity has never been established. As I have said in
the text, Lord Waterford was strongly suspected, but no proof has
ever been discovered to confirm the suspicion. There were various
rumours, one of which was that a number of young men had made a
bet of £3000 that they would in a given time frighten thirty people
to death. But this smacks too much of the incredible.

coffee-room, and started the Highland fling with the usual Gaelic yells, and in his enthusiasm divested himself of his clothes article by article until his shirt alone remained.

At No. 14 Savile Row, Cork Street, the last scene of Sheridan's strange eventful history was enacted. " Nothing could be more wretched than the home in which he lay dying," wrote an eye-witness: " there were strange-looking people in the hall ; the parlour seemed dismantled ; on the table lay a piece of paper thrown carelessly and neglected—it was a prescription." In his dying moments a sheriff's officer arrested him, and would have carried away the wasted body in blankets to a sponging house, had not the physician threatened to make the fellow responsible should his prisoner die upon the road.

But as soon as death had claimed him all this was changed ; there was a pompous funeral, the Duke of Bedford, the Earl of Lauderdale, Earl Mulgrave, Lord Holland, the Bishop of London and Lord Spencer were the pall-bearers ; the Dukes of York and Sussex, and other dukes, marquises, earls and lords followed him to the abbey. One of the very few duties of life which have no *désagréments* attached to it is doing honour to the dead ; it costs nothing, and one has the satisfaction of knowing that the dear defunct will make no further call upon us.

The case of Richard Brinsley Sheridan, however, has called forth more sympathy and indignation than it merits, chiefly excited by Moore's famous " Monody " ;

but we should remember that a poet claims poetic licence, also that the "Monody" was a political fulmination. No more heartless man than this brilliant wit and orator ever existed ; he was utterly indifferent as to the number of tradesmen or others whom he ruined, so that he might live in luxury. He was equally callous to the people who served him for their daily bread. Fanny Kemble in her *Reminiscences* relates how on a Saturday morning the workpeople at Drury Lane would assail him with "For God's sake, Mr. Sheridan, pay us our salaries—let us have something this week". He would faithfully promise that their wants should be attended to, and then, after emptying the treasury of the week's receipts, would slip out of the theatre by another door and leave them penniless.

Nor was his desertion by the great quite so flagrant as is generally supposed. George IV. assured Wilson Croker that Sheridan had more than £25,000 from him alone, and that the only cause of their separation was that Sheridan had appropriated to another purpose a sum of £3000 which had been advanced to him in 1812, to enable him to get a seat in Parliament. After this he kept out of the Prince's way, not the Prince out of his. The fact is, Sheridan was one of those men of whom most of us have had some experience, men in whose hands money dissolves like ice ; give them a thousand to-day and to-morrow they are penniless ; such men are hopeless, and in time wear out the generosity of the most liberal.

And with these moral reflections we reach the end of our pilgrimage, Regent Street. This proud successor of that mean thoroughfare, Swallow Street, though so world-famous, is curiously destitute of associations, and the few it has are evil. The Quadrant was as notorious for gambling "hells" as Leicester Square, and the description of such places given in the chapter on that locality will equally apply to these, although in showiness they more nearly resembled, if with but a faint reflection, the aristocratic Crockford's. Air Street, Princes Street, Cranbourne Alley, Golden Square, little more than half a century ago swarmed with "Greeks," as the professional gamesters, who lured half-intoxicated "swells" and inexperienced youth to the hazard table, were called. Among the notable cases of ruin brought about by these scoundrels was that of Thistlewood, the son of a country gentleman. He was sent up to London when quite young with a large sum of money, some thousands, to place in a certain investment for a relative. Lured into one of these "hells," he was at one sitting stripped of every farthing. Utterly disgraced he drifted from bad to worse, ultimately became a desperado, attended seditious meetings and organised the notorious Cato Street conspiracy, the aims of which were to murder the king's ministers while they were dining with Lord Harrowby in Grosvenor Square, raise an *émeute*, and seize upon the Bank of England. The plot was discovered, the conspirators were captured—they were the last imprisoned in the Tower—and Thistlewood and three of his accomplices were hanged at Newgate, and afterwards beheaded.

The authorities had a hard tussle to break up these dens of iniquity ; doors were lined with sheet iron, and all kinds of ingenious contrivances were invented to dish the police when they made a raid upon the saloons. Some were fitted with a pipe connected with the sewers, down which cards, dice, rakes and all the appurtenances of gambling were thrown at the first alarm ; others had a device by which a roulette wheel could be instantly raised to the ceiling and made to fit into the chandelier that hung over the table. But their day had come, and, thanks chiefly to an inspector of police named Beresford, by the end of the forties they were pretty well rooted out.

It is only upon returning to London after a few months' absence that one fully perceives the vast strides that our metropolis is making in architectural effect. While Paris has been standing almost still since the days of Hausman and Napoleon III., London has been advancing with an ever-increasing speed. Everywhere the dingy and the mean are giving place to the handsome and the imposing ; in all quarters broad thoroughfares are superseding narrow streets ; slums are being swept away, and beautiful buildings are rising up in their place. As a city of pleasure, London is outstripping the Lutetia of the Third Republic, and in the course of another decade it will contest with her the palm of dignity. The dreary London of our youth, of Dickens and Thackeray, is vanishing, how rapidly can scarcely be realised, least of all by the Londoner, who day by day witnesses, without remarking, the vast changes in progress.

The Thames Embankment is unequalled in picturesque effect, and the coming improvements in Parliament Street, the fine thoroughfare that is to join Holborn with the Strand, the superb plans that will convert the eastern half of the Strand, now so miserably mean as to be a disgrace to our great city, into a site that will surpass in grandeur of design any of the *Places* of the Continental capitals, and other transformations which must quickly follow, will render the London of the two thousandth century the grandest, as it is already the vastest, and most imposing metropolis of the modern and perhaps of the ancient world.

THE END.

ABERDEEN UNIVERSITY PRESS.

www.ingramcontent.com/pod-product-compliance
Lightning Source LLC
Chambersburg PA
CBHW030945110726
47900CB00004B/1135